The Wolf
and
The Sheepdog

By John Smith

authorHOUSE®

AuthorHouse™
1663 Liberty Drive, Suite 200
Bloomington, IN 47403
www.authorhouse.com
Phone: 1-800-839-8640

First published by AuthorHouse 7/11/2008

ISBN: 978-1-4343-5512-6 (sc)
ISBN: 978-1-4343-5513-3 (hc)

Library of Congress Control Number: 2008901194

Printed in the United States of America
Bloomington, Indiana

This book is printed on acid-free paper.

This book is dedicated to my wife, for all the love and passion she has brought into my world. Without her, I do not know where my soul would be.

To my mentors, the special people in my life that have given me the building blocks to be a good street cop, thank you.

To my family, for putting up with me during my troubled youth and for tolerating me as I changed because of this life path I have chosen, thank you.

"Good people sleep peaceably in their beds at night only because rough men stand ready to do violence on their behalf." - George Orwell

INTRODUCTION
INTRODUCTION

The calls and situations depicted in this book are only based on actual events.

My name has been changed and my co-worker's names are false ones.

I am still an active member of a police force and because of laws and personal safety I have to keep my identity a secret. I will always refer to my partner as just that: my partner.

I have to protect his identity as well.

I am not a police officer in the United States combating seasoned groups of gang members.

I am not a veteran involved in a specialty unit like Homicide or Drugs or even a detective.

I have yet to be shot at or shoot anyone in the line of duty.

I do not have the combat and street experience of an L.A. police officer, a New York street cop, or a soldier trying to police the streets of a war-torn foreign country. God bless them for the work they do.

I do however work in one of Canada's largest cities, a metropolis that is growing far too fast and is experiencing some serious growing pains. With the economic prosperity come drugs, gangs, and organized crime.

I am a street cop and I take pride in policing the streets of my city firsthand. I walk tall in the dark alleys and decrepit homes of my clients. I am a soldier wading his way through trenches filled with hate, suffering, and filth.

As you read along through my stories you may think that I police the public in a way that you do not approve of. I really don't care.

I police to protect.

My writings may scar what you think policing is about; the stories may even make you wonder what type of world exists in the shadows.

The romantic image that I might make a change in our society by following the rules has long been washed out of me. I follow my moral values, my integrity, and my love for the people I would die to protect.

In these pages I have written what my world is like.

I use the language I use and describe the feelings that are cultivated by dealing with people when they are at their lowest. I describe my feelings that are changed and formed from the things that I see.

This book contains my first five years on the street. I consider myself lucky to be able to be at the right place and time to be involved in such calls.

To be waist deep in "the Shit."

This is my story.

FULL CIRCLE

FULL CIRCLE

Whether it was at dinner parties, drinks at a local pub, or even large social events, people would always ask me:

"What is life on the street like?"

"How dangerous are the city streets?"

"What is the craziest thing that you have seen?"

Because emotions are distorted and exaggerated when mixed with adrenaline and graphic horror scenes, my stories would only skim the top of what I have seen and dealt with. As edited and sanitized as the tales were, people were always captivated by what they heard, trapped by their curiosity about the dark side of man's predatory nature.

I would not let people know how I felt at the calls, about the fear, the anger, the overriding need to shake after feeling the affects of a near-death experience. I was prevented from telling others about this side of my world. I wanted to protect them from the harsh reality of a predator versus prey society.

In all reality I never talked about the emotions because I had them locked away deep inside of me. I locked them away to try to protect myself.

On countless occasions I heard people tell me that I should write down my stories, let people know what the reality is to policing a large Canadian city.

Then the day came I sat down and started to write my book.

I write legal reports for criminal investigations, I articulate myself in court on the processions of events to support criminal charges, so I figured I should at least try to sit down and put my thoughts to paper.

When I started, it was like cracking open a dam, I could not stop. I sat in front of the computer late into the night. Each day I would hear the familiar hum of the computer booting up, the room lit up in the blue-white glow from the monitor.

Minutes would spin into hours. I would walk through old fields

1

that were put far away into the deep dark valleys of my subconscious mind. Memories would flood into me and the weight of those hidden memories would be lifted from me.

Writing became therapeutic, a written prescription for haunting memories that I thought that I had filed tightly away.

I wrote on how my world changed from having adrenalin pumped into my body in a fight-or-flight autonomic response to high-stress situations. The slowing of time, tunnel vision, heightened sense of smell, and the loss of hearing. A world that is filled with distorted time and altered reality.

I put down my feelings of anger, helplessness, and fury that accompany the strange, perverted, and twisted nature of some situations I was called to deal with. I would write on how it has affected me, years after the occurrence had passed.

This book is filled with the transformation of a new recruit to a seasoned veteran. not due to years of sitting behind a computer crunching numbers or hunting down killers from "cold files." Experience gained only from years of street work, filled with an abnormal set of circumstances that allowed me to be involved with the "Hot Calls."

Fate has allowed me to be at the right place at the right time over and over again, situations that some cops will only be exposed to a few times in their careers.

I sit back and consider myself fortunate to be at these calls, while others on the job look at me with a sorrowed gaze for what I have seen. They do not want the danger, the intense excitement. I have experienced this, and now I am hooked on the adrenalin, the near death excitement. I now crave the exhilaration of combat, pushing the danger limit more and more to further the rush.

My book allows a "civilian" the brief and personal insight into the policing world. Reading this book, people are allowed to see the ravishing affects of the drug world and criminal lifestyle. *The Wolf and the Sheepdog* relays the emotional scaring that horrific sights cause, the intimate and life altering encounters that I experience as a police constable.

The pages in my book are filled with the raw emotions of anger, pain, suffering and pity that are created from dealing with people at their worst.

To summarize *The Wolf and the Sheepdog*, it might be easiest to describe it as a collection of short stories that are written in the first person. Each short story covers a call and the emotions that are accompanied with the situation. These are just the calls that I have taken in the past seven years as a constable

Each call is unique. The people and situations are not only described in detail, but the feelings that arise when I handle the calls. My book is filled with raw emotions that are occasionally topped off with the affects of adrenaline. *The Wolf and the Sheepdog* allows the reader to escape into my world, to feel the concrete alleys and the criminal element through my senses.

The Wolf and the Sheepdog also covers the political views of the public, the Police Service with its policies and the opinions of the street working police constables. All of which oddly contradict each other on many occasions.

I hope that you enjoy my tales generated from my own experiences.

DAY ONE

Day One

It was almost surreal. I have just gone through six months of recruit training where you are a low piece of scum that they try to mind fuck.

It is not like the movies.

The instructors do not yell.

They do not use profanities.

They keep you in a very calm and controlled environment. That is the mind fuck. You never know what they are planning, how instructors feel, or what they truly think.

I wanted yelling, I wanted hard, no bullshit instructors, and I wanted stress.

I wanted to be ready for what I thought the streets of a major metropolitan city would bring me. The instructors that felt this way also were kept on a short leash; they were the best to learn from. They too were always weary of their audience.

Fuck, I hope that this is not what policing is about!

I will hate this shit. I thought I had a good idea of what I was getting into but now in my last few days in class I am wondering what the fuck is going on. I have been told that twenty traffic tickets are golden, that the bad guy has more rights than the innocent, and that we cannot go around "jacking up" bad guys.

You see my department is very "progressive." They want to have the public think that the force, or should I say service, is "transparent."

So, instead of fostering a warm brotherhood the way the "Police Service" used to be when it was a "Police Force," they work on building mistrust and deceit. They encourage internal complaints; they promote paper writers instead of mediation.

The whole promotional process is based on "How did you fuck over your fellow man?" They call it "examples." They do not ask how happy are the men under you? How did you promote a high morale in your team? When you had internal conflict how did you solve it?

Nope, not one bit. As a supervisor in my service you will tell the promotional committee that you gave out "negative paper." You "reprimanded" constables for exercising poor judgment, and you enforced "disciplinary measures."

Heaven forbid that you put yourself in the constable's place to see that his "poor judgment" was a product of fear, inexperience, and hesitation. Hesitation that every new constable worries about, because he worries about getting negative paper.

What a royal fuck-up they are causing. The supervisors are trapped high above the streets in a high-rise building. Soaring high above in what we call "The Ivory Tower." They want us to rat each other out, to file complaints against our fellow officer in training, and to fear our partner. What they do not understand is that there is no way to stop this bond between cops.

This bond between brothers forms when you have to trust each other with your own life. No other job is like it, no one else will know unless they have been here and put on the uniform.

Our chief of police actually goes public and tells the citizen population that he encourages complaints against the street constables! Yup, no mention of the good shit that we do, the fact that he is happy with our performance, or even that he might fathom the fact that his words would spew forth a barrage of unfounded complaints.

Nice way to help promote a healthy work environment that collaborates a team environment. Not fucking likely. "The Ivory Tower" is like walking back into time. They are the furthest thing from progressive.

I try to keep the important things in focus. I know that I am the FNG, or "Fucking New Guy." I hope that I get a good team and that my officer coach is good.

"The Shit" is different for every cop.

It is what keeps him awake at night! It is what makes him wake up in the morning with a hard-on to go to work. For some it is a long tedious investigation that nabs a huge fraud file. Front-page shit! For others it is helping kids across the street and displaying a public friendly cop.

For some it is even the thought of going out and setting a radar trap and nabbing high-speed drivers. That shit I will never understand,

I prefer to leave the innocent hard-working public alone. In my eyes they need no police intervention. Sure, if it is through a school zone or an accident-heavy area, cool, but in any other aspect, not my shit.

My shit is combat. I have found my shit to be the up-close and personal stuff that allows you to feel everything, see the eyes of your bad guy, and deliver a can of shit his way. I feed off of the adrenaline dump. I jump at the hot calls and I am all over anything that has a high propensity for violence.

Yup, I want the suicide guys, the crazies, the druggies, and the determined gang bangers. I am eager to get into "the shit."

I want to get bad guys, I want to help the innocent, and I want to see justice and law enforced. The more shit that I experience, the more I want.

If there is a God, he made me to kick ass. He would smile when I get into "the shit"!

I put on my body armor and then button up my uniform. Put on my shiny recruit boots and then I strap on my duty belt.

This action of putting a belt on is not that much different from what a carpenter or electrician does every day. But my belt is grossly different. It has tools made for humans and nothing else.

A set of handcuffs to restrain, a can of pepper spray to blind and incapacitate bad guys (that are not hyped up on drugs or mentally unstable, hmm, not that good of a tool, I guess).

To communicate with my other fellow brothers, a digital radio that surfs thousands of codes to prevent civilians from listening in. Perfect, let's organize the troops and get into some shit.

And of course a .40-caliber Glock, Model 21. A reactive tool that is a poor combat weapon.

"Your handgun is a fucking joke. It has very little killing capacity and has a very low stopping ability. It has an effective range of fifty feet and that is complete shit. Your handgun is a tool needed to get you out of the shit so that you can get a better weapon. This piece of shit will save your life if you train hard and well. But do not count on it! Your mind is the ultimate weapon."

The words of wisdom ingrained in me from an instructor that had enough faith in me to talk to me straight. He knew that he did not have to be politically correct with me. He taught me a lot, and even though he is retired now, I will never forget what he taught me. It has gotten me out of "the shit" on many occasions.

"I do not ever want to hear that you relied on this weapon to stop a threat! I want to hear that you filled the fucker with lead until he fell. Then you watched him bleed out so that you were sure that the threat was gone. No fucking hero moves in combat. You will tell others that you waited till you had enough backup to make sure you could approach the threat with safety, but all you did was watch the fucker die. He did something evil enough for you to deliver your piece of shit tool against him, he deserves to die. Fuck him."

There are others in the locker room chatting away and getting ready for their shift also but I am at the far back row. I am new, no one talks to me. I am new. They are weary of the new breed of recruits coming out of classes. The untrustworthy. I will have to show them that I am a good cop, a solid cop, and a "team player." I am all of these, I just need the chance. I want to get into "the shit."

So, with my kit bag filled to the brim and with its weight cutting into my shoulder I stumble into the "parade room." It is much like any other board room, an oval table that we all sit around and get the latest and greatest information. Usually shit information that is filtered down to us street guys. Information that was already known, passed around in the locker room or over a cup of coffee.

I have a seat after putting my bag down in the corner, and I immediately see that I have stepped over some line. I am early and there are only a few other cops in the room at this time but their conversation stops as I sit down.

A big old-school-looking cop with a full moustache and a barrel chest that fits well with his large "shit locker" (stomach) looks at me:

"You the new guy, eh?" his voice a mellow deep baritone. "Well, just to let you know, that is Lee's chair and he is superstitious about sitting anywhere else."

"What you do with this information is up to you." He made this closing remark as everyone else looked on. He is soon going to be my officer coach, soon to be my mentor. I consider myself lucky now because most other guys I know are getting coaches with only three years of street time. He has twenty-five years on already; he started working the job when I was less than a year old. He already had enough time to retire but loved the job enough he just did not want to leave.

I move and before I sit down again I gesture to another chair, to which the old-school cop gives me a little nod.

"You're a big fucker, eh? That will be good here in the pit, the folks here do not like the cops all that much. As long as you can fight, that is."

As long as I can fight?

These words made me feel better as during recruit class we were told that any situation could be diffused with "verbal judo." A cop rarely needs to get hands-on with their clients. A "Verbal Leash," they called it.

I have only gotten into two good street fights during my entire life before the force. I say street fights, as I have been actively involved in martial arts and of course you "fight" while you train.

But, I am soon to learn that street fighting is way different. And street fighting in uniform is a whole other matter. When you put on the uniform you have rules to fight by. "Use of Force Continuums" under the Police Act as well as case law under the Criminal Code.

Failing to follow these rules in combat will open you up to negative paper, front desk duties, loss of your career, or even worse: Criminal Code charges. Not good. So, not only are you fighting, you are thinking of shit that should never be in your mind during combat.

I sit down and write down my car number, radio identification, and shotgun number into my notebook, just like I was told to in recruit class.

"If it is not in your notes it does not exist. In court a crown or prosecutor will not recognize that you did something unless it is documented." These are words belched out by my criminal law instructor. "Your word in court is not good enough."

What the fuck is that? So, if the bad guy says he did something, which is always a fucking lie, he is believable. But if a cop states that he did something it is a lie unless he wrote it down? That is fucking bullshit.

That is the truth that I will learn in a very short time in court. It is written in stone.

"If it is not in your notes, it did not happen."

Parade starts right on time and I am hooked up with my first officer coach. A mentor, if you will, to help you develop into a good cop. Someone to learn from and someone who, if they are shit, will make you into a shit cop. Not an excuse for all the cops out there that are dog fuckers or shit cops, but I have seen some bad officer coaches fuck a lot of new cops up.

I was lucky, very lucky. My first officer coach is a female and others will mock me for working with a woman. Old primitive cops with the age-old imprint that a female cannot do a man's job. She is switched on, safe to work the streets. She kicks ass like everyone else but she can still tap into the softer side. She was and still is a good fucking cop.

She tested me by fire and put me in the shit right away. Our first call was a domestic. Not all that out of the ordinary, considering that I was placed out in the slums. As we pulled up we parked two houses down from the domestic address so that we could walk up on the address. This allows us to hear what is going on and doesn't let the persons in the residence know we are on scene. Textbook classroom shit.

As I walked up to the residence I started to do what I was instructed to do. I took note of the structure type. What is it made of? Wood, stone, and what could offer protection if someone came out shooting. As I always value my life much more than my grounds for police intervention, I started to think of what my legal grounds were to enter the house if we were not invited in.

But, I did not have to worry about that because as we got to the front door it was opened by a woman in her late twenties. Her hair looked like she combed it with a brick and her eyes were all drawn back. She was skinny and drawn. She was jittery from her recent crack cocaine use and abuse.

My first of many interactions with a person chemically dependent on crack cocaine.

My first crack head.

She wore a dirty white shirt and an old set of blue jeans. Blood dripping from her nose, from her recent fight with her boyfriend, drew long red lines on her shirt that led to droplets on the floor and her feet.

"He is fucking downstairs! I want him arrested. The fucker punched me in the face, I want the fucking asshole in jail!"

"Okay, what is his name and does he have any weapons?" were the immediate questions asked by my new partner.

"His name is Mike and I don't think that he has any weapons on him, I did not see any. Are you gunna go and arrest him or what?"

"Just calm down and let us do our job." Quick, short, precise, and with fucking authority. I loved the way she policed.

I was quiet, not a word came from my mouth. I was busy watching another woman at the end of a long hallway. The inside of the house was very dark, even in midday sun. The occupants covered the windows up with old mattresses to block out light, as crack and meth heads become very light sensitive.

The long hall was only lit up by the ray of light from the front door cutting its way through the dank darkness of the house. This woman was dressed in a long grey t-shirt and wore no pants. Her legs were bone thin and her pale white skin offset by the visible boils on them. She had "crack rot" setting in, it happens to crack heads from abusing their bodies. They get open sores and boils all over them.

Disgusting shit.

She just stood at the end of the hall like a ghostly apparition, moving back and forth like some fucking spook from a horror film. I totally expected her fucking head to spin around and black ooze to come out of her mouth. No such luck. She just kept moving from side to side as if caught in a weird mental loop.

My partner looked at me and I knew in her eyes she wanted me to make a decision. So, I went with my gut, the best decision maker. Always ask your instincts what to do. They will never lead you wrong. Why? Because your instincts are not motivated by hate, jealousy, or lust. They are simple self-preservation programs.

Listen to them and you stay alive.

I want to go down and get the guy in the basement. I want to limit the time he has to think about what he can do. I want him to feel like we are the hunters and he is the prey. The more time he has to think the more he feels like the hunter. I open up the door into the basement and it is a fine example of what hell may look like.

The crackers living here, if you want to call it that, have just thrown their garbage down the stairs instead of outside in the garbage cans. A rush of tiny little fruit flies speckle off of my face as they rush past me to get outside to live their brief life out in the sunlight.

I shine my "Stinger Flashlight" down the stairs. Its high intensity light shows me a world of shit. Garbage was up to the second step on the stairway. Crumbling dirt walls; lined with matted old dust bunnies and spider webs.

The old dirt basement and the smell of dank, musty earth mixes with the rotting garbage. I want to stuff fucking plugs into my nose as the smell hits my olfactory glands. They are telling me this is all wrong, a bad fucking place for me to go into.

But, I cowboy up and make my way down the stairs.

"City Police; show yourself!"

Quit hiding, you fuck! I don't want to wade through this shit. My shiny new boots are gunna get fucked and I hope to God that there are no dirty rigs (needles) down here. I move down the stairs fast. They are a bad place to be from a tactical standpoint. I give a quick glance under the open steps to ensure that he is not hiding there and then I am down into the muck below.

Without hesitation my partner is right behind me covering my back. I scan around and I see something odd. Some of the cob webs are brushed off the wall. A small crawlspace is just on the top of the scuff marks and I throw out my bluff.

"City Police; I see you! I know you are in there, get out now or I will call a K9 unit to get you out!" If this bad guy has been bitten by a dog or even knows someone who has been bitten by a "land shark" he will have the fear of God put into him with that threat!

It works. I hear, "Okay, okay, I am coming out!"

I yell a set of pre-programmed commands that have been instilled into me by good instructors. "Come out head first, let me see your hands, don't fuck around or you are gunna get hurt....Is that clear?!"

The fuck makes his way out. He slowly belly crawls towards me and I shine my flashlight into his face anytime he tries to look at me.

Ha, mother fucker, you want to look at me but you can't. I will take away your vision any chance I get. He gets really close to me now and I can reach him.

Closer, closer, come on, hurry up. I want to drag you out so that I can make sure you are not hiding anything from me! Finally, he is close enough that I can grab his dirty grey sweater and drag him out. I grab tight onto his sweater and start to yank him out of the little hole he shuffled into.

"Whoa, whoa, take it easy! I am not doing anything!"

These words fuck me up. I know my instincts are telling me to drag the shit out and cuff him. To let him know that I am the boss, in control of the situation.

But, thanks to my excellent recruit training I second-guess my instincts. I ease up, I worry that I am stepping on his rights. I worry that I am trotting on excessive use of force turf. I fuck up.

The bad guy reads my hesitation. He knows that I am no longer the predator. He feels his instincts tell him to run. He knows better than to ignore his instincts.

He is off! Up the stairs in a flash and out the front door.

I am like a rabid dog now. I give chase and we both fly out the wooden front door, bursting across the busy street. He is fast, really fast. He runs off of the flight aspect of adrenaline. He is a wiry 180 pounds, with long legs that flow from Olympic runners. I am a solid 250-pound young cop that is really pissed off. I train every day so that I can win in combat. I am a student of combat tactics. Yearning for knowledge to make me better at the shit that I love. I have taken martial arts, pumped iron relentlessly, and read all I can about various tactics.

But, I am not a fucking gazelle. When I run I have been described as the T-Rex off of *Jurassic Park* and even like the cartoon T-Rex off of *Toy Story*. My present partner always has a smart-ass remark when I have told him about the 4 km run I did, one of my two per week.

"Fuck, man did I have a good run today, I did my 4 clicks without major issues."

"Yeah, I know. So did the people in Afghanistan, did you read about the earthquake there?" Funny fuck he is.

He is gaining major distance on me but I keep up a steady pace. I want to get this fuck. I can hear my partner on the radio calling in our foot chase. Over a fence we go. Then another and then I lose sight of him. Risky shit now. Will he still run or will he try to ambush me? But this is the shit I love. I climb the last fence I saw him jump. I now see I will be getting my reward soon.

Down a long gravel alley I see that he has lost his shoes and that his speed is really taking a dump. The fucker is losing steam. I have paced mine; I have lots of distance left in me. Lots left to fight, even fight after this run. I am a dog wanting to get my bite in.

I kick into high gear and now I am gaining on him.

"Keep running, fucker, I am going to fucking kick your ass!" The funniest shit roles out of your mouth when you know you are going to get your game. Ha, not very professional, eh? But it was the truth, I was going to kick his ass for making me run. My first ass kicking to be delivered on the job, I was stoked.

At the time, his next reaction totally confused me but now I know that he had run from the cops before. You see there is this unwritten rule that if you get caught by the police you do not run. The game is up and you are caught. No big thing, those are just the rules. They break the law and we try to catch them. But running after you are caught is going to get your ass kicked. Those are the rules.

We called it "the one-punch rule," you run and every cop involved with the foot chase gets a punch after you get caught.

Just as I finished yelling my totally asinine threat he just stopped and laid down. He went into an immediate fetal position and started begging not to get hit.

What am I to do? I want to clobber the guy but he was giving up. I did not have the grounds to hit, did I? More recruit mental fucking. I ran up, put my knee into his back, and handcuffed him. I totally whored off! I wanted to slap this fuck around. What the fuck was he thinking?

So, as I walked this guy to the scene my partner just looks at me. Her eyes tell me that she is confused but knows why the guy still looks healthy. She knows better than to tell me to punch the fuck. She knows that I will have to cross that line myself. She knows that I am swimming in a pool of educational crap. I have to swim through it myself. No helping hands here.

My partner looks at the guy and lets him know that he is lucky that I caught him, otherwise she would have kicked the shit out of him.

"Fuck you, bitch, I would fuck you up the ass!" are words that escaped his mouth. My world spins as anger floods into me.

What the fuck? You can mock me, you can run from me, your can even laugh at me later, telling your friends how the rookie cop did not kick your ass.

But, you do not talk shit to my partner! She is my sister and you my friend have crossed the line. Now it is my turn to cross the line.

I give a quick glance around to ensure that there are no "eyes" around and I give the piece of shit a reminder that I am on a quick learning curve. No wind up, nothing overt, nothing to make people watch and stare, I drop my right fist deep into this guy's kidney. He feels soft, my whole fist sinks in. And, if the fist fits well, something has to make room for it. Organs move, air gets pushed out, and fluids move.

He buckles over and he is gasping for air. His lungs freeze, his body cramps due to the sudden displacement of fluids. There, you mother fucker, is that up the ass enough for you? My partner looks at me, poised to stop a second shot. For me my point is made. Retribution is done, no need for a second shot. I can see a small smile tip my partner's face, I have walked through the fire and come out unscathed. My first foot chase, my first taste of "The Shit." I am hooked.

Getting back to the car was another thing. When I sat down I was a jittering wreck. My hands were shaking and my knees felt like they were going to fold backwards. I could not write, I barely had enough focus to hold onto my pen.

My partner looked over at me, and when I saw her looking at me I felt embarrassed. I felt like I was out of control, I felt like I was showing her that I was afraid but yet I wasn't. What the fuck is this? I won the fight, I did not run away, why did I feel like this?

"Easy, big guy, no need to write anything right now. It will wear off faster if you don't think about it. So, how do you think you could do that better next time?"

These words were like a solid pat on the back from your father, telling you that he is proud. I forgot my shakes and immediately thought on how I might have fucked up. I never worry about making mistakes, never did. One can only perform to the level of training and foresight one puts into situations. I only had to do my best and I would never lose face with my comrades.

So, my fuck-up was not to communicate over the radio to the other units. I have to learn how to run, watch my bad guy, gather my bearings, and talk on the radio at the same time. My first lesson is learned. I will never forget this day.

Next day in the parade room my partner tells the story at the table of my foot chase. She tells it like it is, nothing blemished, nothing added. Just the tale in its entirety.

I am accepted my second day on the job. My team knows I will not be afraid to enter "the Shit" with them. They know that I am willing to chase, fight, and protect.

They know that I am new, that I have a lot to learn. They know I am eager.

HEAD-ON COLLISION
HEAD ON COLLISION

Where am I?

My mind spins, my hands move over my face as I try to wipe the haze from them.

I smell gunpowder, not from a gun but from the deployment of airbags.

A Ford Crown Victoria, a marked police cruiser, has just rammed a black truck head-on, a combined collision of over 100 km/hr.

The car that I was driving just seconds ago.

I can hear people yelling as I feel my fist crashing through the driver's side car window. I feel no pain because my body is pumping with adrenaline. The glass folds and pops as my fist slams through it. My only focus is to crush the fucker on the other side of the glass.

Why? Because the fucking piece of shit on the other side of that window just tried to run over my partner. I would have seen my brother in blue getting plowed under a black 2004 Ford half-ton truck if it was not for my partner's quick leap between two parked cars.

It was close, too close. If my partner had a fat wallet in his back pocket he would have been tagged.

"Too fucking close!" will be all that will be said in the office later.

I know him as Trevor, I have dealt with him before. He is a cracked-out forty-four-year-old male that uses his cancer as his excuse in court for his drug addiction and his violent crime sprees. It works. His sorry song and dance gets him out in less time than you or I would do for a shoplifting beef.

His criminal record lists assaults, robberies, weapons offenses, drug trafficking offenses, and lots of resisting arrest charges. Ah, the beauty of our criminal justice system. Fucking soft is the best way to describe it.

There is a passenger, I do not know him, but I see him scramble out of the passenger's side door after the collision, right into my partner, who opens up a world of hurt on the passenger. All I catch is a textbook kick into the guy's chest.

The bad guy falls like a sack of shit and my partner is all over him. I cannot see him now, behind the other side of the truck. I have a job to do here on my side, I trust my partner with my life to finish his job. The trust is the same from him.

All this streams through my head in an instant, complete mental clarity as my brain fires off neurons in massive succession. Mother Nature sure created a beautiful drug. I see the eyes of Trevor and they are wide open, lips are curled back over his teeth, and his chin is dipping down. My time on the street tells me that it is fight time as all of these signs are prefight clues. Unconscious signals put out by the human body in preparation for combat.

I see a beautiful star-shaped imprint on the front window of the truck after the head-on collision, caused from his head bouncing off of it. I know that blows to the head will be most effective right now because he has already sustained damage to his head from impacting the window.

Then I get a bigger adrenaline fix, I feel all time slow down, and my face feels hot. I have felt this before and have learned to enjoy the sensation. I know that my body is functioning at 110 percent. I know not to fear the fix. This is when I am the strongest, this is when I feel no pain and my mind is processing information so fast that time seems to slow down.

I call it "Matrix Time" and I love it.

I see the glass cascade down like fluffy snow falling from the sky in a windless snowstorm. A quick glance at his hands on the steering wheel tells me that he has no weapons. Game time!

My left fist slams into his face, causing his nose to bend and suddenly pop under the force. My right fist lines up for a second blow.

I can already see blood flowing from his nose.

"Fucking eh...I broke his nose" is the only tangible thought that fills my mind. The right fist hits solid on his jaw, causing his head to spin violently away from me. He is fucked; I have two or three seconds now. His brain is bouncing off of his cranial cavity and I have two or three seconds to cause more damage to this fuck before his brain even recovers from that blow.

Two or three seconds is a lifetime in combat.

I grab a handful of hair with my left hand and start to yank the ass out of the truck window. I know that he will come out easy as he is stunned and he is not wearing a seatbelt.

He is about six feet tall and 170 pounds but he comes out of the open window like a rag doll. I am a frothing animal now. I am filled with nature's most primitive desire, to fucking crush this guy. Fueled by nature's most powerful drug and motivated by man's oldest emotion, revenge. Here is my chance to get even for all those people this fuck has victimized. For that zit-faced crying kid because Trevor stole his BMX bike. Trevor stuffed a barrel from a sawed-off shotgun into his face. For all those people that have gone out in the morning to find their car stolen so that Trevor could drive around to find his crack or "chip" off of those who had it.

A quick hoot for a ride. And for that family that came home to find that their house, their sanctuary, had been ransacked.

I will extract the payment needed now for their loss of innocence, the payment that the courts refuse to take.

My blows are well placed. I want to have him hurt for weeks. To ache when he roles over at night and to piss blood when he uses the bathroom. I want him to remember me.

A blow deep into the kidneys, an elbow to the ribs, and a final blow into the sternum are all delivered before his body finishes sliding off the side door and onto the ground. I want to keep on going.

I want to yell,"Fuck you, shit bag…it is payback time!" But I don't, I know my limits, I know how to stop, I know how not to be like Trevor, a "bad guy."

Trevor lands on his face and my knee lands in his center back to pin him down. I feel his spine shift and move from the pressure, more reminders from our interaction. In a flash an arm bar is on him. My hand slides behind my back, getting my handcuffs without even a seconds worth of hesitation. It is a task that has been performed thousands of times. The cuffs are on and I immediately feel the dump coming off.

"Shit, the fix is going away. I will get the shakes, I will get the limp knees but I know how to work through this. Keep your shit together; don't look like you are being a pussy. Focus on this important shit."

These words keep spinning through my mind.

I try to not let the side effects of the adrenaline wearing off take me over.

I look around and see a wall of faces from pedestrian onlookers. The only thing that comes out of my mouth is:

"Is everyone okay?"

They all look at me like I am on crack.

"What do you mean, are we okay? Are you okay?" are the first words coming out of a man's mouth who has seen the entire event unfold before him. "You were just in a head-on collision! That guy just rammed your car!"

Oh yeah, I remember now.

The woman that ran out in front of the cruiser with a frantic look on her face, yelling, "He is in the parking lot, he is breaking into my truck!"

I remember my partner jumping out on foot as I reversed the police cruiser into the parade. I remember seeing the black truck turn and aim at my partner and almost run him over.

I remember the sensation of anger flood me as I pressed the accelerator into the floorboard. When I saw the front end of the truck lurch up from the torque given to the rear tires, I knew the bad guy did the same.

I remember the "Oh fuck!" as I pushed myself away from the steering wheel in hopes that I did not collide with it. I remember cursing myself for assuming the guy would go on foot and taking my seatbelt off as I reversed so that I could get out of the car fast when he ran. Assumption is the mother of all fuck-ups.

I remember the car and truck colliding. I see the airbag unfold slowly before me as I crash into it. My body hits the airbag like a cannonball. I slid off to the left, into the "A" post where the door meets the window. I can remember gaining my bearings as I waited to feel major pain anywhere. I read that even under the influence of adrenaline one still feels pain from major bones broken.

"No pain, so I am good, I think." I can still feel my feet kicking the driver's door open as it was pinched shut due to the car's frame bending from the impact. The smell of gunpowder still fills my nostrils as it mixes with the odor of oil and antifreeze from the cracked engine blocks.

My partner's voice echoed in my earpiece as he called for an ambulance and backup. The location and all of the information were called out in perfect succession. We know the air will be tied up with units asking for information because they did not copy the transmission at the time.

I hear the roar of cruiser engines topped off with the wails of sirens. Here come the troops, the cavalry is coming.

My partner and I instantly separate the witnesses and get them to write statements. As soon as the first car is on scene a virtual dance occurs. Every unit that arrives finds a job, gather statements, taking continuity of the bad guys, filling out accident forms, and airing more information for the street sergeant. A well-oiled machine is in action.

"1145 is out, police units are okay, two bad guys in custody. Tell EMS that we have two males that are conscious and breathing but are bleeding."

"1155 is out, roll another EMS this way to check out police units. One member involved in a head-on collision but is walking and talking."

"1121 is out, can we roll Traffic out, this is a police 410 [accident]. Marked unit versus truck."

"1145 can you role two busters [tow trucks] this way, as well as Fire to clean up fluids from the vehicles."

The information pours out in what I am sure is controlled chaos to our dispatch, all the tasks are done. We need to supply medical attention for the bad guy ASAP to show that we actually care for their health. I could give a fuck but that is what the courts want to see and hear.

We also have to ensure that the scene doesn't become a hazard so the fire department is called out to do what they are good at.

The dispatcher replies in a calm voice and with assertion of the tasks to be completed. Our dispatchers are all female and I can tell you nothing more instills calm and confidence than having a woman's voice over the radio that is calm, cool, and collected. I coin it to an angel's voice ensuring you that you are going to be okay.

Every time I have been in a shitty situation I have been happy to hear that voice.

But it is not over yet. The medics check me over and we all agree that I am one lucky fucker as I only have a broken right hand, my fault for punching out the window, and a bashed left knee from hitting the dash when we collided.

Nothing serious, I will heal, and the irony is that I will roll over in the middle of the night in pain, I will remember Trevor every time I bump my hand wrapped in a plaster cast. I will remember Trevor the same way that he remembers me.

I will also have to toil over hours of paperwork, fill in reports, and book evidence. I will hope that the judge imposes my conditions for Trevor's release but I don't have my hopes too high. I know that my request for Trevor to not possess, use, purchase, or consume any drugs or alcohol has a small chance of being imposed.

"Setting up the accused for failure, not rehabilitation" is what I was told once by a judge. I asked him why he did not impose the conditions that I requested. "I will not impose conditions for the accused that will force him into failing. He has an addiction and we all know that he cannot just simply stay away from his crack cocaine. We are setting him up for failure."

No, you dumb fuck! We are going to put him in jail where he belongs. He is a fucking crack head, he cares only for his next fix. He will steal from you, he will hurt those you love, and he will not give a flying fuck. He would rather sell his meal to buy his drugs, even though he has not eaten for days. But, you will never feel this in your secured estate lot. Your kids protected in their chartered school and you in your high-security building.

I still just nod my head and walk away. I know he will one day feel the shit storm that these drugs are bringing. No one is safe for this. Who knows how it will happen to him? A cousin lost to the streets because he was convinced to try the drug to keep him working longer hours? Maybe even his daughter will become a victim to a dirtbag boyfriend who convinces her to try ice or crack, feeding off of her insecurities. Who the hell knows, maybe one day while he is all messed up on expensive booze, wallowing in his own self-pity, he will try it.

Maybe he is just curious as his "buddy" tells him it is a great way to escape.

Who the fuck knows, I have seen it all too many times, and I do

21

not wish it on anyone. One hit and you are done, my client forever.

All police accidents have to be investigated internally by our traffic unit. If it is deemed that I have breached policy or am at fault for the accident, I will get negative paper, be made an example of for some Sergeant that wants to get promoted.

Did I breech policy? You bet, you have to get permission to ram a vehicle from your supervisor.

Will I get negative paper? I hope the fuck not, this is where my talent for articulation comes in.

Think fast, speak slowly, and always make sure your brain is in gear before you engage your mouth.

The key to explaining your actions is to always remember that you are explaining what you felt, what you perceived. To try to explain what other people might have perceived is all wrong, because people's perception is marred by their personal opinions.

Perception is ninety percent of reality.

If you have never seen a fight, watching someone get hit may offend you. You will see it as excessive use of force. But if you have seen lots of fights you may see it as a good use of force. Perception is the key to articulation.

So, how did I "articulate" all of this then? It was easy.

"Yes, Staff Sergeant, I know it is against policy to ram a vehicle unless specific permission is granted from the on-duty supervisor, as stated under section 341, paragraph 12 of the Policy and Procedures Act."

Always, always do your homework! Throw this shit out and the guys in the Ivory Tower go fucking code black. They feel like we are stupid grunts, chucking around dirty bad guys and working night shift because we are thick in the skull. Wrong, we love "The Shit," that is why we are here. Having this information on hand makes them panic because they feel like it is their information only.

"Uh, yes. So why did you ram the vehicle without permission, constable?"

"I did not ram the vehicle, sir. I would not breach policy. The offender in the vehicle rammed me. I was attempting to stop the cruiser when the accused accelerated and rammed me. In fact, sir, I almost had the vehicle in park before the collision occurred, I was in the process of taking my seatbelt off."

Oh yeah, not wearing your seatbelt is also a breach of policy, so I had to make sure I covered that one off right there so that this ass of a leader did not try to get his negative paper on me because of that.

A few more questions go by me but they are just so that the Staff Sergeant can fill out his departmental log. He knows I have done a good dance. He has no shit on me and he knows it. He will usher me off quickly so that he can target another good cop for another possible breach of policy.

Did I lie? No.

I articulated my facts well. I did try to stop the police cruiser just before we hit each other. Out of sheer fear it is natural to apply the brakes before colliding. I did have my seatbelt off, and it would be stupid of me to plan to ram another car and take my seatbelt off, would it not? Besides, it is a known fact that when we are under the influence of extreme stress occurrences become disjointed and slightly distorted.

Lies are those that affect the innocent.

"No, your honor, I did not sell schoolkids crack cocaine, even though the entire police surveillance task force witnessed me do it over and over." That is a lie. I have heard and witnessed the judge believe this shit. Even with seized drugs and statements from some of the now-addicted kids the judge only gave a conditional sentence. Fucking soft.

Finding the Animal Within
Finding the Animal Within.

I sit in a soft leather armchair as I hear the muffled laughter of good friends.

The smell of expensive cigars fills the room, trapped in the thin blue haze that fills the air. Occasionally I catch the smooth odor of high-quality aged scotch that is being consumed in crystal glasses.

I lean forward and place a hot flame to the front of a dark cigar. It has the look and feel of thin leather. The flame dances precariously close to the tip of the cigar. I watch as the heat scars and blackens the exposed tip.

The match burns closer to my fingers as I roll the cigar back and forth, heating the tip to a bright red amber.

I can hear the laughter roll over me in waves as I focus on my cigar.

Everything feels so far off in the distance. Muffled sounds echo to me as if I was locked away in a fishbowl.

Pulling away the flame, I draw on the back of the cigar. The bitter taste of earth and leather fills my mouth as the first plume of smoke enters it. I lean back and blow out the smoke. Its warmth rolls around my face and nose as I let it slowly flow from my mouth.

Sinking into the warm leather armchair, I watch the smoke roll up towards the vented ceiling. The strong smoke flows into the air vents drawing the smoke out of the room; I do not know where the smoke goes from here; I just know that the room is always filtering it out.

I feel a slight pinch on my fingers and I look at them to see the match burning even closer to my flesh. I still hold onto it. I wait for the pain, wondering if I can tolerate it. I watch as the flame gets closer and closer to my fingers.

I let the match burn and I can feel the pain singe through my fingers. I can feel the pain but it is a numb, dead pain. I know that I should be feeling much more.

It hurts but I have felt worse, I have felt much worse. I watch as the flame burns out; my flesh and skin extinguishes the flame.

I look over to the ashtray next to me. Reaching out to drop the black match into the heavy glass ashtray, I see that I was being watched.

I see the face of a fellow named Leo. He is a good man, slim in build but like his name would state he is strong of heart. He is a lion inside and even though he doesn't tell anyone of his sorrows or hardships I can tell from his face that he has endured much.

Leo is easy to talk to and is always laughing.

"Forgot that it was burning?" Leo asks as he sees me toss the match.

"Yeah," I say. Not willing to tell him I held onto it to see if I would feel the pain. My fingertips throb slightly. "I really don't feel much in those fingers since that guy almost bit them off."

With those words I look at my fingers, stare at the tips that have now healed. Fingernails that have grown back, skin that has regenerated. I can still see a light brown ring where teeth dug into my flesh.

Teeth that ripped and crushed my fingers.

My mind wanders back to the call. I can smell the air, putrid with human stink. I can still feel him under me. The thoughts come back like a rush of wind. As my heart beats I am back in my memories, traveling back into time.

"1423 is out," I say over my radio as I arrive in a dark alley. I exit my cruiser as I see a man lying beside a set of green plastic trashcans. I walk up slowly and scan the ground near the male. I look for blood, weapons, and drug paraphernalia, anything that might give me clues to why this male has collapsed here.

He is not poorly dressed and has good shoes on. I see clean socks and washed pants. He is not a homeless person who has had too much to drink or been on a heavy drug binge and passed out.

I close in and see that his chest moves as he breathes in deeply. His chest rises and falls as he breathes hard. He starts to breathe harder and harder. I can see his bloodshot and straining eyes peering at me. His head is tucked away from me but his eyes are open and looking at me. The male starts to breathe harder.

My heart pumps, I can feel the fix coming. My instincts are telling me this is all bad.

"Sir, are you all right?" I say as my hands start to tense under my leather gloves. I can feel his breathing. I can feel it move through me. I sense his anger, his extreme and boiling fury.

Just as I am a few feet away from him he explodes towards me. He attacks like a wild animal. His eyes are wide open, his lips are drawn back over his teeth, and his hands reach for me as if they were tipped with razor-sharp talons.

He snaps his body towards me and lunges for my chest. My hands instinctively come up to protect me. I drive my open hands into his face and force his head back.

This motion slows him down but he still digs his hands into my chest. I feel nothing as he claws at my body armor. I drop my right hand away from his face and arc it back.

I sweep low and then raise my fist to deliver an uppercut. A mere split-second before my fist hits the bottom of his jaw I drop back my left hand that was holding his head away from me. As my black leather-covered hand moves away I can see eyes filled with madness.

I hit him hard and heavy with the uppercut. I drive his head back in a violent contortion. The blow sends him stumbling backwards. His mind is trying to recover from my blow, his world is spinning. I drive forward with two blows to his sternum, sending him further back. I can hear the dull echo of his chest cavity as I slam my fists into him.

He stumbles further back and trips over a full bag of garbage. He spills over backwards and hits the ground hard. His brain was still swimming in a raging sea from the past set of blows that I delivered.

I stop to see if he is finished. I stop to see if he has had enough, if he is going to give up.

My hesitation is going to be a lesson learned. A mistake that I will never make again.

In those brief seconds he was able to regain his senses.

I hear a primal scream as he lunges towards me again. His actions were so fast and unpredicted that I do not have time to move away from his attack. Not enough time to sidestep and allow his attack to be parried.

He leaps towards me like a lion on the attack. His hands lock onto my shoulders and from his forward energy I tumble backwards.

I do not fight the fall, I know that it will happen whether I fight it or accept it. I know that we are going to fight on the ground and I am happy fighting there.

I lock my head into his chest so that my head doesn't whip from the impact and snap off of the ground. I pull tight on his body. I secure my head; I do not want to have my brain receive a concussion from falling. I have had that happen before from sparring in the Dojo. I do not want that to happen out on the street.

If I get knocked out, if I cannot finish this fight, I am a dead man. This deranged lunatic would surely bludgeon me to death. Then he will have access to a gun, a baton, body armor, pepper spray, and other weapons. This is not an acceptable outcome.

We hit the ground hard; I can feel the air try to rush out of my lungs. It is stopped as my core was tight and I was expecting the blow to try to wind me. I kept my body tense and rigid as we fell to the earth. My head holds well in his chest and I do not feel the earth try to split the back of my skull.

We are now on the ground. I am now ground fighting. Not my strongest attribute but still not a place that I hate to fight.

I am brought back to a large gym hall. The yellow lights high above give a dizzying effect to the hard wood floor gym. My instructor's voice echoes over the barren walls. "If a bad guy takes you to the ground don't try to get back up. Lying on the ground is a stable fighting platform. If you are down stay there until it is safe to get back up. I will teach you how to fuck the bad guy up if he decides to fight you on the ground."

I want to fuck this guy up now. I am no longer in the mood to wonder how I can help this guy. I have had enough and I am now feeling a surge of anger inside of me.

"How fucking dare this guy take me down?!" My mind screams as my teeth grit together. "You are mine, mother fucker! I am going to rip you to shit!"

My teeth grit harder. I can feel my heart pounding harder and faster. I feel the air rip through my clenched teeth as my lungs demand more air. I can feel my adrenaline surge into me; I can feel my heart pump harder.

My left hand drives into the guy's face, two of my fingers drive into his right eye socket. He moves away from the pain and sits up on my chest. He straddles my chest and reaches up with both hands to try to pull my hand off of his face.

I drive my right elbow into his exposed quad. His bent leg has the muscle stretched and I drive my elbow hard. I can feel the soft tissue of his muscle move and flex as my elbow is driven hard into him. I feel his body jerk forward as he reacts to the pain.

I keep my grip on his face with my left hand as I pull his head back close into me. I do not want to give him the reach again by sitting up; I want to keep our fighting space small and personal.

I put my right elbow on the asphalt below me. I put my right foot flat on the ground. I chamber my body. I am locked into place; I explode my hips to the side. Driving my body up and over, I throw his body over and down.

In a sudden flash he is now below me and I am on top of him.

My right elbow is then driven into his chest. I squeeze harder on his face and eye. His chest crumples and sags as I force my elbow into his body cavity. I displace air and the rush of hot gas from his lungs is felt on my hand across his face.

I line up for another blow to the chest. I want to finish this fight now. Right fucking now. I want to break ribs and crush his internal organs. I line up, pulling my right elbow as far back as I can take it. I line up my hips and body weight so that I can give this final finishing blow.

Just then I stutter. I jerk as my body sends out major pain signals to my brain. My left hand feels like it is on fire and as I look I can see that the guy has opened his mouth enough to get my index finger in it. I can see that he has clapped down on my finger and is biting.

He is biting with all of his force. He is biting to take my finger off.

Pain, white hot surging pain courses through my finger. I can feel the nail splitting under the pressure of his grinding molars.

White hot pain fills my arm.

I smash him to the head with my right open palm. I want to break this guy's hold on my finger. I want the splitting pain to stop. I hit him again and again but each blow just seems to anger him more. Each blow to the head just makes him bite harder. Harder and harder he drives his teeth into my leather glove.

Deeper into my finger.

More pain.

But as more and more pain is felt I feel something swelling inside of me. It is not my fix, not my body's adrenaline dump. I have felt that countless of times before. It is something else.

I can feel it growing, pulsating deep inside of me. It is anger, fury, and pain all swirling together. I can feel it crashing inside of my chest. It is like an angry beast that wants out.

I have never felt this sensation so strong. It is not panic, it is pure, unbridled fury. I feel the urge to crush, maim, and destroy. I feel like I have a beast inside that wants out, wants to be unleashed on the world to cause suffering.

I still smash my palm strikes into his head. I hit harder and harder and his bite just gets tighter and tighter.

I feel the beast inside and I am afraid of letting it out. I have never felt this before; I worry what might happen if I give in to the sensation.

I hit more and more.

I can feel the fire inside grow. More pain, more fire. My chest feels like it is going to explode. I fear the sensation, but it grows more and more.

The beast builds; it starts to override all my senses. I know I cannot stop it now. I give in as I strike the guy's head again.

I worry that my finger is getting bitten off. I can feel his teeth crush my flesh and mash my fingernail.

My inner animal wants to fight, to destroy. It screams to be released; it tells me that it can take care of my pain. It is a primal beast, one filled with fury and lust.

The animal claws at the cage harder and harder. Like a dam bursting I let out the animal inside of me, the one I have kept buried deep.

It awakes.

A tidal wave washes over me and the beast comes crashing out. Like an orgasm I can feel my world rush around me.

I feel warmth flood into me. I can feel every pore on my body.

I am more awake than I have ever been. My hair feels like it is standing on end, bristled up like the fur on the back of an angry wolf. My heart pumps hard as I become detached from my pain.

I stop hitting the guy in the head. I can no longer feel the pain.

I can only feel the animal inside of me wanting to rip this guy to shreds. I lock my right hand around his face and stand up. I have opened the cage on a beast that has been hiding inside of me my entire life. I have felt it hiding in the shadows. I knew that it was there but never really knew what to do with it. I feared the sensation all the other times it remotely showed its eyes in the darkness.

Without effort I pick up the 200-pound body and lift him off of the ground. I am standing there with an angry male trying to bite my finger off and I pick him up like he is a child in my arms.

"You want my fucking hand? Take my fucking hand!"

I hear a loud gong from his head hitting the hard object; it rings like a bell as I drive the back of his head into the large metal garbage container that is right behind him.

I put my right thumb onto his open left eye and I press hard. I want to see his eye explode. I want to crush and tear this fucker apart.

I drive his head again to the container as I press hard with my thumb. Another resounding ring as the metal container vibrates.

My left hand slides free as he opens his mouth to scream. He screams loud as my thumb presses into his eye socket.

I pull my left hand free and I can only think about damaging this guy more.

I have let my caged animal free and I want to bite, claw, and crush. I feel the rage growing and building.

Rip and tear. I want to see his blood pour onto the sidewalk. I am filled with blood lust. I want to see blood flow. I want to feel it speckle my face. I want to open him up and spill his blood all over the ground.

I hold him hard against the container as I still push into his eye socket. I see the eye start to hemorrhage as small bloody tears flow down his face.

Slamming my left fist into his chest, I punch the air out of his lungs. The blow causes his scream to become a screech.

As he tries to breath in the air that he lost from my blow I drive my fist into him again. I do not feel the sag of his chest this time. I do not feel air rush out of him because there is no more air to move.

I feel ribs bend and a sternum move. I can feel small snaps and pops as ribs separate from the cartilage on his sternum. Without the air in his lungs my blow pummels his lungs and heart.

I feel like I have been possessed by an ancient creature. A primitive animal that is fighting to live, fighting to walk in the sun again. I feel like I am floating in a pool of water as all the sound around me fades to muffled echoes. Time slows to a standstill as I move through the heavy liquid air. My vision is blurred on the edges but everything in the middle is crystal clear.

I can see small drops of blood spray from his mouth as I land another hammer-like blow to his chest. I can smell the garbage around us. It is strong and bitter. I can smell his fear, it is strong and bitter.

I pull his head away from the dumpster as my thumb slips behind his eye ball and finds a strong lock on the inside of his eye socket. I pull his body far back with my right arm. He swings as I pull him; his feet are off of the ground. I feel unstoppable, I feel like I have been struck by lightning. My body is alive.

I have found life in the thrill of death. I am a soldier in combat and I am more alive than ever.

I toss the ragdoll body against the dumpster. I let go of my grip on his face and eye socket as I toss his body away from me.

His body floats through the air. His limbs fall forward as he careens backwards. His head leads his body back to the metal dumpster. I see his hair swirl around his face like sea kelp slowly waving in the ocean. My world moves slowly. I move in the thick waters around me.

He slams hard into the metal dumpster. I do not hear the gong this time. I hear nothing but my deep breathing and pumping heart. I hear nothing besides the animal inside of me yelling for more. My lust for destruction is filling me and I am alive.

Even before his body hits the ground I drive my knee hard into his face. I feel the snapping of soft cartilage vibrate through my knee. I see his head bounce back and ricochet off the dumpster as blood sprays across my pants. His face is instantly filled with a torrent of blood as his nose is badly split and broken.

I grab the rim of the dumpster as I line up for another damaging knee strike. I see his body slumped against the dumpster. I can see in his eyes that he is finished. He stares straight ahead with eyes wide open in an unconscious stare.

I hear my animal scream for more. It wants more blood. I want more blood. I feel the urge to crush flow through me. I want to fight more. I want to utterly destroy this guy.

I want to stop. I worry that I cannot stop this beast I have let out. I have to stop.

I think of my training. I think back.

I wonder if anyone told me how to stop the beast once I let it out.

"Fighting is like a light switch. Turn it on, be brutal and efficient. Then, turn it off. Shut it down so that you keep your ass out of jail. You do not want to cross that line."

I remember the words.

But how, how do I shut this emotion down? I want to stop it now. I want to stop my destruction. I have done enough, the threat is gone, but I still want to pummel this fuck into the ground.

I can feel my teeth grind, I can sense my jaw lock hard as I pull heavy deep breaths of air into my lungs. I feel the cool air move across my lips as they are drawn back over my teeth. I am a bare-toothed animal right now. Teeth flaring and eyes wide open in a maddened gaze. I am an animal and I want to become human again. I want to cage the animal.

I still grip hard onto the rim of the garbage can. I hold my leg back, chambered to deliver a blow to my already unconscious opponent.

My hands grip harder and harder onto the rim. I can feel my left glove fill with blood as my hands squeezes, forcing more blood to come out of my badly damaged finger.

I feel like screaming. I feel like yelling at the top of my lungs. I want to release this energy inside of me. An energy that I worry will destroy me.

What have I done?

Why did I let this animal free?

How do I stop it?

Then I feel calm subdue me. I think about my uniform, what it means to me. I imagine that I was looking at me right now. What would I see? I see no honor, no purpose to my final blow.

I am a professional soldier. I am not a crazed animal like he was. I am not a fucked-up mental case like he was. I am not a bad guy. I have a job to do. I have done what was needed to be done. I have to finish off my job. I am a professional.

I am not a bad guy.

I feel the animal sulk back into the shadows. I feel the fury leave my hands as they relax on the dumpster. My lips roll down over my teeth and my breathing becomes heavy and labored.

I reach down and roll the male onto his back as I put handcuffs onto him. I can see his chest heave as he draws air in. Blood flowing from his nose is sprayed out over the ground as he exhales. He is still unconscious.

I grab my mike and speak into it. I try to speak clearly and calmly. I try to speak without gasping for air but I cannot.

"1423. One in custody. Can you send EMS? Officer is okay." My heart pounds as my words are forced out. My lungs burn as acidic saliva builds in my mouth.

"10-4. Is anyone close to 1423's location to assist him?"

"I am okay, dispatch. Just send EMS for the offender." I can hear sirens start whining in the distance. The troops are coming. They can hear that I am out of breath. They know that something has happened and they all want to come and make sure all is well.

A fellow brother in blue has been in combat and they all want to come to make sure he is safe. They all want to come and make sure that the bad guy is fucked up for trying to go after a uniform.

I lean up against my cruiser. I know what is going to happen next.

I can feel the nausea of my adrenaline rush subsiding. My legs get heavy and my hands shake. I feel like the very ground is drawing energy away from me.

During my combat I feel alive. Now that I have finished and lived I feel like I am dead. As if I wait for death to come walk beside me so that I can feel life.

I shake as my fix leaves me. I fucking hate this part. I have just grown to accept it. I fucking hate it. I worry about people seeing me shake. I worry about people thinking I am weak for shaking.

I shake harder. My hands vibrate as I look at my shiny black leather gloves. Shiny from the blood that covers them. My nausea leaves me but my shakes still fill me.

I see a cruiser pull up at the same time an EMS unit arrives on scene.

Two cops instantly look at me and when I give them a nod that I am all right they move over to the bad guy lying in a fucked-up mess by the dumpster.

The EMS guys move to me right away.

They ask me if I have any injuries and I show them my gloved left hand.

"The fuck tried to bite my finger off. I do not know what kind of shape it is in because I did not want to take the glove off and expose my open wound to his blood."

"Perfect, it is good that you did not take it off. Let's get you cleaned up and then look at your finger."

I walk with the medics over to the ambulance. I feel better now. My shakes are leaving me. I feel better; I hope no one saw me shaking.

I sit in the soft vinyl chair in the ambulance and a medic sprays a solution all over my arms and hands. I can smell alcohol, raw burning alcohol. My skin feels cold from the evaporating mist.

They wipe my skin clean and then spray me again. While they wipe my skin the second time they get me to wash my gloves in a gel solution that also smells of raw alcohol. I roll my hands over and over inside of each other. Globs of gel fall into a bucket placed at my feet. Clear gel that is now pink from the mixture of blood and globs of cleansing solution.

I look outside the open ambulance door and see a second ambulance come for the injured bad guy.

I wash my gloves a second time. My left finger feels like it is made of lead. A stiff stump that is numb and swollen. I do not feel any pain from the injury. Just a thundering throb every time my finger gets touched or moved.

I wonder if I still have a finger. I wonder if his powerful bite has severed my finger from my hand. I really don't care. I am happy that I have lived this fight. A loss of a fingertip is a small price to pay for having an extra day to wake up to.

"Okay, you look pretty clean, let's see what we have going on in here." His hands stretch over and start to carefully roll back my leather glove.

Blood flows from the cuff as soon as he starts to manipulate the glove. More blood drops into the blue plastic bucket at my feet. It mixes in with the bad guy's blood, red pools swirling with pink gel.

The glove is finally pulled off and with the final tug a glob of red coagulating blood spatters into the bucket below.

Fresh blood pours from my finger as the second medic quickly wraps clean white gauze around my meaty finger. He squeezes hard and I just stare forward. I stare forward as I feel a surge of white hot pain fill my arm.

I stare forward as I let the pain fill me. I want it to fill me. It awakens me from this numb world that I am in right now. The pain reminds me that I am alive. It reminds me that I am no longer shaking.

The pain brings me back into real time. It removes me from the downswing of losing my fix. I enjoy the pain.

"Sorry, buddy, but this is going to hurt. I have to check to see what damage is done here." I see the medic look at me. His eyes tell me that he is sincere with his words. He feels for me, feels for the pain.

"No worries, I am fucking exhausted from fighting. I really don't feel shit right now."

"Good." He lifts off the soaked gauze, no longer pristine and white. He looks at my finger. He runs his fingers along the bone. He pushes, prods, and rubs the finger.

Each movement sends pain into me. Each blast of hot burning pain roars into me. I just soak it up. I feel better when I feel the pain. It is only pain, it is not suffering.

He looks at me and smiles.

"It looks like he never made it through the bone. Your nail is pretty well fucked and will probably fall off. I would suggest that we go back to the hospital to get a specialist to check it out so that you do not get nerve damage. If you do not want to go I can stitch it up here and we can call it a day."

I look at my finger. I can see the split skin from his teeth trying to force their way through my glove and finger. I see my fingernail crushed and in two pieces. The large piece is still in place but the small chunk is just barley hanging onto the skin and meat below it.

"What about this fucked-up nail?" I point with my free hand to the jagged nail hanging there. "Can you fix that?"

"I would have to just cut it off. It will probably just fall off on its own but if you want to I can just remove it now. "

"Yeah, take it off. Then let's stitch it up. I am tired and do not feel

35

like waiting to see a specialist about possible nerve damage."

I am tired.

So fucking tired.

I want to lie down here and fall asleep. I will regret not seeing a specialist as I have lost much of my sensation in my injured finger. I feel little from that finger now; it is numb, like I am when I put on my uniform.

"Okay, let's give you a local and wait for it to kick in. Then I will remove the nail."

"Fuck it. Like I said I don't feel shit." I fix my tired eyes on his. I let him focus on my eyes. I let him look into my eyes so that he can see my exhaustion. I never let anyone look into my eyes. I dislike it when people look into them but I let him look through them. "I am finished and all I want to do is get out of this uniform."

He sits there for a minute. Looking at me, deep into my eyes.

He gazes into my thousand-yard stare.

I am beyond tired. I could just curl up here and go to sleep. I have just finished hard combat and all I want to do is sleep. I wish I could just sleep.

"Okay, it is your call." He turns away from my eyes and gets on a clean pair of rubber gloves. "I will make this as quick as possible." His hands move to a plastic box that is located in a sliding cupboard. As he opens it I see a scalpel and a set of what look like to be stainless-steel needle-nose pliers. All of them are wrapped in sealed plastic.

His hands move quickly as blood starts to pour from my finger again. I watch the blood ooze out into the bucket at my feet. It is filled now with blood-soaked gauze, pink gel, my black leather gloves, and other medical scraps. I can hear the tap of my blood dripping into the bucket below.

I don't care. I am too tired to care right now. I want to get this uniform off. I want to remove the sweat-drenched shirt I wear. I want to slide off the heavy combat boots that are strapped to me. I dream of taking my body armor off and hanging up my duty belt. I dream of sleep.

The medic puts another cloth across my finger and squeezes hard again. I feel nothing.

"Okay, here we go." He clamps one off the stainless steel pliers on my exposed fingernail. I feel a surge of pain go through my hand. I flinch from it. The unexpected pain that made its way through my numb body.

He holds the pliers in his left hand and moves the scalpel to my finger with his right hand. He pauses when he has the sharp surgical blade lined up. He looks at me and when my eyes meet his he speaks.

"Whatever you do, no fucking punching the medic."

I laugh and just then he moves his blade across the raw opening of my fingernail bed. I can feel the sharp end slice under the remaining flesh of my nail. I can feel the cut, the cold steel moving through my flesh. I can feel the burn of nerve endings getting exposed to the air. It feels like a blowtorch has been turned on my finger.

I flinch but I am still too tired to care. His movement was fast and calculated. By the time the air is out of my lungs from my chuckle the hanging bit of nail is cut off.

He opens the clamp and my nail falls into the bucket at my feet. I look down as he tosses the scalpel into the heap below. I see more and more blood flow from my finger.

More blood flows into the blue plastic bucket by my feet. I still don't care. I want to go to sleep. I have never yet been so tired after fighting. I feel like my energy has been sucked out of me.

I wonder if letting out the animal inside of me has drained me. I wonder if I could ever get enough sleep to feel better.

I am worried. I worry about how tired I feel.

I am worried about this new emotion I felt. It bothers me because of how fierce it was. How raw the sensation was. And how much I liked it, I felt like I was filled with so much energy that I could have just exploded.

Now I am sitting here with barely enough energy to care about some medic cutting off a broken fingernail.

The medic silently cleans my finger off and wraps it tight with more gauze and medical tape. He hands me a bunch of medical tape, gauze, and antibiotic cream.

"Here, dress up that finger again in about two hours. If the bandage gets too soaked with blood, change it again. Try to leave it alone for a bit." He puts the wad of supplies in a small plastic bag. "I want you to lie back and rest for a few minutes. Keep your hand elevated while you do to slow the bleeding down."

I look at the medic as I lie back on the gurney.

"Hey!" He looks at me when I speak: "Thanks, it didn't hurt a bit."

He laughs. "Yeah, fucking right! No problem. Take care and I will come and get you in ten minutes. Relax a bit."

He walks out of the ambulance and I put my head back on a pillow covered in a starched pillowcase. I can hear the crinkle of the plastic under sheet. My eyes close before my head is even down on the bed. I fall asleep as my head sinks into the pillow.

I dream of nothing. My world is black. I am oblivious to the world around me. I am floating in darkness.

"Hey Smith, enough fucking beauty sleep!"

I hear the voice of my sergeant. I am drawn out of my sleep. I roll over to see my bandaged hand propped up on a blanket. It looks like a mess as small spots of blood speckle the white gauze. Dark purple blotches tell me that the dressing is old.

"How long have I been out for?" I sit up and look at my blood-soaked bandages. The blood should still be red. Dark blotches of purple pudding tell me that the blood has been exposed to air for at least thirty minutes. I have seen enough human blood dry to know this.

"Fuck, buddy. When the medics saw you passed out they told me that they would drive you back to the office. When you did not wake up during the ride back they said that they would come in for a coffee to let you recover. It has been an hour or so. You slept the entire time! I had to come and wake you up so that they could have their ambulance back."

A medic standing outside the door looks at me. "How are you feeling?"

I sit there and assess myself. I look at my finger. I judge my level of energy. I assess my alertness. I feel fucking great! I am totally revived. I feel like I have slept a whole night. My lethargy has disappeared without a trace.

"I feel good, really good actually." I start to get off the gurney.

"I figured so much. Did you know that after combat soldiers always want to sleep? The adrenaline high makes them so tired that all they want to do is sleep. Napoleon figured this out and always kept a troop in reserve to launch a counterattack after the first serge. Napoleon's army would always find the enemy troops sleeping when they advanced the second time."

"No fuck?" my sergeant says. I can tell that he is taking good note of this. He will use this information the next time he sees his men tired from combat. He is a good leader and he knows that information like this is valuable to the safety of his men.

"No fuck. Read a book called *On Combat*. It will let you know about all the psychological backlashes and side effects of combat. The author really focuses on adrenaline highs and lows."

I make sure to remember the name of the book. I will read it. Maybe it will give me answers to what I have just experienced. Answers to why I feel like I do when I get my fix and why I react the way I do when my adrenaline fix dissipates.

I thank the medic again and leave the ambulance. I go into the office and sit down to start my paperwork. My mind is clear and the fog that was so heavy just a few hours ago has lifted.

I sit down and start the paperwork, recalling every event and documenting them.

I sit down and relive the experience. Chronologically remembering the events and writing them down.

I remember the feelings, the desire to fight and crush.

I remember the rush and crash of energy. These are the things I leave out. I hide them and hope to discover in secret what and why this happened to me. I keep them secret because I fear that I will be ridiculed or looked at as a loose cannon.

I worry that what I felt is wrong or bad.

It has been some time since that fight and awakening occurred. I still look back at that day and wonder how I functioned so long keeping the animal at bay.

When I look at myself in the mirror I see myself as more whole, calmer, and more at peace with myself after letting go of the caged primal creature.

I have let the beast out many times since then. Each time I have been able to call it back in. Each time that I lock it back up I am thankful. I no longer fear it. I respect the beast; much like a racecar driver fears the machine he pushes to the limit, or how the hunter respects his weapon that he uses for killing.

I know now the damage that I can do when I let that animal out and I use it as a tool for combat. It is like any other weapon of war. It is destructive, damaging, and, if left unchecked, totally chaotic.

Everything feels so far off in the distance as I draw on the back of the cigar, the bitter taste of earth and leather fills my mouth. The warm smoke rolls around my face and nose as I let it slowly flow from my mouth.

Sinking into the warm leather armchair, I watch the smoke roll up towards the vented ceiling. The strong smoke flows into the air as my animal is locked so far away in my darkness.

CHRISTMAS IN THE HOOD

CHRISTMAS IN THE HOOD

The streets are covered in a layer of sifting snow. It is cold outside and the sun has set hours ago. Any warmth that was generated by it has now been leached out as the chilling grip of winter night.

Our cruiser drives the abandoned streets. It is Christmas night and like the tale goes, all is quiet.

This is the third Christmas that I have worked in a row. I don't mind working over Christmas. The holiday doesn't mean very much to me. No kids, no family, only memories associated with dealing with a divorced family over Christmas, no real reason to like the holiday. I always put my name on the relief board so guys with kids can take the night off to spend it with their families. I always get the days filled.

My partner has just gotten back from visiting his kids for a brief Christmas visit at his ex-wife's house. He has two little girls. Smart and beautiful, filled with fire and beauty.

They have grown up with a uniform in their life.

I like the fact that they just say hello and do not overreact to seeing the dark blue suit that I wear. I make idle chit-chat with the eight- and ten-year-old girls. My partner goes into the kitchen and I can feel the tension build with his ex-wife.

I have heard him talk about who gets the kids on what days over the holidays. I have heard him tell me about the issues as we work ten-hour shifts in the cruiser. I have told him to relax and think more of the kids than the pissing contest he and his wife have. But, he is angry, he is stubborn, and he knows nothing else besides being a cop. So, he doesn't like to lose. He doesn't want to really talk to her, to make her try to understand where he is coming from. And worst of all he doesn't want to listen to her and understand where she is coming from.

I look over and think, "Not here, not in front of the kids. Not in front of the kids. Don't demolish the holiday for them. Don't make them want to work Christmas." My partner looks over at me and he can tell that I am giving him the "better-stop-this-shit" look.

He stops the confrontation and walks out of the kitchen. With a smile and a hug he says good night to his two girls and then says good-bye to his ex-wife. I really think he still loves her and that is why he is so angry but he is hard to be with. His stubborn ways and the "I am always right cop" attitude are things that he needs to work through. He is trying.

No words are said as we pull back into our district; we call our sergeant to let him know we have finished our little trip out of district. He acknowledges and when I run the unit roster (a list on the computer that shows what and where all the cars are), I see another unit book out of district. Another car drives off to see his family and say good night to his kids on Christmas night.

"Thanks," are the only words that roll out of my partner's mouth. I know it is all he can do to let me know that he appreciates me cutting his conversation short with his ex-wife. It would have gotten nasty. I know it as I have heard them fight over the phone in the car.

"No need, brother."

I feel for him. He is lost without his family and lonely without the company of his kids. The service is only a good family while you are at work or out for beers. Past that it is just a job. The guys have families to go home to. If you are a smart cop you hold onto that sanctuary like it is priceless, because it is. Your home, your family is the only mentally safe place that you have. If you fuck up and corrupt that, you are in a world of stress and shit.

My partner slows our cruiser down as we see a figure walking on the sidewalk. Our eyes blink as we try to understand what we are looking at.

Is it an apparition of a late night?

Maybe even an optical illusion from the frost edging that encompasses the corners of our windshield?

"What the fuck?" I say as our headlights illuminate the sidewalk. It is a six-year-old girl walking down the sidewalk. She is holding her Cabbage Patch Kid in her arms and has a little blanket wrapped around her back. She has a pair of winter boots on that look like they are supposed to be worn by a ten- or twelve-year-old. Her face is red from the cold and her hands are clenched in little fists trying to keep warm.

She sees the lights and I can see that she is frightened. I can see the look of fear in her eyes. I can also see that she has the pains of panic running through her as winter's cold breath chills her. Her body knows that out here on the street is going to be a short-lived experience. Mother Nature has no remorse, she takes whatever falls into her arms. Children included.

I open my door and she freezes in her steps. I tell my partner to kill the lights as he steps out of the car also. As the car's headlights dim to a faint red glow she can see who has stopped for her in the middle of the night. She sees the uniforms and she starts to calm down. But with her calm come the shivers from the cold. She just stands there and shakes as my partner rushes up, taking his jacket off. He wraps her tight and lifts her off of the cold concrete.

Her loose boots slip off and land on the ground. The hollow sound attracts her attention and I see a small cold chilled hand reach for her boots. Her little hand is white from the cold but she still wants her boots.

"Don't worry; my partner will grab your boots. Let's get you into our car. It is warm in there." My partner looks at me as I already reach for the boots. I can see the hurt in his eyes. He is worried about what might be going on to force a young child out on the street in the cold.

Huddled in my partner's warm blue jacket I can see her face become a darker shade of red as the blood starts to flow in her again. She stops shivering so much and she is looking more alert. As she sits in the back seat of our cruiser she pulls her feet up close to her body and my partner tucks the bottom end of the jacket under her. All wrapped up she looks like a blue cocoon, her little head the only thing that we can see.

I voice our situation over the air and ask if more units can come in the area to start to canvas the houses in the area. We need to find her home. We need some answers.

As more and more cars come in the area they all start to wake people up in the area. Sleepy residences are woken up to the police knocking on their doors, asking if they know of a little girl that they describe. No success yet.

My partner talks to the girl to get some basic information from her. Her name is Trisha, she is six years old, and she doesn't really know where she lives. She doesn't know her phone number and when he asks her why she is out in the middle of the night she says that she is hungry.

I get out of the car and force my way into the cold blowing wind. With the cold air biting my face I make my way to the trunk of our cruiser. A quick knock on the trunk as the key slides into the lock breaks off a thin layer of ice covering it. The trunk pops and creaks open and I get the cookies and other treats that my partner's ex-wife gave us for the road and the guys working nights on Christmas. I pull out the plastic-covered tin plate and show her the array of Christmas cookies and chocolates.

Her eyes widen as she sees the bright colors of green, red, and white icing. Fancy snowmen, decorated angels, and star-shaped cookies all seem to be too much for her to handle.

Her hand goes out and then she stops. She looks at me as if to ask that it is all right to eat the cops' cookies. I smile and tell her to help herself. I put the tray of cookies beside her on the seat as another cop shows up.

I know this guy, we have taken some hot calls together. He is a mean-looking mother. At only six feet tall he is as wide as a house. His shaved head and broken nose tell you that he is all for the business of combat. He is switched on and likes to go after the bad guys.

He looks inside and sees her eating the cookies like it was the last time she would see sweets.

"Hungry?"

"Yeah, that is why she said she is not at home. She told us that she was hungry."

"Hey, I think I have some chocolate milk in my lunch kit. Would you want some milk to go with those cookies?" The cop leans over and talks to the little girl in the back. His smile and open eyes tell her that she is in a safe place.

Her head nods as a little "Yes please" escapes from her mouth that is filled with sugary delights.

Happiness fills his face as he opens a small plastic container that is filled with chocolate milk and hands it to the little girl in the back seat.

"I have a little girl at home. She is a year older than you and her name is Melody." I move away from the car as this house of a man starts to talk to the little girl. I have seen him in the office talking to his little girl. I would smile when I heard the big rough man talk to his little girl about teddy bears and Barbie dolls.

No one ever bugs you for telling your wife you love her, talking to your kids about toys and imaginary people. You can be the hardest, meanest dog on the block and no one will ever rough you over being soft with your family.

As I walk away I start to track the little girl's footprints in the snow. The boots she wore had a deep knobby sole and it made tracking her path pretty easy. At some points I lost her path as the snow did its best to disguise the trail but then when I would look closely on the ground with my flashlight close to it I would find the track again. The shadows of the imprinted snow would suddenly pick up like dark craters on a white lunar surface.

I let dispatch know that I am tracking her footprints in the snow and give her an address that I am passing. I let her know of the direction and ask that all foot traffic in the area stop. I do not want her footprints to be trampled over by a cop in the area.

My sergeant copies me and tells me that he wants to be updated as soon as I find the end of the track. He knows that my tracking skills are pretty good, developed from hunting game with my father.

I have been outside for fifteen minutes and I am getting cold now. My feet are feeling the ice move through the rubber soles and my ears bite into me. I cover my hands over them to give some heat to them. It helps but I know it is only temporary. I have tracked her footprints for two blocks now and I wonder how she made it so far.

A strong white beam cuts the cold ice-filled air as my flashlight scans the ground for her bootprints. I fear that I may be at the end of my track without success. A snow drift makes its path across the sidewalk and it stretches for the whole block.

"Fuck me, she could not have made it much further. I am fucking freezing and I am much better dressed for the weather than her."

I radio to my partner. "Ask the little girl what color her house is and if she has a swing or other toys in the front yard. Also ask her if her mother or father put up any special decorations in the window."

"10-4; stand by."

I stand there in the blowing snow and I tuck my face into the collar of my jacket so that the warmth of my breath can flow into it. I feel the warm air rush back onto my face and it feels good. I wish now that I had a toque but I forgot it in the car.

"Okay, she has a yellow and white house. She also said that she built a snowman last week in the front yard. She says that she has no Christmas stuff set up."

"Roger that." I scan the street looking for a yellow and white house but under the swirling snow and the dim streetlights, figuring out colors is not going to work. I change my tactics. I look for houses with lights on in the darkness. It is really late so very few lights are on. I figure that a girl leaving the house in the middle of the night will leave a light on. I also figure that if her family was awake they will be up now looking for her.

I see a house at the far end of the block and the stairway light is on and the living room has a pale blue glow of a running television. I make my way for it. If someone is awake maybe they can tell me where the girl lives. It will give me a chance to warm up at least.

As I close in I see the glint of yellow siding through the snow. There are no decorations in the window and I can see a small mound of snow in the front yard that could have been the creation of a six-year-old girl making a snowman.

"I think I have a possible at 133 Cedar Place. I am going to be doing a door knock."

My dispatcher copies and I hear a car's engine in the distance; I know that some other units are making their way over to my location. Everyone is curious to solve the mystery.

My boots crunch under the wind-blown snow that covers the frozen concrete sidewalk. I can see the flashing blue strobe of a television set in the living room and when I glance into the large bay front windows I can see someone sleeping on the couch. I can also see an oval coffee table covered with empty beer bottles, cigarette butts, and a large ceramic ashtray that has a familiar small glass pipe sitting in it.

I can see the white residue of crack cocaine smeared inside of it, the black front showing heavy use. I give another scan through the dwelling and I see no one else in this room. But, there is enough booze here to show for at least two other people.

The heavy foot traffic through the snow shows me that the front door rarely gets used so I make my way around to the side door. As I walk down the narrow path between the houses I can notice two cars parked in the rear of the residence so I make my way to them.

"Dispatch, can you add these plates to the call?" I tell her the license plates of the two vehicles and as I wait for the registered owners' information I can feel the cold bite into my feet again. My hands are getting numb and my ears have finished screaming at me. All I feel now is the ever-present cold bite from the snow and freezing wind. I know I have to warm up soon but I also know that a little bit of patience and information keeps my ass safe on the streets.

A set of lights roll down the alley and then shut off. Peeking my head around the corner I see a marked police unit crawling down the alley.

The car stops as I give my handheld flashlight two quick strobes towards them, letting the car crew know that I am here. I see the doors open and two cops come walking out as they put their toques on. I wish once again I had put mine on. My ears bite from the cold even more.

I keep my eyes on the house and watch for any movement or signs of life from the back windows. I am soon joined by the two other officers and I brief them about what I saw through the front bay window. I let them know that I will be making a door knock on the side door.

They comment on how cold I look. I am freezing now and all I want is to feel the warm rush of air that is being held inside of the house.

Stepping up to the side of the large wooden door, I wonder what clues will soon be uncovered. Answers to the alone little girl, questions on what happened in the house to make her leave. I am so eager to learn the answers, so eager for the warm air within to heat my ears before I get frostbite.

I reach out to knock but I have my arm grabbed by the constable beside me. He points to the door handle and I can see now that the door isn't even locked. The door is slightly ajar and it looks like it's due to a recent strike to the door that it is unable to close properly.

Just then dispatch gives us some more valuable information. She tells us that one of the registered owners to the vehicle is a female with a history of suicide attempts, violence, and drug abuse.

I also find out that the second vehicle belongs to a male that has several warrants out for his arrest and they are for assaulting a police officer, theft, and robbery. I no longer feel cold. I can feel my mind start to fire up my body for this call that could get very interesting.

I knock on the door, banging hard. Another car crew has shown up on scene and is watching through the front bay window. I see him shake his head. I know that the female on the couch is not getting up. I bang again, harder, purposefully pushing on the door to make it swing open.

I yell out to the occupants of the building that it is the city police. No response.

A third car crew has shown up on scene and they take a point at the rear of the house. All the areas of the house are covered.

I look at the other two cops and we all move into the house.

As soon as we enter the back door we are greeted by a scene of depravity and dirt. The whole house is an absolute mess with clothes strewn about, dirty diapers stacked in a corner, and garbage piled in corners. The smells of rotting garbage, stale cigarettes, and old frying grease assault my senses.

I make my way into the living room while the two other cops move towards the rear of the house. They move from room to room looking for more people. I can hear one of them radio that we are inside the residence.

I hear more cops come in from the cold and make their way into the basement. An efficient movement of personnel through the house looking for more people and anything else of interest.

I make my way to the couch where the woman lies passed out, her face swallowed and distorted by a velvet pillow. Her body is twisted as one of her legs is off the couch and the other is jammed into the back cushions.

She lies on her belly and I can see a pile of snot and drool formed on the purple velvet of the overstuffed cushion she has chosen as her pillow.

I nudge her foot with my boot, making sure I keep a safe distance in case she spins around out of fright or drug-induced paranoia to strike me. Nothing.

I kick the bottom of her foot as it lies on the floor. I yell at her to wake up, that the police are here.

Nothing.

I place the heel of my boot onto her calf and role the calf muscle across the sole of it. I can feel the muscle bunch up and spring over to the other side of the calf bone under the pressure and tension. I can hear her groan, but she still doesn't wake up.

I do it again and I can see her eyes open slightly as her brain triggers a pain response to the pressure on her calf.

I reach over to a glass that is sitting on the table. It is filled with ice water, the outside of it is covered with a wet dew from the cold water inside of the glass container. I pour it on the face of the sleeping woman.

Response. She wakes up with a fury inside of her.

"What the fuck? Who is the fuck who wants an ass kicking?!" She then looks at the uniforms gathering in her house. "Oh, um, sorry, I was just startled."

"Yeah, okay," I say with a heavy load of sarcasm. "Do you have a daughter named Trisha?"

"Yes I do, she is sleeping in her room. Why?'

"We found her walking the streets about four blocks from here, freezing."

She knows where this is going. She knows that she has fucked up with her child.

"Who the fuck invited you in here? You cannot come in here without a warrant!"

"Hey, you are telling me how to do my job. Why don't I tell you how to smoke your crack?" I point to the drug paraphernalia on the table. "How would you feel about that? Don't tell me how to do my job again or you are going to piss me off."

"Sorry." She sits up and pulls her tangled hair back into a make-believe ponytail. "This is not my shit." Her hands motion towards the pile of used drug paraphernalia. She grabs a cigarette off the table and lights it.

"Don't fucking lie to me. Don't insult me with that shit. I can care less that you have a chemical dependency problem. I care about a little girl walking the street in the middle of the night looking for food because she is hungry." I let her know how pissed I am going to be if she decides to make our interaction hard because she wants to lie.

"Where's Harold?" I ask her. He is the guy who came back with the warrants for his arrest when I ran the license plates in the back of the house.

She hesitates. I look at her as if I know Harold personally, like I have insider information that he is here.

She still hesitates; she is trying to figure out a lie.

"You know what the best part about being a cop is? People like to think that they can lie to a cop and get away with it. They do not realize it but as cops we are trained to look for small bits of body language. Little clues that people are lying, clues they cannot hide."

She hesitates as I look hard at her. She is thinking of what to say. The truth or a lie.

"Don't even think of fucking spilling some bullshit out of your mouth."

"Harold is sleeping in the main bedroom, my room. He is sleeping in there." She takes a hard drag out of her smoke. She draws deep as if telling the truth has been the hardest thing she has ever had to do.

I look at the cop who just left the main room and he shrugs his shoulders. The cop also knows that we gave lots of warning before entering the house. If Harold had to hide he had a lot of time to cram himself into some small space. The cop snags up his partner and they go back to search through the bedroom once again.

I hear over the radio that the cops searching the basement have found two other kids. Young kids. They ask for an EMS unit as well as CARRT. CARRT is our Child At Risk Response Team. My heart sinks because I know that something bad is downstairs. We only call for CARRT if the abuse is bad. Otherwise it's a Child Welfare call.

"Don't you fucking move." I point to her to stay seated on the couch. I make eye contact with a cop next to me and he knows it is time for him to watch her. He starts to get her name and some identification.

I walk down the narrow stairs to find four cops moving about in the basement. It is a pigsty. The floor is covered with garbage and junk. Small paths are made through the debris, allow for the movement from either of the three rooms down here.

I duck below a low-hanging light bulb, the only source of light for this small dungeon.

I can see a cop holding a small boy in his arms. The boy is about seven years old and has tears welling in his eyes. I can see by the large knees and the slim legs that the young child has not been eating too well. I wonder when the last time he ate was. I look at his face and it is covered in dirt and dried mucus from his running nose.

His hair is in mats as the cop walking with him ensures that it is going to be all right. The boy holds back tears as the cop carries him up the stairs to the awaiting ambulance.

As he passes me I can see anger boiling in his eyes.

"Fuck man, the kid is fucking starving. And check this fucked-up shit out." He holds out the arm of the child and I can see small circular burns on the child's palms and forearms.

Cigarette burns.

"Not fucking right, man. He is just a child."

I say nothing. I know this cop well. He has two kids. A boy and a girl, both around the age of this child. I know he is hurting inside. I can hear the disgust and anger in his voice. I can feel the tears welling up inside of the cop. I can hear him fighting back the anger inside of him, fighting to stay calm and professional.

I cannot feel his pain, I have no kids to make an emotional reference to. I say nothing.

I move through the garbage and make my way to a room that the other two cops are standing in. The inside of that room is illuminated by a small table light in the corner, the lamp shade brown with soot and dirt. The low glow in the room highlights the tension and sorrow that is welling out of the room.

I walk in and see a baby in a crib. It is, from what I can guess, under a year old. It looks dead to me. Its skin is white from not seeing the sun for ages. What should be fat little cheeks is just skin pulled over a small skull. The eyes are drawn into the small face before me and they are lined by red orbs. It has cried as much as it could, but now has stopped. The crib is filled with the waste that the child has put out. No one has tended to this child for days.

I want to reach out and hold it.

I am afraid to.

The babe looks so frail that I worry that moving him will kill him. I can see his ribs as I pull down his shirt. The room stinks. I look away from the baby only to see another cop staring like I was. He has been staring at the child ever since he came into this room.

I know this cop well too. His eyes are circled with dark rims from having little to no sleep over the past month. His wife has just had a beautiful little girl a couple of months ago.

"Mark." I call his name in a low voice. His stare doesn't break.

"Mark." I touch his shoulder.

His head snaps as if he has been awakened from a dead sleep.

"Yeah."

"This isn't for you, man."

"I am okay," he says as he clears his throat.

"I know you are. But this is not for you." I turn his body away from the sight. I push on his back to make him leave. We walk out together.

He looks at me with only confusion in his eyes.

"It is just a child, John. Why? Who? That babe is just a little bit older than mine. It is helpless"

"I know." I want to turn his mind away from this shit. I want him to focus on the good. "How old is your daughter now?"

"Three months." Mark looks at me as if I have gone mad to talk about his little girl.

"She sleep well?"

"Uh? No. She still wakes up at all hours." He still looks at me like I have lost my mind.

"I guess this would be a good time to phone your wife to see how your little girl is doing. She won't mind the phone call." I see Mark's eyes light up. The thought of talking to his wife right now warms him, drags his mind away from the darkness that he has seen.

"Yeah, I guess she would like a phone call. Let her know that I am thinking of her."

"Of course she would, Mark. Let her know that she is doing a great job. Let her know how much you think of her." We walk outside; the cold air now feels good on my face. It refreshes me, cools off the fire I have burning inside.

Mark walks away from me.

"Mark." He turns to look at me. "Talk to her, tell her everything. She can handle it. She will listen. She knows exactly what to say to set you right."

Mark turns away from me.

"Hey John."

"Yeah."

"Thanks."

I walk back into the house. The smell of this place seems to be even worse. I stop at the doorway and step back outside. I am not ready to go back in yet.

I look around and watch the medics move past me to go inside to look at the other child. I can see the boy carried out being attended to by another medic. He looks calmer and happier.

"Smith."

I look over and see our sergeant showing up to the scene.

"Sir," I say as I catch my breath.

"You all good? I hear it is a shit show in there."

"Yes sir, I am good. I think that Mark may need to pull the pin. He needs to go home and see his wife and child." I point to Mark's cruiser. I can see Mark talking on the phone. I see his head dip forward and he holds his hand over his face.

My sergeant sees the same. "Is he messed?"

"Not bad, but this is not good for him. He will not take the last few hours unless you tell him to."

My sergeant is a good leader. He worries about his men. He cares about us.

"I will watch him. If I think he needs to take the last few I will tell him to pull the pin early."

I nod and as we start to make our way back into the house I tell him everything that is going on. I fill my sergeant in on all of the details.

As we enter and I show him around, I see the other car crew looking for Harold has found him. I am told that they found him hiding inside of a large cardboard box in the closet. With Harold they found a bunch of crack cocaine and cash.

My sergeant tells the car crew to gather some of the drug paraphernalia, the small electronic scale on the table, and anything else that will link these two with drug-dealing charges. He voices the fact that CARRT is coming and they will need to know about the possession charges with intent to deal for their seizure paperwork.

"What the fuck! Fuck you! You can't take my kids!"

The mother on the couch has heard my sergeant's comment. She knows who CARRT is as Social Services has warned her that if CARRT shows up her kids are gone. Social Services have tried to clean up this shit show here but they have worse places to deal with first.

She bolts up from the couch. She is furious; she is filled with anger from knowing her kids will be gone. Her maternal instinct overrides the drug haze she has been sitting in.

"Sit down and relax." I step in between her and my sergeant, my hands out in front of me motioning for her to move back.

"Fuck you!" She is getting more furious.

"I won't say it again. Sit down and we talk. If you don't I will put you in cuffs and make you sit down. Your choice."

"Talk? You want to talk? Good for you but where am I going to get my sustenance cash from without my kids?" She starts to scream as she realizes that her source of money is going to be tapped off.

I was wrong. No maternal instincts here.

She just wants to keep her kids in the house so that she can collect her provincial child care funding. My heart pumps hard. I can feel my face get hot from the anger inside of me. I am furious.

My left hand juts out. I grab her by her throat and pull her close to me. Her face is in mine. Her feet come off of the ground as I bring her body up so that she can see my eyes with hers. Her hands grab onto my hands trying to loosen my vice grip.

Her bone-thin hands cannot break my grip, the grip strong enough to hold her, to suck out her breath. A grip that in an instant could crush her.

In a low controlled tone I talk to her.

"Listen, bitch. Fucking shut up or I am going to twist your fucking useless head off right here. I am sick of looking at you. Grow up and fucking be a mother to your children."

With a push I send her flying into the couch behind her. She lands on it hard and gasps as she gets air back into her lungs. She is quiet. She just sits there looking at the floor.

I turn to see my sergeant looking at me. His look is stern, like a father who has seen his son do wrong.

"Sorry, Sergeant, I am going to go outside to cool off. It won't happen again"

"Get some air, Smith," he says in a low and comforting tone. He pats me on the shoulder as I walk by.

I can still feel the anger inside of me. I would have liked to beat her for what she has done to these kids. They will never be the same because of her. They have lost what makes kids so special.

Their innocence.

I walk over to the second ambulance that is on scene and sit on the bumper. I feel the cold air hit me in the face. I feel that chill of winter calming me back down. I see CARRT arrive on scene. I walk towards the big police van. I can see a child's seat permanently fixed in the back. I see a box of lollipops on the dash. The back is filled with kid's books, toys, and various other things to help the children and kids that they seize ignore the world outside.

A female constable comes out of the passenger side of the van. I have seen her before. I know her well.

"Hey big guy, how are we doing?" She can see the frustration in me.

"It's fucking hell in there. You cannot go anywhere without seeing it. It sucks."

"Yeah, we know. We have been working with Child Services over this one but we have been too busy going after a couple of other priority ones."

"I could never do your job. I would kill these people if I could."

"There is a place for everyone, Smith. I never got excited over hunting down bad guys in dark alleys." She smiles and it calms me. That is her gift. Her warmth calms, she is no fighter but she can heal.

We walk back into the house and she asks me to help her gather some information she will need to charge the mother for neglect and seize the children. I know getting my head into business will help me.

She walks me through the house and we gather information. I mark down the fact that there is no food in the cupboards. That there is only a jar of mustard and a loaf of bread in the fridge.

I document the state of the bedrooms. The dirt and filth are photographed by her. I write down the lack of diapers, clean sheets, and even clothes.

I write down what the medics tell me.

A seven-month-old child that weighs six pounds and three ounces. A seven-year-old boy with burn marks to the arms and various other signs of abuse and malnutrition.

A six-year-old girl with signs of abuse and signs of malnutrition. I am focused now at the job at hand and my emotions are in check. I feel much better even though I find information out that I really do not want to know.

During the whole thing, never once does the female cop hate the mother for what she has done. Never once do I hear her hate this house as much as I do. I never hear her say it. I know she has seen worse, for her this is not as bad as the horror gets. For me I have never seen worse.

We finish gathering what she needs and then the female cop goes and tells the mother that she is seizing her kids and that she will be arrested for neglect.

The woman weeps and no one cares. She looks around and sees a wall of faces that don't care for her. She still cries and no one cares. The cuffs are put on and she is moved into an awaiting car. She is carted off and she still weeps. No one cares.

Our sergeant gathers all the remaining members together. Mark stands beside me in the cold snow. I look at him and I see he is much better.

"You gunna go home?"

"No, Sergeant talked to my wife Maggie after I got off the phone and he said that it would be better if I finished off my shift."

I look at Mark and he looks better. But if I was Sergeant I would have made him go home to his family. Right now Mark needs his real family, not the one that stands with him here.

The wind seems to gather its last attempt of freezing all of us, it rages against us. The snow is kicked up as my sergeant gives us directives on what he needs and wants. He tells us that CARRT is following the paramedics to the hospital with the baby. He wants us to take the boy and girl to our district office. Tells us to go inside and gather a bag of clothes and some toys for the kids so that when they go to a shelter they will have something.

He gives out tasks and sends us on our way. He closes his directions with a reminder that he wants everyone to return to the office to get debriefed. He wants us to sit down and vent, to throw our shit out. He does this after hot calls. We all learn, we all share, and we all decompress. He will now do this for this call. Otherwise he will have a street filled with cops looking for revenge on the next person who hurts kids.

A long snake-like parade of blue and white cars fill the street as we all make our way back to the district office. Our car has a small bag filled with clothes for the little girl and boy. As we drive back to the office not a word is said in the car.

It is dead silent. I stare ahead as I drive through the heavy winds and the blowing mist of snow. I seem to be on autopilot as my mind walks me back through the house I was just in.

I can still remember the smell of that hell.

We are the last car to arrive. We enter the back door and put down the bags. Black plastic bags that have a white piece of paper attached to them marking the names of each child. I can hear the station filled with cops. It sounds busy, more people than what were at the call.

Just then my nose is filled with the smell of bread and hot food. I can hear people laughing and then the air is cut with a child's cry. Sharp remarks fly out of the room. I can hear familiar voices say how it sounds like Mark at scary calls.

The station is filled with laughter.

I look at my partner and he too looks as bewildered as I am. We dump our bags and I can hear even more voices not familiar to me. I hear a lot of people, I hear laughter and happiness. The smell of warm food fills the air. Warm, hot steaming food.

All my senses are being bombarded with the sudden contrast from the cold, stale rot that I was just tasting in that house.

As I round the corner into our lunchroom I see it is filled with people. Wives of husbands working the street, small children in their arms. Husbands of wives that work the street, small children in their arms. Little kids from ages five to eight years run around the chairs.

I look at my watch and it is 1 a.m. Everyone is wide awake with an emotion that is rarely felt when we wear this blue uniform.

Happiness.

"It is about time you humps got here." My sergeant pats us on the back. "Look at what these fine people brought us on this cold night. Warm bread, Christmas leftovers, and even hot coffee. It looks a whole lot better than the fucking rabbit food that you eat, Smith."

I look about and now I know why my sergeant would not let Mark go home. He brought Mark's family to work. He wanted to gather his troops and their families so that they could all sit down and enjoy some time together. He wanted everyone to heal together. He wanted everyone to know that the shit we saw can be shared, each of us taking a small piece to remind us of what lies outside. A small piece that will give us wisdom but not rot us.

I see the children we have just seized. Melody and Mike, sitting with other kids their age and playing with each other. I can see that the kids are tired but they revel in the warmth and harmony in this room.

My sergeant's wife walks into the lunchroom with a red bag that we use for collecting food for the less fortunate families. I see the impressions of boxes and a few bow ties sticking out of the top. Gifts gathered from the attending families and wrapped in the room next door.

"Well, Santa stopped by really quick and had to drop off some things here. He is sorry he could not make it to your house earlier but he said that there were too many cops at your house." The room fills with laughter and the kids on the floor spring to life as they know what is going to be in the bag.

"Now, everyone has to wait, as Melody and Mike open their gifts first. After all, they are our guests tonight." Her voice calms the excited pack of kids down. Her motherly tone sets the pace for the kids and she motions for Melody and Mike to come over to get the brightly wrapped gifts, which magically have their names written on the small labels.

A crowd gathers around as the two kids get the gifts and start to rip the paper off in a frenzy. The mass of people close in so that I cannot see the kids any more. I move back away from the crowd. Out of my whole team I am the only single cop here. All the others are much older and have families. I am viewed as the young brother who still has to follow a path they have taken.

"You're a good man; I have never worked for anyone better," I say to my sergeant, who stands beside me.

"Thanks. Just remember this when you are leading men, Smith. This department is changing. They are losing sight of the value of this family in blue. Our superiors want to drive the family apart because they fear the unity of brothers."

"To hell and back for your brother." I say the words that some senior cop wrote on the inside of the locker which I now have.

My sergeant looks at me as if I have incanted some ancient proverb. He smiles.

"That is what they fear."

I see my partner over in the corner with his two girls sharing a cup of hot chocolate. His ex-wife stands there looking at her lost husband with compassion as the hard cop shows his love for his family. She looks up at me and smiles. A little wave from her hand makes its way over to me.

I smile back.

A call is dispatched over the radio for a unit to attend a vehicle accident. No injuries but cars are not drivable.

A hush flows over the room as the family's fear that once again work will cut into the precious little time that they have together.

I quickly key my mike before anyone can answer.

"Yeah, dispatch, this is 1424. I can take that call. Can you mark me as a one-man unit as my partner is still on the missing child call?"

"Dispatch copy."

The call is not in my zone, it is not supposed to be for me to take. I see the cops that work the zone look at me and I raise my hand and shake my head. They know that I will not let them leave this room. I see their wives smile at me and one of them walks up and gives me a hug.

"Thank you, and Merry Christmas." Her hug warms me.

I get a room full of Merry Christmas's from the families visiting. They know I will not be back to see them. They know that I will hump all the calls I can so that they can stay here. I am happy to know that I can do this for them.

As I leave I grab a hot cup of coffee and wave good-bye to my partner. He yells out that if I need help with the call to let him know.

"I am sure I can handle this call." I feel like a little brother who is given the keys to the family car for the first time. I have worked one man many times before but tonight it is just different.

I sit in the car and read the call on the screen. I feel an emotion that I know I will not feel for many years to come. A feeling that is not associated with my work. I am happy tonight.

I drive off into the cold night with a smile and when I get to the accident I exit my car to talk to the two drivers. They are okay and I tell them what I will need to fill out an accident form. I want to get them on their way.

"It is freezing out tonight, aren't you cold?"

I stand there wearing my thin winter jacket with the wind blowing over my face. The crystalline snow gathering on my short hair.

"No, actually I am quite warm," I say with a smile as I walk back to my car to start the paperwork.

TIES THAT BIND
Ties that Bind

I have spent the last three weeks reading a book called *On Combat* by Lieutenant Colonel John Grossman. It is an amazing book that is a heavy read. I can only read ten pages at a time because of the information given.

It is good for me to read it. I am learning that feelings of time distortion, tunnel vision, and muffled hearing or auditory exclusion are all normal effects of adrenaline dumps.

I learn in each page that all the things that I thought were weird are just simple physiological responses to stress, adrenaline, and combat fatigue. I learn more about myself as I read and self-educate.

I sit back and think about all the things I have experienced and all the things that I have tried to hide from my co-workers because I feared that they would mock me or think less of my combat ability. I did not want to appear weak under stress.

I hid what was normal and common. I did it out of fear and ignorance.

Now I am sitting with a cop who just went through some serious shit.

He was a one-man unit and as he conducted a traffic stop the occupant rushed him as he stepped out of his car. The fight was on and for the first time in the young constable's life, he felt fear. Fear of losing, fear of getting hurt.

I sit in my cruiser working one-man because my regular partner is sick today.

It has been the regular shit show of calls. A few domestic calls, drug-related files, some house break and enters, and of course lots of shoplifters.

It is a regular day in the Hood.

I hear a unit call in a traffic stop that is relatively close to me and I decide to cruise by. I know him well and I am hoping that he can meet me for a coffee break after his traffic stop.

I make my way over gingerly, as the traffic is light and the warm sun is cutting into my eyes. I like the warm sun on my arms, the open window cycling fresh air through my car. I am not a big fan of day shifts but if one has to work a day shift this is the best way to work it.

I pull around a corner, exiting off of a busy street. I turn onto the side street and it takes my mind only a split-second to know that all is bad.

Before my eyes a scene is revealed that makes my heart instantly skip. A cop is on his back as a large male is standing over him. The male is bent at the waist and is throwing punch after punch at the downed cop.

The uniform on the ground is set up well defensively, blocking most of the blows that are being driven with punishing force at his head. The blows that I see get through the frantic volley are light and ineffective but one cannot stay in the defensive position for long.

All it takes is one blow to get through, bounce your head off the ground, and stun you. That blow then opens the door for the rest of the hurt to get in.

I am out of my car as the tires chirp from the parking break getting slammed on. I am in a full sprint as I see the flurry of blows continue. I want to stop the bad guy from unleashing the damage.

The uniform on the ground is not only a co-worker, he is also my friend. He has backed me up at hairy shit before. He is my brother. He is in trouble and I am ready to do anything to stop him from getting hurt.

The maddening rush of the attack continues and I can feel my heart start to pound. The male on top is firing right and left blows and he is not slowing down.

I can feel the cold shivers of my adrenaline fix coming. Goosebumps cover my skin as I run faster now. I can feel my legs become powerful, thundering hydraulic pistons working at their maximum output.

My face gets hot as I reach the male. Here it comes, the rush. I can feel the fix flooding me. I can feel my skin tighten, my face become hotter, and my hands become numb.

It hits me. The rush hits me and it pumps through my veins. I remember the love I have for it.

My world slows down as my perceptual distortion convinces my brain that the world is moving in slow motion. I know now that my mind is just functioning faster than normal. Way faster than normal. So fast that I perceive that time is slowing. I understand what is happening and I enjoy it. I crave it now, before I feared it.

I slam into the male at full speed. I put all of my body weight into him and with my 300 pounds of beef, bone, and police kit, I send him flying into the police cruiser.

I hear the air rush out of him as he lets out a low grunt from being blindsided from the blow. I see his body smash into the front quarter panel of the marked unit. Even before he can recover from the crushing body blow I am on him again.

I drive my right fist into his kidneys, I set into him, and I push my fist deep. I can feel my fist sink in up to my wrist before he bends and contorts to avoid any more damage.

He is fucked. His face is contorted in pain. His mouth is gaping, trying to drag in air. Air that was knocked out of him when I slammed into him, precious air that was wrung out of his lungs even more when I drove my fist into him.

I have landed the damaging blows that will allow me to give him the hurt as long as I want to.

My elbow slices into his face. His head snaps to the left and I feel his long hair whip across his face.

I send in another body shot to keep his mind confused. My left fist slams into his sternum. Nothing comes out of his mouth. No groan, no gasp of air. Nothing.

His lungs are still empty, they now burn for air. They are telling him to breath or he will die.

The bright white paint of panic is smeared across his face.

The cop on the ground is now up. I see him coming in from the corner of my eye. I see his fist smash the bad guy in the face.

I turn to the cop and I can see the rage, the anger, and the animal within. I step back.

I step out of the fight. It is not mine to finish. It is for my friend, a fellow uniform to finish. It is up to him to decide how much pain should be inflicted. After all, he is the victim of the bad guy's attack.

I see blows rock the bad guy's head back and forth. The cruiser is the only thing holding the guy up as more and more blows are delivered. The cop is an ex-boxer and he can land the punches better than anyone I know.

He moves from head blows to body shots. Flurries of blows are delivered in a heartbeat.

"Stop resisting! Stop resisting and you won't get hurt!" I yell the commands out loud. I know that if someone is watching my verbal queues will let them know that we are fighting a bad guy who is fighting with us. The verbal direction will also cultivate their minds. They will believe what I yell out.

I see the damage continue and I now know that my friend is letting his beast run wild. I know that the damage is done, any further will be too much.

I calmly put my hand on his shoulder.

"He's had enough now," I say in a low calm voice.

He stops. His right fist is still poised for another blow. His chest heaves as his lungs call for air after the heavy exertion.

"He's done." I lightly push down on my friend's raised fist. I look into his eyes and I can see that the animal that was released is now going away. I can see warmth coming back into his face. His grinding teeth loosen and his jaw relaxes

I step back again and call in our location and what has happened. I ask for an EMS unit for the bad guy. I hear cars in the distance as their sirens go on. I know that no matter what I say on the air the troops are going to come. I let them know that all is well, that they can slow down. There is no longer a rush.

I see the cop walk back to the trunk of the car. I look at the bad guy as he is splayed out on the hood of our cruiser. I walk over to him and roll him over onto his stomach. I take his limp arms and put them into stainless-steel cuffs. I guide his body to the ground and put him there in the prone position. I see blood pour from a shattered nose and I guess that his jaw is broken by the way it sits at an odd angle.

I can see welts already rising on his face. Bruises on top of bruises.

I look over to the trunk of the car and see that my friend's legs are shaking. I can see him standing there holding his knees trying to stop the shaking.

I walk over to him. He turns his back to me slightly and speaks.

"I am okay, just winded from working so hard."

I see his legs shake and I can see that he is trying to hold them so that no one can see.

"Cool. Hey, you know a funny thing about adrenalin? It causes involuntary body functions like body shakes. My hands shake badly when I get my adrenalin fix. I shake like a leaf afterwards. Funny shit it is because the more that I try to stop it, the more I shake."

He turns his head towards me. I look at him and speak.

"It's okay, brother. Your legs shake like my hands do. It means fuck all. I saw you fighting and you did well. The shakes are Mother Nature's way of getting rid of your fix. It means nothing."

He looks at me. I know he is still worried that I am looking at him like he is weak. He is afraid like I was when I first felt the shakes from the adrenaline escaping my body.

I laugh. "I worry about the day I get into the mother of all fixes. A fucking gunfight. I worry because it is normal for a guy to shit or piss himself. Nothing on the fighter's part can stop it. If your bladder is full or you have not taken a dump you are gunna crap yourself. Have you seen the food I pack away on a regular basis? I am guaranteed to shit my pants, man!"

This makes him laugh. As he laughs he straightens out. His legs no longer shake.

"See, the shakes are gone. Normal body functions, you have no control over that. Let's finish off what this asshole started. We have a whole lot of paperwork to do."

"He was on top of me in a heartbeat. I can fight standing up but I was pretty fucked when he bowled me down like that. I was worried that I was going to lose. I was really fucking worried. If you did not show up when you did…"

I cut him off. "You would have remembered your training and taken the guy down. You would have dumped a world of shit onto him. Much fucking worse than what he got today."

I push him on the chest with an open hand. His body rocks back.

"Just because you were on the ground doesn't mean that you are losing. It is just a different fighting platform. You would have adapted and overcome."

I push him again. I wait for him to push back when I push him. I reach out to push him again but he swats my hand away.

"Quit that shit," he says as a smile goes across his face.

I laugh. "That's right, mother fucker. Quit that shit. You are like the rest of us fuckers working in the gutter. The top of the fucking food chain, don't you ever doubt the damage that you can do."

He pushes hard on my chest with his open hand.

He pushes back and I smile. The fight is still in him, the alpha male still thunders in his heart.

I smile and turn to the bad guy. Cars are pulling up as I see a flashing red-and-white strobe light from an ambulance around the corner.

I hear my friend next to me talk to himself.

"Top of the fucking food chain."

An eternal bond gets built under extreme times.

I have heard people talk about friends found in war times. The bond that men and women build when they all rely on each other to survive.

I take pride in the bond that I am able to experience working these streets.

No one can mimic what we go through on the street.

No one can understand the bonds that are built between men and woman that save each other from harm.

No matter how bad the shit has hit the fan I trust the uniform next to me. I trust them with my life.

If we are moving towards gunfire and I am to cover the front I will keep my eyes forward. I know that my left side, right side, and back are covered by my brothers and sisters.

I do my best because they depend on me as much as I depend on them.

No one can know what that is like unless they enter combat with bothers and sisters.

When I see one of my fellow uniform members hurt, I hurt inside. I feel their pain. I wish that it was me instead of them.

No one in the outside world can know what we go through.

No one can feel the binds that are made between us.

THE SOFTER SIDE

If you ever see a serious-looking cop you will also be looking at the biggest kid ever. I take pride in my professional look. My boots are clean, my uniform is crisp, I am in good physical shape, and I am aware of my surroundings.

"Holy fuck, you are one big fucking cop." This is what I like to hear from my bad guys. They will not fight because they know that I am a meaner, bigger, and nastier dog. Step up and I will tear you apart.

I have a belligerent prick in my face.

"You can't take me to jail! Fuck you can't just come in here and take me out of my own house! We were just getting a little out of hand. You can't even be here!"

Oh yeah, a little bit out of hand. That is why we have a woman calling 911 in hysteria. That is why we have to kick the front door in on the house as we hear her scream for help. The bruising around her neck tells me that you have had your hands wrapped around it. The blood flowing from her nose and the cuts to her feet tell me that she has been punched and dragged around this shit pit of a home.

Here comes my one-liner… "Excuse me, what do you do for a living?"

"I am an electrician; why the fuck do you care?"

The ending to that response is the same every time.

"Well, let me come to your work and have me tell you how to pull fucking wire all day. Don't you even think you can tell me how to do my job!" Hah, in your face, asshole. The sentence is finished off with me looking at him in the eyes. I am not giving him the stare-down, I just want him to know that I have seen harder, meaner men and if he gives me the chance I will give him a dishing of what he just recently served to his wife.

He knows that he is no man. He gives up the fight with me. I see it in his eyes. They are not warrior's eyes, he lacks the thousand-yard stare. The stare that one has when he looks passed you, through your eyes. The look that is searching for a weak link. Those are warrior's eyes.

As he turns away from me to have the handcuffs put on he looks over to his wife and fires up on her, the only person who he knows he can victimize.

"Fuck you, bitch, I will be out tomorrow and you are going to pay for me sitting in the tank all night!"

Oh, did I just hear the hero call for an ass-kicking? I am sure I did!

"Hey, butt fuck, you want to be a hero, be a father to your kids and husband to your wife!" My other line, it does one of two things. It will either shut them up or it will twist them into a frenzy. The truth hurts, I guess. My cuffs are not even out yet, they are so far away from being put on. I give him the chance to fight, I give him the chance, and he bites.

I see his feet start to turn first, and then his upper body follows. He spins to face me and as he turns I see his right fist coming out towards my head. It is a wide throw, fucking amateur. His movements are easily telegraphed; I read his actions seconds before they happen. My arms come up to guard my head and I slam my bodyweight forward. I am the fucking predator here, I want in close. I want to have my body touch his, I want to fuck up his personal space.

My brain is now in the fight mode. It only sees targets, computes distance, and logs my movements. It notes the areas of my opponent that are weak; they are highlighted and stored as targeting spots.

His fist loses all of its power as his intended target is way too close. His forearm hits my block and I do not even register any impact. In one step I am all over him. I slam my left elbow into his collarbone, sending his body down. He has lost his fighting platform; he is losing the battle fast. My next blow comes with my right knee. If he is going down I want to set him up.

I want his brain to never be able to adjust to the punishment I am giving him. I hear a gushing of air flow from his body so fast that I see mucus fly from his mouth and snot ooze from his nose as my knee collides into his sternum. He is on the way down when I deliver my final blow. My right elbow still waits for its chance. Down it comes from my head all the way to my waist. It builds up speed as it moves and with the speed comes impact. I have tons of time to target where I want to hit.

I focus on building up my damage. 60 percent of what I can give, 70 percent of what I can give, here we go, 80 percent of what I can give! I have never hit anyone with all that I can give. That magical 110 percent that you can deliver with maximum output on an adrenaline dump. I am curious to do it but I am also afraid of doing it. The right place, the right time, and I will finally see what I can do. This is not the right place nor the right time.

With an odd thump and a sickening snap my elbow finds its mark. I have struck the mid-ribcage, between the shoulder blades. Not much soft tissue to stop my energy, and the tissue that is there cramps and bundles up fast. A light blow would cause a very bad Charlie horse. My blow however was meant to go deep.

The energy passes through the tissues and hits bone. The ribs flex and move but he was not ready to absorb the impact. They snap. I feel them give, I hear them pop, and I also hear the last bit of air come out of his body. He is done. He will writhe on the floor now for at least ten seconds waiting to get air back into his lungs.

I see it in his face that he thinks he is going to die. That look of panic when the body cannot get air. His eyes wide open, his mouth gasping like a fish out of water, and his body shrinking further and further into a fetal position. Air, that is all that his body is thinking of.

He gulps down shallow breaths and his face starts to lose its red hue. The veins in his head start to subside. Air, finally he is getting air.

I watch him stay in the fetal position and then I tell him he is under arrest for assaulting a police officer. He doesn't care, he wants air, he wants to know why it is still so hard to breath. He wants out of his world of shit. I call for an ambulance as I know this guy is going to need a trip to the hospital. He needs X-rays, he needs a doctor's clearance, and he needs painkillers.

You want to know the best thing about guys who beat their wives? The nurses are mostly all women. They hate wife-beaters and well, the chance of you getting any TLC out of them is slim and next to none. The same goes for painkiller, buddy. You aren't getting shit.

Shakespeare said it best, "Hell has no fury than that of a woman scorned."

I look around and I see that my combat has overflowed. I see their eyes looking at me. His kids look on. They have seen a uniform, the only thing that they have been told that will protect them, hurt their father. I wonder to myself how their minds take in this information. Do they see it like the relationship that their mother and father have? Abuse equals love? Or do they see it in its reality. Violence hurts. It destroys a house, it distorts people, and it causes tears. The youngest of their children I have seen before. A young girl about six years of age. I stopped her crying the last time we came here for their parents fighting.

I stepped into her room, her eyes looked up at me with a mixture of fear and abandonment. Her name is Sherri and she was terrified the last time I was here. I know at first my size and look frightened her but as soon as I asked if she was okay she just started to cry. I moved to sit beside her on the bed. I sit on her blue sheets with the Nemo characters on it. I reached over and picked up a teddy bear that was on the floor. He was soft, his fur was so velvety, my hands hold it as my thumbs seemed to massage its belly.

"You know, I had a bear like this once? His name was Max and he was a very special bear. When I was afraid of the dark, Max would always make sure that I was okay. I knew he would help me turn on the nightlight to see in the dark. To see that there was nothing in my room to be afraid of."

"You were afraid of the dark?" she asked as her tears stopped. Her mind moving away from the yelling in the living room.

"I still am," I said with a smile on my face.

"Do you still have Max?"

"Oh no, Max left me a long time ago but he taught me that I can handle the dark all by myself. I suppose that when he knew that I could handle my fears alone he moved onto another kid who was afraid of the dark." I reached into my duty pants pocket and pulled out a plastic metal pin that had "Police Helper" inscribed on the front of it. I learned that long ago from an old partner. A trick to subdue a crying child.

I put the badge on the bear, my thick fingers moving the pin through the bear's velvet fur. "What is your bear's name?"

"Teddy," she said as her eyes widened when she saw the badge put onto her stuffed toy.

"Teddy, you are now sworn to teach Sherri how to fight the things that scare her," I say as I finish pinning the badge on the bear and placed him on my knee to ensure that his badge was straight and proper.

I handed the bear to Sherri and told her that Teddy was going to be on duty from now on but she had to help Teddy. I tell her that Teddy needs her to be strong and always caring because he has fears too.

With that I tell Sherri that I had to go outside and help my partner. I turn my back on the little child when she speaks.

"I know, my daddy is an angry man." Those words carve deep into me. Out of the mouths of babes.

Now I see her looking at me again. Her eyes are wide open as she looks at me. My fury burns out, extinguished by the shame of showing Sherri my animal, the beast within. She has seen too much violence already.

I want to tell her that I am not an angry man. I want her to know that all I want to do is stop the angry man in her house. I can't. No words escape my mouth; I just look at her. I see her bear in her hand. The shiny gold-colored badge sits crooked as she holds the furry bear by his arm.

"Hello, Sherri, how is Teddy doing?" The words croak out of my throat.

She smiles and tells me that Teddy was doing all right and she is not afraid of the dark anymore.

I step over the fallen father. I take her small fragile hand into mine and we walk towards her mother in the kitchen.

"Come on Sherri, you do not need to see this, your mother needs you and Teddy right now." Sherri and I walked into the kitchen, followed by her two younger brothers. When I look at the mother's eyes I could tell that she had enough of the beatings. Enough of the yelling.

She sees the crying eyes of her children. Her most powerful instinct had finally kicked in. The maternal love for her babies now flowed through her. She had the thousand-yard stare. She was ready for any fight.

After that day she never went back to that man.

As I ride in the ambulance with her husband I tell him to look at me. When our eyes met he tried to look away so I grab the back of his head and made him look at me. I wanted him to see that my eyes were empty, that I did not give a fuck.

"You go back there angry, I will kill you. If I ever hear that you have laid a hand on your children, I will kill you. If I ever hear that you are a fuck-up of a father, I will kill you. I know who you are. Be a fucking man." I pushed his head away from me and looked up at the medic that was sitting there monitoring his vital signs.

He just smiles and moves along without even a break in pace.

Ever since that day I have lost something inside of me. The little amount of innocence that sits buried deep inside of me dwindled even more. It is a rare time that I can look at a brown teddy bear and the crying eyes of Sherri do not come back to me.

I smile when I touch the soft fur of the bear, the memories flowing back into me like a torrential rain. I also fight back my own crying eyes.

LOVE FOR LIFE

LOVE FOR LIFE

I love life. I love life so much that I am not afraid to die. I am happy every day that I have in this world.

"Mom, how will I ever know if I love someone?" These are the words of a twelve-year-old boy? These are my words.

"Well, John. You know that you truly love someone if, without hesitation, you will die for them. You will put your life down so that they may live. That is when you truly love someone. I love you because I would never hesitate to have me leave this world so that you could live."

That was some heavy shit for a twelve-year-old boy to try to figure out.

But, at that time I was like many other twelve-year-old boys and never thought about it. Now, over twenty years later I still think about it. Now I see the paradox between my career and my love. I will die without hesitation for a fellow officer. I will put my life in jeopardy for any person who cries for my help. I will run towards the violence while others run away. Why? Because I am willing to put my life down for someone who I have never met, someone who has never met me. I love the people that I have been sworn to protect.

The world is filled with sheep, the innocent people out there who think that world is a good place and they spend their day moving about happily grazing. The sheep know that there is something in the forest that scares them, so they never go into the forest. They feel safe in their green fields.

In the forest lie the wolves. They feed on the sheep. They sneak out of the forest and take what they want from the sheep. Or they would if it was not for the sheepdogs. The sheepdogs are always close to the forest looking for a wolf. They move within the sheep and wait for the chance to protect the sheep from the wolves.

The sheepdog's life is one of solitude. The sheep fear the sheepdog because they have seen his teeth, they have seen him fight the wolves. The sheep also know that the sheepdog is closely related to the wolf. The sheep fear their protector. They would rather have the sheepdog lose his teeth and graze with them.

Out of ignorance they think that the sheepdog is really not needed because they rarely see the wolf.

So, the sheepdog is not invited into the sheep family, and not wanting to run with the wolves, they sit alone. They stand tall during the storms and they stay vigilant during the night when the sheep sleep.

All for what?

Well, that is what the sheepdog was created for. His path in life is to be alone, to not be understood by the sheep, and to be hated by the wolves. The sheepdog knows this, he accepts it.

I am hidden under my blue armor. I put it on in the start of my shift. It is a layer that is removable. Words slide off of me when I take the uniform off. All the shit that I have touched washes off in the laundry and all the crap I have seen stays at work. At the end of a shift I always breathe in deep. I wash out all the evils that I have seen and I look at the pictures I have posted in my locker. They remind me of who I am. They remind me that I cannot bring home the animal that is created at work.

My home is my castle; I am treated like a king when I get home. I am showered with love and affection. I see why I fight out in the gutter. I see what I am protecting. I am thankful every day that I have in my castle. I do not yell in my house, I do not show anger or even give anyone a hint of the carnage that I can release. At home I am a gentle giant.

I fear that my family will see the work side of me one day. Not because of me showing my anger to the people who I love. My family will see the caged animal if someone decides to try to step into the innocent world they live in. Heaven will not follow me the day anyone tries to fuck with my family.

I shut off my "always right" switch. You see in policing you are always right. You have to be. I may have just met you, and now you are throwing me into the mix of ten years of domestic problems. And, you want me to solve them in the next thirty minutes.

Why else would you call the cops?

So, to solve it I am right. No fucking way I will let them tell me how to do my job.

I change who I am when I get home. I am no longer the mean fighting dog that I am at work. I am the dog that comes in from the rain and sits by the warm fireplace. I crave the love and affection of those in my house and I just want to lie there and watch the world go by.

I know that it takes a special person to be a cop but it takes an amazing person to love a cop. The spouse has to be caring, warm, and forgiving. They have to understand the shift work, the violence, and the way that a person changes when they have a few years on the street.

They also have to be independent and carefree.

"Oh honey, you have to be the most independent person to love a cop. I have made it through twenty-five years of loving a cop and the most important thing that I can give to you for advice is that you can never count on him. It is not that he doesn't love you or doesn't want to be with you. The job wants him. He has no choice. He will be there when he can." A line I have heard over and over again from wives of cops,

Words spread to the young wives of other cops.

I married a cop. She is beautiful and caring. She showed me how to love when I thought that love did not exist.

We go weeks without seeing each other when our schedule doesn't fit. I miss her so much, the longing starts to seep in only a few minutes down the road I take to get to work.

Conversations take place with letters left on the table and little notes of "I love you" stuffed into lunch bags. I am a lucky man. She comes from a blood line of cops, her father having a long and successful career in the police force. His words of wisdom I soak up like a sponge.

We have adapted to such a strange life.

I have mentally adapted too.

I have decided that I will sacrifice a small part of my sanity, a part of my soul. A sacrifice needed when someone sees the hate and destruction people do to each other.

Images that eat away at you at night when you sleep.

Sights that haunt you from time to time.

No matter how well you balance your life and decompress, these things will always filter into your dreams.

I am willing to sacrifice this part of me so that the people that I love can sleep soundly at night. So that they can live in a field covered with green grass. A field that has no wolves hunting them.

I have seen a father playing with his daughter in a park one early morning after a long and visually brutal night shift. The smell of human blood still sticks inside of my nose.

A vision of a young girl that was beaten savagely by her stepfather that was messed up on crack. It returns to me at every red light that I sit at. I feel like crawling into a dark room and just shutting down for a lifetime.

I drive slowly by a school. My mind is burnt out, the vision sticking in me. I look into the field and see the man playing with his little girl. I start to slow down.

I see his smile and the beaming smile on his daughter's face as she laughs with her father. I watch as I stop at a four-way stop intersection.

I watch as father plays with daughter. The sight of the innocence, the happiness, and pure joy fills me. It warms me and pushes back the visions that only a minute ago haunted me.

Images that are tucked away inside of me. Images that I know will one day be triggered and resurface. But for now the shining view in front of me has forced the dark thoughts away.

It is then that I realize why I do the things that I do.

I deal with the cesspool of society because of that father and child.

I touch, smell, hear, and see what I have to because I want to make sure that the father and daughter never have to fill their senses with it.

I sacrifice my innocence so that they can keep theirs.

THESE HANDS

THESE HANDS

These hands play with my dog; they also hold my dear wife close to me. They hug my mother and tell her I am fine when she comes to visit me as I heal from injuries sustained at work.

These hands also let me express myself through writing and painting.

These hands will always want to fight. They know the cold feel of a gun. They are trained in knife-fighting tactics as well as how to deliver effective punches and strikes. Once your hands are trained to do something, something you love, they crave the chance to function.

Right now these hands are covered in blood. An unsettling mixture of red as my blood pools with someone else's that I just had a fight with. These hands hurt; they tremble as "the fix" slides away from my body. These hands are happy knowing that they get to go home tonight, to hold all that is so precious to me.

I look down at the guy on the ground. He is eigteen years old. Drunk and stoned on who knows what. His t-shirt ripped and covered with blood. The cheap ironed-on plastic label reading "Way too Drunk" flies like an ironic flag as the blood rolls further down his chest.

He is fucked and in a bad way. It is his eighteenth birthday today.

Happy fucking birthday.

"1161 can you send EMS to our location. One adult male, unconscious, breathing, and bleeding. Offender in custody for assault with a weapon, police units are okay."

"Copy that 1161. So all units on scene are good?"

"Roger that, dispatch, can you send Fire to clean up a biohazard." The blood is everywhere. I can see it up the wall, on the hood of our cruiser, and splattered on the ground. Fire comes out to clean up all biohazard messes, this one not excluded.

Door men from the nightclub near us come running over with bottled water so that we can wash off the blood from our skin.

Fuck, fuck, fuck! I hope that this shit doesn't have fucking hepatitis or AIDS!

Fuck, his shit is all over me.

I scrub like I am covered in human shit, frantic to clean myself as fast as I can. I want all of this off. I repeat this action with more water, some disinfectant gel, and more water. I look at my partner, he is doing the same. I look back down at the kid lying on the street in a recovery position as his arms are shackled behind his back. His head starting to rock back and forth as his wrists strain against the shiny steel bands that are cuffed around them. He slowly gains consciousness.

More cruisers show up as they know that if we call for medics that something bad happened. EMS shows up and then the Fire Department. Now it is a full-fledged zoo. Uniforms are moving about in a semi-organized dance. Strobe lights are flashing everywhere in a dizzy array of red, blue, and white.

We are looked at first by the medics and they give us more disinfectant, some biological scrub pad that foams as we scrub our hands down.

Fuck, does that shit burn. I feel like I am pouring gasoline over my open cuts. Good, I want to kill anything in the cuts. I wash down and I see that my skin on my knuckles has been chipped like bark off a tree. As I pick off the skin to clean out the wound better, the medic pours clean water over my hands.

"Teeth," he says as he keeps pouring the water.

"Huh?" I say as I look up, happy to talk to get my mind away from my aching hands. I hope that I did not break any bones in my hands. I don't want front-counter duty. No fucking desk work for me.

"Teeth, they always do that to the hands. See, you can tell that those marks are lined up. They are his teeth. You have to watch those cuts. If they get infected your hand will fucking swell like a scared blowfish. I have seen it. Bad fucking shit, the germs in the human mouth."

The Fire Department comes over to me as I sit on the rear bumper of the EMS truck, still washing my hands. There are two guys in their fire coveralls. One much older than the other. The young guy is a rookie. You can tell it in his eyes, he looks around with those eager, caring eyes. I can still see the innocence in them. He is a puppy. He wants to look after the sheep in this world.

"And what the fuck happened here? You guys hit the fucking kid with your car?" I look up at the older fireman. Ah, no innocence in his eyes. I wash the last few specks of blood off my tattoos on my arms.

"No sir, the guy tried to stab my partner and me. We went to town on him. All we need is to get some of you guys to clean up the biohazard after we get some photos of the area."

"No shit, eh? Lucky the little fuck is still alive; you guys okay?"

I look over to my partner, who is letting some attending units know what happened. He looks okay.

I drift back now to the front of the bar. Before my uniform was covered in blood. Before my hands hurt.

"Hey guys," a door man shouts as he waves his arm in the air to get my attention. "We just had a couple of guys kicked out of our bar and they just pulled a knife on Mike."

Mike is a good door man, I have never seen him go heavy on anyone in the bar. He has always been even tempered and a good guy to deal with. His quick wit seems to deter stupidity from the clients in the bar. At six feet, eight inches Mike could be a prick, but he is a gentle giant if I have ever known one.

"They just booked down the alley when you guys pulled up."

As I get out of the car I call in our location to dispatch and let them know that we are looking for two males that are involved with a possible weapons offense. She acknowledges my transmission and asks if we want other units to attend.

"Negative on that, dispatch, the offenders have fled the scene. I will let you know if we spot possible suspects." The street is busy, I do not want to tie up manpower on this.

As my partner and I round the corner Mike runs up beside us and points down the alley.

"That is one of the guys there!"

Now, let me explain something. If you are ever pointing out a bad guy to the cops, the difference between "that is one of the guys" and "that is the guy with the knife" is night and day. The first is not as much of a high risk as the second.

I yell at the kid not to move, that he is under arrest, and that he is dealing with the police. All in a standard format, a well-rehearsed set of words. I have to do this because I do not want this kid to get off in court by telling the judge that he did not know we were the police because we never told him. Heaven fucking forbid the uniform, the gun, the duty belt, and the shoulder flashes don't tell him that we are the police. But I have had my bad guys get off on that. Like I said, fucking soft system.

As my partner and I get close to him I target glance his hands, I see no knife, no weapons, and just empty hands.

I have worked with my partner long enough that I know what he will do without having him tell me. He knows what I will do, we read off each other and function as one. I grab the kid's left arm, my partner grabs his right.

Like all things in life, what happens next comes without warning. No words from the kid's mouth, just sudden violence. He pulls his arms away and comes out swinging. I lock on his left arm again and drive home a knee strike to his quad. I felt his femur, my strike went deep, that should cause his quad to cramp. I can feel his body jerk from my partner's same strike.

We want him down on the ground. A better place for us to fight. We want him down so that he can get cuffed and under control. The closer we are to the ground for a fighting platform the more stable we are. Besides most people do not train for ground fighting. They are out of their element and I want that.

"Get down, get down, stop resisting!" I blurt the commands without thinking. Training, I train with these commands. I want them to flow out of me when I fight. I want my witnesses to testify that I was telling the bad guy what to do and that he was resisting me. Why? So that some soft fucking judicial system doesn't drop the charges because the bad guy tells the judge that he did not know what to do because we never told him. The bad guy would say that he was not fighting with us, he was just confused. Are we starting to see how the system works?

"Knife! Knife!" my partner yells. His voice dry, his body just dumped a shitload of adrenaline into him. The dump makes your voice go dry. His command is perfect, a product of training. It is like a warning call for all those in the area. There is a knife in this combat now. Not ours either. I quickly look over and see that my partner has grabbed the bad guy's right arm. In the guy's hands I see the knife.

My brain dumps the mix into me. It tells my body that it is afraid now. A knife at this close range is deadly. It is deadlier than my sidearm. The knife doesn't jam. The knife doesn't need to reload. The knife has excellent targeting ability. Where your hand is, the knife is. The knife is the preferred weapon of choice in close combat. My sidearm is a piece of shit.

Time slows down, I am in "The Shit." I float on autopilot. I feel my face get hot and I know that I am at my peak, my 110 percent ability. I want to shoot this fuck. My training tells me to dump my hollow point Spear Gold Dot .40-caliber rounds into his chest until he drops. My training also tells me that using my firearm now is a bad choice. My partner and I are fighting side by side. If he moves to the right while I fire I tag him in the back. Body armor or not, tagging your partner in the back is not good.

Decision is made. No time to access other tools and no room for them either. This is an up-close and personal fight. Bad guy with knife, cops with fists.

The hammering starts. I have fought with my partner enough to know that we are both going to pound this fucker into the ground. I know that my actions will follow his. I know that what he does will not get in the way of what I do.

As my world spins in slow motion I feel us push the kid back to a brick wall. He doesn't want to go down so we will use the wall as our platform to fight from. I see my partner trap the guy's arm and weapon on the wall with his right fist, I can see him moving for an uppercut.

Space is limited and we want to keep it like that. I aim for the head also. I want to shut this guy's computer off. Take away his ability to fight.

It was like I was watching a face made of rubber when my partner made contact with the uppercut. It was a money shot. The kid's head snapped back like a whip. His head ricocheted off of the brick wall as his face twisted and contorted from the blow. My fist followed immediately afterwards. Just as his head made it back from bouncing off of the brick wall my right hook caught its mark on his jaw. It spun his head violently to the left. His chin snapped and I felt his body start to go limp.

Come on, mother fuck, pass out, you don't want more of this. But he holds on to his reality. His eyes are rolling back in his head but he still stands. He still pushes on us. He is going into his primitive world. For him it is fight or die. His body is running off of the Mix too.

I drop a blow into his kidneys. The hollow thud echoes and then I drive up my elbow to strike his head again. Have to keep hitting this guy. I cannot stop to let him gain his bearings. My left fist hammers his sternum and I feel the chest fold to let air out of his body. Keep hammering him. Keep fucking this guy up until the knife is dropped.

My partner drops a solid knee strike into the guy's thigh. The force knocks him to the ground but not the way we would want it. He is on his back, facing us. He has a good fighting platform. His mind no longer has to think about standing to fight. No need to think about balance. Fuck.

My right fist slams into his face as he lifts his head off of the ground to try to get his bearings again. With a crack sounding like a coconut hitting a floor, his head bounces off of the concrete.

Excellent, a double concussion.

The brain sits in a vat of fluid and floats there in its protective bone case. If you shake the vault the brain bounces off of the bone, causing a concussion.

Now if you combine that with a solid object on the other side, the brain bounces twice, you get a double concussion.

One will always remember the sound of a head hitting the ground.

Our blows continue and this guy still refuses to drop the knife. I wonder to myself what kind of drugs this kid has flowing through him. Does he even feel what we are doing to him? Is his brain just confused at why the world is shaking so much?

Two more blows crush into this guy's chest and then I hammer his head back into the concrete. I see my partner place both knees onto the guy's forearm and pry the knife out of his hands. I glance over and see that my partner has secured the knife, the threat is over. As we roll the guy over to put cuffs on, my adrenaline dump starts to wear off. I stand up to walk off the effects and to try to get my breath back.

I look at all of the blood on me and then I look at my partner. I check him over as he looks at the blood on him. I cannot see any wounds on him but we both try to get rid of our adrenaline fixes so that we can now feel pain. Under extreme stress and adrenaline fixes, the human body doesn't recognize pain. It is not important to you at the time. Survival is the only thing that is important, and knowing where you were hurt will only matter after you survive the encounter.

We check each other for open wounds and sudden "leaks" that may appear.

"Always do a self and buddy check after a deadly force encounter. Under an adrenaline-induced state the body will restrict the flow of blood to certain parts of your body. This is a survival program that will give you more blood to your heart, limbs, and lungs.

"You could have a hole in you that you do not know about. When you calm down you will start to bleed, you will spring a leak.

"Your body will pull blood out of your stomach, internal organs, and your ass. If you have a full bladder or haven't taken a shit in a while you will piss or shit your pants. If I ever hear that you mocked a fellow officer after he has survived a deadly force encounter because he defecated himself I will personally come over and shit down the stump where your head used to be. It is a natural reaction and is not a sign of cowardice. He has shown he is no coward by winning the battle." The words of a good instructor, they will flow through my mind till I die.

Now that my time becomes normal again, now that I know I have survived this encounter, I remember things that are so important for me to fight for. I remember all the people that I love.

I look at my hands and they are covered in blood. They are cracked and chipped. They are rough and harsh. I wonder why anyone would love these hands and their owner.

Months have passed now and my partner and me are testifying in court.

We have gone through so much with this offender. He filed an excessive use of force complaint with our Internal Affairs department. My partner and I could have shot this kid, killed him outright, and we would have been covered in every aspect. Our use of force was far below what the Criminal Code states we would be legally allowed to do.

We are still investigated and even though the investigator tells us we are "all good" I do not believe him. This is Internal Affairs, the stepping-stone for guys to find "examples" and get promoted. The enemy here is behind you, in a blue uniform, and he is more deceiving and cunning than the bad guys we deal with on the street.

He is a wolf in sheepdog's clothing.

"I am here to talk to you about the punishment beating that you guys dished out." This was the opening line from our investigator to my partner and I as we sat down in a large board room to be served our internal investigation documents. My partner was quick to let the investigator know that it was not a "punishment beating," we acted in self-defense and professionally.

The next words out of our mouths drew our line in the sand with the investigator.

"I will not provide a voluntary statement, and I request legal representation from this point forward."

Nothing more is said as we are delivered paperwork and we leave the board room.

Our complaint will not be fully investigated internally though, as the complainant, the eighteen-year-old male, cannot get his lies straight and his story falls apart. The witnesses that were supposed to come forward telling the investigator how eight cops beat the "victim" as he begged us to stop, never came to fruition.

Why? Because they did not exist, he found no one who would want to lie on paper to an investigator. The complainant fails to return the calls from the Internal Affairs investigator and the file is closed.

Now I look at the same young man sitting across from me as I explain every little detail again and again to the judge as his lawyer continues to try to find a flaw in my testimony. He fails over and over again, I tell the truth. The truth has no flaws because it is burned into my mind, forever etching into my dreams.

The day is over and the judge finds the accused guilty for two counts of assaulting a police officer with a weapon, two counts of resisting arrest, and one count of possessing a weapon dangerous to the public. Sounds like the hammer will fall, right?

It never falls, the accused gets six months probation for his sentencing. No jail time, no real punishment for such behavior. Just a six-month promise: that he will be of good behavior, not consume alcohol or drugs, and oh yes, a written letter on how he was wrong to fight with the police.

Looking back, have I learned a lesson? Yes, I now know that if I am ever put into that same situation again I will not risk my safety or my partner's life on fighting with the offender. We were lucky, very lucky. One of us could have easily gone to the hospital or even worse cast his blood all over the street as an artery is severed.

Next time I will use the appropriate force. I will take a mother's child, a father's son, another man's brother from the world of the living to stop his threat to me.

When I get home I tell the tale to my wife about the sentencing that was handed down from the judge to the offender and she becomes infuriated.

I reach out with my hands and touch her face. I tell her that is the way the game is played and it is not in our control. I calm her animal within, the tiger that lies beneath her beauty.

Her eyes close as her hands hold mine close to her face. Her cheek rests in the palm of my hand as her words spill out, words that echo in my soul like the whispers of a thousand angels.

"I love you; I just never want to lose you."

Both of my hands hold her face as I move forward to kiss her. In our small quiet exchange that doesn't involve any words I let her know that everything is fine.

I look at my hands as they rest on her soft smooth skin. They are cracked and scarred. They are rough and harsh.

I wonder why anyone would love these hands and their owner.

WARRANT FOR ARREST

WARRANT FOR ARREST

The sense of humor that is created on the job is like no other. When I went to serve my first warrant I soon realized what this sense was.

I was nervous as my FTO (field training officer), my mentor, my coach held out the pink warrant notice.

"Well, you are going to be having a whole lot of these in your career so we might as well start you off right away," she said with a smile on her face. "It is no problem, just knock and ask if the guy on the warrant is in. If he is you arrest him for the offense listed on the warrant."

I reach over and take the warrant and give it a quick overview. I am more interested in the offender's name and take most of my time to remember it.

"Okay, let's go," I say as we exit the cruiser and start to walk towards the residence. I ran the guy's name through the computer before we left the car and went to the residence. I wanted to know his whole criminal history before we went to the house, just to be on the safer side. The guy had been convicted of impaired driving with a criminal negligence beef attached to it. He probably was driving drunk and then hit and killed someone during the process. My FTO was happy to see me take the extra few minutes to pull up this information. She knows that I will play it safe.

As we make our way down the sidewalk between stacked condos that look like small bird houses filed neatly in rows. I keep track of the numbers as they go by and in a few minutes we are out in front of the door that I am going to be knocking on. I am nervous, not the afraid nervous but the type of anxiety that comes with doing something that you have never done before. I guess you could simply call it performance anxiety.

I look at my FTO and she gives me a reassuring nod as I reach to go knock on the door.

My hand raps the wooden door three times. As I wait for someone to answer I rehearse the lines I am going to be saying. I am mentally prepared and I am ready to arrest this guy for his outstanding warrants. I run through the handcuffing procedure. I decided that to handcuff this guy outside on the sidewalk is the best. Room for my partner and me to deal with him in case he decides to get stupid. By taking him out of his house you remove him from all the weapons inside, take him away from his cave, his comfort zone. More control on my part if it is done outside.

I go to knock the second time when the door creeps open. I see no one as I look forward and my eyes follow the opening door down further to the ground. My eyes stop as they see a guy in a wheelchair. He has no arms and no legs. His motorized chair is humming as he moves backwards with a slim rope in his mouth. The rope is attached to the door and is fashioned in some way to unlock and open the door.

"Hello there, can I help you?" he says as he looks up at me.

I pause for a moment as my mind adjusts to the different scene in front of me.

"Uh yeah, is Robert Hellinger in, please?" I am happy that I can remember the guy's name that the warrant is out for. I want to impress my FTO anyway I can.

"That's me, what can I do for you?"

I really pause now. I was fucked. I had no mental plan for this to happen. I look down at this guy and I just say what comes to my mind next.

"Robert, you have a warrant out for your arrest." Arrest? How the fuck am I going to arrest this guy? How would I fit the chair and him into the car? Not fucking possible. I guess the need for handcuffing is out of the question, if not impossible. I try to figure out a way to deal with this if it comes to an arrest.

"A warrant, what for?"

I was so worried about remembering this guy's name, I totally forgot what the warrant was for. I pull up the pink sheet and read down the lines until I get the offense information. I almost choke when I read it.

"Uhh well," I say as I rub my head with my right hand. I can feel the short stubble from my fresh haircut. "You, umm, well, you failed to show for a fingerprinting date." I could not have felt dumber if I tried. There I was standing over a guy in a wheelchair. His arms and legs no longer belonging to him. There I was telling this guy that he had a warrant out for his arrest for failing to attend an act that he could not do no matter how hard we try. Failing to attend for fingerprinting? What fingers?

"Well, I can see why that might be a problem, officer," he said; his short stubs are raised towards me as he tilts his head like a dog wondering what that strange noise is coming out of your mouth when you hum.

"Yeah, I can see that also." I look at my FTO and she just looks back at me like nothing is out of the ordinary.

"Well, what are you going to do, Smith?" is her reply to my look for help.

"Well, let's just take this as a reminder that you do have this outstanding warrant for your arrest. I think that you might have to go get this taken care of." I do not want to take this guy to jail. I know that I would be the fucking laughingstock of the district if I did. I would also feel like an ass for doing it. I want out from this and away from here. I look at my FTO and shrug my shoulders.

"Thanks for your time, sir, and make sure you call our Justice of the Peace and see how you can take care of the warrant." I exit the steps and make my way back towards familiar ground. I sit in the cruiser and wait for my FTO to sit herself down.

"What the fuck was that all about? That was some weird shit, eh?" I am in total shock right now as I actually thought on how to arrest the guy. My FTO bursts out into a hysterical laughter. Her hands wrap around her belly as if she needs to hold her body so that she doesn't explode. I look at her in confusion. Why is she laughing at what happened? What is so fucking funny?

Then I get it. I was set up. This was a prank that was to not only test my sensibility but it was done to amuse my FTO.

"Oh, fucking nice!"

She is still roaring, her laughter becoming contagious as my face starts to break a smile.

"You should have seen your face when he asked you what the warrants were for! Fucking priceless! You almost fucking fainted!" was all that she was able to gasp out between her laughing fit.

She continued to laugh even as we pulled away back onto the main street. Even hours afterward she would still giggle, when the memories crossed her mind.

It could have been worse. I have seen FTOs tell the new guy that he has to acknowledge the Queen before serving a warrant. Then a card is passed over that has this long convoluted speech on how under the Queen's direction and power a warrant is served and enforced. It must be some excerpt from a 1600 medieval document. I have to say it is funny to hear the FNG go through this because the mike would always be keyed open when the new guy read the speech.

No matter what you did you always stopped to listen and laugh. I am happy that I was never given such a task. Maybe she knew that I would just not do it or ask her to do it first. Either way I am happy that I never had to even worry about doing it.

So, here I am now. I sit beside a shiny new guy and he is a good guy. He will be a good cop as he has a solid head on his shoulders. We pull up to a row of condos that look much like bird houses.

I look forward to meeting an old friend too, and I am sure he looks forward to the day the cops come again with a new guy. A FNG that will come and knock on his door to serve him a warrant. A set of circumstances that are played over two or three times a month as we always have new guys coming onto the street. I am sure it is Robert's only interaction with people nowadays and I have talked to him about it before. He enjoys the cordial visits.

I look over at the new cop sitting beside me. I have my line well-rehearsed so that it flows smoothly off my tongue. No hesitation or stuttering. No clues of a lie.

"Well, here is your first warrant for you to serve. You are going to do a lot of these in your career so we might as well get you used to them right now." I hold out a pink warrant form. I hold back my smile.

HOMELESS
HOMELESS

I believe in giving a hard time to a subculture that most people fear. Fear when they are approached by them on the street, but feel sorry for them as they sit in the comfort and safety of their own home. This subculture are the homeless people.

We are slammed with a huge homeless society as we have three brand-new homeless shelters and the city is looking to build a fourth.

"We have had a sudden increase in our homeless population over the last two years and it is still growing. We need to have more shelters for the less fortunate people in this city." Who wrote that news blurb up? Who has their head up their ass? ("HUA" as it is abbreviated on the street.)

First of all let me cover something here. Less fortunate? The less fortunate people here can eat five free meals a day, by simply walking from one shelter to the other. Thank god the city engineers decided to build all of them in a five-block triangle. Heaven forbid we make them walk from one place to another. But I guess it is easier for the rich and the important to not see these people walking about. That is why they want them contained. I could go on that they do not pay rent, have clean clothes, and get free use of showers, etc. I would be surprised if they used these facilities. It seems to be a prerequisite that if you are a street person you have to be smelly, dirty, and of course reek of urine, shit, and body odor.

Heaven forbid they get a ticket for drinking alcohol in public, being drunk in public, or have been dealt with by the police. They even have a lawyer that is supplied to them. Hmm, I cannot remember a guy coming forward in traffic court asking for his free legal counsel. Nope, my friends we are the less fortunate. We work for every dime we make. We have to pay for the roof over our heads and even the water we drink. They sit at the corner and ask us to give them some of our hard-earned money.

Second, if you build it they will come. I hope that one day someone of political importance will come forward and see that building homeless shelters in our city is just like hanging a big welcome sign. Hell, if I was homeless I would make my way over to this city. There are lots of places for me to stay, lots of meals for me to eat. I know that once the fourth shelter goes up then the politically correct will be wanting a fifth. The cycle will continue until we come up with a solution.

Third, ever do the math on the strain that a homeless shelter puts on a city's emergence response units? I know that we (the police) go to our shelters at least three to four times a day. The usual stay there is about an hour, not including the three hours lost with the arrest as well as the paperwork. So that makes it four hours per car, four cars in a day, so the total for that would be sixteen man-hours lost. And since only two-man cars are sent into the shelters because the people there in general do not really like the police, we can double it to thirty-two hours lost. Per day, so the next time your city taxes go up, the next time it takes the police an hour or two to show up you can thank that homeless stinky guy on the corner.

I will not even touch on the medical response or the Fire Department's response to the facility. They are there as much as we are. They have to help out those who smoked too much crack cocaine, hopped on too many "meth" rides, and even those who just got their ass kicked in a drug deal gone bad.

Don't get me wrong; I truly feel that there is a need to providing housing for people that for whatever reason have become down on their luck. I fully believe that some people do fall and need a hand up. But there are questions we need to ask ourselves. Why do we build homeless shelters in our downtown core? How can we stop the panhandling issues? What can be done to reduce the amount of homeless people?

Why do we build shelters in our downtown core? I have no fucking idea. It takes up prime retail space, it makes the core look like a shit pit, and it does nothing to help the image of a city. The lineups, the degradation of the surrounding area, and not to mention the high level of drug traffic in the area. All these things dump down your property value in the area. Then the effect of that is that rental housing in the area is lowered, attracting another level of clientele, and so on and so on.

So why do we build homeless shelters in our core? I guess it is, once again, to cater to the homeless people.

I mean why make these less fortunate people walk to the outskirts of the city to get their free bed and meal?

I don't even want to get into the mass of car prowling and panhandling calls for service that they generate. Oh, that is right; we do not want to see them walking our streets.

The next two questions are easily answered and I guess to me it is black and white. Not a whole lot of confusion in my world about how to handle the panhandling issue and the homeless issue. Build the fucking shelters out of the city core and in an industrial area.

This would allow those who are really homeless, really down on their luck to have a place to get set up as they get back on their feet. I would install bylaws that would not allow bars, liquor stores, and general stores around it. No bottle depots to return the bottles from a day's worth of bottle picking to get more drugs or alcohol. That would allow the staff to help treat a crowd that is not under the influence of alcohol or drugs.

The drop-in centers and homeless shelters can now focus on those who do want to get better.

I would also install bylaws that would state that if you are in the area you will have picture ID in your possession and that you must produce it upon demand of a police officer. It would reduce the drug dealer crowd. If they lose their ability to remain anonymous they do not like to stay in the area.

I would also state that the area is not slated for any type of living accommodations so that slum housing could not open. Crime in an industrial area is harder to commit as most industrial areas have full-time security, have a full shift of people that are active 24/7, and most areas are gated.

The more people about the better chance of you getting busted for illegal activities.

In an industrial area the traffic is very limited and it is easy for police to monitor the vehicles in the area. This makes it easier to target drug vehicles or vehicles of interest. This makes it harder for the illegal activities to happen. The harder it is to run your illegal business, the less business you will run. Simple stuff.

As far as public transportation in the area goes it would be strictly enforced that "No cash, No ride." And it would also be noted that if you are giving the persons on the bus a hard time in any fashion the bus will stop and police will attend.

A zero tolerance policy.

The restriction of the public transit to law-abiding citizens for the area would prevent the less fortunate from hopping a ride downtown to get money through panhandling, theft, or other crimes for their drugs and alcohol.

And if they do go downtown to get their drugs and come back on the bus drunk or all doped up, they are off.

They lose their ride.

As far as the panhandling thing goes I prefer to get to the source of the issue. Educate the public on giving money to the less fortunate. Inform them on the issues at hand. Inform the public that giving money to the guy begging will only fuel his chemical addiction.

Let the public know that if they truly want to give, give to the shelters. They can use their money better at their end.

And for those who need an excuse or someone to blame for not giving money to the homeless guy they can blame me. I would make it against the law in my city to give out money to a panhandler. Yup, a fine for those who are seen by the police giving money to a homeless person. Right at the root of the problem, it gives people an out.

"Sorry sir, but I cannot give you my spare change because it is illegal for me to do so."

What will the simple move of a homeless shelter do?

Lots.

We already allocate a lot of resources to the less fortunate and it is a growing problem because we cater to them. If we cater to ourselves we can reduce the issue and make it easier to handle.

By removing their ability to beg for money, feed off of the innocent, and commit crimes which are needed to supply their chemical addiction, we remove a lot of the other issues attached.

By making it hard for these people to get money for drugs and alcohol, we now make them clean up or move on.

By making it hard for them to get their alcohol and drugs, they will move on. Where will they go? Oh, to some city that is building its fifth homeless shelter.

A DAY OF SHIT

A DAY OF SHIT.

I like to focus my energy on the drug addicted, the gang bangers, and the drug dealers. I cannot remember the last time I recovered a stolen vehicle that did not have crack pipes in it. I cannot remember the last time I took a home break and enter that did not come down to a drug-addicted person stealing for cash. I cannot remember the last time I went to a shooting that was not gang related and I surely cannot remember the last time that a drug dealer cared about selling crack or meth to the thirteen-year-old girl prostituting herself out on the corner.

But I do remember the time that I can make the lives of these people living hell for them. I am a royal pain in the ass to these people as I want to make their world a tough place to do business. A place of shit for them to get high in, to sell their drugs in, and to continue their illegal activities in. I can make a small dent in their activities; I can make a larger change in the end of the chain reaction.

Do I think that I can make a difference? Not any more I don't.

I cruise the alleys of the dirtiest areas to find my clients.

As we drive through one of these areas, a long alley tucked behind a bar, we find some of our regular clients. They are hidden in a corner smoking crack. The area reeks of urine and shit. The dumpster near here is used as a regular latrine for these people, and it is a hot summer day.

Pulling closer we see that they have just sparked up and then they spot us. It is like turning on a light in a dark room filled with cockroaches. They want to scatter. They want to just move on and not get dealt with by the police.

"Don't you guys just fuck off on me like that! Get over to my car!"

They stop as they hear my voice. They know me. They know the rules. So, the group of five come over without any real objections but here is one new face in the crowd.

I have not seen him before and I want to know who he is and why the fuck he is here.

My partner makes all of them sit on the stairs with their hands on their knees so that we can watch them. I call in our location and what we are dealing with.

"1166 we are out with five suspicious males at the corner of 17th Avenue and 5th Street Southwest."

"10-4, do you want other units there?"

"Negative, dispatch" is my only response to her question. We are outnumbered but the situation doesn't warrant us to ask for backup. Yet.

I call each one over to ask them their name and date of birth as well as what their criminal record is to match their information up on our computer. None of them have ID, they never do. I also never ask if they have a criminal history, I just ask what their criminal history is.

They all have criminal records, that is a trait of being homeless.

As I call the second one up to the car my partner starts to zone in on the new guy. I can tell by my partner's movement that something is wrong. I get out of the car fast and start to close the distance between my partner and me. I also make sure that the guys sitting stay seated and with a pointed finger I tell them to stay seated. Some of them were already putting their hands down to the ground to push themselves up. With the quick and concise direction they know that they have to stay sitting down.

I hear my partner start to tell this guy to get down from the top of the stairs. As the bad guy makes his way to the top of the loading dock stairs he turns around and starts to do his imitation of Mike Tyson. He throws a few air jabs in an attempt to tell us to back off. His lame show of force, an attempt of telling us that he is a meaner, better dog.

My partner cruises up the stairs while watching this guy for his next move. I start to close in to the railings of the steps. There is not enough room on the steps for two to fight and I have to stay in a position where I can still watch the other guys still seated.

I see my partner start to fight with this guy and the bad guy goes down hard onto the steel grate of the steps. I want to get a piece of this guy bad. I look at the seated group and I tell them to get lost, and without a moment's hesitation I see the group scatter. Fucking cockroaches.

I now focus on helping my partner out. He has the bad guy down and is landing some solid blows. I reach through the railing so that I can take this guy down to an area where two cops can deal with him. As I pull him through he locks his feet into the railing so that I cannot pull him to the ground. He is flailing around. He strikes me twice to my chest but they are ineffective blows. His reach is compromised as he cannot get a full swing in and his blows are more of an annoyance than anything else.

I grab his left arm and let the right side of his body hang to the ground. I want to open him up as my reach is also short and I do not want to hit him too many times. If someone is watching it looks bad. So once his body bends, his obliques stretch open as his body dips to the right; I wind up with an elbow. My right elbow starts high and when I get close to landing my blow I even add some more damage to it by putting my body into it. My elbow hits hard. It sinks in, it slides deep into his body cavity.

I drive it in further, trying to keep it in the body as long as I can. I want his body to give way to me, I do not want to lose any of the energy that I have delivered to him. His body folds and bends around my elbow. I hear his air get forced out of his lungs and I also hear him let out a huge gas expulsion from his ass. Body has to make room for my elbow, and room it does make.

He comes crashing to the ground. I follow him down so that I can put my knee into his back to pin him. He flips like a fish and tries to get back onto his feet. The fight is still on and we both go tumbling to the ground as I trip over him. As I hit the asphalt I lock his head into my chest and flip myself over. I am back on the top, back into a fighting position. I slam out two open-hand blows to his forehead, which make his skull bounce off of the solid asphalt. The echoes of these blows bounce down the alley. My partner is now behind him, I catch the red stripe of his uniform from the corner of my eye. This guy is done, I flip him over and cuff him.

As I get up I look at my body to ensure that I have not been hurt in this altercation. I am not hurt but I have been smeared with human shit all over my shoulder. It is smudged into my uniform. This guy wanted to fight behind the dumpster as he knew I would get covered in shit.

I look at him and he just smiles and looks at me.

"Looks good on you, fucking pig!"

I feel anger erupt inside of me. I look at my partner, who starts to look around in all directions. He is looking for bystanders, for eyes that may watch us. He gives me the nod and I know it is time for me to make sure this loser doesn't try this again.

I move over to this guy lying on the ground, hands cuffed behind his back. His look of delight changes to a look of fear as he knows I am so ready to open a can of shit on him.

As I grab his shirt to give him a couple of head blows my partner blurts out:

"The puddle, the puddle!"

I look behind the dumpster; I see a puddle. Not a puddle from rain or a leaking water pipe but a puddle of human refuse. As if we were sharing the same mind, at the instant I know what my partner wants me to do. It is a great idea. I drag him over to the puddle and dump his face into it. He squirms and tries to stop this but I have a hand full of his long greasy hair.

He has to get his licks now. Pay his pound of flesh.

I shove his face in it and then I drag him through it. He is covered and I have a few more smears on me but at this point I do not care. I am already contaminated.

One final dunk of his face and I talk to him.

"Hey fuck, how is that mouth working for you now? I think this is a new look for you too, asshole!"

I drag him over to the car, almost lifting him off of the ground as I carry him by his belt and jacket. I pitch him into the back seat and thank my partner as he gets out a tub of disinfectant wipes.

I can clean myself off as well as I can. In the back of the car our bad guy is now quiet. He knows that he has stepped out of line with the wrong car crew.

I retrieve some newspapers out of a dumpster and cover the passenger's side seat.

As I gingerly slide myself into the seat my partner keeps asking what cologne I am wearing today. He has a fucked sense of humor.

"Hey, what is that you are wearing? It smells fucking awful! You smell like rummy guy!" These words barely escape his lips before he starts to laugh his ass off.

Just as I go to tell him to shut up and drive, I see our sergeant drive down the alley. Before I even know what is happening he has a digital camera out and is taking pictures of me and our bad guy. He is laughing hysterically as my partner keeps telling me I smell really bad.

I just want to leave, I am covered in shit. I want to go to my locker and change. I want a shower, but I know that this is a long way away. I would have told the entire district to come see my partner if he had shit on him, and he has. Car after car comes by to smile, they all wave and point. All these actions were followed by a resounding laugh.

Oh well, I would have not cut my partner any breaks either. I suck it up and laugh at the situation too.

Steak Sauce, Anyone?

STEAK SAUCE ANY ONE?

Just about anything can get a nickname on the job.

Our Glock pistol is a "chunk."

A car is a "veh" or a "cruiser."

A criminal is a "bad guy" or a "shit bag."

A young criminal is a "puke" or a "YOA."

A pedophile is a "skinner" or a "ped."

Extra stuff we carry is "kit."

The list goes on.

Everything gets a new name. We have 10 codes for calls and we even speak to each other with the codes.

We have our own language, our own rules for behavior, and our special sense of humor.

We call those large cans of bear spray "steak sauce," and I carry one. You know the huge cans of pepper spray that you can get for backpacking and hiking?

Well, they are really popular weapons of choice for street people because they are effective and cheap.

Want to rob someone? Just blast them in the face with some bear spray and off you go.

I have seen it countless times.

So, I always carry a can of bear spray in my kit bag. A kit bag is used when we have a call that involves a gun of some sort, so you fill an extra bag for the days that you are trapped outside watching a house for a guy that may be in there with a gun.

I have mine filled with knee pads so that I don't temporarily cripple myself kneeling for long periods of time. I also have a rain poncho, extra shotgun ammunition, crowbar, gloves, water, and some other weather gear.

A kit bag is a bag that is filled with "stuff." Nonissue stuff that we spend our own cash on.

I put the bear spray in my kit bag because it is a place where most people never look. It is my personal kit and the chance and the need for upper management to look in it is next to none. I am really not supposed to have this piece of "kit."

The reason I carry the bear spray is more for an easy room-clearing device than anything else. We have several crack flop areas and what is getting popular with the crack heads is to find a storage shed, abandoned garage, or even an old construction site. They move in, set up shoddy traps, leave dirty rigs on the ground, and litter the floor with broken glass and human waste. They sleep in the garage rafters and hidden under old mattresses that they bring from dumped garbage sites. It takes about three to four days for them to totally take over any little nook and cranny that they can find.

So instead of putting me at risk, as well as any other cop that would have to go in and route these crackers out, I figured out a fast, safe, and efficient way to get all of the guys out of the places they wish to hide.

I find an opening and give a quick three-second blast of this shit into the room in question and like magic the coughing starts. Then the people flow out one by one until we have all the coughers outside and no one inside. I think it is rather ingenious as the room is clear, the bad guys are out, and well, the best and most important part, the cops are safe and healthy. Works for me.

If the "Ivory Tower" found out about this they would freak! To them this is a bad way of doing things but they do not have to go in and do the clearing, so fuck them.

So, now I am walking to our cruiser with my lunchbox in one hand, Code 600 bag in the other, and a shotgun stuffed under my left arm. Full load capacity is where I am at. My partner has his lunchbox, his duty bag filled with all sorts of paperwork that we may need for the day, as well as his 600 bag. He is also at full load capacity. We can carry nothing more without falling all over our own kit.

Into the trunk all this shit goes and as I put my 600 bag into the trunk it is just not sitting right. And, if the trunk is not packed properly all your shit will fly all over the place when you are driving hot to a call.

I give the bag a good shove on the top to jam it down into the already stuffed trunk. So, if Murphy really hated cops, which he does, what law could he instill on us just before shift?

Murphy could give me the "what the fuck law." As I push the bag down, the safety on the bear spray can disengages. The can gives a full burst discharge in my bag. That in itself would have been enough to remind us about good old Murphy's Law but no. The bag is slightly unzipped and the spray comes gushing out of the open area. A blast of bright orange mist comes bellowing out of the can and the stream strikes the spare tire in the trunk. The high pressure stream of particles hits the spare and ricochets off the tire, striking me right in the face. My eyes instantly slam shut as I have just gotten a good hit of pepper spray into them.

The burn is horrible. I have been pepper sprayed before. Once in recruit class, and three other times voluntarily, just to see how I could work through the pain and discomfort of the spray. I also have been Tazered, tear-gassed, and hit by a multitude of "special munitions" and "less lethal" weapons. They all hurt, they all make your world fucked, but out of all those things I dislike pepper spray the most.

"Hey, John, what is pepper spray like? I mean does it really hurt that much?"

"The only way to describe the spray is that if I had a warm bucket of piss to detoxify with I would stuff my head into it." I guess that is the best way to describe it. It makes people realize how much of a hurt this shit puts on you. Although, if you are mentally unstable, very combat motivated, or high on a narcotic, the affects are reduced or even none. If you are to spray someone you have to take into account these factors. To tell you the truth I have only sprayed two people out of five years on the street. I think that is a good reflection of what our clientele base is like.

So as soon as I feel the hit to my face and the instant burn with it, I know what has happened. The smell, the cough, the mucus building in my nose, and the instant tearing in my eyes. I definitely know what is happening.

I force my eyes open and reach for my lunchbox. I see the world as a blur, a foggy haze that is caused by the spray. I relax myself and keep my eyes open because I know that once I let them close I will want to keep them closed.

I reach into my lunch kit and pull out my bottle of water. I then take a couple of steps back and start to slowly pour the water over my open eyes to try to flush out as much of this shit as possible.

I cannot stop laughing. My partner is walking around the car coughing his lungs out because of the cloud that enveloped him when the can discharged. He is also laughing.

I pour half of the bottle on my face and I know that I have gotten as much of the product out of my eyes as is possible without going to the bathroom inside to detoxify. No fucking way I am going to do that. This is fucking bad enough without having everyone ridicule me further. We get into our cruiser and my partner is still coughing a bit.

"That is fucking funny shit!" he bellows out between hacks. "What are the chances of that!"

He starts to laugh even harder when he looks over at me and my face is all red and puffy from the contamination. I pull down the visor to look in the mirror to see what he finds so funny.

"Ah, fuck! Look at my fucking eyes, man, they look like I have been smoking green all day." They did. They were so red that I am sure that you could have seen them in the dark. I look at my watch and have to squint to make it clear. 1349 hrs, I will be all good at 1409 hrs. I know that these affects will wear off in about twenty minutes. Ah fuck, does this shit burn. I can taste it on my lips, the spice burning my tongue. I can feel it in my scalp and I can feel it burning the fuck out of my eyes. Oh well, still really funny shit.

"Hey buddy, hit the road so I can decontaminate my face better. I know that the wind will take the remainder of capsicum particles off my face." So, he starts to drive while he cannot stop laughing and giggling at me as I stick my face partially out of the window to get a breeze. It is fall out and the air is a frosty 4 degrees Celsius. As the wind moves past my face I get the cool air on it, which helps with the burn I am experiencing.

The funny thing about pepper spray though is that your face becomes so sensitive that you experience "wind friction" on your face from the air moving. It feels a lot like you have a really bad suntan on your face and then you stick your head out of a moving car as it is raining. You can feel the wind rub on your face.

Nine more minutes, I look at my watch again but I do not have to squint anymore. I am on the downside of my detoxification; I am feeling much better now. My partner and I laugh all shift about this. No matter how hard one tried, you could never duplicate a set of circumstances like that again. Murphy fucking hates cops.

"Fuck, buddy, you know what? We need to get another can of steak sauce, I tossed that one out!"

These words bring forth a roar of laughter from my partner. He knows that the last thing I want is another can of spray after our unfortunate experience.

CHRISTMAS PARTY

Christmas Party

I sit there in a suit and tie.

It is Christmas time. I am out with my girlfriend, socializing at her friend's work Christmas party. I am surrounded by laughing people, great food, and luxurious accommodations.

I feel safe and comfortable. My work, the street, is an alien place that seems so far away as I sit with what I call "civilians." I am involved in conversations of politics, renovation projects, and, of course, golf. A topic I know very little about but I still involve myself with the topic.

I want to be a civilian. I want to just blend in.

Then it comes. The hammer falls. A question comes from a well-dressed woman in her forties. With rosy cheeks and an innocent smile bent large from a few glasses of good wine.

"I was just talking to your better half and she tells me you are a police officer?"

The crowd I am talking with gets quiet. I know what will happen next. The group will start to poke and pry into a world that they see as closed and private. A place that they only can see on television and movies. I know that I will be bombarded with questions like:

"Have you ever shot anyone?"

"Do you ever get scared?"

"What is the worst thing you have ever seen?"

I reply back to her hoping to avoid the barrage of usual questions.

"Yes, I am a street cop in the core of the city."

Due to their innocence they want to know what happens when the sun goes down. They are just curious of the unknown. It is human nature to seek for answers. I do not blame people for prying, because they are innocent of the evil that lurks in the forest at night. It is their innocence that I work hard to protect.

"You must see some horrible things. Do you find that you have become immune to the stuff you see? You know, desensitized to it all?"

My mind is suddenly flooded with the worries and fears that hide inside of me. Fears created by what I have seen on the dark streets I work in. My heart pounds and I can feel a cold bead of sweat roll down my back. My tie feels like it is trying to strangle me, cutting off valuable air I need.

My mind creates the fears and then sends them on a freight train into my heart.

I think that one day my unborn child may be working the streets because of drug addiction. The vision is so clear and punishing. Dirty hands with cracked fingernails, hair frizzled and woven into small knots for days of walking the streets. I can see her all gaunt and skinny from lack of food. I can smell the human stink from not washing for days. Her lips are cracked from a hot glass pipe that feeds her crack and crystal meth. Her eyes are empty and lost. She is caught in the hell of her addiction. She has lost it all. I have lost part of my soul. I can feel my heart pound harder now.

Fear.

Of having a wife. A person I dearly love becoming a victim of some fucked-up home invasion rapist. I can imagine it all. A horror movie scene running through my head but each scene is highlighted with the smell and taste of fear and destruction. Scenes I have seen before, I am now just filling the victims' faces with the faces of people I love. Their house changes into mine. My clean walls are filled with blood now. Carpet is stained. The sanctuary is lost.

My minds races, fear builds.

My dogs, getting killed and beaten by some sadistic little piece of shit. I can hear their whines and whimpers, the same ones I have heard before when I have stroked a dog's head before having him die because of the injuries they have received at the hands of their twisted owner. Looking into innocent eyes, I cannot forget those eyes as they fade to black. The old anger I had felt then is replaced with the fear of losing my pets, which have become family.

Fear builds.

I can see myself looking at a young man, who is paralyzed by a drunk driver. I can smell the chemical odor of the hospital cleaner. The stale must that fills every corner of the rooms. I know the smell as I have been there. Getting a statement from a young kid. I write as he nods his head to say yes and a small shake to say no. That is all he can do. His youth crushed like his spine.

I can still remember his mother telling him:

"You are doing a great job. You have to let the constable know what happened so that the guy who did this can pay for his sin."

Her words echo in my mind.

Sin? I had no heart to tell her that no one pays for their sins anymore. She soon found that out in court.

My mind works the worst fears into my heart and I feel like my chest is going to explode. I feel my inner animal wanting out.

I feel like I need to leave the room. Run away from the questions that will wake up old sleeping demons.

I want to run out into the vast quiet wilderness that surrounds the exotic resort. I want to let my animal out.

My animal wants to run; it wants my legs to pound though the stinging branches of old growth. My animal wants to burn my lungs with cold winter air. It wants to run through the dense forest. My animal wants to run free. No tie, no suit to hold it in. It wants out.

I can feel my heart pound.

But I have no need for this animal right now. A beast bred for combat and war. It is an animal that can be let lose only when the time is right.

I breathe in deep. I hammer down my animal. It is not time to run. It is not a time to let go of the leash. Don't worry old friend, I will let you out soon enough. We will be running through the concrete forest soon enough.

I force down the fears. I lock the doors that they hide behind. I put them all back into their dark places. My heart rate slows. My flood is over and the waters inside of me return to the calm that I am accustomed to.

A quick cough clears my throat and I reply with what comes to mind first, a lie. I lie to protect them from the reality of a burden that I have voluntarily agreed to carry. I lie so that they are not shaken out of their innocence. I do not want them to think that they need to help. They cannot help me, I am not of their breed. I am a soldier, a man of the sword, created to protect them.

So I tell them what they want to hear.

"Yeah, you get a little cold to it all, I guess. I only care about my family and people I know."

I sit back in my chair and reach for my coffee. The bitter taste slides over my tongue as the warm fluid comforts me.

What I would not give to be alone right now.

The questions start. I have heard them all before and I know how to answer them. Each innocent question opens a locked door and I get a brief glimpse of the demon that is hidden there.

I shut down my emotions. Detach myself from the nagging fear that sounds inside of me. I don my stone face, my professional guise, my bulletproof mask.

The questions come to me as expected.

Here we go again.

I wish I was alone right now.

FIT FOR THE FIGHT

"Are you fit for the fight?" Bob questions us as we run our sorry asses up a hill. We are running our last recruit qualifier. I am busting my ass hard to improve my time from the last qualifier but to Bob it looks like a regular day in the park. He is able to run and talk to us, give us the right mind set to complete the run faster.

I cannot even say a thing as my breathing is heavy and labored. I hate the running shit. Mother Nature did not make me a gazelle. It made me the bear, thick and powerful, and fast if only on the short haul. I love the weight-lifting sessions, the anaerobic sprint running, these are what my body is good at. Long-distance running, man that is way too hard on my body. My knees will ache and my feet will be telling me all day how upset they are with the run.

"Come on, recruits, you want to win the fight? You have to have a solid cardio foundation to be able to get those bad guys if they start to run!"

Now only five years after that run I know how wrong Bob is with that statement. All the fights I have been in since those virgin days have been a matter of skill and power. Not an issue of staying power during a run.

I can tell you, no matter how good of a runner you are, load forty to fifty pounds of gear onto you and you suck. Any run becomes a science of pace and developing a new running style as you have a radio, magazine pouch, and other various tools around your waist. No efficiency of movement here. The rabbit you are to chase is a bad guy all hopped up on drugs and adrenaline. He has nothing but his clothes and running shoes. If you cannot get him in the first 100 feet you are not going to get him at all.

It makes more sense to call in his description, direction, and why you are chasing him. The troops will come and that is good tactics. Let the rabbit run right into the mouth of another lion. All cops are fresh for the fight and the bad guy is burning off his steam. That is good combat tactics, running your ass off to try to get the bad guy is just bad tactics.

Engaging in a foot pursuit is also bad tactics as it allows the bad guy to choose when he wants to fight. And his timing will be all on the fact if he can ambush you, he will. Once again, bad tactics.

I strain under the weight of the bar. I push myself harder, to lift more, to have more explosive strength. I push myself to work past the pain, I want to learn to like the pain more. I crave the sensation of hitting the wall. A few more reps and my daily workout is over.

I hit my legs today and they feel like they have been pounded to smithereens. This is day six of a six-day workout routine. I will take tomorrow off as every leg day seems to totally wipe me out. I need a day off of training after the sixth day.

I feel the hot water of the shower fall onto my face. I close my eyes as I let the warmth cascade over me. I drift off as I rest my forehead on the cold shower tiles.

In a hushed voice I let the other four cops around me know what is going on. "OK, we got a fucked-up crazy guy in there and he says he will kill any cop who comes to stop him from killing himself."

"Tell me why we have to save his ass again?" my partner asks.

We all glance at each other and know that we just have to. Somewhere some loser decided that if he wants to kill himself it is the cop's job to try to stop him. It is our duty, after all, to protect life, isn't it?

I cast a glance at my partner to remind him that this is all business now, no fucking around here. "TAC [our name for the better-known SWAT team] is busy on another call so our sergeant has put us together to go into the residence to get this guy.

"He is on the Suicide Help Line and has told her that he is hiding in a closet and has a knife." What a joke: Suicide Help Line. It should be called a "Cry for Help Line" as all of the suicides that I have seen are successful.

I mean the ones that want to do it, they just do it. No warning, no phone calls, just the standard: oh, life sucks, you deserve it, I hate you for ruining my life, I have no other choice, blah, blah, blah fucking bullshit.

"He has a history of violence and he is off his medications. We have an unlocked back door so we are going to move in. Remember, slow, steady, and control your fucking breathing. No heroes here tonight and we all get to go home. I don't give a fuck about this guy, but I want to make sure we can all go for beer later. Agreed?"

Successions of head nods go around and I can tell that we are ready as ever to go in. The hardest part about this is that you never really know how well trained the guy next to you is. Is he calm, is he collected, is he confident with his weapons? Or is he "cannon fodder," a fuck-up that talks well and writes good paper that has made his way to the streets?

Too late for any of those questions now. We are in. I take the lead and we move down the back hallway like a human snake. I look forward and see piles of old junk. All the way to the roof, it is like a maze through a solid mountain of garbage.

James's voice breaks the silence. "Fuck, maybe we should just hold this until TAC shows up. This is fucked-up shit."

I know James is now questioning his combat ability. He has fear, so do we all, but he cannot control it. He wants out and in a big way. He is a liability. The weak link in this chain we are in.

"Too late for that now, James, but I need you to hold a point at the stairs to make sure this guy doesn't come up behind us." I give him his out; I hope that he takes it. I have three other good cops with me and we all want to go in and get this guy. We do not want to wait outside for another five hours to have the TAC unit come in.

"Yeah, okay, I will hold the rear while you guys move forward. I will let you know if I see any movement downstairs," James says as I look into his wide fear-filled eyes.

"Excellent, you let us know then." I know no one is downstairs. There is a layer of dirt going down the stairs from years of neglect and there areno footprints in them. No signs of being disturbed. To have James hold back is good for the rest of the team. He would have stalled and held us up.

I take the lead again as we make our way through all of the trash this psycho guy has collected. There is everything here. Old televisions piled high, boxes crammed right to the ceiling, and even stacks of magazines that lead to the stippled ceiling like trees in a forest.

All the lights are out and the place is in darkness. All the light switches I have seen are dismantled and have the exposed wires hanging free. A good booby trap, I think to myself. Touch those live wires and you would let out a good yelp at the very least.

Slowly we move, taking corners with caution and stealth. We move so that we have the best cover and concealment possible. We are hunting a predator in his own house. He is waiting for us. We can only react.

As I pass by a switch on the wall I recognize it as a thermostat. I stop, causing the rest of our line to stop. I get a bewildered look from one of the other guys in the line. I reach over slowly and turn up the thermostat.

Now even more confused, they all look at me, as if asking, "What the fuck are you doing?"

Once the temperature is turned up all the way I point at my eye to tell them to listen and I give the flat hand signal telling them to wait.

Then we all hear it. The furnace kicks in. The roar of the fan sounds like a distant train. They all know now what I was doing. The noise from the furnace hides some of our walking noise. It covers the squeak of our leather belts and the floor creaks from our body weight.

A moment of genius?

Nope, I read it in a book and hoped that I might be able to test it once. I had no idea if it would work or not. But, it did so I don't look like a fool.

I get the thumbs up and we all set off to move again. As we move down a long hall, I see three doors. I motion to the first door and we all know that is where we are to be going. I have to open the door and clear the area behind it. Then the number two guy flows through to start to clear the room. The others will follow except the last guy. He holds the entrance so that no one can come from behind.

I can feel my heart rate start to climb as my hand reaches for the door handle. I start to turn it then it stops. Locked!

I can feel the bind of metal on metal the instant it hits. My brain tells me that the door is locked and it also floods me with all the other vital information that it can produce. Locked door equals someone locking it. This is where the bad guy is. He has locked himself in.

I step back and my right foot goes crashing into the door. I hit the money spot, right beside the door handle. The door splits right by the door knob and the door bursts open. If I kicked the interior door anywhere else the door itself would have given way. I would have probably launched my boot through the door. I would be stuck with my boot through a hole and still have the door locked. Not a very good situation.

As if hit by a train the door slams hard on the wall as we all come bursting through with flashlights creating an eerie strobe-like effect in the small room. We all move through the door and every second guy goes the opposite direction of the first. It looks like a work of art to me. Everyone who enters the room finds a job to do, muzzles pointed in every possible threat area.

But no bad guy, just a locked door and now we have broken our silence. It is a mixed blessing as now we can communicate openly, talking to each other to ensure we all know what is going on. No more hand signals, it makes our movement much easier. But the bad guy now knows we are here, he gets time to plan.

"Clear!"

"Clear here!" says a younger guy I have never seen before as he looks under a bed frame in the corner.

"Police! Show yourself! You are considered armed and dangerous! Show yourself and you will not get hurt!" I toss these words out in my best authoritarian voice to let this guy know we are here on business. I also know that these words will cover my ass in court. There have been countless cases where a guy, who has been told over the phone the police are coming and has been challenged over the loudspeaker, has killed cops and gotten off.

How? Well, he tells some fucking soft judge that he did not know that it was the police in house and was acting out of self-defense. Some even go as far as to say that they shot at all of the people in his house because he thought it was a rival drug gang coming to take away his stash of drugs. It works, as fucked up as it seems, it works in court. Bad guy kills a cop who is just trying to do his job and gets off.

Could you see the headlines if a cop took the stand and told a jury that he killed a group of males because he thought that they were bad guys? He killed them because they did not identify themselves as good people? What a shit show that would become, so why is it so different for the bad guys?

"Police! We do not want to hurt you, show yourself!" is the last command that I give this puke. I want a piece of him and I want him really bad now.

I can hear the rest of the team breathing hard as they are working through the last dump of adrenaline we got entering the room.

"Okay, guys, just like before. Let's look sharp here and take a second to slow our shit down." I can hear the breathing relax, I can feel my breathing slow down. In a matter of five seconds we are all focused, we have all passed our adrenaline fix, and we know it is time for the next task.

I am back on the point of this sharp stick. I am lead man and even though it is the hairiest place to be, this is what I want. I want to be the pointy end of the stick.

We slide out into the hall again, moving at an even pace. I control the pace so I move at the best pace for me to cover ground but to still have a steady shooting platform. I watch my chunk, if it starts to bob up and down I slow my shit down.

We are approaching the next door and I can once again feel my heart rate start to jack up as I start to reach for the handle. I can see my fingers reach out for the brushed silver door knob. As my hands is a mere centimeter away from grasping it, I detect movement. The door handle is turning!

Here it comes again. I know the feeling all too well as my body pumps the adrenaline into me. It is time for the fight! The dog inside of me is frothing at the mouth.

I let my body go, I let it go into autopilot. My time slows down, I feel like I am working in water. As weightless and slow as I feel I know I am still moving fast, still computing information clearly. My boot once again slams into the door. I blast the door back right into the face of the guy who was opening it.

I follow the door in. He is still in the way so I give the door a heavy shoulder, which snaps it off of its cheap factory hinges. I can hear the door itself creak and snap as it bends under my weight and the bad guy's body.

The force knocks him back into the room. I can see his feet come off of the ground as he lurches backwards. I can see blood leak from a cut over his nose and forehead. I can see that he has fear in his eyes. Under the acute awareness of an adrenaline fix my eyes deliver information and my mind absorbs it all. I feel euphoric, I feel like I am weightless. I do not feel the cumbersome fifty pounds of gear that I wear.

I am now the hunter here. I want to tear this guy up. I watch his body slowly cascade to the floor and as his arms stretch out to brace his fall I see a knife fall from his hands. I can see the black plastic handle, I see the six inches of steel that are attached to it. I can even see the "Ginsu" writing on the blade. My world is crystal clear.

"Knife! Knife!" are words that flow from my lips. An autonomic response from training. We are trained to yell this if we see a knife. We have to let everyone else know that there is a weapon here. "Train like you are in combat and you will fight like you train." More words from the wise, never heard that from a pencil pusher in classes.

I let my primitive mind take me over. I know that if I do not let my training and instincts take over I will slow down, I will second-guess myself, and I will not be as fast and fierce as I want to be. I float even further into my self-administered drug haze. I am aware of what I am doing but there is little conscious thought to my actions. I am relying on my skills.

The bad guy lands hard. I can see his head snap back as my gun finds its holster. I know it is locked in and now it is time to get close and personal with this fuck. He is still stunned as I close in on him. He locks eyes with me as my knee slams into his chest. I pin him down as I pound my whole body weight into his ribcage. I can feel the ribs pop and dislocate.

I feel a spray of spit hit my face as all the air is crushed out of his lungs. I know that I do not want his fluids on my skin but that is something that I will have to take care of later.

I can see feet move past me in the room. Red stripes making their way around me as the rest of the team moves about clearing the room. I can see the heels of the issued boots; I know that because I can see their heels, they are facing away from me; I know that they are covering my back. I can hear the calls of "All clear here" as I am working this guy into the ground.

His head turns to look for his fallen weapon and I can see his eyes target it. His right hand juts out towards it as I drop my right elbow into his face. This was a hard blow, as I threw my whole body into it. The tip of my elbow hits his nose and left cheek. I feel his head snap back and bounce off of the floor. I chamber again with my elbow as I still have room to hit him again.

My second shot was not as effective but it still rocked him hard. I saw that he was still functioning, his insanity complied with his own fight-or-flight drug that was keeping him going. I grabbed onto his long hair and jerked his head towards me with both hands. In a simultaneous succession I forced my left knee forward. I almost picked my body off of the floor as I drove my knee into his head. I wasn't aiming for his face. I wanted to put my knee into the back of his skull.

My energy traveled far into him as my knee wanted to still drive to its intended target. I felt his hair rip out of his skull. I felt his nose pop and snap under the blow. His body went limp under me as his mind shut down from the blow. This fuck is done. I want to fuck him up more, the dog inside of me wants to be let off of the leash. I reel the animal in. Take control of the raving mad dog that wants to take another bite out of this guy.

Once my fury is locked up I roll the suicidal male over and slide my cuffs out of their leather holders. The cold metal cuffs slide on as the sounds of the locks make an echoing tick in my ear.

I now close the door on my inner dog. I can still feel him barking and pissed behind the door but I know that he is locked up. I lean back to fill my lungs up with air, to slow my heart down, to quiet the barking dog. I scan the room and see that the room is secure. The cops here are making their way to me, one scoops up the knife and secures it in his duty belt. One takes a point at the door as the rest of the house is cleared, and another one talks to our sergeant on the radio, letting him know what is going on.

"One in custody, needs EMS, members are okay."

"Are you all good?" A hand touches my shoulder to ensure that I am still here. To make sure that I have not drifted off to some field to run with my inner dog, as some cops do after a good fight.

I look at my knife-resistant leather gloves. They are covered in hair and chunks of skin. I see blood spattered on the wall in front of us. This is all his shit, he fucking lost. I focus on feeling if anything hurts. I focus on if anything is bleeding or if I can feel wetness from an open wound under clothes. Nothing, I don't feel shit.

"Yeah, brother, I feel fine. Do you have some ISAGEL to wash the fucker's fluids off of me?" In a flash I get a small container of gel from another cop. They all wait to see me clean myself off. I know they are looking for wounds on me that I may not be registering. I want to look at them and give a resounding "Hey, enough mothering, you fucks, I am good to go!" but I don't because I see the look in their eyes. They are looking at me the same way I would look at a daughter or brother if they fell. They are worried for me. They are my brothers and we all worry about each other.

"Okay, I want those units to hold their point as we have a TAC medic coming in to assess the subject." A TAC medic is a medic who is trained with all of the tactical knowledge so that he can assist police in calls like this. They have received extensive training on safety issues, cover, and concealment.

I have no idea why they do not carry a chunk.

They would make a great cop with the knowledge they possess. But he has found his calling, as I have found mine.

I hear that uniforms are coming in and that we need to check our targets. I hear regimental numbers get called out before a thumbs up gets shown at the end of the hall we just came down. We don't want to shoot anyone that doesn't need to be shot. I see two more uniforms flow into the room as well as the TAC medic. He instantly comes over to me and checks me out.

"I am all good, man."

"Shut up and be still, you are all good when I tell you that you are."

Fuck, this guy is the shit. No fucking around with him. He has protocol to follow and he lets me know right off the hop that no matter what, he has a job to do. I shut up as I know any griping from me will just slow him down. His hands run over my elbow and he tosses me an instant ice pack.

"Put that on your elbow so that the swelling will go down. You are going to have to get that checked out later. It looks pretty puffy and if you do not take care of it, I guarantee that it will turn to a swollen piece of shit. Fucking front desk for you if you are not careful."

Magic words, I put the ice pack on my elbow and the cold forces its way into me. I can feel the throb of my elbow now and I know that with the ice I will be fine as long as I did not seriously fuck anything up. No fucking front counter for me.

I know that my ass-kicking session for the day is done. The medic tells me that this guy needs to go to the hospital.

"This sack of shit is seriously fucked up. He has a split forehead, broken nose, and some fractured ribs. We have to get a stretcher in here and move this guy out ASAP." All of this is relayed to the constable next to me and the information is tossed over to our sergeant.

"Roger that, send two more men inside with a medical team. I want the rest of the residence locked down as we move the guy out. I want the injured member out also. The fresh bodies will finish clearing the house once our bad guy is taken out."

CHESS, ANYONE?

CHESS ANYONE?

It is like a game of chess. An age-old game where bad guys try to get away with crime and police try to catch them. But the difference is that unlike chess, where the rules are old and unchanging, today's game is always changing. The Queen and King are always making new rules as they are protected behind the Pawns and the Knights.

So, you want to play this game with me then? Well, I fucking cheat. I want to win and when you are not looking, when the Kings and Queens are busy hiding, I will cheat.

I will not play by the rules because I know that they are always going to change anyway. There is going to be a monthly crown memorandum telling me that the way I used to do things, the way that they said to do things, is now wrong. Some lawyer has convinced a judge that we are now supposed to do things a different way.

To me I have the best game of chess with drug dealers. They are out to sell some fucked-up chemical concoction that will fucking ruin someone. I am out to stop them, catch them, and get them to jail. In theory, the criminal justice system should allow me to do my part in this game of chess.

But because we live in reality, the criminal justice system only makes the game of chess very lopsided. The courts have taken away our ability to move. The courts have removed our ability to make proactive decisions. The justice system has made the game of chess impossible to win. They make it so hard that even when we get a good move in and remove one of their players, the courts just give them a one-turn timeout. After that the drug dealer is allowed back into the chess game.

If we make a mistake, if we fuck up, you can bet it is game fucking over for us. No second chances The public, those we are here to help, fuel the fire by thinking that they are like the bad guys. They feel like the cops are there to control them, to remove their rights and freedoms.

Why should they not? The news tells them that the police are going to do it. They show white cops arresting a black man. That is fucking news, man. Cry out racism and then the camera phones fly into your face. Everyone wants a little moment of history captured on their camera. A two-second real TV clip, fucking bullshit.

I can tell you I have never jacked anyone up who was not a bad guy. I have never put an innocent person into my game of chess. So, if you want in on my game, get ready for the repercussions. If you are a bad guy I will harass the shit out of you. I will make your life a personal part of mine.

So, here is my chess board right now. I have two Kings that I have to try to get. They are a crew that call themselves "One Ten" and have a marker of "110." The second is a crew with no street name but flies under a longtime dealer called "LA." These two Kings are playing their own game of chess on the streets, looking for a little bit more turf to sell their shit on.

I am also hunting a couple of chess men, Knights. Each has a set of enforcers. Their street names are Big Mike, Red Top, Staz, and Little Moe. Big Mike and Red Top play for 110, and Staz and Little Moe play for LA. These guys are the bill collectors and they are some mean mother fuckers. They are fueled by drugs and the lifestyle that comes from hanging out with the Kings.

Now 110 has taken a path that, in this game, they are going to be very publicly visible. They complain about police harassment every time the police deal with them. They get the attention from the news and it makes our superiors in the Ivory Tower shit their white linen shorts because they want to avoid the public nightmare.

"For no reason whatsoever, these cops pull us over. Man, they are doing it because we are black, man. Nothing else. They stopped us for no reason!" The guy on the other end of the camera is S Dog. He is the King on his chess board and right now he is telling the media that he was a victim of police brutality. "The cops just stopped me and I did nothing. They called me racial names and then told me to f--- off!" The camera bleeps out the word, which we are all too familiar with. But the bleeping adds to the Effect. It makes the viewers think that it is a word that maybe they never heard. A really bad word.

"I am an honest businessman, these cops here are racists. They cannot stand the fact that a black man drives a nice car and makes an honest living." I wonder if anyone believes this shit. There he is all decked out in known gang attire, telling people how he was unjustly stopped and harassed by the police. I wonder if the public can just take a moment to step back and see through all of his lies. I mean, do people honestly think that we have enough time on our hands to randomly pick on people?

Can the public honestly believe that this guy is just accidentally driving through one of the highest drug-trafficking areas? That this honest businessman is so popular in this city that all the drug-addicted people seem to know him by his street name?

I hope that our chief of police will come forward and tell the public that this honest businessman has five criminal convictions for drug trafficking, three convictions for assaults, as well as a multitude of other convictions, all closely associated to the drug trade.

I know better though. Our chief is a politician. He plays the same game that the lawyers and judges do. He wants things to slide away into the darkness so that he doesn't have to be a leader and deal with them.

The word comes to our district the next day. S Dog is suing our department. He is saying that we beat him and disgraced him when we gave him the ticket. Believe me when I say that I would love to beat the fucker into the ground, but I also know that there is a time and place for that part of the game.

I tell my sergeant that the guy had a fucking video camera in my face when I issued him the ticket. That they yelled and called me "fucking pig" for the entire time. I tell him that the guy is a huge dealer and if left unchecked he will get way too out of control. Without some repercussions he will think he is winning the game and he will get more and more aggressive.

"You are talking to me like I give a fuck. I have gotten this right from the corner pocket [our inspector] so you will cease and desist all activity with this guy. I don't want my ass chewed out because I have some fucking cops who will not listen to what I tell them they need to do. Clear?"

"Clear, Sergeant." I am fucking fuming.

I get into the cruiser with my partner and he endures my fucking rant about how fucked up everything is. How fucked the courts are. How fucked the system is, and then how fucked up our service is. He sits there and drives, just listening.

"Well, it looks like we are just going to have to leave this fucker alone and play by their rules then." My partner knows precisely what he was doing. He knows I would never leave this fuck alone. But, he also knew that I needed to vent, a chance to focus, and a chance to see the grey zone, the flaws in their plans.

We have worked in the same car, for forty hours a week, for the past year. He knows me, he knows that I will brew on this until I find a solution. He always tells me that I think too much.

The next day I get to work with a smile on my face. I have found a solution, a way to get around this issue. As soon as my partner sees me he knows that I am up to something. We just pass each other in the office, and as I slide my key into the front metal clasp of my duty belt he gives me this look.

He looks at me like he is waiting for an answer.

"What?" I ask as a smile stretches across my face. I cannot keep my excitement in. It is the mother of all plans, one that will allow me to sleep well tonight if it works.

"Don't fucking 'what' me. What the fuck are you up to? I have seen that smile too many times before." My partner points a pen at me like it is a magic wand that has a built-in bullshit indicator.

"Don't worry, brother, it is all good," I shout out as I quickly leave our office, "and hurry your ass up or we are going to miss parade."

Our parade, or daily meeting, was like all the others. We share information on who is who and what is what. Jokes fly and insults are thrown about, all in good fun. We share a few of last night's hot calls so that everyone can learn from it and share in some of the funny ones. Having the boys leave the table with smiles on their faces is always good. Humor lifts the soul.

One could never guess how our faces were filled with smiles and energy as we leave the office. Not if you could see us come back after a shift. Our faces are completely opposite. They are drawn, empty of all life, and the eyes void of all compassion. At the end of the day we are dried up. How we can recharge within the next few hours for another shift I can never know, but it happens. We all come back to work excited as ever. Most of us, anyway. The guys going through divorces, domestic situations, and home problems are always empty. They are tired. No recuperation for them.

"So, anyone looking for someone? Anyone have anything on the go?" This is the way our sergeant closes up the bullshit session. Hell, we could sit here all day and shoot the shit, sometimes I wish we could.

I speak up, just to let my team know what I am going to be focusing on between dispatched calls. "Yeah, I am going to be working on Memorial Park. I have some complaints there from the community that the crackers and hoes are making their way back into the park. I have to get some cleaning up done there."

"Okay, anyone else got shit on the go today?"

Others toss out their plans for the day but most of the guys here will just surf the streets waiting for the calls to hit their screens. They will not hunt for the shit. They will just put the time in and go home. I never understood that but I guess some guys feel that they are in a losing battle and they are going to do just the minimum. They have lost hope and in that they have lost their community.

I see it like they have given up on the little girl who is getting targeted by the crack dealer to be his next street girl.

I feel like they have given up on the next guy who lies bloodied in the gutter holding his guts in. His body bleeding out as he begs for someone to help him. His words a mere whisper as he has been rolled for his cash and then stabbed afterwards. All this for a piece of rock for a chemical addiction.

I pray I never give up, I know I will never give up. I am a warrior and my battle ground is the streets.

I slide myself into the passenger's side of our cruiser as we are getting ready to leave our lot to start our police work. The sign that hangs on the gate before us reads: "Act as if everyone is watching, because they are." It is a friendly reminder that no matter what happens we have to try to remain professional.

"So, what shit are you going to get me into today?" My partner is still prying, the fact that I will not tell him what I have planned is driving him nuts. He knows that if it really involved anything really stupid I would discuss it with him.

"Fuck, relax, buddy, we are just going to clean up the park like we did last year. That is all. Oh. We are going to meet a friend for coffee at 2100 hrs."

"A friend? Nice, thanks for the information. What are you up to? You and I both know that 110 work the park now. After that ass ribbing the sergeant gave you we have to back off those fuckers."

I know that. My partner knows that I know that. He heard me bitch about it all last shift. He also knows that I love to think of new ways to solve a problem. He knows that I will find a way to get around the issue.

"Like I said, relax, brother; trust me."

"Yeah, famous last fucking words. Don't you start thinking too much! You know that a big fuck like you should not think so much. It is not good for you and, most importantly, me!" My partner drives out of the lot onto the streets. I look at him and smile.

He just shakes his head and starts to drive to the rundown area of the city we call home.

"Who the fuck did I piss off in my last life to get you as a partner?'

I smile even more. He is a brother to me. I know he likes the shit we can stir up, and I know that he also wants to get the 110 guys. He has not given up on his community.

We pull into the park and it looks like shit. I hate to see it this way. Strung-out crackers everywhere and hookers working the corners. Garbage from the homeless floats across fresh-cut grass, the tumbleweeds of the twentieth century. We had cleaned up this place two weeks ago. Kids were playing on the grass that now has dirty needles strewn about. Couples walked on sidewalks now littered with passed-out druggies and crack pipes.

I shake my head as we get closer. "What the fuck, man, we just did some heavy damage here. Why are these fuckers back?" The park is easy to clean up, relatively speaking.

It has places where public eyes cannot see. It's cast in total darkness during the night. In certain areas the fences, tall hedges, and rocks make it impossible to leave once you get in. It is like a lion's den. For the druggies it allows them a place to hide to fix up their drugs.

But it was a false sense of security because once we came in and closed off their routes of escape they were in our den. The lion was here and the damage would start again. We would clean this place up in a few days.

Word gets out fast when some people go to jail, some asses get kicked, and names are taken for the next round.

"Hey, Kirby! What the fuck are you doing here? I told you to get the fuck out of my park!" A head spins to look at the voice who is talking to him. He knows who it is but really doesn't want to know. Kirby was a heavy hitter when I came downtown. A cracked-out steroid monkey that the uniforms on the street would not deal with unless they came in force. He wanted to fight the cops any chance he could get and he is good at what he does. He and I had it out a long time ago and he lost. In a big way, so he knows his place with me.

"Hey, RC, I am just…"

I got the street name of "Robo Cop" when I first came down. Now they call me RC.

"No fucking excuses, Kirby, you know the rules. Give me the shit straight." I give Kirby my rules off the hop. He knows that I am here to clean up this shit.

"Sorry, boss, I am here to get some crack, man. You know how it is."

I know that Kirby is a dealer, not the worst one for me to deal with so I turn a blind eye to him if he feeds me good information and just supplies the hooked. He knows if I find him out of his area he gets a bad ass-kicking.

I have taken the devil to bed, I know that drugs are here to stay and I have made the decision on who can and will sell the shit in my area. If I see him trying to get new clients I will fuck him up bad. He knows that I will do it with a smile on my face.

"Okay, Kirby, but why the fuck are you back here? I told you to beat it last week and you cleared out. Why are you back, man? This is going to turn out bad for you."

His hand rubs his jaw, a nervous habit he has picked up since I broke it the last time we met. His brain is reminding him of the weeks of slurping up soup through wired teeth. "I know, RC, but to tell you straight, the 110 is here selling shit and they are taking my market. It is business, man. A guy has to survive."

"I know 110 is here. I know they are selling in my park. I also know that their shit is getting old and I am on them. They are on the out and you better get your ass back to the Center of Dope. That is where you work, my friend." The Center of Hope, or better known as "the Center of Dope," is a homeless shelter that is well known for the amount of drugs that move through it. If you go there for a place to sleep and you are not addicted, you will come out a cracker or meth head. It will fuck you in a heartbeat because of all the drugs there. It is acceptable and commonplace there, part of the center's subculture.

And of course, when in Rome…

"Okay, okay, I get the point. Hey, you want some shit on the 110?"

Ah, here it is. Kirby is good for information. He hands it out to me when he thinks that the information will pay him in the end. He will "rat" out any of his competition and they will do the same to him. There is no honor amongst thieves and there definitely is no honor among drug dealers. It is business for them. Who gets to have the best places to sell, who makes the most cash, and of course who has the reputation that if you rip them off they will kill you.

"What do you have for me, Kirby? It better not be some chickenshit information either, I am not in the mood."

"You know S Dog runs the 110 crew, right? Well, last week he goes into the White Room [a local bar in the area that gets the nickname from all of the cocaine and crack that moves through it] and pulls out a sawed-off twelve gauge. He points it around the joint and then warns everyone that if they fuck with him he will fucking shoot them."

The White Room is a hangout for crack heads and they even score and use in the bathroom there. It is a hard place for us to get into and now that 110 is selling there it is even harder for us. They are better organized and have a "six man" lookout at the front. They see the cops and all illegal activity stops. This joint is really hard for us as the owner knows what is going on but wants the people in it buying her booze.

"So why should I care? I know 110 carries heat. You have to do better than that." I know that Kirby likes to impress with his street knowledge so I bait him a bit. Damage his ego a bit to try to get some more information.

"Yeah, well, after S Dog leaves the bar I see him put the shotgun in the center console of his Lincoln Navigator. It just popped off and he slid it in there."

Good stuff, that is good street information. "Well, Kirby, that is good shit. Just hidden right in the center consol area, eh?"

Kirby smiles and nods. He has gotten his praise and now he wants out. He looks around to see who is around and waits for me to give him his out.

"Get the fuck out of my park! I don't want to see you here any more, Kirby. Last and final fucking warning!" I say loud enough that the other crackers and hoes in the area can hear if they are listening.

"Okay RC, chill, man. I am getting lost," he says with a smile and he is off into the shadows again.

My partner and I make some more rounds and in a few minutes the park is empty again. But we know that this is a band-aid solution. We know that as soon as we go the crowd will slowly filter back. There is a supply of drugs there and they have the demand for it. More drugs and they will follow.

We pull into the Starbucks across the street after I explain to Howard that we are supposed to meet my friend there in a few minutes. The bell above the door chimes as we walk in like a small warning token to all who sit there. As it rings people look at the door to see who is coming in, a natural reaction for a people-watching environment.

You can see it on all of the faces. The look of wonder.

Why are the cops here?

You can see then eyeing all of the gear that we carry. Kids stare at the uniform and little boys will always look at our sidearm. I guess the fascination comes from seeing a real gun in an era where boys cannot even play with toy ones anymore.

When I grew up my father placed a very big gun in my arms at a very young age. I was so eager to shoot it, and after walking me through the shooting procedure he loaded one round into it while I held it tight against me. Once it was loaded he told me to aim and fire. It felt like the gun exploded. I was ten years old and this was my father's hunting rifle. The recoil slammed into my shoulder and the sound of the discharging round echoed through the valley. I was so shocked at the energy. I was scared of the destructive power, and I was fascinated.

In a heartbeat I learned how powerful this tool was. I was afraid of it and I learned to be respectful of it. I cannot even remember if I hit anything or not. That did not matter to my father that day either. He wanted to take the curiosity out of the gun. He wanted me to know that this tool will destroy whatever is in front of it. He wanted me to respect the tool.

As we walk by the tables I laugh and joke with my partner to let the others in the coffee shop see that we are here for coffee, not business. I can see the faces relax. I see the mothers with their children lower their anxiety. They go back to tending to dirty mouths and giving cautions over the hot chocolate that the kid is trying to drink from.

A quick smile to the young lady working behind the counter and I can tell that she recognizes us. We were in this place every shift for the past three months while we cleaned up the human refuge outside. We would grab a coffee to go and then ask the employees what was happening in the area. We would make sure that they were not having problems with any of the crackers outside and if they were, we wanted a description and what they are doing. We received stories of aggressive panhandlers, vehicle prowling, and even some attempted robberies that happened in the back parking lot.

That was the first place we cleaned up. The back lot was filled with drugged-out clients. The druggies slept there, passed out, slumbering by cars. Tucked behind garbage cans and even propped up against the back door.

We came in like a tornado. I have zero tolerance for this shit.

The people parking here, walking past this filth, are honest, good people. The flock that I am protecting doesn't need to see this. They do not need to tell their kids not to look as their walking pace picks up to avoid any confrontation. The druggies learned hard and fast that this place is out of bounds. They learned the rules fast and moved out after only three days of work.

"Hey, Trish, how are we doing today?" Trish is a young cute girl who served us countless coffees while we worked the area. Her light attitude was always a pickup when we were tired but her naivety always aggravated me. She believes that no one can do wrong and that everyone deserves help. This attitude made our job cleaning up the parking lots hard as she would feed the "poor homeless" people out back the expired pastries and cookies. She would even look at the people we would remove with sorry eyes and ask us why we were so cruel. When she said that I wanted to just turn around and tell her to beat it. Tell her she floats in a dream world. But I couldn't. Her innocence is something that I would guard even at the cost of her telling me that I was a cruel man. I knew in her eyes I was a harsh, cold cop and she wished she could help me. Help me like she helps everyone.

All that changed when one night my partner and I were parked in the back alley working "dark": our headlights off and all interior lights out. Our windows rolled down listening and the radio off. We were hunting, waiting to ambush our prey if they came our way.

I saw Trish come out with her bag of goodies for the homeless out back. There were less and less to feed every night she came out because of our policing the area. As she looked around for someone to take her donations a male approached her.

His body language was all wrong. He was walking head on with his chest squared to her. His arms hung low and his hands open. His chin was dipped and his eyes never left her. He was set to attack. He was ready to grab her if she bolted in any direction. The wolf had cornered the deer and did not want it to get away.

I was out of the car making my way over on foot. My pace was fast as I moved through the shadows. My partner was close in behind me, as his instincts told him that this was all bad.

I saw Trish's instincts tell her that this was not a good place to be. I saw her feet shuffle as her brain was telling her to run. Telling her to be a deer and run away from the predator. But her good will took over. Did she tell herself that she had nothing to worry about? Did she tell herself it would be rude to run away from this guy? Did she tell herself that she did not want to be cruel? I never asked.

Just as I came into the light of the parking lot I saw that he was up close, really close. His dirty unwashed hands grabbed her by her shoulders and pushed her into the dark rear vestibule. Her eyes were wide open. Fear had opened them and now she knew that she was too late to react. She was frozen, even though she could still fight. I am sure she was asking herself why this was happening to her. Then she saw me. Her eyes locked onto me and I could see the cry for help.

I was in full crushing mode. I wanted to tear this fucker apart. My pace was already fast. I wanted to have no more of this shit happen. It already went too far. When I closed the distance, the bad guy still had his back to me. He was focused on his prey, not paying attention to his surroundings.

My first blow was a heavy right fist into his midsection. I could feel his body allow my punch to travel deep into his side. It was soft as my fist traveled into his body cavity. I could feel his lower ribs bend to my pressure. He curled around my blow, his body arching as his face contorted with pain. My left hand went up and dug into his face. My leather-covered hands found holds in his eye sockets, my thumb locked into his jaw, and my index finger twisting his nose into another handle. I pulled back on his head, taking his body back with it. I wanted to remove this piece of filth from Trish. I wanted to tear his head right off.

I saw red, this wolf was going to pay for going after the sheep.

As his body folded backwards, arching back against all natural biomechanics, I pushed harder to get this guy's head to the ground. His head hit hard. The sound of his skull striking the pavement reverberated down the alley like a bat hitting a homerun ball. I saw my partner move past me to grab Trish, to make sure she was okay, and to move her away from the fight.

I dropped my fist again in the stomach of the bad guy and then gave him one more strike to the sternum. His body was soft and limp. All my strikes landed without resistance. His muscles were not ready for the hits and his organs and bones suffered for it. Without muscle tension, the fluid in the body becomes like ripples in a pond. The strike causes these ripples and the energy in them cannot be stopped. The body absorbs it all.

"Mother fucker, stop resisting!" I said as I slammed his head two more times into the hard black asphalt. He wasn't resisting. His brain was still trying to recover from the blow on the ground. He was still conscious but his mind did not know what was up or down. I wanted to just take a little bit more of this fucker before I stopped.

I rolled him over and put handcuffs on him. He was fucked. He just laid there on his side, groaning and curling up into a fetal position.

"You ever think of doing that again I will fuck you up worse. I never want to see you again," I whispered into his ear as I got up off the ground. I looked at Trish, who had her face covered in tears.

Her hands trembled like mine. My hands shook from anger, hers from fear. But our hands both trembled.

She was safe and sound. We brought our bad guy to jail for sexual assault. I am sure his cruel words still sit in her thoughts even though he never had the chance to do to her what he said he would do.

"Pretty good, John. Venti bold and a tall mild for you guys today?"

"Yeah, thanks, Trish. So, everything all quiet here?" I asked. More to ensure that she was getting over her experience, not that she remained a victim.

"Oh yeah, I still park out back but the manager has put a lot of lighting up and I carry some, what did you call it? Steak sauce?"

I smiled as I heard her call it that. I smiled that she now carried pepper spray, that she was now a deer that would listen to her inner voice. I frown because she has to live in a world where the shadows show the evil that can leer in them.

Just as I grab my coffee, I see Mike, my coffee appointment, come in. He is an editor with our local newspaper. We have done some good work together as he tries to educate the public on the drug issues in our city.

I can feel my partner's eyes burn into me. He hates the papers and rightly so. No matter what we do in our uniforms, we are wrong. Bad cop stories sell. We shoot the bad guy, we are wrong for shooting. Why not shoot him in the leg? Why not talk to him longer? If we don't shoot him and he hurts someone, well, you can see how the story would read.

"Hey, good to see you, let's grab a chair." I pull out a chair and slide it over to my partner. He grabs it in reluctance and puts himself into it, all the time looking at me. He is not too happy with me right now.

"So, Smith, I don't want to be rude but I have to get to another meeting so we have to talk business right away." I feed him information on dealers, crack hot spots, and even get him in to do surveillance on these areas. He prints good articles and we both do what we can to fight this war.

I look out into the dark streets, scanning for what I want to show the always eager journalist.

Like a blessing my target shows up. The ivory Escalade comes into view. The 110 guys are here and they are openly loading up their sellers.

They feel like they are untouchable because they know we have been dragged upstairs to Internal Affairs. They know we have had the heat turned up by our own service.

"Right there," I say as I point out the window and tell him about our little incident with IA.

"Are they loading right on the street?" he says as he looks closely. He nudges his co-worker and in a heartbeat the young assistant is out of the café and into the SUV parked out front. The camera comes up and the tape is rolling. "Why the fuck are you not stopping that?"

"I told you, we cannot deal with these guys. Not without valid reasons even though we know what they are doing. You know the game."

"I sure do," he says and reaches into his pocket and pulls out his cell phone and dials a number. "Hello, City Police? Yes, I want to report a guy that is selling drugs right outside of the Starbucks coffee shop. Yes, it is an ivory Escalade, license number…."

He talks on as I look at my partner. He smiles and he starts to get out of the chair. The call will be dispatched soon and for some reason we will be in the area. We wave at Trish and she tells us to have a good night. Getting into our car we hear the call get forwarded over the air and we see it pop up on our computer in the car.

"Dispatch, we are in the area; we can take that call."

"10-4, 1144, caution; check on that license plate. Violence, offensive weapon, and trafficking offenses for the driver. You want me to send a unit your way?"

"10-4 dispatch, that would be great."

My partner reminds me that the guy is still videotaping and I give a smile. "That is all good buddy. Play it cool and see how they like to be on camera."

"Dispatch, could you put us out with that vehicle on the corner of 11th and 4th Street South West, two occupants."

"Copy that and 1155 is on the way."

1155 is a good car crew. They are switched on and ready to rock in the shit. I am happy that they are coming. I feel that we may need them today. As we pull up the dealers that once flooded the sidewalks now are nowhere in sight. They have disappeared like phantoms in the fog of the city. They have an uncanny ability to lose themselves in this jungle of lights and concrete.

"City Police, you are under investigative detention for possible drug trafficking. Can I see your driver's license, insurance, and registration? While I deal with you I want to see your hands at all times, are we clear?" My eyes zone in on the interior of the SUV. My eyes scan for a weapon that I know is in the vehicle somewhere. I watch his moves, I read his body language. I can feel some adrenaline start to flow.

My instincts are telling me this is all bad. They are screaming at me to do something. But, all I can do is wait. A judge will never understand that I yanked these guys out of the car, searched them because my instincts told me that they had a weapon. I have to wait, I can only react to his attack. I have to wait for him to attack me. Fucking sucks but those are the rules.

"Hey fuck you, pig, I know you! You are just pushing the black man down, you fucking racists." S Dog's movements are fast. His face is filled with anger. He tries to get me to look at him. He wants to see my eyes leave his hands. He is trying to distract me; he is trying to see if he can get a drop on me.

"We have had a complaint, are we clear on the rules?" I still watch his hands.

"Fuck you, mother fucker!" he screams as the second unit pulls up. My partner is set off to the passenger's side door and points to his eyes as the second unit arrives. He signals that we are being watched. A small gesture to tell everyone to keep their mouths and attitude in check. They nod and move into tactical positions. Our floodlights aimed into the car's mirrors to blind the bad guys. I am set off to the side of the lights so that if and when he shoots he has to shoot into the light. Less of a chance of a good shot. But at two feet, skill is not a necessity to hit your intended target.

I feel my heart pump. I know this is bad, I know that I am just standing here to be his target so that I can deal with him. I breathe in slowly, lowering my heart rate. I calm myself down, I just wait.

I do not know if S Dog took my breathing as a sign of weakness or of complacency but he springs to life. He throws the door over as I take a half step back. He comes out with empty hands but pissed off. He is putting on a show for the dealers. He wants to show that he is not afraid of the cops. He wants to let all see that he is not afraid to deal with "Robo Cop" and "Bond."

I tell him to relax, I tell him not to get back into his vehicle, and I tell him again that he is under arrest. He keeps ranting and raving. He yells every obscenity I know at me and in configurations that I could not even think of. Good on him, his verbal diarrhea is something to be admired.

I keep my guard up in high alert. My eyes scan his pockets, stream across his beltline, and keep his waving hands in sight all at the same time. I stay calm and professional. I don't like this at all. His baggy clothes could hide a weapon with ease. His low-hanging pants allow him to store drugs and weapon easily in his groin area. The puffy jacket distorts the contours of his body to allow for more areas of concealment.

Do you think that gang bangers dress like that for fashion? Nope, tactically sound clothing.

"Fuck you, pig! I want my lawyer! You can't fucking arrest me, mother fucker!" He knows just what to say. He is not threatening violence, otherwise I could crush him. He just talks shit and yells. That is when my mind spins. It is working out facts, body language, and this situation in every angle. My inner voice scrambles to tell me that there is a reason why he wanted out of the driver's seat so bad. I target the area and I see it. The butt of a sawed-off shotgun. The worn black hockey tape that is wrapped around the handle, the gun metal blue of the top receiver. I can see half of the weapon and almost like I have x-ray vision I can see the rest of the weapon under the seat.

S Dog sees me look there and he knows that I have seen the weapon. Just as I shout, "Gun!" he bolts for the driver's seat. I have a huge adrenaline dump, I get the fix that I have been trying to keep at bay for so long. I accept it, I let the warmth flood into me. Matrix time kicks in. His jacket swirls like a slow-moving sheet in the summer breeze. I see his dreadlocks flow away from his head as he spins. His hands reach out to the weapon, fingers wide open on grasping.

I move fast in this world. My left hand rockets out and locks into a fist full of dreadlocks. I know not to grab the baggy jacket. I have had too many bad guys slip loose from a big jacket too many times. As soon as I make contact with the hair, I pull back.

Control the head, you control the opponent. His body is jerked to a sudden stop. His head snaps back and his upper torso starts to fall backwards. His feet still move forward as his body falls off-balance.

I want more adrenaline, I let my autopilot kick in. I am once again floating in my state of combat euphoria. I yank on the hair, pulling him further back. My right elbow slices the air towards my target. I think of where to strike. To the face, break some bones? Nope, too solid, I don't want to fuck up my arm. To the throat? Watch him die as he gasps for air under a crushed larynx? Nope, hard to articulate without a weapon actually in his hand. Chin? Drive it hard into his chin! Break or dislocate the jaw? Yes, that is the best spot.

My left hand holds his head by his dreadlocks as my right elbow thunders into his chin. The contact is perfect as I see his head snap violently. I see teeth slam together and I can hear the sound of bone on bone. My left hand is free of its hold. My fist is still closed and I can see that protruding out from the fingers are cords of hair. Ripped out from the blow and now I have lost my control of his head.

He falls onto his back and his head snaps off the pavement. He is still dazed but not for long. My senses pick up a fight with the passenger and that someone is closing in from behind me. I do not know who it is but I keep focused on S Dog. I am confident that if someone is behind me, it is a uniform. If it was someone else they would have to deal with the guy who is covering me. I place my life on this trust.

I drive my elbow again into the face of S Dog, making his head bounce off of the asphalt once more. He is stunned but I have to keep working him. I want this guy to be out. I don't want him to have the chance to pull out a knife or another weapon from his body. I drive my left palm into his head, rocking it one more time. Like a spike being hammered into the ground I stamp my right elbow into his chest. I drop all of my body weight into it and I can feel his chest tense as the impact comes. S Dog has fought before and his mind knows how to try to protect itself from severe damage. The reaction comes too late as ribs break under the pressure. Two of them snap and his chest now has an odd dent in it with the ends of the bones protruding out of the skin.

I see his eyes bolt open as his body recognizes the pain signal sent to him from his ribs. I lock his left arm as it reaches down to cover the damaged area. I then shoot up from my knees and his body flips over onto his belly. His arm locked close to my body, the flip takes very little effort. He is on his stomach and I can hear a sickening wheeze come from his mouth. Lung has just been punctured by the broken ribs. I reach over and secure his other arm. The handcuffs slide on. I put him in a prone position before I can even figure out what has happened. My autopilot switches off and I glace at who is behind me. I can see another cop hovering beside me, waiting to get in on the action but knowing that his turn only comes if he sees that I need help. He doesn't want to mess things up by getting involved when I don't need his help. He knows that through experience. He calls in for more units and EMS, and updates the street sergeant. He finds a job to do and he goes about it with ease and expertise.

S Dog is down and out. His passenger, who I find out is a shit rat from Vancouver, is also down and out. Both of them seemed to feed off of each other and fought at the same time. They are now face down on the asphalt. Their night is done now.

I look across the street and I see Mike's camera guy still taping. For effect and of course evidence, I reach into the truck and pull out the sawed-off shotgun. I move so that the camera guy can get a magical shot of the weapon.

I know Mike is probably twisting in his boots with the video footage he just got.

More units come and the truck is towed so that we can secure it. I know that a mountain of paperwork is ahead of me as I have to get a warrant to search the rest of the truck. I still have to book my bad guys in, take care of that paperwork, then I can tackle the paperwork for the SUV. It is going to be a late night.

I look over to my partner when we both sit in our cruiser. "You all good, buddy?"

"Of course I am, how are you? That was some hairy shit that just went down."

"All good here. That was fucking fast paced, man." My hands are still trembling a bit. I wait for the fix to leave before I start to write some quick notes in my notebook.

We pull an extra four hours on our shift and after a sixteen-hour day we finally can stop. Our warrant is passed and in the center console we find a bunch of crack, a whole shitload of methamphetamine, some green dope (marijuana), and about sixty grand in cash.

All that is just a day's pay for this fuck.

When I got home at 7 in the morning, three hours past my home arrival time, I was greeted by a house just waking up. It was nice to walk in and see my wife moving about doing her thing. I just sat and watched, happy to have this chance.

"Late night, babe?" my wife says as she hugs me from behind. She is prepped for her shift, her police uniform crisp and perfect. I feel her duty belt push into my back as her arms wrap tightly around me.

I smell her perfume and feel her breath on the back of my neck. This is why I work the streets. I work these hours, deal with the scum of the earth, so that my house can stay safe. I stay awake all night so people can wake up in the morning and get ready for another busy day. Because of what I do, people can safely sleep at night.

"Yeah, I am beat!" I say as I kiss her lightly on the lips. I get out of the kitchen chair, knowing that I have to get some sleep in. "Catch you later. I will be gone by the time you get back from work. I will call you when I book on from the car." We go for weeks like this sometimes.

I cherish the time that we have off together and not a moment is wasted.

I slide into bed, so tired that I do not stir until my alarm clock goes off. I still ache from last night's work but I drag my feet out of bed. The warm sheets call to me like a sunny beach. I just want to lay back and fall asleep for a small eternity.

My body armor is still warm from the night before. I slip it on with the rest of my gear and I wonder if any other clothing in the world could feel more uncomfortable. I slip the black laces of my Danner boots through the eyeholes and cinch them tight. I check my pockets to ensure I have everything, then I go over to the loading box. Drawing my chunk I rack the action and pinch check the slide to ensure that a round is in the chamber. I holster my weapon. I am now ready for work.

Downstairs I stop in the main office to get my daily mail from my pigeon hole. In it I find a CD from Mike. I know what it is, the footage from last night. A perfect little gift.

"Hey Smith, nice TV time you got today. You're a fucking movie star."

"What?" I say as I am still trying to gather my thoughts from my lack of sleep. I have a hard time moving, let alone working into a conversation.

"Mister, mister, can I have your autograph?! You're my fucking hero!" says another guy in the office as he runs towards me like a little schoolgirl. He holds the morning paper out at arm's length and bounds up to me. He bats his eyes like a girl who is in love.

I push him lightly back. "Fuck off, what does it say?"

"Oh let me see," the cop clears his throat. "Constable Smith is one hot cop. He is so cool and fit. He is our hero even though all he can do is beat innocent people up!"

"Piss off!" I say as I crack a smile and laugh with the rest of the office. I just see the headline of, "Park Drug Dealer Busted!" with a split picture of S Dog in cuffs and a still of me holding the shotgun. I want to read it all but the room hushes as someone walks into the room.

It comes like a sledgehammer to an egg. The moment is shattered as our staff sergeant comes into the office and we can tell that he is pissed. "Smith, my office now."

I hear taunts as the crew knows that I am getting set to have my ass ripped up for the incident last night. But, I know that I am covered, I have something in my hand that will cover my ass. As I make my last few steps into the corner of the building where all of the brass have their office, known as the "corner pocket," I see my partner standing in the staff's office.

He looks at me and I look back but give him a little wink to let him know all is good. All I see is him raise his eyebrows. We have been here before and for some reason we always seem to get away with no damage.

My partner tells everyone that the reason he is partnered with me is to keep me out of trouble. He is a good guy to have in your corner; he does keep me out of a lot of shit too.

The ass ripping starts as soon as the door closes. The staff fires right up into a frenzy about how we were given orders to stay away from this guy. How this is our second complaint and now we have even hurt this guy. He says how much of a media nightmare this is going to be. He gets all wired when he talks about giving out negative paper, busting our asses so hard that we will be happy working front counter filing traffic complaints.

As I stand there I think to myself how this guy probably has the negative paper already generated. He probably sparked a major boner this morning when the complaint rolled his way. He sees this as an excellent opportunity to generate his package a little bit more for promotion.

I let him go on his tangent. I want him to blow all the steam out of his ass. Then I will give him my blast. I told myself to be calm and cool. If I blow up I can get negative paper from him for poor demeanor.

"So, what the fuck do you guys have to say for yourself?" are his finishing words.

I speak up right away, knowing that my partner would rather keep his mouth shut. I am sure he wants to tell the staff to fuck off also but he has much better verbal control than I do.

"Are we getting negative paper for this?" I know the answer, I am curious if he already typed the fucking thing out.

"You bet your ass you are!" The sheets of paper slide across his desk, the staples holding the white pages together as they try to fan apart.

"So, how far was this investigated? Did you interview all those on scene to ensure that the complainant's story matches what independent witnesses say?" I want to catch him. To burn his ass a bit.

"Are you questioning my investigation? Are you saying I did not do my homework?"

"I am saying that you are on a head hunt building your package, sir. But if I do not doubt that you did your homework and are filing proper negative paper because of a good and thorough investigation. I am sure you have followed all of the necessary steps." I say all this as I reach over his desk and turn his computer monitor so that we can all see it. I slide in my CD into the computer's drive and boot it up. In a flash it is filled with pictures of a screaming, frantic bad guy. His words are clear and precise. The whole scene unfolds like my report says it did. Hard video evidence that my story is right, the truth.

I see the staff's eyes widen. "Were did you get this, and why is it not in evidence?"

"I just got this today, dropped off by an anonyms citizen. Just at the right place at the right time, I guess. How is that investigation of yours?" My hands reach across the desk and grab the negative paper. I secure it in my pocket.

"I am going to need those back, Smith."

"Sorry sir, I was served my paper, I will keep it on file." He knows what that means. I have something to hit him with if he fucks with me. The Ivory Tower plays a game and I will play it back. Always find a way out of the box. If he comes at me or my partner again I will go to the association, our union, and explain how he is generating a "negative workplace environment." That of course would get the Province involved to complete an investigation, and he knows that all this shit would come to light. He jumped the gun, making the paperwork before finishing or even doing an investigation.

I have my "leave me the fuck alone card" now.

My partner and I get into our car after strolling out of the staff's office. We are calm and collected. All of the rest of the office staff wonders what has happened but we just leave. Better to not spread stories. If they think that the staff gave us shit that is okay because we are fucking Teflon today. Nothing is going to stick to us.

I look at my partner as we wait for the cage gate to open to let us go do another day's work.

"Funny how all of that turned out, eh?"

"You fucking think too much, Smith." I can see him try to hide a smile.

"Maybe, but I think there is a park to clean up. But let's get a coffee first."

We drive out of the lot, both of us feeling new and fresh. No matter how little sleep one gets, when a plan works properly and the bad guy goes to jail, it feels good. Every once in a while you can start work feeling good.

S Dog dropped his charges against the Police Service, stopped the legal battle, and no longer deals out of the park. He is still selling but every time I see him I can see the hate in his eyes. He has lost street credibility, he has lost face in the courts, he has done some time, and he knows that we are on him like flies on shit. He doesn't complain anymore but he is still a major ass to deal with.

Every time he fires up I remind him how bad I kicked his ass. I ask him if he wants to get fucked up again. I always do this in front of others. They all heard how he was in the hospital for two weeks as his ribs and lung healed. I can see the hate in his eyes.

He will do anything to get revenge on me. I have crushed the image he had generated over the years of dealing. It took a mere few seconds.

Since then I never take the same path home twice and I heat check all of the time when I leave work. I now take my chunk home every night. I know he and many others want to gain their street credibility back.

Fighting Superman

Fighting Superman

My mind wanders while I sit back holding a cold glass of beer in my left hand. I can feel the cold numbing moisture role off the frosted glass bottle. A fog drifts off the neck of the brown bottle as I raise it to my lips.

As I tilt the bottle back to let the cool liquid slide into my mouth, I look out into a vast expanse of trees and mountains. My soul floats through the valley as my eyes trace the outline of green pines matching the varied shades of brown rock silhouetting the backdrop.

I am at peace here, a small bit of heaven hidden away in the mountains.

I draw a deep breath as my peace is shattered by a sharp jagged pain.

I look at my right hand that is strapped tightly into a plastic splint by bright white Velcro straps. Where the splint and bandages stop, purple fingertips stick out. Swollen and fat from broken bones pinned together. I look at the mess of my right hand and ask myself if it is all worth it.

Is this lifestyle worth a smashed hand with metal pins sticking out of it to hold bone so that it can fuse together again?

Is this lifestyle worth the pain and suffering of rehabilitation?

Is this really worth it?

I raise my right hand, lifting the mass of plastic and tensor wraps to eye level.

I focus on the fingers that stick out like mountains silhouetted against the clear blue sky. I think of seeing them move, feeling them twitch slowly The sharp pain creeps back into my hand and rolls down into my arm. I grit my teeth as the pain grows and throbs in rhythm to my beating heart.

I fill my lungs slowly with air as I deal with the pain, move the suffering away from my mind.

I start to gaze past my hand. I trace the outline of the majestic landscape strewn before me. My eyes looking past the granite and slate, I move through time as the mountains blur and the clear sky fades into grey concrete walls.

"Check that shit out." I point to a hunched-over figure at the far end of an open-air parking lot.

In the dusk we can see that the figure is blasting off. I can see the bright flame from his red lighter touch the tip of his glass meth pipe. From the distance I can see the flame bend and reach for the glass pipe like a fiery finger.

As our cruiser gets closer to him he draws the pipe away from his face and lets out the hot gas from his lungs. His head rolls back and he faces the sky as if the gods were coming to rescue him from the hell he lives in. Clear grey blue smoke escapes his lungs in a maddening torrent towards the heavens.

I see his shoulders fall and his face relax as his hit surges through his body.

I know this guy. I have seen and dealt with him before. He is a full-blown junky. He lives on the street, never showers, shits behind dumpsters, and begs on various corners for enough money to get a rock to smoke.

A fucking pitiful way to live a life but he chose his path long ago. Now he has to live with his decision. We all have to live with the decisions we make, unfortunately his act of trying this drug has put a craving into his soul.

I get out of the cruiser and walk over to him as my partner starts to put the junkie's information into the computer to see if he has any warrants out for his arrest.

It is a strange thing. I almost always forget birthdays and anniversaries of friends and family. But out here, in this jungle, I deal with these people so much that I can remember their date of birth and first, middle, and last name. In most cases I will know distinguishing features like scars and tattoos.

I figure this is because of the reputation of the information dealing with these clients forty or more hours a week. But it is also good policing and officer safety, always remember your opponent and you are one step ahead.

"Hey, Trent." My voice echoes in a low bellow, covering the dull noise of distant traffic.

Trent spins his head towards the set of cops now standing right in front of him. His body still hunched over, knees on the ground as he worships his chemical addiction. His head tilts back and eyes try to focus on us but the drugs surging through his body are messing up his vision, his grasp on reality.

I continue to converse with Trent as my partner goes back towards the driver's side of our cruiser to run Trent's name through our computer system. I reach down and grab onto his arm to pull him up from his knees. "Come on, Trent, stand up. We have to talk now. You have any warrants out for your arrest?"

Without a moment's hesitation Trent unleashes his caged animal. The beast locked up inside of him that has been poked and prodded. An animal that has been made fierce and wild from the constant punishment delivered by the crack and meth he drives into his lungs. Each high, each single moment of drug-induced paranoia has triggered the animal to grow more insane and uncontrollable.

Now the animal is unleashed. Its collar snaps off as fear of the police turns into a maddening paranoia. Trent has binged for too long and now he is delusional and paranoid. He thinks that the uniforms here are going to kill him, take him away, and execute him. So, Trent lashes out, in his mind he is fighting for his life.

All of Trent's 158 pounds are crammed with meth. He feels nothing, he fears nothing. Trent thinks he can stop bullets and that he can do anything he wants. His brain cannot read the electrical impulses that tell him that he is in pain. His muscles will not be able to tell his brain to stop lifting when they rip. His body will be unable to tell his brain to stop punching or fighting because bones are breaking. Trent is Superman.

I feel his hands grip my utility belt, pinching the hard stiff leather into my hips as he secures his grip. My first instincts fire. My right hand covers that back strap of my sidearm, locking down my gun firmly into my holster. I don't want Trent to try to grab my gun from me. My left arm bends and tucks into the side of my head in case Trent tries to hook me in the face with a sharp right fist.

No fists fly at me. Trent is simply working on primitive plans. His hands locked firmly on my belt, he lifts me up off of the ground. I am tossed aside like a rag doll. A 305-pound rag doll, that is. My adrenaline kicks in and time instantly comes to a standstill. I feel the heavy water of my body's own chemical fix close in around me. I float through the air, towards the windshield of my cruiser. My feet are level with my body as Trent's hand let go of my duty belt. I am completely airborn.

I see Trent slide away from me as I collide into the front windshield of the cruiser, the sound of cracking glass fills my ears. My head slams into my arm that is tucked in close to it. I don't lose my visual on Trent. I am focused, I am fixated on my target.

As my body starts to slide down the shattered window I let loose my inner animal. The dark caged beast that I keep locked behind so many vaulted doors. I can feel my heart pound and my breathing rumble in my lungs through my nose. My jaw clenches as my teeth grind together. The animal is set free.

Trent's eyes flash his insanity as he braces for my attack. Like a tiger lunging from its high perch to ambush his prey, my legs snap straight. I burst forward with my hands stretching out towards Trent. I want blood, my animal is set free, and I need to feed it.

Trent and I go crashing to the ground as my body weight slams into him. My hands lock onto his neck as he topples back towards the earth behind him. I feel Trent's fists slam into my body armor, his unbelievable strength pounding its way through layers of ballistic protection.

Pain fires up to my brain but I ignore it. I am focused on my prey. My animal cares not about pain. It cares not about the body suffering. All my animal wants is to crush, destroy, and maim.

As we impact the solid ground behind Trent, I land on top of him. With my left hand locked tight onto Trent's neck and my right hand clenched tightly into a fist, I start to land blow after blow into Trent's face. I stab my knees high into Trent's armpits so that he loses any mechanical leverage to kick me off of him. I sink all of my body weight onto his chest to sap his strength, rob him of his breath. Short gasp for air is the only thing his body can do as my weight pushes relentlessly on his lungs and diaphragm.

My fist slams into Trent's face. His nose bridge splits as raw white bone pokes its way through paper-thin skin. Blood spurts out of his mouth as teeth smash and shatter. I drive blow after blow into Trent's face, I want to have him remember me. Never to fuck with me again.

I feel my partner's hand lock onto my left shoulder. This link to reality, the lifeline of a friend, allows me the split-second to slow my animal down. I cage the beast in an instant. The heavy water feeling of my adrenaline fix ebbs away. My tunnel vision on Trent's face expands. I see the parking lot again. The rocks, the concrete barricades, and the lonely trees all come into clear focus.

"Hey brother, take it easy. The fuck is out for the count. Lets roll him over and put the cuffs on him.""

I stand up, straightening my bent legs that have Trent trapped to the solid earth below him. Reaching behind my back with my right hand to get my handcuffs out as my partner rolls Trent over, I know that something is wrong. Horribly wrong.

Fingers skip off of the hard leather cuff pouch. I cannot take my handcuffs out of their container because my hand is fucked.

"Hey, man. You have to cuff this fuck. My hand is messed up," I tell my partner as I support my right hand. Black leather work gloves hide what damage there is.

I walk back to the passenger side of the cruiser and sit down. I cradle my right hand in the palm of my left as I relax to try to feel what damage there is. A medieval systems check, if you want to look at it that way.

I try to move my fingers, pain.

I try to make a fist again, pain.

I try to roll my hand over, pain.

"Okay princess, let's see what you have done now." My partner slides into the driver's seat as his eyes make their way over to my cradled hand.

I carefully pull off my leather glove as pain shoots into my arm and surges into my body. I suck it up, pain, suffering, weakness, is not something that is shown on the job. No one cares about how bad you were hurt. They look at all injuries with compassion, but if you cry, then you are fucked. You will never live that down. No one cries, at least not here.

The glove is finally pulled free and I see the damage I have done. My hand is broken and badly. I see the pinky finger knuckle and the index knuckle are pushed far back into my hand. The two fingers look to be an inch shorter than the other fingers. Swelling is already kicking in and my hand is puffing up like a balloon.

A mass of purple and red blotches make their way into my hand as the swelling starts to stretch the skin to its limits. In a matter of seconds it looks like someone hooked up an air hose to my hand and just keeps pumping it up.

"Oh, fuck" are the only words that escape my partner's lips as he directs me to the back of an attending ambulance.

With a smile sheepishly I hop up into the awaiting blue vinyl seat. I know that I have to accept the help that is given to me by the EMS personnel.

I have been in this world before. I have learned that humility is a lesson to be learned when you are injured. I know that I will need someone to tie my shoes, to do up my zipper on my pants.

I will need to ask to get my steak cut for me instead of spearing it with a fork and eating it like a barbarian teleported to the twenty-first century.

The ambulance rolls forward as the medics start to ask me the questions listed on the check sheet before them.

As the answers fall from my lips I just gaze out the side window. I wonder how long this injury will take to heal. I wonder if I will get full use and mobility after mashing it so badly.

My mind drifts off to my home. The smell of sweet honey that comes from flowers that grow in the back yard. Beautiful clumps of green rose bushes that have bright bursts of red and yellow flowers speckled on them.

I can feel the cool morning mist that rolls off of the mountains to the west cover my body as I stand out on the wooden planks of my deck. Hot coffee sitting in my hands as my wife wraps her arms around my chest. My thoughts instantly fill with the woman I love.

I float to a better place, one without pain and suffering.

I think of my wife, her warm touch and gentle smile push away all of the pain I am feeling right now. I put my mind in this place because I know that I will not feel the pain. I know that love relieves suffering.

Looking out into the vast expanse of trees and mountains, my soul floats through the valleys of green pines and brown rock.

The Cavalry Comes

The Cavalry Comes

I travel through the dark alleys of the Hood. They are narrow streets that are filled with potholes and large frost cracks that make the tour in the alley a bumpy unpleasant experience. I am hunting "slow and dark." My lights are off, my computer screen is closed to remove any interior lighting, and I am letting the car's idling engine slowly move me forward. All my windows are down so I can hear all that the street has to offer.

My cruiser rocks and jerks under the uneven asphalt, filling the night silence with the sound of the cruiser's shocks and struts trying to compensate for the uneven surface. The squeaks and groans sound like small apologies from the car for giving me such a hard ride.

My eyes watch for movement, look for anything that would be out of place. I am hunting these alleys, I have been hunting them for over three years now. The high-rise condos on each side block out the eerie glow of the main street lights. Shafts of light cut the darkness as people live their lives inside the small cramped rooms of the low-income housing developments.

I can hear laughter from kids echo through the alley as a family enjoys the simple things in life. So many simple things that people forget. Family, friends, and the love that is generated in a warm caring environment.

In dark contrast the laughter is drowned out by the yell of a man's voice followed by a rash of obscenities from a woman. Laughter is replaced by violence and harsh words as a couple sort out their issues through barbaric means. My eyes follow the sounds up to a fifth-floor apartment window and I see a man and a woman fighting. It is not physical but the words are getting louder as the body language gets more extravagant. Arms wave, fingers point, and eyes flare as they become more heated. But no violence, yet.

I chirp my siren and shine my light into the fifth floor. They both look out and see the police car. The voices drop and the blinds get closed.

One noise dies down to be followed by another. It now belongs to an old woman. "It is about fucking time you shut those people up!"

"Hmph, nice mouth, grandma," I say to myself in a low voice as my spotlight dims to a faint hot glow as I cut the power to it. My tires rustle forward as my brake releases and I start my hunting again.

The radio suddenly belches in my earpiece. To anyone else it would have sounded like a squelch, a half second of radio feedback. But to me and all of the other uniforms listening to the radio, it was was a sound that we never like to hear.

I have heard it before, a signal for help from an officer that has just enough time to key his mike in the heat of combat. A mere half second of air time is filled with screams and sounds of panic.

My heart skips and I put my foot on the brake. My ears strain for any other information. I lift my computer screen open and I pull up all the units in the area. I look to see what calls they are on.

Like an angel's voice the dead air space is broken by our dispatcher.

"1444?"

I scan to see the address of unit 1444 and I see that they are at a noisy party complaint a few blocks from me. I slam down the accelerator, throwing up a rash of gravel and broken asphalt. I flick my headlights on and toss the switch for my light bar.

My siren roars and the nauseating strobe of red and blue fills the alley as my speeds top over 90 km per hour. I am coming in hot and I approach the main street. I push the breaking capability of my cruiser to its threshold. My tires vibrate as the antilock kicks in and I slow down enough to ensure that I do not hit anyone in the area. A quick left and right check and my foot is down on the accelerator again. I can hear my engine roar over my sirens. I see the lights ahead of me flash to green as I blast through the intersection. The uneven pavement tosses my car around like a ship on rough seas.

I can feel my seatbelt yank tight on my body as inertia tries to throw me up off of my seat. The front end of my cruiser hits hard on the other side of the intersection and then my foot once again pushes the gas pedal to the floor of the cruiser.

I watch the street signs pass in a blur. I listen to the radio as Unit 1444 still fails to respond to the dispatcher. I can hear sirens in the distance. They are flowing in from all over, cars with cops filled with the same goal as me. I want to know what is going on, I want to know that my fellow brothers are safe, and I want a piece of the fuckers that are trying to hurt them.

Three blocks. Two blocks. Last block and then a hard right-hand turn. The rear end of my cruiser kicks out and I slide around the corner. My car is angled and my mind is screaming at me to let off the gas. It wants me to slow down. But my training has taught me to push this car much harder and faster.

I push the last bit of accelerator space I have to the floor. The engine whines in excitement. I can smell the engine, the hot smell of metal. The acidic smell of superheated brakes and the odor of burning engine oil as the transmission oil reaches its breakdown temperature.

I am going well over 140 km an hour as I see the house in the distance. It sits at the end of a cul-de-sac and I see a swarm of people outside. They can hear my sirens and see my lights, and they are making for the hills.

It is a house party gone bad. Hundreds of teenagers, filled with violence and courage that stems from alcohol or drugs.

They are all running about like angry ants as I close the distance. I can tell that there is pure chaos happening at the front door. The human ants are flowing back and forth as if they were awakened from someone driving a stick into their nest.

The front end of the car lurches forward as my brakes try to lock solid but the marvel of mechanics will not allow them. The antilock system vibrates my brake pedal as the last few kilometers are burned off under the mechanical pressure of the brake pads.

I jump out of my car as a cloud of blue smokes rolls past me under my cruiser. The rubber strips from my hot tires trace lines on the road to my car from my sudden stop.

My eyes focus on the front steps as I burst into a run. I can see two blue uniforms. One is on the ground wrestling with a young male and the other stands over his partner. His arm slams into the back of another male that has wrapped himself around the waist of the cop. The standing cop is ready to fall over under the weight of the tackle.

As I close in I call for backup. A firm word is out that the world here has gone to hell. I now no longer care about the radio on my hip. My right hand reaches down to my baton on my left waist. I feel like a barbarian that is running into battle as I crash into the crowd ahead of me. My left hand reaches for the first body ahead of me. I grasp a hand full of hair and the butt end of my baton crushes a collar bone. A hard yank and the guy falls back, his brain too worried about the injury to continue fighting.

Anyone who is not running away is fair game. My right hand, which is wrapped hard around the five-pound piece of collapsed metal, thunders into the chest of the next person. I see his eyes widen as all the air is compressed out of his chest. I toss him to the side.

Sensing that something is wrong, one of the swarming males turns to see what is causing the crowd to break up. He wants to know why this human swarm is thinning out. All he sees is an object for his hate, a person in blue, another cop trying to crash the party.

He swings at me with a sloppy punch. It rounds through the air and holds all of his strength. It is slow and has no form but if it would connect it would be one hell of a money shot. My left arm arcs up and creates a barrier between his strike and the intended target, my head. My forearm lands into his, the energy from his blow absorbed. My right hand starts low. It chambered from my waist and I force it upward to his jaw. I aim his nose, knowing that the metal base of my baton will hit him a few inches under his chin.

I feel his chin give as my baton hits it marks. I see his eyes roll back as his brain shuts down. The blow fractures his jaw. The surge of pain from his broken jaw and the mad rush of his head snapping back shuts down his brain.

He falls straight down at my feet. I try to step over him but I am rushed by two other males. The first slows as he sees the body ahead of him crumple to the ground. The second continues his advance. I am halfway over the body on the ground when I am again involved in direct hand-to-hand combat. I cannot move laterally, I cannot change my stance without risking tripping and falling over the body below me.

Two hands grab at my neck. I can feel one grab my shirt collar as the other one finds its mark just below my chin.

My baton is still closed, I prefer it this way, I have no room to swing it here anyway.

As my left hand grabs the fingers of the hand on my neck I drive the tip of my baton under the ribs of my assailant. I can feel the baton drive in deeply as it enters the lower part of the ribcage. I give my wrist a quick twist, arching the baton so that it tries to exit the body cavity through the ribs.

His other hand springs open as he twists his body to try to ease the pain he is receiving. I grab hard with my left hand still holding the hand that was on my neck. I grind together his fingers so that they mash into each other. I turn bone onto bone until I feel snapping and popping. I can feel his fingers dislocate under the pressure. His body now lurches forward to try to stop this pain.

I yank his hand hard to the ground and he follows the flow of my energy. His dislocated fingers rolling freely in my hand. As he follows my downward direction the other male tries to enter the fight. But his fellow combatant is in his way. He stumbles against the body that is now dragged to his knees. He cannot enter the fight, his ability to strike me is removed due to his distance away from me.

But I am not controlled by the range. I swing my baton hard out to the right in an arc. The inertia causes the baton to expand as it flows through the air.

His arm moves to block my blow. He does not know yet that he is attempting to block a piece of steel that is designed to break and punish the human body. All I see is his hand touch his bicep as his arm snaps under the baton.

I hear his scream as he rushes off to the side, cradling his broken arm close to his body.

I am now close enough to see the two cops. The one on the ground is blocking blow after blow that is intended for his head. His assaulter is sitting on his chest with his legs straddling the cop below. The other cop has crashed back into the wall under the weight of the male that was trying to tackle him. His body is stuck halfway into the wall behind him. He sits in a hole carved between the studs of the wall.

I close in to the cop on the ground and let go a kick any soccer player would be proud of. My size twelve Danner boot collides with the ribs of the guy straddling the cop. The weight of my leg slams the body off to the side and the energy focused on the tip of my combat boots punches in ribs.

I grab the male that is on the cop that is stuck in the wall and drive the base of my baton into his lower back. My intended area is the meaty part of the back between the hip and the bottom of the rib cage. All I feel is soft human tissue giving way. I see the body in front of me let go of the cop and arch backwards. His hands rush behind him to cover the area that I hit. I see his mouth open wide with pain. His eyes are slammed shut as he keeps reeling backwards. The cop in front of him, now free of the wall, slams his elbow into his attacker. The strike hits the male in the face, splitting his face open over the brow.

Blood flows across the room. It paints a red speckled stripe across the ceiling. I spin my body around to put my back against the wall, only to see a whole wall of fresh new faces. The crowd has grown again and they are all functioning with the same primitive brain. The mentality of this mob is one of blood lust and revenge.

I reach for a fixed blade that I have hidden on the left side of my duty belt. I will start to cut those who enter my range. If I go down, I will die here tonight. I will now smash skulls with my baton and cut bodies with my knife. I must not fall.

Just as my fingers wrap around the hilt of my knife I see other cruisers pull into the cul-de-sac. I see a river of red and blue lights coming, and over the roar of this crowd, I can now hear all the other sirens coming.

I let my knife stay sheathed and I give a smile to the next person who lunges forward. I know the cavalry is here and that I do not need to worry about falling. With the wave of blue that will be coming in here to spill blood I cannot lose this battle tonight.

I know that the cops here see the same sights and feel the same way. A fire rages in them as the three of us unleash on the crowd ahead of us. Fists are flying and batons are crashing into bodies. I punch a male to the face as he gets within range and I feel the pop of his nose in my hand. I see the rush of blood flow from the nose and when my second blow strikes the same spot, a red mist of blood creates an earthy halo around his head.

He starts to fall and I drive a third blow into the face again and I can see that his nose sits on the side of his face. It is folded over as the bridge of it lies raw and exposed. The bone sharply protruding outward.

I will strike anything that comes into my range, and when my targets start to get out of range I reach forward with my left hand and pull them close to me. I am now filled with a combat lust. I can feel my brain moving from autopilot to a primitive animal. I start to lose my tactical ability and my fighting is moving to a place where I never want to go.

I want to spill blood. I want to let out a roar from my lungs, and I want to rush forward and crush everything. But what I really want to do is stop. I have gotten close to this place before but I fear it. I do not fear it because I do not like the sensation. I fear it because I like it too much. I fear that once I travel this path that I will want to walk it again.

I fear that once I let the leash off of the dog that I will never be able to get him back again. I will be trying to cage an animal that I have set free.

I toss the next body that crosses my path to the ground.

Breathe it out, breathe it out. Slow down the heart rate and focus. Get your shit together.

I can feel my heart thunder in my chest, I can feel my lungs burn for air. I can feel myself coming back. I look around me to see a world of carnage. The wave of blue rolls in like a tsunami. The bodies that were once blocking my path are now all pushed aside, washed towards that back of the house. The swarm breaks and runs but they just run into the blue tsunami that has wrapped around the house.

There is no escape now, they have lost their chance to run away. I see bodies getting swept under. I see some try to fight the growing wave but they fall. Engulfed in our own swarm, victims of our mob mentality.

The radio buzzes with directions from an attending sergeant. He gives out orders and ensures that everyone keeps their inner animal tethered. He holds the leash on these dogs of war.

He controls this mob and soon, the chaos is over. Ambulances pour in and medics look at anyone who was involved.

"Hey, big guy, step on over."

"I am okay," I say; my mouth tastes like acid from the mucus that is moving up my throat from my lungs. They burn like I have been breathing gas.

"Whatever, cowboy, get your ass over here. Let me clean you up a bit at least."

I look at my leather gloves. I see the shine of blood on them as I roll my palms up toward me. My forearms have blood streaked all over them. I see hair and more blood splatter on my uniform. It looks like a red morning dew that has settled on my dark blue uniform.

I am sure that none of this is mine. Well, pretty sure.

I walk over to the medic that is standing next to the ambulance. I sit on the back bumper, a place that I have sat many times before. I toss my soaked leather gloves to the ground and wash the blood from my arms.

"Follow my pen light with your eyes."

"I told you, I am all good."

"Hey, I do not tell you how to do your job, so don't tell me how to do mine, okay, cowboy?"

"The name is John," I say with a smile. I would never want his job. I was not made to do what he does. I give him what he deserves. The utmost respect.

"Okay, John," he replies with a smile. "I know you're all good but your hand looks a little bit fucked." He points at my right hand with his latex blue gloves. His palms and fingers streaked with the blood that is covering my body.

"Ah fuck. That is not fucking good!" I see the side of my hand is bent in a way I did not think was possible. My knuckle is pushed back and when I push on the area my hand sinks and folds. I am still wired with adrenaline and do not feel a single thing.

"Don't do that, you stupid shit! That is fucking disgusting!"

I chuckle to myself. Disgusting? This? I am sure he has seen things that would make the most iron-clad stomach break. He has seen the human body twisted and broken in thousands of ways.

I wrap an ice pack around my hand as he looks me over quickly.

"Keep that pack on your hand and don't bend or touch your hand like that again." He pats me on my back. "You're all good, cowboy." A quick smile crosses his face as he walks over to another cop who has blood running down his face.

I look about and see all the cruisers, all the cops who have come from everywhere to help out. I can hear our police helicopter overhead and the radio chatter never ceases.

I am tired and I can now feel the throb of my broken hand pulse its way up my arm.

"Fuck, it looks like some front-counter desk work is in the works for me." I squeeze that ice pack harder around my hand. I want the cold to sink in.

And on the Seventh Day the Lord Created... The Police Officer

When the Lord was creating peace officers he was into his sixth day of overtime when an angel appeared and said, "You're doing a lot of fiddling around on this one."

And the Lord said, "Have you read the specs on this order?"

"A police officer has to be able to run five miles through alleys in the dark, scale walls, enter homes the health inspector wouldn't touch, and not wrinkle his uniform. He has to be able to sit in an undercover car all day on a stakeout, cover a homicide scene that night, canvass the neighborhood for witnesses, and testify in court the next day. He has to be in top physical condition at all times, running on black coffee and half-eaten meals. And he has to have six pairs of hands."

The angel shook her head slowly and said, "Six pairs of hands...no way."

"It's not the hands that are causing me problems," said the Lord. "It's the three pairs of eyes an officer has to have."

"That's on the standard model?" asked the angel.

The Lord nodded. "One pair that sees through a bulge in a pocket before he asks, 'May I see what's in there, sir?' (When he already knows and wished he'd taken that accounting job). Another pair here in the side of his head for his partner's safety. And another pair of eyes here in front that can look reassuringly at a bleeding victim and say, 'You'll be all right, ma'am,' when he knows it isn't so."

"Lord," said the angel, touching his sleeve. "Rest and work on this tomorrow."

"I can't," said the Lord. "I already have a model that can talk a 250-pound drunk into a patrol car without incident and feed a family of

156

five on a civil service paycheck."

The angel circled the model of the police officer very slowly. "Can it think?" she asked.

"You bet," said the Lord. "It can tell you the elements of a hundred crimes; recite the Charter of Rights in its sleep; detain, investigate, search, and arrest a gang member on the street in less time than it takes five learned judges to debate the legality of the stop...and still it keeps its sense of humor.

"This officer also has phenomenal personal control. He can deal with crime scenes painted in hell, coax a confession from a child abuser, comfort a murder victim's family, and then read in the daily paper how law enforcement isn't sensitive to the rights of criminal suspects."

Finally, the angel bent over and ran her finger across the cheek of the police officer. "There's a leak," she pronounced. "I told you that you were trying to put too much into this model."

"It's for bottled-up emotions, for fallen comrades, for commitment to that funny piece of cloth called the Canadian flag, and for justice."

You're a genius," said the angel.

The Lord looked somber but smiled.

"I did not put it there," he said.

Unknown Author.

FROM THE HOOD TO THE PIT
From the Hood to the Pit

I have worked four years now in the Hood and it was time for me to leave. I was burning out. I had reached the point of not wanting to come to work and deal with the same shit group of people all over again. I wondered after awhile if I would be invited over to their houses for Christmas and birthdays. I felt like an integral part of their family. I was in their houses so much that I forgot what mine was like.

My sergeant saw that I hit my wall. He saw my dragging feet and the loss of passion in my eyes. I, of course, did not know that I was burnt out. Sure, I felt tired, my temper short, and all I really wanted to do was crawl under a slab of concrete and hide. But, I only knew the Hood. I did not know what was happening to me.

So, one day I came to work, dressed for another set of domestics, assaults, drug-induced fits of violence, and the regular shit that happens in the lowest income part of the city.

I strolled into my sergeant's office the same way I have done for over four years. But this time he just sat back in his chair. He said nothing, just stretched out his arm and offered me the best gift he could have delivered me. It was a blue departmental envelope and in it were my transfer papers.

"Smith, you are a solid cop, and it is time for me to push you out of your comfort zone and transfer you. I talked to the brass downtown and told them a bunch of lies. They think that you will do well down there." He smiled as he told me this. I did not know what to do. I just took it and made sure that he was not transferring me because of lack of performance. He again assured me that he was happy to have me as one of his men but it was time for me to leave. I was to go downtown, to the Pit.

I felt like a wolf cub that was kicked away from its pack. I was given the rest of the shift off to clean out my locker and transfer my paperwork. Word spread fast and I was sure that everyone knew that I was transferred far before I was told. I received handshakes and smiles from everyone. I still felt like I was walking into a call without my brothers beside me.

I still see my sergeant on a regular basis as we cross paths in court and when calls cross imaginary lines that carve up the city into sectors. When I saw him after working in the Pit for six months, I thanked him. I told him that I have matured more as a cop and my desire is back to full strength. I knew then what he did was the best for me.

So when I was transferred here, I set out to set my reputation in stone. Deal with me straight and I am a good guy to deal with. Fuck with me and I will turn your world into shit.

I wanted to find Kirby when I first came downtown. I learned from my old partner that when you go to the Slums, the part of downtown that the shit flows in, you get a street name for yourself. The street zombies give it to you as they find it difficult to remember your name. Even in the Hood where I worked before it was the same. If you were a wimp, a pushover, they called you a pig. Be a fuck-up and get a nickname like "pork chop" and "tubby dog." Those who were afraid to deal with the assholes are well known to the bad guys.

I found Kirby on my first shift downtown. My partner at the time was confused about why I wanted to find Kirby so bad even though I never even dealt with him.

"His reputation in the Hood is that he is a mean mother fucker," I told him.

"You got that shit right, he is a mean fuck. You want to try to rip a piece off of him?" He had heard that I too was a mean mother fucker.

Bad guys travel the city and they will tell you who is a bad ass to deal with. You can see it at cells. The congregating place for all bad guys when they get arrested. We process all of the assholes here. It is a production line and once in awhile you will get a junior cop or an FNG who doesn't know how to control his fish (prisoner). Now if this guy is firing off and he isn't your fish you do not deal with him. If the cop has the capacity to let his bad guy mouth off to him, fine; let him take the abuse. It is his fish and he can deal with him.

If his fish targets you then you have to ask if you can deal with his fish. It is a common courtesy practice. So sometimes a guy's fish will start to talk shit. It will fire up the rest of the fish because they will see what they can get away with. I have zero tolerance for this. I have told more cops to deal with their fish than I can remember. I will also talk to the cop in the back room after letting him know that he has to get a leash on their fish so that they do not cause all of the other assholes to suddenly get a pair of man balls.

But word spreads when a mouthpiece comes in and he is talking shit. A mouthpiece that I have dealt with before, a mouthpiece that is pushing his envelope hard. I just call his name out, and when he looks at me I tell him that if doesn't check his shit now, he will be my fish. I remind him of the way things went last time I dealt with him. I also remind him that the cop he is dealing with is a much nicer man than me. It works most of the time. They shut up and put their head down. That is how cops you have never met know that you're a mean dog and you are not afraid to bite.

"'Try' has nothing to do with it. If he is good to go I will want to get a piece of him," I said with a nod. I will never second-guess my combat ability. "Try" doesn't exist in my world. "And, I don't want you into my shit when I start. It is him and me." I did not want to tell him that my new reputation was on the line and I did not want him to mess with it.

When we saw Kirby I was impressed by his build and size. At six foot, one inch and 210 pounds Kirby is an enforcer on the street. He deals the crack and he makes sure no one jacks him up or rips him off.

As we pull up Kirby holds fast to his ground as all the other crackers around him fuck off. It is like turning a light switch on with a room filled with cockroaches. They scatter and disappear with almost a mystical ability.

As I get out of the car Kirby makes his way over. He knows the routine, he knows he is going to get jacked up. If he has no drugs or cash to lose he will tell us to do our thing. But if he has anything to lose he will fight. He hates jail time and he hates losing money. We make eye contact and I see his hands flex and relax a couple of times. He is getting ready to fight. I can tell by his posture, I can see it by the way he lowers his chin to protect his throat. Little clues given off that we do not know we are doing. Primitive self-preservation items we have programmed in the deep dark recess of our mind.

"What the fuck?" Kirby yells. "I am just walking down the sidewalk. Fucking jack me up for that?" His arms move fast and out to the side. He is posturing now. Trying to make himself look bigger, like a peacock does to scare off other predators. He is loud, testing my steel against his roar.

We close in on each other as I hear my partner call out our location on the radio and who we are out with. He wants other units to start to come in. He knows this is going to turn ugly. I keep my mouth shut as I keep getting closer. Kirby knows now that I will not back down. He knows that it is go time and he better put up or shut up. His hands come up in fists. His guard is good and his feet are well planted. He has used this fighting stance before and he knows it works. I blade myself to him, keeping my gun side away from him. I do not want him to try to access my chunk in a desperate attempt to get a weapon.

Kirby is a big powerful man that has street combat experience. He lacks, however, self-control and inner calm. He lets his animal out right away and lets the beast run rampant. He still has to learn that the animal can only get let off the leash for seconds at a time. Let the dog out to bite but then drag him back in to keep the guard up. It is a controlled chaos inside but once you get ahold of time, fighting becomes a game of tactics.

He lunges forward but as his dog is out wanting to bite he thinks not of protecting himself. His guard is open and since my brain is functioning on tactics I see the chance. His arms are high and he protects his head well. But, his legs are open and free to be damaged. As his weight comes at me like a raging bull I snap out my left foot. I aim for his shin and the timing is good. My hard rubber sole slams into his raw shin bone and I can feel the solid strike try to push the energy back into me. His eyes spring open as he registers the pain.

His hands drop a bit but I do not go for his head, not yet. My kick has stopped his momentum, his body lurches forward from the sudden stop. I slam my boot down his shin, raking the flesh under his jeans with the side of my work boots. I see his eyes widen more. Now with all of my body weight I finish off the movement by stomping hard on the top of his foot. I can feel the small bones shatter in his runner. His eyes cannot open any further as he lets out a loud yell. He is no longer worried about fighting, his brain is telling him that some severe damage has occurred, and it wants him to protect it.

His hands drop, they reach to prevent me from stomping on his foot again. Now I go for his head. Now is when I let my dog out to bite. I start low with my strike, to generate speed and power. My fist forms at his belly as both of my legs bend to chamber energy. My fist follows the path up his chest and strikes him under the jaw. His mouth slams shut like a steel bear trap.

The blow sends his head rocking back and his body follows. His senses are lost and he doesn't know what is up or down. He crumples backward further and hits the cold concrete sidewalk with a thud. His arms hit the ground after him, his brain not even able to compute enough information to try to break his fall.

I reel in my dog, his fight is over, time to lock him back up. I look down at him, and I see his jaw is set off out of where it usually sits. It is already swelling badly and the colors of blue and purple are starting to mix in the area. His eyes roll about and his mouth just whispers small groans. He is still not back with us in the real world. I roll him over and cuff him.

EMS is on the scene as they were just around the corner. They check me out first and then they take Kirby. His jaw and foot are broken. He needs to get to hospital. My partner tells me he will go to the hospital and I nod my head. I have paperwork to do now.

I am still coming down from my adrenaline high when I feel a slap on my back. "That was some fucking cool shit, Smith." I see my partner with a huge smile on his face. "I have never seen Kirby get his ass kicked like that."

"Yeah, just lucky today, I guess." I never boast about handing out an ass-kicking. It is bad luck, karma will dish you out an ass-kicking if you cannot stay humble.

From that day on Kirby and I have an understanding. He doesn't fuck with me and I have gained the reputation downtown that I want. Don't be an ass with me or I will fuck you up. Respect is given if you treat me with the same.

I smile as I think back to the first day I had in the Hood. "Not much different," I say to myself.

"What was that, Smith?"

"Oh nothing, just thinking out loud." I look around at the squalor of the downtown slums. I see so much to be done. See so much that can be fixed, so many people that need to be dealt with. I am excited to be here. My fire has been rekindled. I smile.

Hang Your Soul at the Door

After a hard day at work a lot of guys like to go home, turn on the television, and watch whatever they can with a cold beer. They sit there and try to shelve what they have seen into a hidden filing cabinet somewhere in the dark recesses of their minds.

The best way for me to end a long day is to lie in bed with my wife, just lie and talk. She listens to all that I have to say and if she sees that I have become quiet and withdrawn, she will even work a bit to pry the information out of me.

When I tell her what has happened in my other life, my life on the job, I don't edit it for her. She is a cop too. She knows how to be safe, how to fight, and that bad people roam the streets. But I still try to keep my stories sanitized.

I leave out the blood, the smells, and cries of the innocent as their sterile world has just been shattered. I know that she knows these senses, that she has experienced them as well. I just want to protect her, keep her safe from my suffering.

Tonight I have had a long shift dealing with a full variety of calls. No violence, just a lot of paperwork and of course drug-related issues.

She has just laid there for the last twenty minutes listening to me talk about the youngest crack cocaine-addicted person I have ever dealt with. For me the story has value and interest as I am always amazed how the new level of street drugs pass all social boundaries. These drugs do not fit into any age or financial group. It affects small towns, big cities, the rich, and the poor. Now I have seen it affect the very young and I have already seen the very old addicted.

Now this drug has passed to Amanda. This young girl is eleven years old and got hooked when she was ten years old. Her older sister, sixteen at the time, wanted to go to a house party so she brought her younger sister to it. So piece of shit guy gets the younger sister to smoke crack and as she draws the hot chemicals into her lungs the rest of her life has just turned into a living hell.

If I could travel through time I wish I could go back to that time and place to kill the sick fuck who decided that his world might be better if he gets more people addicted to the drug that he uses and sells.

Amanda is now on the street and left to fend for herself. I have talked to her family in the past when I have arrested Amanda and they are good people. The father almost breaks down every time I call him to let him know when and where I have seen Amanda. It was his request from me the first time I talked to him.

He has told me that he had to let Amanda go to the streets because no matter what they did, no matter what social programs they tried, Amanda would just run away the first chance she got. She always went back to the streets and found the addiction that called to her so much.

I try to understand her world but she knows nothing else. Some people fight the call as they remember better days. They remember their family, their house, their car, and all the other things that they had before becoming chemically addicted. To her she wants and needs this drug. She knows that the rest of the world cannot understand her, that they lack the ability to understand her desire for the drug.

At eleven years old Amanda cannot understand that she is killing herself. She doesn't understand that she has to fight the call of the drug to try to beat the hold it has on her. Try to get an eleven-year-old child to stop eating their favorite cereal and you have issues to deal with. Imagine an eleven-year-old addict?

Amanda does understand that there is a demand for child prostitutes, she understands that she can survive on the streets, and she understands that when she smokes crack the cravings go away, if only for a short time.

Amanda knows no other world. She is maturing in this world and it is filled with street prostitution, drugs, and violence.

As I finish off telling my wife about meeting Amanda she asks me if I care about Amanda.

"No, she is a client. I cannot bring her into my world as she will use me, take from me, and then just run off to get her drugs. I am no different to her than her family is. I just was amazed how young she is. It is a note of interest, I guess."

"It is okay to care, everything will be all right." She is a better person than me; she still cares about the fallen. She is hard as stone when she needs to be but she still knows that it is good to care about those who are not so far gone.

I have heard her say that before. I usually hear it when I bring home my uniforms and plop down the black plastic bag by the washing machine. My wife washes my uniforms for me. She takes the extra effort for me because she loves me so much. She has put in a long day at work too, working in the same shit pit I walk in.

When she opens the bag the smell of unwashed human flows from it. The sweet stench of human body odor that is permanently stuck in my blue uniform from all the unclean, unkempt people that I deal with. The last thing on a chemically addicted person's mind is to wash, change clothes, and even sometimes clean out their pants after they have pissed and shit in them. They exist for their fix and when they are high they may just shit and piss themselves. They do not care, they are high.

Her face always crinkles and mashes into a contorted mix of disgust when she opens the bag up. Her clientele base is not like mine. She works in a different part of this metropolis, she doesn't deal with the homeless and drug addicted like I do.

A routine is built; she washes my uniforms like she washes hers.

The uniforms are washed alone and she doesn't even touch them. She rips open the bag and dumps them into the washer. I know that she runs the washer empty after they are washed just to make sure the street slime is rinsed out.

But this time, when she tells me she that everything will be all right, I can hear some despair in her voice. I know that she says this with pity and affection to me. This time it is different, she is telling me that everything is going to be all right but she sees what it does to me. She knows that I am an animal at work. She knows that I inflict violence to those wolves.

Her lips spill out soft and comforting words. "We are different that way, John."

"What do you mean by that?"

"Well, when I tell people I know what you see at work and deal with, they ask me if you have changed since I have known you. Of course you have changed, we all have. People change as life shows them different learning experiences. They ask me if you are cold and hard.

I tell them that you always bring lots of love home when you come home. But, last week I was asked how you could be so different at work and at home."

"So, did you find an answer for that?"

"I thought about it and I know how you can be so different. When you come to work, you stand at your locker and change into your uniform. You hang up your normal clothes and you put on your duty belt and put a loaded gun into your belt. Your tools are meant for people. Not a pen to strike financial deals. Not a wrench to fix mechanical things. They are there to be used on people and usually when they are at their lowest. I know that because I wear the same tools."

I smile. I am happy that she is able to see my world. I have never tried to hide the reality of my work from her like some other guys do. I cannot, she lives in my world also. I smile that she knows what it is like to start my shift.

I smile because it is nice to be understood.

"Then after you take your uniform off the hanger and put it on you hang up your soul. You go to work with no soul so that no one can hurt you. No one can make you care, and you do not worry about dying if you have to. You take your soul off and lock it up to protect it."

I am quiet. I lie there staring up at the ceiling as I digest the information. I am not bothered by what she has said because I know that it is true. I wander the street with no compassion, no soul, so that I can survive.

I reach out so that I can put her face in my hand. I run my fingers across her face and I see compassion in her eyes. I see her sorrow for me, generated because I have to do this every day I work. Sorrow because I have to lose part of myself to do my job.

She knows the softer side of me. The loving husband that is a warrior, fighting the same battles she faces. I have come home with broken bones and surgery scars. She tells me that she likes the battle wounds, that they are marks of a soldier.

I tell her that I love her as she reaches over to turn off the lights. She knows that I do but I just needed to tell her. The room goes black and I lie there staring at the ceiling.

I can hear her breathing go into a slow rhythmic pulse. She is in a deep sleep and I lie there staring at the ceiling. I worry that one day I will not be able to find my soul in my locker. I am worried that I will come home the same man I am on the street.

I roll onto my side and fall asleep knowing that the day will not happen. I will never lose my soul as long as I know that after work I have my home to come to.

SNIFFER HOUSE
Sniffer House

"Sniffers" are guys and gals that feed their drug addiction by sniffing glue, gas, and anything else that causes a high from its corrosive vapors.

You can see them walking the streets holding their hands in front of their face, almost looking like they are trying to keep there hands warm. But, what they are really doing is sniffing model glue from a plastic bag, thinners or gasoline from a rag soaked with it.

Every drug makes its users react and act a certain way. I can tell if you are on green dope (marijuana), crack cocaine, methamphetamine, acid, P and D's (Percosets and Demerol), or a full book of a variety of drugs by the way you walk, talk, move, and think. All these drugs cause different side effects and behavioral changes.

Sniffers are in a class of their own. Most of the narcotics that are highly addictive cause increased awareness, hyper reactions, and increased euphoria.

Sniffers are in the complete opposite area. The glue and gas that they sniff makes them brain dead. It destroys the mind and its ability to function. When they are really high they can be violent and when they twist they, like most of the other chemically addicted people, have a huge tolerance to pain, and near super-human strength.

My partner and I are responding to a call where the neighbors have called the police because of a strange chemical smell emanating from a house. Fire is on the way but we are out on scene first.

As we park about four houses away from the residence my partner and I discuss the fact that this might be a methamphetamine lab. If so we are going to secure off the area and get the Hazmat team in. Meth labs are chemical bombs waiting to explode. Add some extra air, some source of spark, even from a light being turned off or on, and boom. You're done, your partner is done, and probably the house next to this one is done also.

A quick death but one that I do not want. No chance to put up a good fight, just a sudden flash of light and I am snuffed out.

As we get closer I see no red iodine lines on the window and no other flags that there is a lab here. I sift through the garbage and I see just normal household trash.

I shrug at my partner as we decide to do a door knock on the residence. I peer through the window and see what looks like a drug flop house. Two people passed out on the couch in the living room and I can see two more people passed out in the kitchen.

"I have two bodies in the living room and two more in the kitchen."

My partner nods and raps on the door twice. I watch for movement. Nothing.

He hits the door hard now, kicking it with his boot, and I still see no one move.

"They are fucked, buddy, I do not even know if they are alive." They looked okay, pretty peaceful sleeping there but dead people look peaceful most of the time if they die in their sleep.

"Is 1101 on the air?" I hear it resonate from my partner right next to me. Then two seconds later I can hear it over my earpiece. Pretty confusing when you first start to use these radios, the two-second delay, but you get used to it pretty fast.

"Go ahead for 1101."

Our sergeant on duty is Sergeant Walker. He is a good shit and he will let us take this call to whatever extent that we feel confident doing. He is a good man that knows that we will function with common sense and that he can trust our decisions.

It is a dangerous thing to let some car crews do what they feel they can handle. Our force is so junior that some cars have two guys working together with less than a year on each. Scary shit, the blind leading the blind. But we have proven ourselves to him time and time again. Taking immediate action when it has to happen and then waiting for better tactics when it is needed. He knows that we are not cowboys or chicken shits.

"Yeah, 1101 we have done two door knocks with no response, but we can see people throughout the residence. No one is conscious here. Requesting permission for a door kick."

A brief wait occurs over the radio. He ponders what to do. If we kick the door in, the city pays for the damages and he has to get some paperwork on the go. Obviously he doesn't care about the extra paperwork.

"Does Smith have his camera on him? If so, ensure a photo of the damages is taken when it is good to do so."

"Roger that, 1101, we will take the photos and if you can, forward the paper to my mailbox. We can complete it for you."

That will make him happy. No paperwork for him, we will take care of it, and he doesn't even need to show up as I have a digital camera to take pictures of the damage we will do.

"I will give it one more knock, then you can kick it." The door vibrates again with the heavy boots that hit it. My partner looks at me when he is done kicking the door. He looks at me and steps back a few feet.

"It's all yours." His hands extend forth as is he was welcoming me to a dinner party.

I turn my back to the door and measure out the distance so that when my foot hits the door my leg will still be bent. I want my leg to be at about a 25 degree angle when I hit so that I can deliver door energy and still not hyperextend my knee. I look like a mule getting ready to kick an unsuspecting person who walks behind him.

"Ready?" I ask my partner as I reach up and grab his shoulders for support.

His legs bend to give him a solid stance and he gives me a nod.

My right leg blasts back and rocks my boot back onto the door. My foot hits right beside the door handle, right on its mark. If I kick to the center of the door, the door just bows, taking the energy out of your blow. A hit at the door knob will not allow a flex in the door, it will deliver the energy that you have given it to the door knob and the lock.

The locks and the knob will usually hold but the framing around them will shred. The door slams into the locking mechanism with my kick. The door knob bends and turns in the door, snapping itself free from the wooden hole where it sits. The deadbolt lock edges back and twists in its hold. The twisting of the two locks splinters the door and pops out the thin wood frame that holds it into place.

The door bursts open and small wooden splinters fly out into the short hall on the other end of the door. With the sudden rush of swirling air from the door flying open I can smell that we have a problem here. The odor of model glue wafts out from the house.

My eyes water right away and I can feel mucus flowing into my nose. I choke on the fumes. I can see that the same effects are given to my partner. We move away from the door and go for clearer air.

"1411 to 1101."

"Go ahead for 1101."

"We are going to need Fire here, the place is filled with fumes and we don't have the right gear to get in and out of this place safely." I catch whiffs of model glue fumes and I wonder what the heck is going on in the house. Are those people all dead inside? Is there a can of solvent or glue that was opened in the residence accidentally? Or, is this place rigged to kill, has someone set up something to kill everyone here? Lots of questions with very little answers.

Fire shows up and into action they go with the right equipment for the right job. They march into the residence with their breathing apparatus and protective gear. I move towards the lead officer for the Fire Department. He is an old fellow with a big belly and a set of aging eyes. He is listening to the transmissions on the radio from his men inside.

I hear the belching of codes; the talk of chemicals and explosive limits catches my ear.

"So, what is the scoop, Chief?"

He looks at me and smiles.

"You are not going to believe this shit. I don't think I can explain it to yah. My guys are venting the building right now and I will walk you through it as soon as possible."

"I have to update my sergeant; are there any fatalities in there?"

"There fucking should be from the sounds of it but none to say so far. All those guys in that house are all fucked up on solvent."

I update my sergeant and let him know that we are going to enter with Fire as soon as it is safe to do so. I now wait anxiously as I can see the windows open up on all levels. People gather as they see the big pump truck with all the fire guys running around. To me it looks like chaos but one can still tell it is organized chaos. High-powered fans are set in the doorways and as they are turned on a rush of air flows into the house.

The house is getting vented with such proficiency that the curtains blow out from the house, swinging from the windows like cloth-covered arms waving for help.

The fire chief pats me on the back and tells me that the place has been vented enough for us to go in without any protective equipment. As we enter the house through the side door I can see a kitchen that has been under neglect for weeks. A moldy loaf of bread sits on the counter; empty food containers fill the table and are thrown in the corners.

The floor has a clear path made through the trash from the fire guys working in the area. As I make the short two steps that lead up the back door to the kitchen the fire chief motions to the pot on the stove. I walk towards it and even with the fans blowing the house full of fresh air I can tell from the chemical odor that this is the cause of the smell. From here is where the chemical contamination starts.

I see a clear fluid in the pot, looking much like a pot filled with water. I dip a large wooden spoon into it that I picked up from the side of the crusted stove and I can tell that this is not water. It is thick, a mass of hot glue. I swirl it with the spoon and I can feel the thickness try to slow the spoon down. But the fluid is still hot, off-gassing its fumes under the low heat of the stove.

"Fuck me, this is fucked, man."

I look at the fire chief as I can tell that my eyes are starting to feel the effects of stirring the foul concoction on the stove. The slight agitation of the fluid released a plume of vapors.

"I know one hell of a way to kill yourself, this is the weirdest suicide attempt I have ever seen. It is like a cult house that everyone wants to die in."

I know that this is no suicide house. I look around and I see the faces of those passed out in the house. They are regular customers of mine, long-time sniffers.

"Oh, this is no fucking suicide attempt, Chief. These guys have set up the biggest glue bag ever. They are getting high in this death trap."

I can see the fire chief look around. His eyes moving over the passed-out people that are now being attended to by the Fire and EMS personnel that have arrived on scene. His brain is taking in the senses delivered to him by his nose, eyes, and ears. To him the easiest thing to understand was that the people here were trying to kill themselves. It is a hard fact to see that these people are just sniffers trying to get high.

"That is just fucked," the old man says as he moves back outside to co-ordinate his men to clean up this mess.

My partner calls me over to a guy lying on the couch. Two medics are standing there with a look of utter surprise cast upon their faces.

"What?"

"Check this shit out. When you were over there chatting to the fire chief I came over to help out these medics waking up these fucking zombies. So, I just walk over to this guy who has the fucking thousand-yard stare going on and kick his feet to try to stir him up. Well, check this shit out." He taps the guy's foot with his boot and his whole shin moves. But not in any natural way. The shin shifts from its middle, the area that is supposed to be solid bone. The foot rolls from one side to another as his leg stays in one place. The foot rotates without any resistance.

A medic now sees the same expression on my face that I saw on the fire chief's. I know that his foot and shin should not move like that but my mind is trying to imagine what is going on under the grey sweats that the guy is wearing.

"The shin is fractured. Looks pretty fresh, maybe a day or two old. This guy doesn't even know that he has shattered his shin."

I look at the medic and then my eyes flow over to the guy lying there. He is about twenty-five years old, Caucasian male; I have dealt with him before. I recall memories of him and me having a little fight outside of a convenience store. He was arrested by someone in store security and when I showed up he was scrapping with the security guy. Not much of a fighter and he got his ass kicked.

Now he is lying here all fucked up on glue fumes. He is staring up at the ceiling like he has X-ray vision and can see the clear blue sky outside. He has no idea we are even here. He hears nothing, feels nothing, and sees nothing.

A medic comes to assist and he starts to cut off the sweats to see what is actually going on. As his scissors move up from the ankle to the fracture area his foot swings from side to side without any resistance.

Once the sweats are cut high enough up that we all can see what is going on under the concealing cloth, we all take another moment to look at the sight. It is a mural of blue, purple, and green. There is severe swelling in the area and I can see the sharp bone beneath trying to poke its way through the thick flesh and skin.

I look again at the guy lying on the couch and he doesn't move. He doesn't feel his injury at all.

The medics go to work and dump chemicals into his system to try to bring him back to reality. An IV is started and fluids move up his arm into his bloodstream.

I think that this is such a waste of time. I imagine a mother in labor, an elderly person lying on the ground with a fractured hip from taking a recent fall, or a child hurt from playing outside. I imagine them waiting for medical attention because this useless piece of skin here is soaking up resources.

I look about and see more medics arriving on scene to try to revive the residents of this house. All of whom put themselves willingly into this state of oblivion.

"What a fucking waste, we should just pull the pin and let these fucks rot." I look at my partner, who nods his head in agreement.

But, as I look into the eyes of an attending medic who overheard my statement, I can see that she is appalled. I can see that all she wants to do is what she has been trained for. She wants to save lives.

In her world there are no good people, no bad people, just sick and injured people. She has been given a gift to help and cure people when they are at their worst. And now she looks at a cop who wants to leave these people to rot. She turns her head away and moves over to another drug-induced coma victim.

I shrug my shoulders and wonder what it would be like to actually care about these people. I shudder at the thought. I do not want to care, if I do I will bring this shit home. Caring causes you to think about it after you're done. It makes you wonder how you can help, change what cannot be changed. It will drive you bonkers.

I look around me to see a variable dance of medics, firemen, and cops. More and more personnel show up on scene and more jobs are getting done.

I walk over to the medic that seems to be getting all of the information and logging everyone's status.

"So, anyone going to code here?" I know their language, it only takes being at one fatal accident to understand what "coding" is. The word is yelled out as the patient slips from their reality in the shadows that wait for them. A frenzy of activity always follows those words as professionals try to hold onto the slipping patient. He will tell me if he thinks anyone is even close to dying at this scene, he knows I need this information for my sergeant to allow him to organize units for continuity.

"Nahh, these guys and gals here are really fucked but no one is going to die. We are going to transport three of them to the hospital for assessments and detoxify, though."

"Okay, copy that; thanks."

I make my way back to the guy lying on the couch to see him getting loaded into a gurney. His leg has an air cast on it and his arm is now prepped with an IV tube. One medic places the IV bag by the guy's head and then he is hoisted up.

I just finish radioing my sergeant when my hand grabs the side of the gurney to help the medics take this guy out of the house. I look down at him and the scene is more fitting for a psychiatric hospital than a medical emergency scene.

The bright orange body straps wrapped around his arms, chest, and legs looking like tentacles from some strange deep ocean beast.

His eyes still haven't moved and I am startled to see that he has just blinked. That was the first sign of life I have seen from him besides his slow rhythmic breathing. I look into his eyes only to see that the void still lingered there. How much of his brain matter is gone after this little episode in his life?

He gets loaded into the ambulance like a slab of industrial beef. I take out my notebook and start to jot down the medic's regimental numbers, the ambulance numbers, and the numbers listed on the big pump trucks from the Fire Department. I ask over the radio for anyone with victim information to send it to my car.

I already know that the next two hours of my shift will be taken up by this call. The paperwork is already being formulated in my mind and the forms that I have to fill out in triplicate are mentally stacking up. I curse this fucking house and its occupants. Besides taking up valuable time from the fire guys, it has filled hospital beds that are already packed to capacity. Now it will take me off the street to do the paperwork on it. What a waste of resources.

I saw the couch guy again about a month after that call. He was holed up behind a dumpster sniffing gasoline from a dirty rag. I just moved him on from that area, hoping that he will find a place that people will not see him and call us to deal with his stupidity.

It is now three months after responding to the sniffer house, and I am driving through ice-covered streets. It is winter now and the wind billows through the empty alleys. Snow swirls and dances across the hard ground until it finds a place to rest.

As I drive by a stack of garbage cans that are piled up against an old half-rotten fence, I see a pair of worn boots sticking out from the corner. I stop and as I get out of my cruiser and put on my winter jacket I can see that the snow has found small a crevasse around the boots to rest after its long dance down the street. I know that these boots have been here for a long time and have not moved.

"Looks like another corp-si-cal," I say to myself. During these cold times homeless people that are way too fucked up to get into one of our many homeless shelters will freeze. I guess on average two or three will be found during our winter months.

As I round the trash cans I find the couch guy lying there. His arms are curled tight around his body, as if tied there again by the straps on the medical gurney. His hands are blue and they too are pulled in tight to his body. His fingers are locked out like his last attempts were to grasp at the cold coming in on him.

In his right hand I see a plastic bag filled with frozen glue and across his face I see strips of glue stuck and strung out in thin lines like a spider has spun a web across his mouth and nose.

I radio dispatch that I have a body on the corner of 18th Avenue and 64th Street in the alley. I let her know that it looks like this guy has gone down from the cold. I also let her know that I am going to be setting up a barricade around this guy to hold the scene until the coroner comes.

She acknowledges my transmission and so does my sergeant. He asks if I need additional units and I decline. This guy isn't going anywhere and it is so cold out no one is on the streets.

I pull my jacket up to fight off the cold that wants to make it down my back. Pulling the zipper up high to prevent the cold from seeping in any more, I take one last look at the frozen guy. I find it funny how even in death his eyes look the same. They stare off to the sky seeing something that we cannot see.

"It is about fucking time you died. What a piece of work you are. A total fucking waste of skin," I mumble under my breath. I hope that he can hear my words as he goes to some unknown place.

After stringing up the police tape I sit in the car rubbing my hands together for warmth. As I hold them over a roaring heat vent in the car I look back at the dead guy. He is just lying there in his contorted form. I pull out my notebook and start to write my notes. I will have to wait for the coroner to show up and tell me that this guy died from the cold. Then I will have to wait for the body removal guys to show up to haul this sorry fuck away.

Then after all of that, I will have to go and do the paperwork on this call.

I curse this fuck for wasting my time. Even in his last moments he has the ability to throw away society's valuable resources and suck the life out of an already taxed system.

WHEN I DREAM

WHEN I DREAM

"When I dream, I dream of killing."

When I hear these words I have to catch myself. I almost fall off my chair. I sit tall and at attention, but what I really want to do is look around at all the other recruits in class and ask them if I have heard this instructor right. Did he just say that he dreams of killing? Is he some sort of sociopath?

"I have dreams that I am in combat. That someone is trying to kill me or kill those who I am supposed to protect. I dream of killing them. You too will one day dream of killing, if you are good enough cops.

"There is not a day that goes by without me thinking of how I would move to close the distance. Where I would move to have optimum cover from fire and how I could kill someone. That is thinking tactically. That is thinking smart."

I am thinking right now that he is insane. How could someone go through his day-to-day life thinking about killing, about fighting all the time? Wouldn't that "on edge" attitude drive you nuts?

"The only time I feel safe is when I am at home with my wife and kids. Locked up behind my metal door and knowing I have a gun or weapon to protect the people I love the most."

It has been two years now and a lot of learning since I have heard those words from my instructor. I have seen him lots after classes but I still say very little to him. He is my mentor now, a decorated cop that did his time in the Tactical Unit and on the street. He is a switched on, determined, and driven cop. He trains hard, he thinks straight, and he stands for what is right.

When I am around him I just listen, I am still a student and always will be to him. I want information and I listen to every word he says as if I am looking for the meaning of life.

His name is Allen and he is respected throughout the department. He has walked the streets for over nineteen years now and has never had any of that respect lost or even wavered.

Now, when I am walking up to a house to deal with a domestic call I scan the area. I look into windows for shadows in the darkness. My eyes follow dark areas to see if anyone is hiding to ambush me, I trace the front steps to see if anything is out of the ordinary.

I process information, the steps are concrete, good cover from gun fire, a place I will move to if shooting starts at the front door.

There are some large trees in the front, good for concealment but poor for ballistic protection. Better than hanging my ass out in the middle of the lawn. No dogshit on the lawn, no "beware of dog" signs to warn me in advance of possibly having an animal used against me as a weapon.

My ears pick up yelling and I listen to hear what the conversation is about. Just two people yelling, no threats of death and no pleas for help.

I look over to my partner and I can see he is thinking the same as we follow along the dark part of the yard, away from the streetlights to close in on the house. We take every domestic call like this, never do we think that we are going to another routine call. That mind set will kill you.

My partner walks up to the door and stays to the side. I take a position further back on the lawn where I can see the windows, the side gate, and the side door of the house. I give a quick nod and my partner knocks on the door.

"Who the fuck is it!?!" A male voice, angry and full of alcohol-driven anger, yells out.

"City Police!" is my partner's only response.

I can hear the shuffling of a kitchen chair on tile and the movement of feet. I can see shadows move from the kitchen to the living room, back into the kitchen. I tell my partner that I have movement in the living room.

The front light turns on and a male comes to the door. He looks at my partner.

"What the fuck do you want?"

"We got a call that people are fighting here."

"Well, we are all right, so you can hit the road, man." The male goes to close the door, but in a flash my partner gives the bottom of the door a solid kick and the door flies open in a sudden rush, striking the male in the head with the corner. I rush up to the door because I know that we are going in.

My partner moves in and I am just a few paces behind him as he breaks through the doorway. Just as the guy shakes the strike out of his head he see two cops in his house now. He only saw one before as I was tucked away in the shadows. I can tell that he is wondering where I came from, and if there are more of the men in blue waiting outside.

"What the fuck did you do that for? I got fucking hit in the head with the door, man."

"You know better than that, trying to slam the door on the police. What the fuck, man, I know that you know better than that. Doesn't matter if you're angry or been drinking too much, there is no excuse for that shit." I deliver the words to him on a silver platter. A mind fuck that gives him the out to excuse his actions, the little brain tease because he knows that he did wrong. I also want to remind him that there are rules to this game and if he doesn't want to follow them he will get hurt.

"Yeah, fuck man, sorry for trying to slam the door. I am just a little bit pissed, ya know. A few too many beers."

I smile inside, I gave him the bait and he took it. So, now that he is listening to me, my partner moves off to the kitchen and talks to the woman there. He stays within my visual to watch me and knowing that I will be watching him out of the corner of my eye.

"So, what is going on tonight?" I look at him like all I need to know is what is happening and I will fuck off right away.

He pauses, not a good sign, he is thinking of a lie to tell me.

"Not much, just family shit, ya know." He turns his head so that his voice can be projected into the kitchen where his girlfriend is. He wants her to hear his story so that their stories match.

"So, what family shit may that be? I have just walked into your house here and I have no idea what is going on. I need to know a little bit more than 'family shit' so that I can leave knowing everyone is going to be all right." I give him another out. I want him to think that if he tells me what I want to hear that I will just leave.

He pauses again, formulating more lies. He wipes his hands through his hair. Not good, he is getting nervous. His palms are sweating and he wants to dry them off. He is thinking of what he needs to do and he is getting prepped for a fight if he has to. You cannot fight with sweaty hands. His subconscious knows that.

"Ah, fuck, we are just fighting over money. Bills and shit. We are both okay, no one is going to get hurt tonight. It is just a stupid fight."

"Good enough for me. Do you have some ID for me so that I can know who I have talked to tonight?"

"Right over here." He motions over to the living room. We walk in and I break my partner's line of sight, I can hear him move slightly so that I can still be within his peripheral.

As the male moves over to the couch that sits like a brown leather brick in front of the bay window, he picks up his black leather jacket. The jacket is well worn, the sleeves are creased with grey lines, and the leather is soft and limp. I see nothing that would indicate a weapon hidden in the pockets. No heavy sagging from the weight of a gun, no stiff lines in the pockets from a knife. But I am still focused in on him. I know that he is trying to hide something. He is nervous. He runs his hands through his hair again as he tosses his jacket onto a matching brown leather recliner. He is holding his driver's license in his right hand when I pick up on something.

I got him! I now know his hiding spot. The recliner. He walked from the couch, away from me, and then tossed his jacket onto the recliner. People are lazy by nature. They do not want to use extra energy unless they are trying to hide something. He just gave up the game without even knowing that his actions told me a whole story.

I look at the license and then write his name down. I act as if nothing has changed.

"Let's go into the kitchen and see what my partner is doing. We should be out of here in a flash." I motion to the kitchen with my left hand holding his ID. I keep my dominant hand free in case he decides to fight. I can still see he is nervous but he is relaxing. To him the light is at the end of the tunnel. The cops are telling him that they are going to be leaving soon.

As I walk into the kitchen I see the woman sitting at the kitchen table. My partner has put her as far away as possible from the counter and has the table between him and her. Good tactics. Kitchen counter equals lots of knives and other weapons. The table gives a barrier between him and the female in case she decides to go stupid on us.

"Why don't you just have a seat by your girlfriend as we tie this up?"

The male sits by his girlfriend and I can see that they both look at each other with fear and panic in their eyes. His hands touches her thigh and he gives her a light grab. The type of grab that says "everything is going to be okay."

I hand off the driver's license to my partner as he changes his radio to a different channel to put both of these names through our computer. In a moment I will have their criminal history and I am hoping that I can build my grounds to look in the cushions of the recliner.

Without my grounds I will lose what I will find in the recliner. I cannot use it in court unless I build some sort of legal ground to look in that area. The courts do not believe in good police skills or police intuition. They want grounds, otherwise we are invading his rights and all will be lost in a court system that really doesn't work anyway.

My partner turns up his radio as he finishes giving the person on the other side of the channel the information needed to be put into the computer. He wants me to hear the same information that will be aired on the radio soon. It will be in our codes, a language we know very well and most other people do not. A string of numbers that will tell us what they have done in the past.

As the words come over the radio my partner and I know that both of these people have had police come into their house dozens of times for domestic problems. They both have violence, drug, and theft criminal histories. Not enough to build my grounds for looking into the recliner.

Then the gods smile. The male has an outstanding warrant for his arrest for a cheesy bylaw fine. Parking in a handicapped zone without a proper permit. I smile and look at my partner. He knows that this warrant is an easy solve for the domestic call. Bring him to jail for the night, she sleeps off the booze she has dumped into her system.

"1099," I tell my partner. It is our little code for us to keep our heads up. Something that we tell each other when things are going to get interesting, a code that tells him that I am up to something.

"Okay, you have a warrant out for your arrest. Why don't you just come with us so that we can take care of it? I am sure you knew of the warrant so might as well just get it over with tonight, so that you don't have to worry about it all the time when the cops are behind you." I give him another out. I make up the excuse why he should just take care of this warrant. I make it sound like it is nothing and of course, he wants us out. If he has to go with us to get us out of his house, away from what he is hiding, that is good with him.

"Let's take care of it. I should have just paid the fine a long time ago."

We walk to the front door. I can see that he is trying to act calm. But he is way too calm. He is now laughing to himself. He tells me how he knew that he was going to be caught one day on this warrant.

As he starts to put his shoes on, I motion to my partner to watch this guy.

"Oh, it is fucking cold out; let me grab your jacket for ya."

"No worries. I ...." He moves towards me and my partner cuts him off. He tells the guy to put his shoes on, that it is really cold out and that he is going to need his jacket.

I close in on the recliner. I hold his ID in my left hand, and as I pick up the jacket I look around me.

"I am just going to put your ID in your jacket pocket." I look at him to make sure he is looking at where I put his ID. I am acting like I am going to be a really nice guy and put his ID in his jacket and bring it to him. Then, with the best theatrical "Oops," I drop his identification onto the recliner. It falls where I wanted it to, right into the side of the cushion.

"Ah, fuck. I dropped it," I say as I reach for it. I pull back the cushion to get it out and I see what the mystery prize is. A bundle of cash, a bag of white powder, and another bag of chipped-up crack cocaine. Bingo! I now see what had been so important to hide.

I am also legally covered, this is now what is called "plain view doctrine," and it allows me to charge both of these losers, as it is in plain view. The way it became in plain view was of course a matter of Murphy's Law ,but nonetheless it falls into a legal category.

My partner instantly tells the guy he is under arrest and puts his hands on him to let him know that he is not going anywhere or doing anything.

His girlfriend just looks like she has seen a ghost. She just stands there looking at us, and she seems to be contemplating her sudden change of fate. Her mind is just trying to figure out how all this is happening.

Or is she? My skin tightens on my neck, making the hair on the back of it feel like it is standing up. My internal instincts are telling me that something is going to go bad. My subconscious is reading body language from her that my conscious brain is not telling me. I can feel the adrenaline starting to dump into me, and I still do not see anything that I would feel is a threat to me.

I move in, I want to close the distance on her, put my hands on her, and let her know that there is nothing that she can do. I want to be close so that I can control her actions if I need to.

I feel like I am floating across the room in slow motion, my world distorted by my adrenaline fix. My eyes zoom in on an item on the table that was covered before by a newspaper. I see the black handle of a kitchen knife. Now I see what my subconscious was picking up on. Her eyes were constantly glancing at it but I was not able to see the knife handle from my angle.

Her knees start to bend as her body dips to deliver energy to allow the burst of speed to move to the knife. Her motion is filled with intent, she has made up her mind now. She wants to fight, all her body language is telling me that. Her eyes are wide, her lips are drawn back over her teeth to allow better air flow, making her look like an angry dog.

Her slender arm juts out and grabs the knife, she needs an equalizer for this fight. One on one with me would have been a bad decision; the knife puts the odds in her favor.

Without thinking I yell out "Knife" at the top of my lungs but it comes out like a small screech, as my mouth is dry from the heavy adrenaline surge I am getting. My world slows down even more. I feel like I am in a dream world that is filled with water. I feel like no matter how hard I push myself in this dream I cannot move fast enough. I can hear my heart pounding in my ears, I can feel my face become hot, and right at this moment I have a million thoughts running through my mind.

I need to make my decision: stop and get some distance and a barrier between us, or go into her threat zone with the knife.

"Thirty feet is a threat zone with a knife. If you have your gun holstered and someone attacks you within thirty feet with the full intention of killing you, studies show that you will be able to get off maybe one shot before they close that distance. And a knife never jams, it never needs to be reloaded, and it requires very little skill to kill." The words of my instructors echo in my mind. I know that I am too close to disengage. I am in no position to think of anything besides fighting.

Just as her hand grasps the handle of the knife I am only two feet away from her. She swings at me in a wild roundhouse punch. The knife is in her hand with the blade cutting a deadly path through the air towards my face. My left arm comes up to block the punch, just as my training has programmed me. Just like the years of martial arts under my belt has programmed me to do. I turn my arm to allow the outside of my forearm to be exposed. No vital veins to be cut there. I know that it is the best part of me to sacrifice to the knife.

She wants to kill. She wants to kill me so that she can kill my partner. Her act is not one of impulse, it is a premeditated act. One does not pull a knife off of a table and push the shard, pointed end of into the face of a police officer without thinking about doing it.

I want to kill. I want to kill her. My wanting to kill her is an act of impulse, there is nothing premeditated about it. I want her to stop the action she is taking against me. I am furious that she is trying to hurt me. That she wants to stop me from walking on this earth.

Her arm collides into my forearm, the blade of the knife passing a mere inch from my exposed forearm. The blade comes to a thundering halt as her arm is stopped. I can see the tip of the knife right in front of my left eye. I can see the serrations on the knife, I can even see the maker's brand on it.

Before she could pull back to try her strike again I use the few inches between us to chamber for my blow. My bent legs start to expand. The muscles in my calves tighten as my quadriceps and hamstrings follow suit. I can feel energy building from my feet up to my elbow that is racing to her chest.

My hips start to turn as they ready themselves to lock out in the final few movements as my elbow enters her body. I target the inside of her chest. I want my energy to stop when my elbow is inside of her chest cavity. I want the elbow to lock into place and I want her body to have to give way to allow for the sudden intrusion.

Her arm starts to move back, her hand getting dragged far behind her as she winds up for another stab at me. I see her face contort and shift as she builds up power to strike me again.

Just then I have hit my mark. My right elbow contacts her sternum. It flows into the hard mass of bone that sits cradled by cartilage. I can feel the popping as ribs dislocate from the sternum. I see her face change from anger to pain. Her mind knows that damage is being done.

I still move further into my target. My body weight shifting as my hips finish the twist to finalize the blow. Much like a golfer's swing, I have just contacted the ball. I follow through to get the maximum effect from my blow.

I can feel hot damp air rush onto my face as I force all the air out of her lungs. The force of my blow is now snapping ribs and crushing her lungs. The energy is pushing her internal organs against the moving sternum, her heart expels all the blood that was just madly rushing through it. Her body starts to fall away from me as it moves away from my blow. Her arms now lash forward in recoil from the sudden delivery of energy.

I don't stop though. She is not down, her threat to me is still apparent as she has not dropped the knife. I deliver my left elbow next.

I cut a wide high arc through the air. I follow the path she just took towards me. I send my elbow into her face, striking her cheek and sending it skipping further down into her collarbone. I am much taller than her so when I hit I slam my body weight down. My arc is completed when my elbow passes through her body. Her mass of skin, bone, and flesh make way for my strike.

I hear the knife hit the floor, it sounds like a small metal bell being struck. I hear nothing else. I see her body fall back in slow motion. Her center mass leads the ways as her arms and hands follow in a slow wave. I can see blood starting to pool from her cheek where I hit her. I can see that her eyes are rolling back as her hair flows around her head.

I have never hit anyone as hard as I have hit her. I know that I could have hit harder. I know that I had much more resources to call on, more energy to tap into. I know that I still held back because she is a woman and I have always been told to never hit a woman. Never before I started with "the Service," that is.

I have been programmed that someone who wants to kill or hurt you or anyone else is just a target. They are not woman, child, elderly, or man. They are a threat. I have to dehumanize my opponent, then I can kill them if I have to.

From all the books I have read I know that the human race doesn't want to kill each other. It has to be programmed to do so. If we had the kill switch inside of us to turn off and on at will that would not be very good for us to evolve, to continue our existence.

All animals are like that. Two bull elk will fight but only with their antlers, they will not kill each other. But, have them attacked by a wolf and they will gore them without hesitation.

As she falls I wonder if I have killed her. I wonder if my blows have caused so much damage that she may die tonight.

I do not care; in fact I am happy when I see her limp body hit the cold linoleum floor. I am happy to be alive, to have survived this attack.

I grab her arm and slide her onto her belly. Her body is a limp doll. Her eyes are open, locked in their gaze as the brain did not have enough time to close them before shutting off. I slide her arms behind her back and lock the stainless-steel handcuffs around her wrists.

As soon as she is secured I reach over to the knife on the floor and secure it into my duty belt. I need it for evidence.

I feel my partner's hand land on my shoulder I can see his mouth move but I cannot hear his voice. I am experiencing "auditory exclusion." My mind has shut down my hearing, it was not valuable to me when I was fighting for my life. I soon learn how to overcome this effect of heavy adrenaline dumps.

His voice starts to float to me like he is coming closer to me in a fog-filled field. I am calming down, I can feel my body starting to come back to speed. My senses return to normal. I know I am going to crash, my high is going away.

I can feel my legs start to shake and my hands tremble like I have been struck by an internal earthquake. I can feel my partner's hands move me to a chair, and force me to sit.

"Are you all good, buddy? I can't see any cuts anywhere, did you get cut?" His voice now floats to me in waves as I look at my arms and see no blood flowing from me. I run my hand over my left side of my face to feel for a cut that I was sure was there. Nothing. Not a scratch.

"Fucking crazy bitch," I say, my heart still crashing in my chest. I look at my hands and they are shaking like mad. I try to close my hands into fists to hide the shakes that I have. I feel like I am a child that has been chased by a dog. I feel like a weak boy right now. I do not want to shake.

"Don't worry about the shakes, John. We all get them. Just don't fight it, they will be gone in a second." His words pull the shame of my shaking out of me. I know that he doesn't see my quivering as weakness. He knows what I am going through. He has been there too. He pats my shoulder twice and smiles at me.

"Good fucking job, soldier. Good job."

I can hear the wail of sirens and the low growl of police cruisers racing to the scene to help in any way they can. I see the red lights of the ambulance flood the living room as they arrive.

I am looked at right away by the attending paramedics; they check my body to make sure that I was not cut. I still move about in a haze. My mind working out information in this reality, a reality that is not filled with such immediate danger. I feel like this world is slow because no one is trying to kill me.

I sit in the passenger seat of the cruiser that we arrived in and look at my hands. They have stopped shaking. I pull out my notebook and start to write out what happened. I know that what I write now will not be as clear as it will be tomorrow. One always remembers these fearful times better after the mind has a few days to sort things out.

My leg hanging out the cruiser door, I see my sergeant walk over to me. He looks at me like a worried father would. "You all right, Smith? I heard that it got pretty hairy in there."

"I am good, I am not hurt." I seal my statement with a smile.

"Good to hear, and just a small FYI for you, the chick is not going code on us. She is pretty fucked up but we are not going to have to call out Homicide."

I feel better knowing that. Not because of the investigation that will not occur but because she is still living. By every right she should have died but it was just not her time. She tried to take my life and I should have taken hers. We are both lucky tonight.

When I get home I am wide awake. I pace around the house. I cannot sleep. I ponder a cold beer or a stiff drink but I know that it is a trap that I do not want to fall into. Alcohol is not a way to decompress, a way to deal with stress. I have worked all night and as the sun comes up I have no desire to sleep. I am wired.

My wife walks downstairs and greets me with a loving smile. As soon as she sees my eyes she knows that something has happened. Something bad happened last night at work. I feel her arms wrap around me, her strength pulling my splintered soul back together.

We stand there for an eternity and hold each other. Her perfume smells like heaven, her warmth fills me, and the sensation of her face against mine reminds me of why each day I live is so valuable. I realize that every day that I have to walk here is a gift. I will never forget how precious this time is for me.

"So, tell me what happened." Her voice calms my inner beast.

"Well, babe, it was a really busy night..." I start to tell her what happened and I can feel my inner storm release. I can feel the warmth of my calm flow back into me. I am walking on my beach again with the sun cresting the horizon and the cool ocean breeze pressing on my face. I am walking with my inner peace.

As I talk my hands start to shake.

Her eyes look at me with sorrow and pity.

"Oh, never mind that, babe, they will stop shaking soon. It is just a side effect from the fighting."

I don't fight the shakes. I let them pass as I tell her what happened.

Years have passed since that fight. I lie in bed wide awake from a dream that raised me from my sleep. I walked through that very house, following the very same path of events that occurred. I can smell the cooking that was on the stove, the odor of open beer and cigarettes filling my senses.

But this time, like all other times I dreamt of what happened, I kill her. I have lived the experience dozens of times. I have stabbed her with my duty knife, I have shot her with my sidearm, and I have struck her harder and in more vital areas. In each dream I am victorious, I have killed her for wanting to kill me.

I dream of killing.

KAZI

His name is Kazi and he is a man to be feared in the criminal world. In some ways I look at his criminal history with respect. You see, Kazi is a crack head. Nothing too special there but Kazi also slams steroids and anything else into his body to make him a top-of-the-food-chain predator.

Kazi's crack cocaine habit is a large one by most standards. He needs about $150 to $200 a day to keep himself baselined. Without that amount of crack to smoke he starts to get edgy and jittery. He moves into discomfort and withdrawals without his fix, and he is not a nice man to begin with.

So, what does Kazi do to supply his habit? He is not patient enough to sell to skim the profits to smoke the junk so he preys on the dealers themselves. He steals, robs, and maims anyone who might have drugs for him to steal. Kazi has become a major pain in the ass for the drug dealers here, to the point that they have filed police reports to get us after him.

Getting jacked is just a price of doing business for your street-level dealers, but last night Kazi busted into a high-end west-side house. Once inside he tied up the owner and his family and used some pretty interesting means to get the drugs that were hidden in the house. Interesting means would include a bullet in the knee.

On Kazi's side he did not threaten or hurt the wife or the kids, but in all reality they are not players in the game and Kazi should have done his business without them.

Kazi left the house with about 500 grams of crack cocaine and over forty grand in cash. The victim, if you want to call him that, is now crying to the police so we have to take this guy down. I really hate doing business for the bad guys, considering that this is the drug dealer's shit storm. But, the line was crossed and the family was targeted so Kazi needs to be locked up.

Some simple math would conclude that Kazi will not be active now for about half a year but when he is in the money and drugs he will party harder and use up his stash at an alarming rate. I figure Kazi will be at it again in about two or three months with the stash he got from the home invasion.

"Here we go, guys," my sergeant says, sliding a picture of Kazi and some related information on him across the table. "Right up your alley. This is one nasty mother fucker and if he is holed up in a hotel or house I have strict orders that TAC will do the entry."

I nod my head as I grab that folder on the desk.

"Are we clear, Smith? His ass is for TAC unless you have no other choice." My sergeant looks at me hard, making sure I make eye contact with him. He wants the point driven home.

He knows that I am no cowboy, that I will not put myself or anyone else in jeopardy to get a piece of Kazi. But, my sergeant also knows that I am eager to get into the shit, that I will not avoid conflict with this fellow.

"Yes sir, we are clear on that." My eye contact with my sergeant is long to let him know that I am not fucking around. I want a piece of Kazi because he is a mean mother. I want to go toe to toe with him because he is a respectable opponent. I want to get into "the shit" with him so that I can test my abilities, and I want to tear him apart. I also know that if the TAC guys get him he will be torn apart. Fucked up from his brief interaction from the world of shit the TAC guys will set upon him. Either way we win, so I really don't give a shit.

Once my partner and I get into the car we thumb through the photos and the information. We start to set a plan into action as to where we are going to look for this fellow.

My mind races to where he might be crashing. My partner says that he is probably hiding at a friend's house but I quickly disagree.

"Word is out the Kazi has hit a big fish for his dope. The crackers on the street all know that if they are found with Kazi they are fucked. His friends will be his friends no longer."

As we drive and clear some calls that are on the computer to be handled I still swim in my thoughts, trying to put myself into Kazi's shoes. Where would I hide if I was him? Where would I want to bed down if the streets were too dangerous for me to play on?

Kazi has the cash to sit in a hotel for quite some time and enough drugs to keep him warm for a while. But he still needs food and booze. He will be on a party rush right now as his world is all good. Not so good as to let him walk the streets for the next few weeks though.

"Hey, let's stop at the local dial-a-bottle and see if they have had any large orders lately. Maybe we can hit him through the booze and shit he will be ordering."

Our marked cruise rolls up to the store front that has "Kings Dial a Bottle" displayed in bright red neon lights. I know the owner fairly well as he gets robbed in this area a lot. I have taken my fair share of calls from him after he has been robbed. Owning a liquor store in the Hood can be prosperous but also a very risky venture. Some people's addiction to liquor can be as dangerous as a hard-core drug addict's call for his drugs. Theft and violence are just tools to get the booze so that they can reduce the pain of withdrawal.

"Hey officer, how can I help you? I have a great special on beer tonight!" The heavy East Indian accent topped off with the sarcasm he just directed at me makes me smile.

"No, no beer for me tonight. But I am looking for someone, maybe you can help me out."

"Oh yes, I would be very happy to help you out. Who are you looking for? Is he a bad man?" I can see the owner's interest peak as he now has the chance to help me instead of asking me for help. This may be the time that he can repay us for all of the times he had to call for help. To him, the ability to give anything to help me is a way that he can feel like he has repaid a debt. I never feel that anyone owes me anything, I am just doing my job.

"Well, this is a bad guy," I show him the photo and hand it over to him to allow him to look at it closely. "I want him because he has hurt someone's family and terrified their kids. He is a piece of shit that needs to go to jail."

The owner looks at it more closely. He is taking his time and I glance over at my partner, who is sitting in the car getting some of last night's paperwork done. I know my partner is just putting up with me as I try to find some leads on Kazi. I also know my partner thinks I am wasting my time, he feels that Kazi has headed for the next town. The heat too hot in the city for him to stay here.

I let the owner look at the picture as long as he wants. He moves the photo from near his face to a full arm's length away. He then lifts up his glasses and looks at the photo with his normally poor vision.

"Actually, I have seen this man. I dropped off an order for him last night. He was a nice guy, tipped well also." He turns his back to me to look through a pile of receipts that are sitting on the counter behind him.

I cannot believe my ears. I have totally lucked out, and I now have an actual location for the place Kazi may be at. Kazi broke a major rule, never do anything that will make people remember who you are. You tip average, you talk average, and you dress average. Kazi has made that fatal mistake that will cost him his freedom.

"Oh yes, here we are." A receipt is handed over to me and I jot down the address into my notebook as well as the owner's name and the time that I talked to him. I will need all of this to get a warrant to enter the address if we are going to get TAC in.

I thank the owner several times and tell him that he is a good man. As I leave the store I can see him brimming with pride and I am sure as soon as I leave he will be on the phone to his wife to let them know that he helped the police tonight.

I walk back to the cruiser trying to hold my excitement in.

"So, what did the owner tell you? Anything good?"

"Fucking jackpot, man!" I say with a smile across my face. I hold up my notebook and read out an address that I want my partner to confirm and run checks on. "The guy in there tells me that he dropped a whole shitload of booze just last night. He totally recognized Kazi from the picture."

"Hold up, Smith, I know you are anxious to kick some ass but we have to make sure this is a good lead before we call TAC out and get the shit rolling. We have to make sure that the guy in the store is not trying to be Mr. Good Samaritan and tell you a load of shit to make himself feel better."

He has a good point, I have a reputation to hold onto and I do not want to risk it on this guy's information. But, I still feel good about the information I have gotten. It feels right.

"You bet, let's go do some reconnaissance on the joint and see what we can stir up. But we should tell our sergeant what we know so that if the shit goes down and turns sideways he will have a grasp of what is going on."

I let my sergeant know what we have and he tells us that he will be sending another car crew to back us up. If we see Kazi in the residence he wants us to call in more cars for containment and hold it until TAC comes.

I flip the cell phone shut and lock it back into our car holder. I am getting pumped. The information sounds good and everything feels good. I know that something is going to go down tonight. My partner can feel that I am anxious, he can read my body language, as we have worked in the same car now for two years with each other.

"Jesus, Smith, you would think that fucking Christmas is coming."

"I tell you, this is good. I can feel it. We are going to get this fucker tonight."

I call in the turns to take as I follow our car on the computer screen. Our in-car GPS shows us where we are and due to the gift of modern technology our computer shows us the best route to take. As we get within a block of the house that the store owner told us about, I slide the car into a parking lot and slip it between two other parked cars. I try my best to hide the marked cruiser from view.

My partner pops the trunk and tosses my Code 100 bag. It is filled with binoculars, ground mat, raincoat, and other miscellaneous items to assist us with a reconnaissance of the residence. "Okay, let's take the alley and stay in the shadows."

"You all wired tight?" I ask my partner. I know that he has a bad habit of not using his ear mike and lets his speaker on the radio make noise when it shouldn't.

He reaches into his vest pocket and pulls out the wire for his earpiece. He screws the wire into his portable radio. He slides the earpiece into his left ear. "I fucking hate this thing."

Now we are all wired tight. No noise from equipment. No keys rattling and no change to jingle in pockets. I slip off my shiny name tag into my shirt pocket. I do not want any metal to glimmer.

I can still see my instructor walking down the line of a few cops that decided to take more time at the range to shoot. The same set of cops that work late at night on their hard skills. Fighting, combat skills, and weapons tactics are the thing we loved and wanted to learn more of. This instructor saw this in us and gave us all the information we could absorb. "That, my friend, will get you killed." He points to the shiny steel tabs on our duty belts. "Darken out all that fancy stainless steel you have on your kit. Tie up those keys, ear mike that radio, and for fuck's sake keep your mouth shut. If you are hunting, silence is your friend. If you are with someone who doesn't know how to keep their mouth shut, send them back to the car. You do not need them for the call. They will not keep you safe with the bullshit chatter."

I now look at my partner and I can see that he too feels like this is going to turn into something. I can see that he has his game face on. He is now in full hunting mode. We are set, total focus at the job at hand.

The only thing that we can hear is the crunch of loose gravel under our boots and the soft squeak of our leather belts. Combat noise, the silent noise that slips out while you move. Clothes rub, leather bends, and rocks and rubber on boots squeak. To anyone else this would seem minimal but to me I feel like I am walking around with a bell on. I know that this is as quiet as I can be at the speed we are moving at.

As we get within two houses of the residence our speed slows down drastically. Our combat noise is now reduced to a slight whisper of cloth and leather.

There is a fence that surrounds the house we want to peer into. I spot a small opening in the fence that is used to place garbage cans out into the alley for the city to pick up. It is dark there and the garbage cans are gone. It looks like a great place to hunker down to watch the residence. Just as we start to make our way into the small opening, I see a car coming down the alley, and from it I can hear the chatter of a police band radio. I look at my partner and he too knows what is happening. The backup is not as switched on as they need to be and are driving right past the residence to see if Kazi is here.

We duck into the garbage chute and hope that these guys do not stop here to talk to us. I pray that these guys have their heads so far up their ass that they miss us. I feel the frustration build up in me as they get closer. I can hear the car slow down as they get closer to our target.

In a low whisper my partner lets me know that he is also pissed off.

"Why the fuck don't they just shine a light in the house while they are here?"

As if they heard us the car slows even more and a ray of high-intensity light flares from the car's spotlight. The beam kills my eyes as they try to adjust to the sudden change of light. I am now even more pissed as my night vision is fucked and I know that I will not get it back for at least two minutes.

"Fucking assholes," is my whispered comment. "They are going to fuck everything right up!"

The light turns off and the car moves away. It is a miracle that they did not see us.

My partner keys his mike and in low steady tones tells the car crew that just drove by that they are not needed. He tells them to leave the area. I know that everyone that heard his radio chatter knows that something bad happened. You only get called off of a hot call if you have fucked up. I know there is going to be some harsh words sent about in the locker room with that car crew at the end of the shift.

My partner pulls on my shirt to tell me that we should book out. That our plan has been fucked and that we should just move out. I pull him back and tell him to keep still. I tell him that my eyes are fucked from the bright light and we have to wait here until the bright purple orbs leave my vision.

So we sit there. My partner keeping his eyes on the house as I let my vision come back. Just as the last remaining blob of purple leaves my eyes I catch something out of the corner of my eye.

I saw movement. Nothing small like an alley cat or a dog. It was slow and cautious but I saw it. I slide my hand onto my partner's shoulder to tell him to stay still. It is my warning that I have seen something and we have to stay still. He reads me and I can hear his breathing slow down.

I peer down the alley looking for what has caught my eye in the heavy darkness. I scan from side to side looking. Then I see it. A human silhouette breaks the shadows. I cannot see who it is but the person is trying very hard to hide from any eyes in the area. He walks crouched over and he is definitely on the prowl. His head moves from side to side as he scans for any warnings. I can see he is on the prowl, he is hunting too.

From his silhouette I can see that it is not another cop. I do not see the familiar outline of a radio or gun holster.

As he gets closer I can tell that my partner has quietly turned around in our small wooden box. I can feel his breath on the back of my neck. I know he is now looking at what I am looking at.

The image is walking right towards us and he passes through a brief ray of light that is cast by an illuminated kitchen window. I know who it is. Kazi.

He must have been out on foot and hid when he saw the cruiser coming down the alley. I am sure his curses were just as many as ours were when he saw the cruiser slow down and light up his place of hiding. He is stalking his way up here because he knows that we are hunting him now.

Kazi is taking as much time to cover the distance as we did when we made our way up to the house. My legs are cramping and my calves feel like they have gasoline burning in them. The position we are crouched in is not natural and it is wearing on me.

Kazi now slows down even more. His instincts are telling him to stop, go back. His internal warnings know that something is bad here, like a deer in the cross-hairs of a hunter's rifle. For some strange unexplained reason the deer always seem to know that they are being watched, even from hundreds of yards away. Mother Nature's sixth sense that society has cultivated out of most people.

But he still moves forward ignoring the screams from within to not go forward. He still moves in closer, his walk slowed so much that he seems to be standing most of the time listening.

My heart starts to pound with excitement. I can see him come closer and closer. I can see his face, his clothes, and his hands. I can even see that he has a gold ring sitting on the thumb of his right hand. He is getting even closer now. I can see his eyes wide open, looking for what his inner self is warning him about. He is close enough that I can see his ripped jeans, the worn patches on his boots, and the white worn areas on the leather jacket he wears.

My eyes target his jacket again. Like a methodical computer my eyes have picked up on something. I see a bulge in his jacket, a heavy object sitting against his body. Is that the gun Kazi shot the dealer with? Or is it a bottle of beer? I do not know but all my internal instincts tell me it is not good. My eyes widen to take in more light as I purposely try to keep my breathing from becoming accelerated. I feel my heart pick up pace and I fight it. I control my breathing, control my heart rate. I need to stay calm and focused. I am a mere second away from getting in the shit.

I am the closest to Kazi when he opens the gate to his back yard. Just as the gate swings open I can see a look of relaxation on his face. I am sure he felt like he ran the gauntlet and made it through unscathed again.

As his face relaxes I drive my legs to force myself up. I feel the blood pump into cramped muscles and burning calves. My hand slides over to my gun and I have my chunk in my hand even before I am fully erect. My legs are bent, chambered for more action. My stance is solid and my gun is out. We are only four feet apart and I can see the fear hit his mind.

His relaxed face is filled with fright. His eyes are wide open, his mouth is gaped in a contorted mouth wide open frown. I see his body shudder and curl from the sudden startle. I know that his body has just dumped a huge amount of adrenaline into him. It is fight-or-flight time.

A pronounced voice thunders through the alley cutting through the silence of the night. "Police! Don't move!." The sounds come in harmony as my partner and I yell it at the same time. I sense my partner moving to the left of me. I pick him up in my peripheral vision. He has cut off Kazi's escape route by taking a simple step to the left. With my body on the right and my partner on the left Kazi will have to go through one of us to get away.

I am jacked, full of the same body drug that my prey is filled with. I want to fight or chase. I want to use the chemical running through me.

I yell my second command since Kazi is looking right at me. "Keep your hands away from your body!"

I can see Kazi's mind swimming. He is stuck in a loop and is trying to figure out what to do.

Then, he knows what he wants to do. He is ready to fight. He wants to fight, not run. He knows that running will not help him. He thinks that there are more cops here, as it always has been. He is willing to put his best foot forward and have a go with these cops. Kazi will not go to jail without a fight. Even if he loses, he will fight.

He lunges forward towards me. His hands move out in slow motion towards my extended gun. He doesn't have far to reach as he tries to grab onto my gun. Both of his hands reach out as if grabbing for a life rope. As his hands come forward, my gun moves back into my body. It is a mad game of catch as his fingers trail inches behind my chunk.

As my chunk closes into my body my left hand releases and drives forward into the face of Kazi. My autopilot has kicked in and I am running on pure training.

I remember sitting on the blue foam matt in the Combative room listening to our close quarters combat instructor. "Some fucker wants to grab your gun, he means to take it away from you and kill you with it. FBI studies of convicted criminals who attempted to take away an officer's gun all stated that their full intent was to kill the cop with it. If someone reaches for your chunk it is now a deadly force encounter. No fucking rules any more. Do what you have to do to stop the threat."

No rules, no worries about where I hit Kazi, how I hit him, or if I kill him. It is fight time and thanks to him I do not have to worry about my use of force. I can articulate all the damage I do by starting my story with the fact that Kazi tried to grab my gun from my hands.

"Gun grab!" Trained response to when someone tries to grab my gun. I have done this hundreds of times in training and have mentally run through this type of scenario. My yell lets my partner know too that the rulebook has been thrown out the window. It is game time.

I am filled with total exhilaration as I know that this is going to be a great fight. I am filled with fear as I know that he has something under his jacket. I do not know what it is for sure, but I do know that it is bad. I have to keep his mind away from whatever it is.

My left hand finds its mark. I aim for the cheekbones with my fingers splayed apart. I feel my fingers hit the hard bones of Kazi's cheek and then I can see them slide up his face into his eyes. Three of my fingers find the goal I wanted. Two go into his right eyes and one more finger forces its way into his left eye. I feel his body jerk as my digits poke into the eye sockets. The sockets feel warm and wet. His head moves back to try to rid his eyes of the foreign item. But his forward lunge keeps on coming so he is unable to move out of the strike.

I grab hard, I do not want to lose this strike. I know that with my fingers in his eyes he will not think about grabbing onto the item concealed in his jacket. My thumb locks onto his chin and my fingers drive deeper into small openings that now hold his eyes and my fingers. I can feel the eyes slide up to make way for the grip I have on him. I wonder if his eyes will slide out. If they will simply pop out of their natural place to allow my fingers the room that they are demanding. I do not release my grip, if the eyes come out, they come out, that is for him to deal with later. A simple mathematical equation of combat. I win, he loses.

Both of his hands come up and grab my left hand. They lock around my wrist and forearm, trying to release my grip that is sending his brain into a whirlwind of pain. I grip harder and I hear a shriek of pain come from his mouth. My right hand slides my gun back into the holster.

A movement done thousands of times before at the range.

A movement done a thousand times before in combat training scenarios and still done a thousand times more in my dreams. The gun locks into place in the three-stage locking holster. I do not do the strap up as I have no time. I have firmly set the gun in place. Two of the mechanical locks in the holster take effect, it will not come out of its designated spot as long as I keep the pressure on the gun.

I pull his head to the left with the lock I have in place. I feel his body flex and bend as my partner delivers blows to his body. I can feel Kazi's mass move under the pressure of my partner's strikes. I know that this is not going to take long. Kazi has lost, he lost when he decided to try to grab my gun.

I crash his head into the fence post and my grip still tightens on his face and eye sockets. I deliver an open-hand blow to Kazi's neck. My big fleshy palm hits the side of his neck and the kinetic energy sends all the blood in his carotid artery rushing into his brain. The pressure from this surge shuts down his brain. His television is off as his body slumps downward.

I cannot hold onto him and my left hand slides free of its grip. His body falls down to the ground and as he tumbles backwards over his legs his head snaps off the ground with a hollow coconut sound. My partner secures an arm as I grab the other. We roll him over onto his belly as Kazi starts to come around. He is getting conscious just as we put the handcuffs on.

He turns his head up towards us and fires off a wad of blood-filled spit. His eyes are turning red with the blood as internal hemorrhaging takes place.

"Fuck you, pig." The biohazard spit lands on my pants.

"No, fuck you."

Our blows land into his kidneys and he curls up into a fetal position with his hands behind his back. His lungs gasp for air as the strikes to his abdomen pushed out all the air in his lungs. He gasps and wheezes, his lungs demand air but his contracted body cannot relax enough to feed the desire.

I am on the radio now letting our dispatcher know what has happened.

"1445 we have one in custody. Need EMS for the accused. We are fine."

I can hear the sirens closing in. I check myself for injuries and my partner does the same. Then with flashlights out we check each other out.

I pat my partner on the back as we stand there victorious. I look down at Kazi and he is still lying there twisted up. His chest is heaving as his lungs are filling back with air. I reach into my pocket and pull out a spit sock. The fine mesh slides over his head and the elastic bottom holds the bag into place. He can breath through it, he can see through it, but he cannot spit at us anymore. The sock also tells all that he is a "spitter."

As my partner pulls out some disinfectant wipes for us to clean our hand off with, I lift up Kazi's jacket to access what he had hidden. The item that I zoned in on when I first saw him.

As the heavy leather jacket is lifted up I see what I had expected to see. The gun metal black of the 9 mm Berretta gives a low luster under the glow of the yard lights.

"Oh, fucking nice" are the only words to run out of my partner's mouth.

I take out the gun and release the magazine. I work the action to release the slide and I eject one shiny 9 mm round out of the chamber. It was locked and ready to roll. If Kazi had reached for the gun there would have been a good fire fight. I slip the chambered round into my breast pocket and I hold the magazine up to the light to see how many rounds there are in it. A full magazine, I can tell from the brass showing through the round counter holes in the rear of the magazine.

"Fuck me, Kazi, fifteen in the mag. And one in the spout. You think that is enough ammunition?"

"I wanted enough to kill as many fucking pigs as I could."

My boot lands hard into his face. I hear the pop of his nose and hear his head ricochet off of the ground. He groans in pain.

I lean over and grab Kazi by the bag that is over his head. The bright red blood from his broken nose is seeping through the closely knit mesh. "Are we learning something yet, Kazi? You are not the top of the food chain, mother fucker. We are. You want to fuck with us, you are going to get your ass kicked all of the time. Next time you interact with the police remember the ass-kicking that you got tonight. Learn how to fucking behave." I push his head back into the ground; his broken nose hits the ground again.

EMS shows up on scene and Kazi is no longer an asshole. He is quiet and courteous. He is a beaten dog and he knows who the bigger dogs are. He knows that if he pisses us off again we will break more of his body.

I ride in the ambulance with Kazi. We are off to the local hospital to get Kazi's eyes and head checked for the damage we caused him.

Kazi's spit bag is off and I can see his eyes swelling shut. The cornea is blood red and blood oozes out every time he squints his eyes shut. A glint of white shows from his split nose, the bone protruding through the skin.

The medics are fast at work, adding ice and pressure bandages to his face. Kazi groans as one medic feels his ribcage. The medic looks up at me.

"You really fucked this guy up."

Kazi mumbles through a swelling face. "You bet, doc. I have been arrested many times before but I have never been fucked up." Kazi cannot see right now. He cannot see I am sitting quietly beside him.

"Yes, Kazi, but did we learn anything tonight?"

His head jerks back as if he is expecting another blow. "Yes sir, not to fuck with the police."

I look at the medic as I shrug my shoulders. The medic just shrugs back, "Excellent."

Ballistic tests show that the gun that I seized was the weapon used to shoot the other guy in the leg. In the house we found almost all of the money and about half of the crack cocaine. During an interview by detectives following up the arrest Kazi admitted to smoking about 60 grams of crack that day.

Kazi also admitted that he wanted to get my gun to kill me. He did not want to use his gun because after he shot the other guy he thought that his gun was not powerful enough to kill.

The lawyer that Kazi hired was good enough to know that going to court would be a bad thing to do.

"My client was on a heavy drug binge and lacked all moral capability to make proper decisions. My client is afflicted with a chemical dependency disease and is making valid attempts to keep himself clean and rehabilitate. I give to you, Your Honor, that my client pleads guilty to the charges before him. I also ask of you, Your Honor, that you take into account my client's three-month medical rehabilitation as he recovered from his injuries from the arrest. These three months were served in a secure medical institution. I would ask that Your Honor take this into account for the sentencing."

The judge looks at Kazi with a stern gaze but I have seen this judge hand down sentences before. A stern look and a finger wagging is all that Kazi is going to get.

I lean over to my partner and whisper, "I know this judge; he is going to do fuck all. I bet for time served and a conditional release."

The judge leans over to the accused and speaks in the best solemn tone he can. "Your actions before the court today are inexcusable. I accept your guilty plea before the courts. I also take into account what defense has stated about your drug affliction. I am going to give your penalty as time served with several conditions for your release."

I lean in once again to my partner. "You owe me coffee."

The judge rambles on about how he wants to see Kazi enter a drug rehabilitation program and get his life back on track. All bullshit.

Why? There is no accountability for the judicial system. I say, if a judge thinks that a guy is safe enough to enter society, that is all right. But if the guy reoffends not only should the offender make the news but so should the judge's name and decision to release him. Make him think harder if he wants to release a violent offender.

As we leave the courthouse my partner tells me he is so frustrated sometimes with the courts.

"Buddy, the courts are soft. There is nothing we can do about it. We do our job and bring the bad guys to jail. If the courts do not want to keep them there, oh well. Fuck all we can do about it. Besides, job security, man." We both laugh but we know that we want these guys in jail for a long time. To keep them away from the innocent people we are here to protect.

So, Kazi walks that day a free man with some conditions for his release that he gives a rat's ass about.

Kazi that night goes out and hits a drug dealer for his fix and cash. The word is out that "Crazy Kazi" is out and he is preying on all. All but the police.

The next time Kazi is arrested for breaching his conditions and is confronted with the police he puts his hands up high and follows all of their commands. He did learn something after all.

THE INSANE

THE INSANE

The sun is out in full bloom. The orange light of the early morning warms our cruiser as my partner and I make our way through the dirty streets of the Hood. The radio plays a Top Forty song but my partner and I do not talk. We are looking around, scanning the buildings and shops that litter this part of the main street.

Patrols regularly take us by this area as it is a high drug trafficking zone fueled by a transit rail line. It is filled with junkies, drug dealers, criminals, and good people. A bad mix, one that we are trying to slow down but is spinning out of control.

The rails allow for fast movement of product, the most of which is crack cocaine. With the access to the train system the dealers move about freely, the buyers move through the area, and the criminals have a steady supply of unsuspecting victims to feed upon.

I have arrested countless criminals here for a variety of offenses. The violent ones, the ones that are the biggest threat to civilians, are the ones I really worry about. I have tried to place conditions for their release to prevent them from coming to this area. A "No go" deal that if I catch them here I can just arrest them for breaching their conditions. But I never get the conditions in place. A judge always hears the sad story of how the bad guy needs the transit system for work purposes, family needs, etc., and the conditions never get put on.

I find it ironic that if you have been caught drinking and driving that your license is immediately lost. No chance for excuses like family or business. But, if you violently assault someone, steal from them, or victimize them in any other way the courts will give the bad guy a second, third, and fourth chance to repeat his crime. No thought goes into the victim here.

So, I have taken it upon myself to start to deal with the regular offenders. I will personally make this a well-known "No go" place for the bad guys. Word will spread that if you go here and victimize people

I will cause violence upon you. End of story.

Our car stops at a red light and just then I can hear a commotion. I look over my right shoulder to the transit platform and I see two males fighting. The punches are being thrown as we jump out of our cruiser and head towards the waist-high concrete median that separates the cars from the rail tracks. As I swing my legs over the median I am reminded by a large sign that this is a live track. "Watch for Trains" looms above my head as we duck into the hazard area that is void of any people. I quickly scan right and left to see if there are any concerns and I do not see a train coming. Up and over I go to the platform and in a flash I am running towards the two fighting men.

My brain and eyes scan for any hazards. No weapons can be seen. Bystanders are staying clear of the frenzy and it looks like the two men do not have any companions with them to interfere with what I need to do.

An echo passes into my ears as my partner calls in the fight. I can hear other sirens in the distance making their way here. They know that crowds can turn even if we are just breaking up a confrontation. I have heard it more than once where we are there just to stop the fight, and as soon as you lay your hands on someone, a dick in the crowd has to yell "police brutality" or "Rodney King." Then all hell breaks loose. The crowd will turn on you and soon you have to cause pain and suffering on those who originally had nothing to do with the occurrence.

There has been more than one time that I have felt like just looking at the crowd as we arrest someone and yelling, "Fine, you fucking deal with this! You want to call the shots, you arrest the violent bad guy."

But I never do. I put up with the ignorance of the public. I tolerate the badgering and the yells of "Fuck you, pig" and all the other racial slurs thrown my way. I tell myself that they hate the blue, not me. I always tell myself that they are ignorant of reality.

I am closing in on the bad guys now. Really close. I recognize one guy right off the hop. He is known as Styles. He is a regular bad guy on the tracks. He lifts wallets, does purse snatchings, and roughs up kids for whatever he can take. I have tried to get "No go" conditions on him several times.

I yell out our trained police command: "Police! Don't move." My baton gets extended. I am ready to fucking draw blood on Styles. He is a piece of shit that needs to realize that this is a "No go" area for him because I say it is so.

The two split. I see Styles has taken the worst of the fight. He is bloody and his clothes are fucked up.

The guy he was fighting with is a huge man. Not one of Styles's regular-looking victims. The man is about six feet, two inches in height and at least 300 pounds. Not a fit man by any means but still huge, lots of mass to the guy. Even though I know Styles is violent I keep facing the big guy.

Something is not right, my instincts, or what we call "Spidey" senses, are yelling at me to keep an eye on this guy. I listen to them, they have saved me countless times before.

My partner takes Styles down hard as Styles starts to run away as soon as the big guy lets go of him.

I can hear Styles yelling at my partner.

"I had nothing to do with this, man! He just started to fight with me."

I also hear the familiar noise of the metallic zipper sound of cuffs getting locked on. Without even looking back I can tell that Styles is in custody because of the noise and the fact that my partner is relaying over the radio that he has one in custody. I can still hear the sirens in the distance. They are getting closer.

"Are you okay?" The big guy just stares at me when I ask him the question. My hair stands up, I feel that all is wrong with this guy but I cannot pick out exactly what it is.

I get a response from him. His low voice matches his huge frame.

"Are you the real police?"

"Yes," I say in a slow monotone voice. My mind is screaming, "This is wrong, this is bad. Do something!" My conscious is telling me I cannot do anything yet. My conscious is telling me that I do not have legal grounds to crush this guy even though my mind is letting me know that I should.

My conscious is going to be the death of me one day.

I stand prepped, my legs are slightly bent, they are chambered like a coiled spring, ready to deliver energy. I know that I can only react to what this guy is going to do next. I stand in a state of readiness. I somehow know that combat is coming but I cannot back away, I cannot attack. I have to stand and wait.

Then it comes. I see the lumbering giant awake. His eyes open up and I can see madness in them. His eyes are filled with frenzied anger, insanity.

He lurches forward with both arms. His huge hands grasping at me. I know how this guy fights. He fights like all other big guys do with very little combat training. He uses what works well for him. His size.

He wants me in close. I used to fight like him before I started to study the art behind combat.

He expects to grab onto me and pull me in close. He expects that I will use all of my energy and time trying to break free of his hold. He will keep on the attack so that I will use my time to try to defend myself. He has fought guys before and this is the way it goes.

I like to be up close and personal. Hand-to-hand combat is just that. I want to be able to touch him. I want to be able to use all the tools that I have for fighting. Hands, feet, elbows, knee, forehead, and even teeth if I have to. To me close is good. Real fucking close is better.

My arms rock up to protect my head and his heavy arms come crashing into them. I am bounced around in the protective cage that my arms have built. I can feel the energy of his blow travel into my arms. They absorb the blow.

His hands grab onto my shoulders and pull me into him. He expects me to stop this attack but I welcome it. My left hand slides out of the protective block that it once stood firmly in.

I reach behind his neck and grab hold of the mass of flesh and fat that holds his big head up. I lock in my hand and pull his head towards me. In harmony with this I drive my right elbow into his face. The contact is one of pure flowing energy. He is pushing himself forward while pulling me in. I pull him in as I push my elbow forward.

Combat symmetry. I connect with a sharp strike to his face. I aim to stop my blow far behind his head. I want to flow through him, cause his head to snap back. A violent snap of the head causes the brain to slide inside of the cranial cavity and bounce around. This bounce is a concussion.

The laws of physics override the laws that govern this big man's insanity. My blow stuns him and I am now on the attack. He is using his time and energy trying to ward off my attack against him. He is way out of his element now.

I drop a second elbow back into the same spot. Driving it hard again. I feel teeth fold in as my bony elbow slams into his face for the second time.

His knees buckle. His brain is now starting to shut down. I need to keep up the damage so that his brain finishes shutting down. If I stop now he will recover. His insanity will fire his brain back into the madness that drives him.

I roll my elbow up high as his body slumps down towards me. I keep my left hand locked in place. It controls his head and I turn his face away from me so that he cannot use his eyes to target me. As I turn his head I also know that I am making him lose balance, adding more confusion to his brain.

I let my chambered legs release. I jump up in the air to gain the angle that I need to deliver my next and hopefully final blow. As I reach the apex of my jump I drive my elbow down again. I strike deep into the collarbone of this guy and with all of my body weight behind it. Three hundred pounds of force delivered as my full body weight combined with duty gear lands on his collarbone. A bone that can snap with a mere twenty-five pounds per square inch of force.

I sink deep and through the bones on my arm I feel a pop. I can feel the collarbone break as I sink deeper into the big man. His head slides free of my left hand as his body slumps down. The last blow sends pain messages to his brain, and that is the breaking point for him. His brain shuts off, his television goes black.

At my feet lies a mass of dead body weight. Unconscious.

I move quickly to get the cuffs on him, and as soon as the cuffs are on he is back into fight mode. He is furious. He rants and raves. He yells how we cannot take him back. He screams his delusional world out for everyone to hear.

I can scarcely make out that he thinks that he is going to be cut open for testing. That we are trying to steal his thoughts and that he doesn't want to be examined again. I feel for this man. In his world he thinks that he is going to die. He thinks that we are going to take him away and perform medical experiments on him. He will do anything to escape, that is what makes him so dangerous.

I ask for a unit with a van to come and take this guy for us. A car will not be big enough to move this man to jail or the psychiatric ward.

Styles keeps on saying that it was not his fault. He keeps on repeating that he did nothing wrong this time. I can see it in his eyes, fear. He knows now what it feels like to be a victim. I tell him to keep quiet. I tell him to remember what it felt like to be attacked, that is the way he makes his victims feel.

It takes four of us to move the big man as he tries to spit, bite, and yell his way to freedom. We drag him over to the stairs and people are starting to gather. He thrashes, screams, and yells at the top of his lungs.

Then I hear it. The voice of ignorance. It comes from a guy who has just gotten here. He sees only this one brief second of an occurrence that has played itself out over the last few minutes.

"Hey, take it easy on him. Fucking four on one, real fucking fair. Fucking police brutality if I ever saw it."

I want to stop, to let this guy go. To take the cuffs off of the mad man and tell him that the guy who just opened up his mouth is the source of all of his troubles.

I would love to stand there with the rest of world and watch the crazed giant kick the fuck out of this guy.

I would love to put my hands up as people look at me and wonder why I do not stop the violence. To just say that I would not want them to see police brutality. I just stare at the ignorant man.

Then as if my mind was read, a woman steps forward. She is older, in her mid-sixties. She is strong willed and doesn't let this goof fire off any more.

"Hey, listen here, let them do their job. That guy is unstable and they are just doing what they have to do." She points her finger at him and I can see the crowd watch what happens next.

If he touches her they will lynch him. He knows it. It is like his mother is telling him to grow up, to sit down, and behave. You cannot touch your mother. He stays silent.

I make eye contact with her and through the screaming and yelling of the mad man I thank her. It is like the world stops and the sounds stop. My words seem to travel across to her in perfect clarity and she just smiles at me.

I can hear his screaming again. I lock hard into his body to try to slow his thrashing but his weight tosses us around. Without real control or grace we finally get him to the van. The back door is open and he sees it.

He gets absolutely hysterical. He panics. His world is over, he is going to die. We are going to take him away to torture him for what secrets he knows. I feel for him.

More cops come and now we have seven to try to control him. Each of us has an arm, leg, body, and head. He is overpowered; we are like ants on a worm. We attack, hold, and secure him. He fights with all of his might. He is going to die.

We toss him into the van and he slides to the back like a slab of industrial beef being shipped. I grab the door and swing it shut as fast as I can because I know he will try to escape. He is going to die. He is going to be tortured. I would try to escape too.

I try to close the door fast, but not fast enough. He is up and rushing to the door full steam. I know that I cannot put the locks in place before his full body weight forces the metal doors into me. He will escape into the arms of the other officers and we would have to do this all over again.

I swing the door open as he rushes at me. I drive out my left arm into his face. It is a perfect blow. My palm strikes his face and I feel his body lurch as his brain gets rocked again. He falls to the side and my hands slide off of his face. He falls and I try to pull my arm back but it gets pinned between the cage and his body.

Fuck! I feel my shoulder pop. I see my arm twist in a way I know it should not move. Fuck! My brain sends me pain. Fuck!

He falls back away from me as his body jerks back to avoid another strike from me. I jerk back as my left arm swings to my waist. It hangs there only supported by tendons and flesh. The ball of the joint no longer sitting in the socket.

Fuck! I reach over and hang my arm onto my duty belt. Jamming the hand into the place were my baton sits. I still have work to do. I cannot move back yet, I have to close the cage.

Pain! Fuck!

I reach over with my right hand and slam the door shut. I twist the lock into place and I see the mad man get up and attack the door again.

He smashes his body weight into the steel frame with a crash.

I move back and see my co-workers stare at me. My world slows down as adrenaline pumps into me hard. I feel like I am moving through water, sounds are muffled, and movements are slow.

My partner grabs onto me and walks me to the cruiser. I just walk along, my mind in shock. It wants out from the pain.

I look down and I see that my arm has fallen out of the spot were I set it. I see the bulk of meat swinging away as other cops look at me in shock. I grab my arm again and hold it close to me.

As soon as I am in the cruiser my partner drives hard. He is heading to the hospital. He knows I am hurt and hurt bad, He can see it in my eyes. I am trying to make the pain flow through me. My body is a sponge; I will absorb the pain.

I have been hurt before. Broken bones, cuts, and bruises are marks of my business. The byproduct of combat.

My partner hits a turn hard with lights and sirens blaring.

The first words to escape my mouth since I got hurt.

"Fuck! Jesus!"

"Sorry, brother, but I got to get you to the hospital ASAP. Hang in there!"

We slice another corner and my mind yells at me. I can feel my bones move, I can feel the tendons stretch, and I know that the damage is getting worse.

I gasp. "No worries, man. I am all good."

He laughs. "Yeah, fucking right you are. Fucking cowboy."

I groan and laugh. I am fucked. I am in pain and I laugh. I laugh when I move and it hurts more. I still laugh. I am now insane, I am being driven to madness by pain. I laugh as we come to a fast stop.

My partner gets out and rushes into the emergency ward. I get out of the car. I lock my arm into place and I sweat. I feel my lips sweat. I can taste the salt from my sweat. Keep fucking walking. Not time to quit. I am a sponge, I soak up the pain.

The medics come rushing towards me as I walk behind my partner. He looks at me and he is pissed.

"I fucking told you to stay in the car!"

"I am okay." I did not hear his words. I was too busy going insane.

A wheelchair is propped up behind me and I sit down. I am getting wheeled into thehospital.

"If you fall down, you big fuck, how will we get you back up?"

I laugh.

We get into the ward and I move myself into a bed. I look at my partner and he is pissed again.

"Fucking gronk! You will never ask for help, will you?"

I sit up on the bed as the medics go to work cutting off the layers that hide my injury. My dark blue shirt is cut away. Then my hard ballistic armor is removed. Then my soft body armor is cut off. Then my black undershirt is cut off. Like layers to an onion my uniform is removed. The clothes hit the floor and like a gift being unwrapped I can see what has been done.

"Fuck me." I look at my left shoulder. The place were my arm was attached is now a skinny tube of flesh. No bone sits there. I see blue blood pooling. I am going insane with the pain. I lean my head back and laugh.

"Okay, son," says a man wearing a white coat. He looks at me in the eyes. "I have to set the arm. You have tendons and ligaments sitting in the joint and they are getting damaged. I have to put the ball back into the socket and I do not have time to give you painkillers for it."

I have had bones set without painkillers, I have had stitches without painkillers. I want painkillers right now. I soak up the pain. I want to throw up.

"Do what you need to do."

I see more medics come in. They hold down my feet and my good arm. I do not like the feeling. I do not like to be held down. I feel rage building. I look at my partner.

He can see my soul asking for help. He knows what is happening inside of me. I cannot focus on the pain and the feeling of helplessness from being held down.

In a calm cool voice he touches one of the medics holding down my good arm.

"He doesn't need that. He will be fine if you let him go."

I can feel the medics look at the doctor as my partner tells them this. I roll my head back and soak up the pain. My sweat runs into my eyes. Sweat runs down my back. My shoulder burns, hot lava is rolling in the joint.

The medics let go and I hear the doctor.

"You have to relax, it will make things go better if you do."

I inhale and think of the pain washing over me. I think of nothing but the white burning lava I feel. My heart slows, I exhale.

The doctor pulls down on my arm.

Fuck! Pain. I am going insane. I laugh. I groan. I try to hold in my pain. I want to vomit.

I feel his free hand grab my shoulder blade and roll it upwards.

I groan. I do not laugh anymore.

I keep my eyes shut. All I see is a blinding white light.

I feel the doctor roll the socket around the ball of my shoulder.

I groan deeper. I see the white light. I am blinded.

My lungs hurt, my teeth hurt, my mind screams. I am going insane.

Then, my bones sit where they belong. The light disappears. I want to throw up, I might throw up right here. I hold my mind steady and focus past the nausea. I don't want to do this. Not after what I have been through. Just hold fast, I don't want to throw up.

I open my eyes and I see the doctor beside me. I laugh.

"That feels much better now, I bet," he says.

I laugh. I am high. I am swimming on endorphins and I am high. My stomach settles, I am not going to vomit.

I look around and I can see people stopped in the hallway. I can see eyes looking at me through the curtains. My groans were loud. They were strained and filled with pain. My low moans have silenced the emergency ward.

The doctor turns to the nurse beside him; he lets loose a ramble of acronyms, codes, and procedures that he wants done. He places his hand on my back and tells me that I will be feeling the painkillers that I just recieved.

"If you were a smaller guy they might have kicked in before we set the shoulder. I want some tests done on your shoulder because I think there is tearing in the rotator cuff area."

"Thanks for the good work, sir." I put out my right hand and shake his.

He smiles and shakes my hand.

"Thanks for being such a good patient."

He leaves and I feel the ebb of the painkillers soak into me. I am washed by a wave of drugs that make me not care about my injuries. I look over to my partner. He is just standing there looking at me.

"I am fucked. Can you take my chunk back to the office?"

"Don't worry. I will take of all of that."

I drift off to sleep. I am exhausted; my walk through the valley of insanity has worn me out. I fall into a deep sleep.

A week later I sit at a desk. My arm tied close to me. I am fucked. My shoulder is done. I am breathing shallow as I have stopped taking my painkillers. I hate the feeling they give me. I have no real control in me when I am on them. I feel like I am being held down.

My pectoral tendon is ripped off and my bicep sits near the base of my forearm. It is severed clean off. My rotator cuff is torn and I am slated for surgery next week. I have to wait to get the best surgeon that our compensation board can get. He is the best, and I am sure he can fix me.

I will spend one month at home after the surgery. Five more months at a desk as I go through rehabilitation, then I will be back on the street. I miss it already.

I look at my surgery scars. I run my fingers over the thick scab that surrounds the black stitching. I imagine the four titanium pins that now sit in me. They are my companions now for life, screwed deep into my bones. Anchored to allow the tendons a point of attachment, secured in to allow my body to work properly again.

The scars are my reminders of the events that occurred. The scars on my shoulder stand with the scars on my hands, my knees, and the hidden scars of built-up calcium from bone fractures.

These scars stand with the other deeper scars of emotional burns and unknown trauma.

I breathe shallow as I work through the constant pain in my shoulder that travels through me. I can't wait to get back to the street.

On the Mall

On the Mall

There is a beautiful street that runs through my zone. It is filled with trendy shops, posh restaurants, and well-decorated light standards. Old-growth trees that have indigo blue strings of lights give the whole street a mystic glow. The open-air market greets tourists and welcomes the regular shoppers and diners.

Driving down the street is like being invited into a mystical wonderland.

Then, in drastic contrast to the sandstone buildings, the druggies and homeless have invaded this space. The pillars that line the walls of old banks now converted into luxurious restaurants offer hiding places.

Dark corners form little meeting places were crack and methamphetamines are sold. Inside the solid stone walls the chatter of the rich and innocent flow. Outside the violence is boiling, waiting to make a new victim in the night.

My partner and I have been hitting this area hard but it is proving to be a challenge. Our street reputation still clears out most of the regulars but the rest hold fast. The money for the dealers is good, the flow of pedestrian traffic allows the predators to find victims, and the unique structure of the long street makes it hard to target and deal with the offenders.

If an education is needed there are too many eyes watching. Too many people that do not know what they are seeing that will quickly yell "police brutality." Too many eyes that will complain when we are just doing our job of jacking up bad guys.

The criminals use this as a shield, the very sheep that they prey on. They hold them up in front of us when we start to show our teeth. The sheep cry and we back off.

This has become a huge problem and we are getting flack from all angles.

The shop owners complain to the chief, he shits on us for not cleaning it up.

The civilians complain to the chief about police in the area jacking up "innocent homeless people." He shits on us. Our chief of police also lives in a personal bubble. He is no different from the people in the restaurants. He sits there, talking with other suits looking out the window of his stone-walled cave.

He looks out and sees only the well-lit streets and sees the police drive by, occasionally talking, dealing with bad guys. He thinks he knows what the streets are like.

It has been years since he has policed, since he has had to arrest a person. Years since he made personal contact with someone. Years since he experienced combat.

He has no idea what it is to deal with belligerent kids that will swarm and attack the police. It never happened in his era.

He has no idea what it is like to deal with a guy hopped up on meth or crack. It never happened in his era.

He has no idea what it is like to have a police hater infected with AIDS or Hep. C, who is focused on doing what it takes to infect us. It never happened in his era.

He has no idea what it is like to try to police when civilians stuff cameras, tape recorders, digital cameras, and other electronic devices in your face. All of them trying to get that magical money shot for the news. It never happened in his era.

So, there he sits looking through the plate glass window, watching the well-lit parts of the streets. He never sees the dark alleys or the drug-induced violence that it holds. He runs our service and he has no clue what we do out on these streets any more.

Our cruiser edges down the busy street slowly and my eyes are focused on a male in particular. He is about five and a half feet tall and weighs no more than 140 pounds. At his actual age of thirty-six he looks more to be in his late forties, the byproduct of heavy drug abuse.

His pale skinny arms are loaded with track marks and his face is filled with boils and sores from his methamphetamine addiction. I have dealt with him before and I know that when he binges he is a violent man. But, I guess if any of us went for five days without sleep and food, we would driven to insanity from a chemical that screams for us to take more and more. Forced to wander around because a chemical keeps us awake and hyper, no matter how much our body or brain wants to shut down. I guess we would be violent too.

I call him over to the car and I can tell from the way his body moves that he has been on a heavy drug binge now. I have seen him worse but I know he is on the path to violence and self-destruction.

"Tyler," I call out. He looks at me with far off eyes that are sunk into dark black pockets. They jerk from left to right. He is paranoid, his hands twitch. He is "sketching," I know he is not far off from falling apart. One or two more days and he will be a ranting raving lunatic.

"Tyler, come here," I call again and he seems to set back into reality. He comes over to the car and I start to talk to him about his drug abuse. I want to feel out where he is at, how much of a threat he is becoming.

My partner puts Tyler's information into our computer to see if maybe he has some warrants for his arrest. A day in the tank will help him sleep and recover from his binging. No such luck.

Tyler's actions are unpredictable and agitated so my partner and I get out of the car to talk to him. If Tyler flips at least we will be out with him. Having to get out of the car is risky when someone is waiting for you.

I stand there as my partner tells Tyler that he is not supposed to be on the mall and that he has to leave.

A well-dressed male in his late forties walks by and overhears our conversation. For some reason this guy, this ignorant man, decides that for once in his life he will stand up for what he perceives is wrong. He never before decided to do this. Never when an irate customer bastardized a teller. Never once when a youth was acting like an ass. Never once when he saw a rude action. He never decided to speak out when it was right to.

But, now he sees his chance to get a jab in. Why? Who knows. It may be to get a word in the last time he got a speeding ticket. Maybe because the last time he called for the police we took a long time to show up. Who knows, but now he decides to speak for this chemically dependent fellow we are dealing with.

"Hey, cut the poor guy some slack." His comment is simple and short. He keeps on walking past me when I look at him. I call him over to me.

He points to himself as if I was talking to someone else.

I nod.

He walks over and I keep my voice calm and relaxing. I do not want to scare this fellow off for the one time in his life that he has decided to have some balls and step up to the plate. Even if his courage is very misplaced.

"I am curious why you said what you just said."

He pauses.

Come on, buddy, get some balls. Let's talk.

"Um, well, I think that you guys don't need to give the poor guy a hard time."

"Okay, fair enough, but do you know this guy?"

"No."

"Do you even know why we are chatting with this guy?'

"No."

"Okay, so without me even telling you what this guy's history is and that we deal with him on a regular basis, I have a question to ask you."

"Okay, what?"

"If you think that this guy is so nice and innocent why don't you give him the keys to your car?"

"What?"

"Yeah, you seem to think that we are just picking on some poor guy so why don't you give him the keys to you car and let him come over to your house?"

"Are you kidding?' His eyes are looking at the ramble of a man in front of him. He sees the dirty hands, the human waste stains on his pants. He now sees the bags under the eyes and the crazed stare of the "poor guy."

"Nope, I am not."

"No way." The business guy pulls back in horror of the thought.

"Well, now. I guess this guy is not just some poor fellow we are giving a hard time to." I slide the comment in with no sarcasm or undertones. Just simple facts. I can see that it registers. But I know I have to praise this guy somehow so that he doesn't build a wall and ignore what I have said. I don't want him to be offended and lose on this learning lesson.

"You see, your judge of character is good. Once you actually look at this guy you can tell that he is a drug user. That he has a criminal record and right now he is so far gone on crack or meth that he is dangerous." My verbal reward. I feed him another pat on the back to seal the lesson. "You should wear this uniform. Your ability to judge character would be a really good tool for you on the street. You would make a good cop." Perfect. He is rewarded and praised. He doesn't feel like I stepped on his pride.

"No thanks, I could never do your guy's job. You guys take care and have a good night." He walks off with some knowledge. He walks off knowing that I told him he would make a great cop. His ego is intact and he never lost face in the conversation. A happy police and client contact.

I look back at Tyler.

"Time to beat it, Tyler. People don't want you here."

Tyler shrugs and moves on, walking further down the street to find his place in one of our homeless shelters or a local crack flop house.

We get back into our car and cruise further down the strip to keep moving out and dealing with the drug dealers, drug users, and other criminals that walk the mall.

In a short time we have found a guy with some warrants out for his arrest and we are off to cells to process our guy.

On average we hit our cells two or three times a night. Some cars will only get to cells once a month. It depends on your work ethic and if you like to deal with the bad guys. I have no issues with it. If you are a hand-shaker type of cop good for you because we need the hand-shakers. Better you than me.

Once we are out of cells, and a little chit-chat session is had with the staff in cells, we are out back on the street.

Deep inside, something tells me to drive the mall again. There was just something about Tyler that I did not like. It might have been the fact that he is so close to "tweeking." Becoming violent from several days of violent binging.

I have talked to many meth heads after they have tweeked and they all have the same stories to tell me. I know what Tyler will be experiencing when he loses his grip on reality. His mind will be gone. He will be moving in world that is filled with a high-pitched whine, much like the whine from your television when it is not on a receiving channel.

His eyes will only process partial information, so he will be looking at the world as if a strobe light is going off. Only getting bits and pieces of information. If you move fast it is almost like you have teleported from one spot to another.

He will be filled with paranoia and delusions. He will think that he is going to die or maybe that he needs to kill. He wants more drugs but he wants to sleep.

Tyler will have a high level of pain tolerance. He will be strong and he will be able to take an unbelievable amount of punishment. He will not care about injuries, and to top it all off the burning fire of violence will surge through his body. I have seen him there before. He is a raging animal.

I pull back onto the street, which runs the length of the open-air mall. My eyes gaze down the street and are filled with the tree lights, the dazzling store fronts, and the slow-moving pedestrian traffic. I drive slower because of the amount of people that zip from one side of the street to the other.

Women in black evening gowns are escorted along by men in high-priced suits. High heels and leather loafers click down the streets as a low rumble of conversation echoes off of the walls. It is a surreal scene.

Just when I start to feel that my sensation of worry was false. Just when I start to doubt the inner warning system that I have developed from working this job. I see Tyler.

He is face down on the concrete. He has crumpled forward and lies on the ground like he has died praying on his hands and knees. My partner sees it too and I pull our cruiser up to Tyler.

As we walk up to him I can see a meth pipe lying next to his right hand and a lighter next to his left. A large amount of mucus is coming from Tyler's nose.

"Hey, buddy, heads up. He is really fucked," I say to my partner as I point to the drug pipe near his hand. A quick nod tells me that he is ready to deal with Tyler.

I grab Tyler's shoulders and heave his light body onto the bench that he has fallen off of. My black knife-resistant gloves dig into his shoulders, and through the clothes that he is wearing I can feel bone and very little muscle tissue. Tyler is wasting away, his body is feeding off of itself to live. He is starving because he only wants to feed his great need for drugs.

Tyler wakes up from the lift; he instantly sits upright on the bench. I am on Tyler's left and my partner is on Tyler's right.

"Tyler, are you all right?"

These are the only words that get out from my partner's mouth before Tyler springs to his feet. I try to stop the upward motion but my upper body strength cannot hold Tyler's lower body power. He stands.

I grab onto Tyler's right arm to try to get him seated again and Tyler pulls his arm away. My grip is broken without any effort from him.

His hand juts into his jacket and I try to stop him. Both my hands on his arm barely stop Tyler from reaching into his jacket.

Now the warning signs scream at me. The same signs yell at my partner as I hear him say one word:

"Down."

It is not meant for Tyler. It is meant for me. I know that our efforts now are no longer to keep Tyler seated but to take him to the ground. We want him down and we want him down now.

With that command our energies are harmonized. We do not pull in separate ways, we do not waste energy on conflicting motions. A fluid motion that can only be developed after working with the same partner for a long time.

We drive Tyler to the concrete. On the ground we can secure Tyler. On the ground is where my partner and I know how to fight together the best.

Tyler goes down hard. I hear his body slam into the concrete. The air rushes from Tyler's lungs as his back hits the solid sidewalk.

The fight is now on. Tyler swings wildly and frantically. His blows hit my sides and my shoulders. My body armor soaks up most of the energy and only a little bit of air escapes my lungs.

I get jerked forward and his knee strikes the hard ballistic panel that I wear over my soft armor. The hard ceramic panel that is designed to stop rifle fire and trauma from high-caliber rounds takes all the pain out of the blow.

I feel Tyler's body jerk as my partner's knee strikes into Tyler's ribs.

My partner is working low on Tyler so I start to drive open-handed palm strikes into Tyler's face. I wait till Tyler lifts his head slightly off of the ground before sending a blow into his face. I hear his head bounce off the side walk.

Tyler is not fazed. His head snaps off of the ground like a water-filled basketball and he still is in full fighting order. Normally two or three consecutive blows like this will crush a will to fight. I have shut down some of the best fighters on the street when I can land these blows.

The damage is just too high and disorientating. The brain is just suffering too many concussions to keep the will to fight.

Tyler's brain is suffering from the fourth blow. His brain has suffered a fourth concussion in a matter of two seconds. Tyler's chemically filled body doesn't care.

My tactics have to change. Tyler's fist lands square into my jaw. It is a hard blow but I am not fazed. I have been hit harder, much harder. I switch to pinning Tyler's arm to the ground.

I have been hit harder but I still do not like to be hit. I drive another strike into Tyler before I move to trap his arm to the ground. I drop my body and land a left elbow hard into Tyler's sternum. I land with all my body weight and I compress Tyler's chest.

I feel his chest shrink under the weight and force of my blow. I hear Tyler grunt as I drive the air out of his lungs. His body loses momentum and it gives me the split-second to trap his left arm under my knees.

I have his arm pinned under my knees, the full weight of my body on top of his one arm. I look over to my partner and see he has done the same.

I see him key his mike with his free hand and a call for backup is aired. The cavalry is on its way. Only through sheer manpower can we control Tyler. We have to swarm on him like ants and hold him down.

With my free left hand I grab onto Tyler's throat. My right hand grabs onto Tyler's pinned arm at the wrist.

My hand wraps tight around Tyler's neck and I squeeze to cut off air to his body. On the street this move is called "the C clamp" or "turkey claw." I have used it a lot.

"If some fucker is on his back and is getting to be more than what you can handle I would suggest a 'C clamp.' Choke the fucker out." My recruit instructor looks at me with his battle-hardened eyes. I am sitting across from him having lunch. It is only a week before I hit the street and this instructor allows me to sit and have lunch with him. He took me under his wing early in the training and has been a great mentor to me.

"Now you have to be careful because our agency doesn't train you in this. So if you crush the fuck's throat and kill him you will be hung out to dry. Actually if you ever inflict violence on anyone our department will hang you out to dry." My mentor's finger stretches out to point at me to drive this fact home.

"Our agency doesn't give a fuck about protecting you from the job you do. They eat their young here.

"But, back to the C clamp. Grab the fucker's neck and squeeze hard on the side and a little on the front. Squeeze until you can feel your fingers touch and then watch his eyes. When he is out, stop fucking squeezing and give his air back. Choke the fucker out." My mentor's hands curl into a claw-like hand as he mimics the movement. I can see it in his eyes that he is traveling back in time remembering all the people he choked out.

My left hand tightens. Harder and harder like a vise slowly closing. I feel my fingers touch and I just apply a little bit more pressure until I can see Tyler's mouth move like a fish out of water.

I take away his ability to breath. Seconds now before he passes out. In his state of heavy breathing and combat his lungs demand air for the body. His air is cut off, just a matter of time before he passes out. Then the cuffs will go on and we can control him better when he wakes up.

I hear the sirens in the distance, seconds now.

I see Tyler's eyes widen as his brain panics from the lack of air. I see his cornea open as he starts to slip into unconsciousness. I keep my grip steady and hard, I can see he is going to slip into the darkness.

I hear the sirens coming closer.

I am choking Tyler out.

I see his cornea grow, he is slipping now. I feel his arms start to go limp and his body starts to relax. He is slipping.

Then as if his mind recoils from the lack of air I see life and fire come back to his eyes. He is going to give the fight one last go before he slips into unconsciousness.

I am lifted right off the ground. My knees still propped up on his arm, my whole 300-plus pounds in full kit is picked up off the ground like I am a rag doll. My shoulder slams into my partner as he too is being lifted off of the ground in the same fashion.

I don't let go of his throat, I cannot let go. I cannot give him an ounce of air. I cannot give him anything that will help him win this fight. If I let go Tyler will be on a rampage. In his state of delirium he could only be stopped by having some lethal force being delivered upon him.

I seal my grip on his airway harder as my body slides onto his chest. I keep my right arm up to block Tyler's now freed left arm. A wild blow comes crashing into my guarding arm and the force is so great that it still makes its way to my face. His hand once again crashes into my jaw. I can hear teeth grind and my jaw slams shut. I can taste blood.

My animal fires up now. I am mad and furious. Fucking pass out, mother fucker! I grit my teeth, I can feel my lips stretch back over my mouth. I know what I must look like now. I have seen the primitive face of combat on others.

I know the face well. Eyes wide open, teeth showing, and lips curled back. I look like an angry dog and I want to tear this fuck to shreds.

I smash an open hand into Tyler's face, his head tries to twist but my grip on his neck is too strong. I pull his head up with the hand gripping his neck and slam his head down onto the concrete.

I do it again, and again. The clashing of skull onto concrete can be heard down the street.

Pass out, come on, Tyler, and give in to the darkness.

I smash his head again and I see blood squirt out across the sidewalk. I am in a fury. I smash his head again. I see more splatter fly across the grey concrete. I can feel the fury build.

Tyler's body starts to go limp. His eyes start to roll back and his cornea starts to widen. Tyler is now falling into the darkness.

I smash his head again. Fuck you, Tyler!

Tyler now goes completely limp. His body has moved into the

black, his mind is shutting down from lack of oxygen. He is now floating in the blackness of unconsciousness. Do I deliver him into the light of death? He is close, I know it will take just one more strike to the concrete. A few more seconds of no air will force him there.

I am still furious, my animal is still released. I am still wide-eyed and bare-toothed.

I let go, I give Tyler his air. His mouth gasps even though Tyler is unconscious. He breathes in the gift of air. His lungs scream no more of the fire that was burning inside.

I pull in my animal. I pull hard on the leash and drag my animal inside again. It has done its job, now I have to lock it up again. I have to stuff the beast into my darkness. Keep it hidden.

It will lie there sleeping until I open up the doors again and awaken the animal in me. I like to release it but it scares me when I do. I fear not stopping it, not being able to control the beast when I let it go.

My partner reaches into Tyler's jacket to pull out whatever he was so concerned on getting to when we first dealt with him. I see a large hunting knife get pulled out. My partner looks at me and secures the knife in his duty belt.

"Fucking lucky," the only words that I can say. I see it in my partner's face that he too feels like we lucked out that Tyler never accessed this weapon.

We roll Tyler onto his belly and as the cuffs are going on more and more hands are reaching for limbs. The other units are arriving and as the first cuff goes onto Tyler he starts to wake up. More and more hands reach out to pin legs, hold arms steady as the cuffs go on.

I step back as another cop motions to take my place. Tyler fully awakes. Tyler's beast is still out, he is in a rage. His screams fill the street. He sounds like a wounded animal, a baby that has not been fed. His screams make my skin crawl.

I stand back to get more air into my lungs. I am exhausted. I roll my head back to get more air, my lungs burn.

I walk over to the cruiser to sit against the hood of the car. My adrenaline fix is going away and I am shaking. Give it time; I know it will go away.

I pull off my leather gloves and wash my hands in the alcohol-based gel that my partner pumps into them. I slide my hands together to spread the cold gel about. I spread the antiseptic wash over all of my exposed skin, hopefully killing any contaminated blood that may have sprayed onto me.

I wash, my hands shake. I wash more, I see no blood on me, my hands shake.

I lean against the car and I can taste the blood in my mouth. My hands are still shaking. I reach into my mouth with my fingers to see if I can feel any loose teeth. My tongue travels my teeth to feel for chips or a crack. I can taste blood mixing in with the antiseptic gel on my fingers. A mixture of acidic blood and burning sour chemical scours my taste buds.

I feel nothing. My face hurts and my gums bleed. Nothing serious, I control my breathing. I look at my hands, the fingers stained in my own blood. I am happy, my hands have stopped shaking.

I spit a mouth full of blood, gel, and saliva into the sewer drain. I wipe my face with an alcohol wipe that another member hands to me.

The streets are still filled with Tyler's screams. He is insane now. Pain, drug abuse, and combat have driven Tyler to insanity. A mob of cops are holding him down as he thrashes and still tries to fight.

Medics roll onto the scene. One comes to me, the other goes to Tyler. A third goes to my partner, who is sitting in the driver's seat of the car holding an instant ice pack on his knee.

I make eyes contact with my partner and he gives me the thumbs up as a medic pushes and prods my jaw line.

"Nothing broken." The medic cringes from one of Tyler's screams. "Just put this on your jaw so that you don't get a bad bruise there. It will also keep the swelling down." He hands me an ice pack.

As I put the ice pack onto my face and spit one last time into the sewer drain to clear the blood from my mouth that was pooling while the medic checked me out, I look up into a large plate glass window.

A restaurant window stares at me. Its shiny face filled with all of the open eyes inside watching the spectacle. A sea of open innocent eyes look through the window, their eyes wide and hollow like a mass of fans watching the best game of the season.

The crowd of high-end suits and black dresses are all still piled around the glass window, looking at what they never get to see. The real world, a world hidden in dark alleys and shadowed corners. Violent, cruel, and savage, Mother Nature at her finest. It is displayed in full view behind the large window they hide behind. Real television at its finest.

I scan the faces of the crowd and I catch a familiar face. It is the face of the man that I had talked to earlier. The suit that gave us a hard time for telling Tyler to move on.

He is not looking at the hustle of the medics or the mass of cops restraining Tyler. He looks right at me. He is staring at me as I wipe the blood from my lips. He is looking at me with eyes that are lost.

He is just staring. He doesn't even know that I am now looking at him. He stares.

I see pity in his eyes. He looks at me with sorrow and compassion. He can see I have been hurt, the bulletproof blue uniform of political power that he viewed before is hurt. It bleeds like all the other people he knows. I have moved from a uniform to a human being in his eyes.

The transformation of the uniform has made him think of what it would be like if he was wearing it. Makes him think about what it would be like to have gone through what I have gone through. He feels for me like people do when they read about other people's losses in books or see it on television. He is able to put himself in my place and he feel feels sorry for me. He wishes this world did not need people like me to do what others are too afraid to do.

I stare back and when he realizes that I am looking at him, he looks away and slides back into the crowd. He moves back into the mass of faces, blending into the innocent.

Tyler's screams are now faint and sullen. He is chemically sedated and his limp body is getting loaded onto a stretcher.

I walk over to my partner, who sits there with an ice pack on his knee.

"Aren't we a fucking sight?" he says as he looks at the ice pack on my face.

I laugh and pat him on the shoulder.

"Fucking wild shit, eh?" I say as I sit in the driver's seat of our cruiser.

We both laugh.

Morning comes and I sit at the breakfast table eating a bowl of oatmeal. It is soft and warm. It feels good because all my teeth hurt when I chew anything solid.

My neck hurts and when I got out of bed this morning I was crunched over like I had aged thirty years. My hands are sore and my face feels slightly puffy and numb. I am thankful that I slept well and that I took some Ibuprofin before I went to bed. A household remedy for waking up better after a good fight.

My wife walks into the kitchen.

"Busy night?"

"Yeah." She always has a knack of knowing if I had violence in my night or not. "Nothing major, just a meth head that went out of his cake. It was a good go, babe."

I smile as I eat my food. We talk a bit more and then I switch the conversation to her day off from work. I want to know what she will be doing, I want to know her plans and what is happening in her world.

When we talk we try not to talk about work too much. We both work hard at trying to keep our heads clear from the demons that haunt us. We know that there is more to our world than policing.

She knows far too much of mine, because she lives and works in the same world.

Policing has already ruined her innocence by letting her know what the shadows hold.

I leave for work like any other day but today will be different. I am sore and so is my partner, and over a quick phone conversation with him we decide to take the day off. We decide on a trip to a doctor so that our soft tissue injuries will be documented. Our bodies ache, our minds are not clear from yesterday's fight. We are in no shape to be safe street cops today.

Our sergeant has no issues with it as long as we stop in to get the file finished and to pick up our Worker's Compensation forms for the injuries.

We stop in the office at our agreed time. When we show up our sergeant tells us that he got a phone call from one of the bystanders that watched our arrest.

"Oh, what is it?" I am bracing for a complaint. Another "those cops should have left that poor guy alone" stories.

"This guy phones me and tells me that you guys did a great job. That he is happy to see the Service do such a good job at protecting the public. He told me that the guy was totally nuts and would have killed the next person who came along to help him. He goes on to say that he is grateful that there are guys like you working the streets because he could never do our job."

I smile, I know who phoned. The suit I talked to. I feel better now, my injuries melt away under the pride of doing my job. I know my partner feels the same. A small gratification like this will sit inside of me for a long time. A little pat on the back from the innocent puts all the other shit and abuse we get from the public behind me.

WOLVES AND SHEEP

WOLVES AND SHEEP

I sit in the cruiser looking down at my notebook as I detail the evidence for the robbery charge I am investigating.

The accused sits behind me, his breath creating a rim of fog on the rear passenger window. Through my rearview mirror I see him gaze far off into the distance. His eye fixed with a thousand-yard stare as the world passes him by.

"Tim!" I raise my voice enough to work its way past the steel and Plexiglas that separates us.

He leans forward and winces as the stainless-steel handcuffs pinch his wrists locked behind his back.

"Yeah?"

Tim is an intellectual, he thinks about his world and why he is there. He just cannot kick the habit he has.

"Why do you rob people? This is the third time I have scooped you up for robbery." I am waiting for him to tell me that he has a chemical addiction issue. I wait for him to tell me that he needs to get cash and this is all he knows. But, Tim is smart. Very smart, smart enough to know that he is hooked on crack and that he is fucked. He has told me that before. We have had conversations in length on the way to jail.

"If God did not want us to shear them, he would have not made them sheep."

His eyes catch mine in the rearview mirror. I look into the eyes of the wolf and I see no pity, no suffering consciousness. I see a predator.

We both sit in silence as his words echo.

The world is filled with basically three categories of people. The first and most prominent are the sheep. These are the innocent people in the world. The sheep move about in the fields with big innocent eyes and they graze happily. The sheep know that wolves lurk in the forest that surround their fields, but they really do not want to know more than that. They make up the masses.

Lurking in the shadows are the wolves. They prey on the sheep. The wolf will work alone but hunts better in a pack. At any opportunity the wolf will victimize a sheep. The wolf waits and scours the land for a sheep that has strayed from the herd during the day. When night falls it is time for the wolf to attack. The wolf hunts the best under the cover of darkness.

Now we come to the sheepdogs. These are the police. We are here to protect the sheep. Help the sheep out in times of need. The only thing is that the sheep see the sheepdog as a white wolf. We have teeth and we fight. We bite and we attack. So, the sheep fear us, view us with suspicion because they see that we can be violent and vicious.

Sheep know that they need us but they really wish they didn't. The sheep want us to look less like sheepdogs and more like sheep. They want our uniforms to be less paramilitary, they want us to use less force when dealing with wolves. And they want us to show respect, courtesy, and compassion for the wolf. The sheep think that the wolf can be cured if they are treated like sheep.

The wolf grows stronger while the sheep try to help them. The sheep want to re-educate them, rehabilitate the wolf to be a sheep. It can never happen. The sheepdogs always look at the sheep with disappointment when they welcome the wolf out of the forest. We know that the wolf will attack. We know that we will respond to the cries of the sheep and fix the chaos that they have created by inviting the wolf into their fields.

But the sheep also want to rehabilitate the sheepdog. They want us to dull our teeth and lower our suspicion of the wolf. But we cannot be sheep, we cannot change because we know that the wolf is coming soon. So, the sheep force us to live on the outskirts of the herd.

To sit in the rain and snow while the sheep sleep. We sit alone and force ourselves to stay awake so that the sheep can sleep quietly through the night. And if by chance they see a sheepdog attack a wolf they are terrified, they voice their cries towards us for our violence. They cry out to leave the wolf alone if we strike first, before the wolf attacks them. Cries of "excessive use of force" and "police brutality" echo.

But when the wolf attacks, the sheep cry. They cry about the wolves' upbringing, social injustices, and lack of rehabilitation programs. The sheep make excuses for the wolves' behavior and the wolves use these excuses to continue committing atrocities against the sheep. A wolf is born a wolf. It makes a conscious decision to attack the herd. It cannot be changed like the sheep wish it could.

When the wolves do attack, the sheep cry for us. They want to see the sheepdog come and protect them. They want to hear the barks and see the dog in front of them. They need to hide behind the sheepdog. This is when we are our finest. Our life has meaning and if the wolves attack we will fight till our death to save the sheep.

But when the fight is over and our teeth are bloody from fighting and our hair is still up on our backs, the sheep fear us. They see too much of the reality to their world so they push us away. Our job is done so they force us to move to the outskirts again. The sheep want us to be more like sheep again. The fear of us is again fueled.

What the sheep fails to understand is that life as a sheepdog is meant to protect the sheep. We have been programmed, trained, and naturally cultivated to protect them. Our whole existence is to protect. That is why we are so lost when we get too old to protect and we leave the field to sit on the Shepherd's bench. We are lost because we know nothing else. We were created to help the sheep.

There is a balance for all things in nature. There are the sheep, the wolves, and the sheepdogs. The sheep have been trying to change this balance for generations now. The attempts to change the balance have only done what we as human beings do the best. We have destroyed the balance.

Pedophiles are roaming the streets controlled only by a piece of paper telling them not to victimize children. We know that they reoffend, we know that they will prey on the innocent as soon as they are released. But the sheep still hopes that this time it may be the one magical moment where the pedophile is cured. Then the sheep cry when another child is destroyed for life.

Drug dealers are free the same day that they are caught. Selling the poison to the sheep as soon as they are released. They do not fear the system because the rewards of selling the death that they deal in far outweighs the price of being caught.

Gang bangers still spray bullets into the houses of the sheep and kill without regard or remorse. The violence that they create and live by is of their own making. They use the violence as an excuse to the sheep.

They tell the sheep that they live this way because they have no choice. The wolf has grown up in a violent place so they must continue to be violent. But, the gang banger chooses his path, it is not chosen for him. He decides to carry the gun. He decides to pull the trigger.

Rapists still attack and rape because they do not fear the sheep's criminal justice system. They know that if they say that they are sorry for destroying the life of a sheep that the sheep will hold them, comfort them, and allow them to take a course to become rehabilitated. The rapist knows what to say so that he can move back into the forest and start hunting again. For the victim the world has changed and the innocence is lost. The other sheep mourn for the victim but they secretly thank God that they are not the victim of the wolf.

The list goes on. Drug addicts, pimps, thieves, killers are just a few off the top. A natural balance has to occur to reduce the wolves. The sheep have to step back and let the balance restore itself. This will not be done by more rehabilitation. This cannot be done by open arms welcoming the wolf into our houses.

What the sheep have to do is know that the sheepdog is there to protect them. The sheep have to remember that the sheepdog is only out there to hunt the wolf. Let us hunt them. Let the wolf know that if they stroll out of the forest they will be hunted by the sheepdog.

Let the wolves know that if they want to hunt the sheep, a mean vicious dog will come and make it so that they will never attack a sheep again. Take the reward away from the risk that they take to commit their crimes against the sheep.

KING OF THE RING

KING OF THE RING

In the city I live in there is a provincial fighting association called "King of the Ring." This association is a knock-off of "The Ultimate Fighting Championships" that you always see on television. It is filled with skilled fighters that train relentlessly in the cage and gym for upcoming bouts. I have seen a few of these events and have enjoyed them all.

To see skilled combatants in a ring pitting wit and stamina against each other is truly riveting.

But, in this group, as with all groups, there is a bad seed. His name is Shane "The Snake" Slinn. Shane is a semiprofessional fighter going for his pro card in the King of the Ring. His aspirations are to become a UFC fighter. He wants to make a career of fighting.

Shane also has a huge anger management issue and, after a few beers, gets himself into a domestic conflict with his common-law girlfriend, Sherri. Sherri is an attractive girl who thinks she really loves Shane but she is caught on the emotional roller coaster that abused women find themselves in.

He hits her, she fears and hates him.

He is sorry, shows great affection for her, and she loves him.

He hits her and she fears and hates him. The cycle continues until he kills her or she leaves when she finally sees the light.

A vicious circle that I see on a day-to-day basis while I work in the Hood. The bulk of our calls are domestic related.

Some days, especially around the holidays, I will deal with this type of abuse four to five times in a shift. Basically defusing one then completing the paperwork and then off to another domestic. It wears thin in the beginning but as time goes on you care less and less about these clients. You realize that no matter what you do, you cannot make either of them see the light. They have to see it themselves.

I have stopped caring for many years now; I look at the complainants and victims with blank, hollow eyes. Seeing this shit for years has made my eyes cold and that, unfortunately, is just a sign of an experienced cop.

So, now my partner and I are driving to the house of Shane and Sherri. A tenant in the basement has called for the police to attend as they have heard a large fight happening over the past thirty minutes. The caller states that he has been hearing crashing noises and screams for help.

It makes me wonder why people wait for so long to call for the police when they hear breaking furniture, crashing bodies, and yells and screams for help.

So, now we are driving to the apartment building with our lights and sirens going on. We are screaming down the road to get to the call as fast as we can.

I read off information to my partner, who is driving. I tell him of the room number, the location, and all of the other garble that is coming over the radio and computer. I let him know who else is being dispatched to the call.

When we hit intersections my head gets out of the computer and I watch traffic. I look for that one person who always has their head up their ass and still goes forward while others stop.

It never fails.

"Hold on! Car on the right!"

My partner slams on the breaks as a midsized car flows through the intersection. All the other cars have stopped but this driver is lost in the clouds. She zips past us looking at our car with the funny lights on the top and the loud siren.

Her blank sheep eyes look at us like we have done something wrong by expecting her to stop. She has no idea how close she was to getting creamed by our car. She has no idea that her stupidity has cost seconds off our travel time to a hot call.

"Fuck, stupid fucking bitch!" My partner slams the accelerator hard down onto the floorboards to get us up to speed again.

I glance over and score the license plate off of her car. I scribble the number down on a scrap piece of paper. I will deal with that issue later.

My partner's special skill for this job is his fantastic driving ability.

He has a natural talent to push our cars hard, never lose control, and keep the ride as smooth as possible. I do not know anyone else on the job that can drive the street cars harder than him. For him it is a natural skill, a gift.

As we get closer to the call we cut the sirens. We do not want to let the offender know we are close, that we are coming. The reasoning behind this is that the offender doesn't set a trap for us. So that he or she doesn't just kill the person they are fighting with, and to allow us to have the advantage of surprise.

Our car comes to a fast stop outside the apartment building but no screech from the tires is let loose. It is a hard, controlled, quiet stop. We get out and close our doors with control. No slamming, just a click as the doors locks engage.

I run up to the door as a person is waiting for us. He swings the door open and with a great look of panic in his eyes almost yells at us, "They have been at it for almost an hour now. She sounds like she is terrified."

I can see panic in his eyes and hear it in his voice. I click my radio and tell the dispatcher that we are out and heading to the apartment number.

My partner kicks the hallway rug into the door jam so that the door cannot close and lock up. The bunched grey carpet will hold the door open for the next attending unit.

Our ascension up the stairs to the third level is speedy but not so fast that our breathing will become elevated. As I climb step after step I can hear the battle in the apartment.

I can hear a man screaming at the top of his lungs as glass smashes.

"Fucking bitch! Fuck you!"

Another crash is heard and a large thump echoes through the halls. A thump I know. It is a body hitting a wall. It sounds like a large piece of padded furniture hitting a solid wall with force.

I look at my partner and he knows what we are to do. We have had this type of call before. The door holder has followed us up the stairs but has stopped on the landing. That is as far as that sheep will go, his courage has brought him here, but no further.

My partner puts his back against the wall as he faces the apartment door. I step in front of him and put my hands on his shoulder to stabilize myself. I put my back to the door. I lift up my right leg and line up a kick that would resemble a horse kicking the door.

"City Police! Open the door!"

I hear the command given by my partner and I lash out my horse kick. I strike the door near the door handle and the force blows the cheap door apart. My heavy combat boots twist the door so that the wood around the lock splinters and sags. The doorframe splits and the door flies open with tremendous force.

I spin around as my partner dashes by me. He is in first and he cuts to the left.

"City Police! Don't move!" my partner challenges him.

I crest the corner right behind my partner. I look in all directions as my partner shouts more commands to the male. I look where his eyes are not, for other threats.

What I see is a war zone. The furniture is over turned; blood covers the walls and the old brown carpet. Tables are smashed, and table lamps are twisted and shattered. Holes made from punches and heads fill the drywall. The head-shaped ones have a ring of blood around them and locks of brown hair dangle from the rough corners of the shattered drywall. Her hair.

Any picture that was on the wall is broken and the floor is littered with broken glass and blood.

I see a woman trying to find shelter in the corner. Her long brown hair is stuck across her face. Blood and tears hold it in place. Her eyes are filled with terror and helplessness.

I can see bruises already forming on her face and her arms. Her legs are cut and she is bleeding onto the floor.

In her panic she tries to get up but when her hands touch the ivory walls a streak of red just follows. Her hands are covered in cuts and the flowing blood is slippery. She cannot get up, she is in terror, a place we call "Code Black."

Total panic, total terror. A place that is dreamlike. You want to run but you cannot. You want to scream and fight but you cannot. Terror is gripping her heart because she was looking at death. She never thought it would happen to her.

She cries, a mass of tears rush down her face.

"Thank God, I was screaming for help! I was screaming for help!" She sits there and sobs as she uses her bloody hands to pull her legs close into her body. "I was screaming for help."

I turn to my partner and his task. I see a caged animal looking at the barrel of my partner's .40-caliber Glock pistol.

I see a powerful man in a maddening rage. He is cornered as we are blocking his exit. I know he wants out, to run, because his eyes glance towards the broken door, then to us. He glances back and forth. His body is covered in sweat, his chest is heaving harder and harder. He is getting filled with Mother Nature's fight-or-flight drug. In seconds I will know what way he will go.

His eyes stop. Shane looks at us and then focuses on my partner. His shoulder rolls forward and his jaw drops. His hands clench into fists and he brings them up. He is setting to fight.

"Fuck you, pig! What are you going to do, shoot me?"

Shane knows that we cannot drop him. He knows that unless he has a weapon we cannot articulate shooting him. As strong as he is, as hyped as he is, as good of a fighter as he is, we cannot shoot him.

Then without hesitation Shane marches forward. He doesn't run into us, he just marches towards my partner. He is closing the distance like a veteran fighter. He doesn't want to waste his energy running at us. He only has a few feet to close in.

My partner side-steps when Shane gets close. The side-step not only allows my partner to get off of the line of attack from Shane but it opens my ability to fight Shane. I have no gun to put away; I will do the fighting until my partner secures his weapon. A weapon that is useless for this type of combat.

Shane's eyes are focused on my partner as he turns with his side-step. Shane only trains for one-on-one combat, and in this situation that training is no fucking good.

I step in and just as Shane looks towards me, recognizing the threat, I drive forward a hard front kick. I strike into his stomach and I can feel a solid mass of muscle under my boot. I have struck hard and fast but I know I have done very little damage. Shane's last-second constriction of his muscles have sucked up the energy. His fighting instincts have saves his insides from feeling my boot against them.

He is pushed backwards but I do not follow him. His arms are up and he lashes out with a right hook that if it hit would have hammered me. I know better than to close in such a fresh and fast fighter.

Shane regains his composure and with lightning-fast speed lunges for my legs. He lurches forward to hook my legs to take me to the ground.

I drive my hands out into his face and push him towards the floor but the strike is expected by Shane. He has calculated for it and his hands still grab the back of my legs.

Shane is about sixty pounds lighter than me but he is skilled and fast. In a ring he would outlast me, outmaneuver me, and outstrike me. But we are not in a ring. We are fighting on a carpet filled with glass and blood. We are engaged in primal combat, man's first primitive program. The only survivor will be the one who has the better tactics and skills. The one with more ambition to win. Determination is the key to this game.

I grab Shane's head and tuck it into my chest. I crush his nose against the ballistic panel that I have in my armor. I can feel his nose snap as I grind it hard onto the panel.

Shane slows just a bit but he is used to the pain. The momentary stop of his takedown is barely noticeable. But I feel it, his hands don't dig into my legs as hard and fierce. His arms slack just a bit as his brain tries to figure out why my chest can break his nose. As primitive as this combat is I have tools, and I know how to use these tools.

I feel his strength coming back and I know that he will dig his hands into my legs again. I know that he will want to take my body down to the ground and that he expects me to fight this tactic.

But I don't. I drop my body down, let my weight fall as I lock harder onto his head. I roll the face against me back and forth, grinding the broken nose more. My fall is controlled, my momentum is under my control.

The ground rumbles with a thud but I am fine. I fell when I wanted to fall and I knew that I was going to fall. My head was curled in, my stomach was tight to take the impact, and my brain knew what was happening. I too have trained to fight on the ground.

Shane functions on simple training reflex. He has been taken to the ground thousands of times before. He hits the floor with me and as soon as we are horizontal his legs splay out. He is stable and comfortable where he is.

His arms reach around and try to lock under my chin. He wants to grab my chin and twist my head back. He wants to peel me back like a skin on an orange. He wants to break my hold on his head.

My teeth grind as I exert more force on his head. I grind his nose again into me. I can see blood covering my arms from his gushing nose.

As a set of iron-like fingers make their way under my chin I can feel the dig into my skin. I can feel my skin stretch and start to rip. I can see my partner closing in, I hold the pain of the grip back. A few seconds more and I can switch my attack.

I see my partner's baton exit his holster but he doesn't expand it. My partner knows all too well that in such a close fight swinging a baton will probably hit both of us.

My partner drives the closed baton into the kidneys of Shane. He jabs it hard like a warrior that was piercing a fallen dragon.

The blow is fierce. The hard metal tip drives its way into Shane's body. Shane jerks as his brain tells him that he has been hit hard. Shane was not expecting to be hit from behind. Shane only trains for ring combat. He is not prepared for two opponents.

As Shane lurches back I let go of his head. He lifts it off of my chest and I spin my right elbow at him. I use the ground for my platform and drive it hard into his jaw. His head snaps and twists. I can feel his hot blood splatter across my face as his head swings. His nose pumps out blood in volumes.

I reach up with my left hand and palm strike his nose again. I push my blow upwards to force blood into his eyes. I want to remove his ability to fight. Take away his vision.

My partner drives the baton tip again into his side and I can tell that Shane has had enough of these damaging blows. He spins with a hard left hook and strikes my partner hard into the chest. The blow rocks my partner back and he stumbles across Shane's splayed legs.

Shane's fury is now back to me. He wants to drive my head into the ground. He wants to crush my skull. His teeth are showing as his lips are dragged back. His eyes, filled with his own blood, are open and crazed. His right elbow chambers back and his whole body bends like a golfer looking to hit a long, hard drive.

Once at its apex his body starts to uncurl. I pull my arms up to my head and make a cage around my head with my arms.

I brace for the impact of his blow. I tuck my chin into my chest so that my head doesn't snap back and pull hard on my abdomen. I brace for the blow. It takes what seems like a lifetime to hit me.

When it does, it hits hard. My forearms scream and his elbow crashes into it. He slices across them and I can feel his bone rub and grind against mine. An electrical shock is blasted into my hands and my clenched fists spring open. If this blow would have connected with my head I would be working just to recover. I would have been hurt and in a bad way.

Even though I have successfully blocked his blow to my head I know my forearms have been heavily damaged. I can feel the muscles cramping from having the blood forced out of them so violently. I try to focus past the gut-wrench ing cramps that follow. I cannot close my hands, I cannot make them work.

I drive my putty-like hands hard into his face again and as his head is jerked backwards I let my fury out. I have been keeping it trapped, hidden in this fight. I wanted to keep calm and cool because I felt that this fight would be short-lived. I expected the fighting ability of my partner and me in tandem to finish this fight fast. I assumed that there would be no need for the animal. Assumption is the mother of all fuck-ups.

I can feel it taking me over. The anger, the rage, the animal that is caged. I have poked it with a stick for long enough and now when I open the cage it rushes forth. I cannot stop it now, it needs to feed.

I drive my right palm forward again into Shane's face. He lurches further back. Then I switch. In full glory of combat lust I slam both elbows into Shane's quads. He had dragged them up high to allow him to sit on my chest so that he could drive his elbow into me. Now I have other things to punish.

I see Shane's face contort as I strike deep into his quads. I drive hard and far into the big lumps of meat. I squish the muscle into his femur and force blood out of the large muscle group. Shane is fighting with the gut-wrenching cramps now. His legs are screaming for blood.

My right knee comes racing into Shane's back, getting more power as my left foot pushes hard into the brown blood-stained carpet. His back arches as my knee hits him high in the back. Air gushes from his mouth and sends a spray of blood across the room. I feel the warm droplets splatter on my cheeks. The animal wants more, it wants to feast.

Just then a solid kick comes from my partner and Shane goes sailing off to the left of me. His body is launched off of mine. I turn on the carpet and I am on fours. I lunge forward and close the distance as Shane's body hits the ground. I pounce on him like a rabid dog looking to rip the throat out of his prey.

I am on top of him. I drive my right fist into his face. I feel the smashing of soft skin, bone, and slippery blood under my fist. I chamber back and drive my fist again. I grab a hand full of hair and pull his head forward as I drive another blow into his face. I hold his head steady with my left hand gripping his hair. I drive my fist again.

Blood sprays onto the wall next to me. His blood. I can see his face. A face that has blood pooling in the eye sockets. Lips swelling from the blows and brow split from the strikes. I drive my fist again.

I want to scream. I want roar in rage and fury. I want to pound his head into a soft pulp. I want to crush him into oblivion. I am engaged in nature's oldest lust, the lust for blood.

I have won! Fucker! I am high on combat lust and I have let my animal go.

Then, I hear a voice. It is low and calm. It doesn't command me; it just calls back the animal.

"He's had enough."

I look up to see my partner looking at me. His hand touches my shoulder and he gently pulls me up to my feet.

I stand there with blood streaked across my face and my chest heaving from the heavy exertion.

I stand there with the animal caged again and the adrenaline escaping my body.

I stand and I can feel the shakes coming on. I hold onto my inner will and hold it down. I keep the shakes from taking me over.

I open my hands, releasing the tension from my fists. My angry hands are opening and I look down at them.

I see hair fall from my left hand. Hair that has blood and tags of skin on the ends of it. Hair ripped free when I was delivering blows to his head. Shane's hair.

Rolling over my open hands I look at my palms. I see blood smeared inside, coating my skin with a sticky crimson paste. I see the clear disinfectant gel ooze out into my hands. A cop arriving on scene has seen my blood-covered hands, and he knows I have to get this shit off of me as fast as I can.

I float back into reality. I have locked up my animal and as the adrenaline wears off I can feel my mind and body return.

I rinse my hands and as I roll the gel about I can feel pain shoot through my right hand. I look at the swelling coming in and the odd blue-green color making its way through to the top of my hand. I know my hand is broken. I have seen and felt this injury before.

More and more cops come on scene. I can see some take away the injured woman, others secure Shane and drag him out to the awaiting ambulance.

Without a word I turn to my partner. I hold my hand close to me and I walk past him. Without exchanging words we talk to each other.

He pats me on the back and holds a door open for me. He tells me without words that I have done a good job. He tells me he knows I am hurt and he also tells me that everything will be okay. I walk up to an ambulance and look at a medic.

She is young and her uniform is shiny as if it was just out of the box.

"Hi there," I say in a calm tone. "I think I might have broken my hand."

"Oh!" she says in a startled tone as she gently takes my hand in hers. She is barely over five feet tall and I tower over her. She looks up and asks if I want to sit down. She asks in such a way that it is a direction, not a question.

I sit down as she gives me a bag of ice to put on my hand. Another medic walks over and I recognize him.

"Hey there, big guy! What did you do to yourself now?'

"Fucked my hand," I say as I raise my hand holding the ice pack around my broken hand. I can feel the throb of a broken bone. I have felt this before.

"It looks like you might have cut your face," the female medic says as she gingerly wipes the blood off of my face with a cold wet cloth.

"Nah, I think this is his blood." I point to the guy lying on the ground outside. Shane is just lying there in handcuffs as another medic checks him out.

She looks over. I can see that she is shocked at what she sees. She sees the damage that one human can do to another. Damage that she will one day look at without caring or emotion. She will get the eyes of an experienced medic. They too will be cold.

"How did you get his blood all over you?"

"Splatters from hitting him. I broke his nose and it was splatter after that."

"Splatter matters," says the seasoned medic. I have not heard that in a long time. A saying that I usually hear at bad car scenes when some idiot has forgotten to wear a seat belt. His body splattered across the road.

"Oh, nice," she says as she laughs an uncomfortable laugh.

"She is new." The senior medic pats her on the back and I can see that she is offended to still be called new. She has done hundreds of hours of class time, studying, and practical work. In her mind she is not new.

I calm the fire inside of her.

"Oh, really? I couldn't tell. You are way calmer than any new medic I ever met. You seem on the ball. Thanks for your help."

I see her smile at me. She probably knows I am full of shit but having me back her up has made her feel better.

She tells me how to care for my hand and she washes the last bit of the blood off my face. I walk over to my cruiser and take off my uniform top. I grab a biohazard bag out of the trunk of the car and slide the blood-soaked t-shirt into it.

Another cop comes over and tells me that he is going to seize that as evidence because of all of the glass and blood stuck in the back of the shirt. It also gives evidence to the fight that I will have to articulate in my report.

I am standing close to the second ambulance and I can hear Sherri tell the medics of what she has just been through. I wash my arms with water to clean off the blood that has soaked through my long-sleeved shirt.

245

I hear a tale of Shane driving her head through the wall. Stuttering as she speaks, she explains how she was thrown around and how Shane choked her into unconsciousness several times. Only to awake to Shane slapping her face or from cold water in the shower as he held her in it. She cries as she says how many times she had to scream for help. How long the police took to get there to help.

I look over at the computer screen in my police cruiser and see the license plate of the car that almost hit us in the intersection. The car that slowed us down coming to this call. I sit down and write out a summons for her traffic violation and ask a good friend on scene to go deliver this to the female driver that is registered to the plate.

I wipe a cold ice bag over my head and my partner walks up to me looking at my arms.

"Well, buddy, I think it is time to take you to the hospital. You are going to have a cast on the hand and you should have your arms looked at."

"My arms?" I roll them over in front of me to look at them. A huge raised bruise is forming where Shane landed his elbow. I see the swirling colors of blue, black, and red filling the puffy flesh. I squeeze my hands and I can feel the gathering blood. "Yeah, I guess so, eh? It doesn't look too healthy, does it?"

At the hospital I arrive with Shane and Sherri. Shane is having his blood drawn to see if he has any blood-born diseases. Sherri is being admitted for her injuries, and I am getting checked to have my hand set and a cast put on.

As I wait for the cast to harden I begin to shake. I am thinking of what I will have to endure if Shane is positive for a disease. I will have to go on to a chemical soup, which we call the "cocktail." It is like an intense chemotherapy session that goes for one month. If I start as soon as possible, I can be rid of the disease but I will be super sick.

Some cops who go onto the cocktail don't finish.

I shake and wait. I shake and build myself for the worst news. I imagine myself looking at the doctor and keeping a smile on my face as I tell him to hook me up.

I shake as the doctor walks in.

"Good news, constable, all tests come back negative for Shane."

I still shake and I smile.

"Thanks, that is great news."

I walk out of the hospital happy. I know that I will have to sit behind a desk for a month or so but taking everything that could have gone wrong, I am happy.

It has been three weeks now since that fight. I have a rock-hard cast on my right hand that has been decorated by cops drawing on it. It looks like a ghetto graffiti topic but I smile as I read what people have added.

Little taunts like "Bird Bones" and "Flower Hands" remind me that if your fellow cops do not poke fun at you they do not like you.

I stand in line at traffic court. I see the woman that I issued the traffic summons to for "failing to stop for emergency vehicle" too. I walk up to her.

"Hi there, I am Constable Smith. I issued you the ticket and I was wondering what your plans are today." I want to know if she is hear to plead down the fine, plead guilty, or to just plead not guilty. I want to know if I will be here for long.

She looks at me. She is angry. "This ticket is bullshit. I am not going to pay a $600 fine and get demerits on my license for this. It is not like I caused an accident."

"Yes, but you did stop me from attending a very important call. Your actions cost valuable seconds to a person in need."

"Oh, well, it was no time at all, I don't deserve this ticket." She waves the yellow piece of paper in front of me. She spins away and sits down. Her arms crossed like a child in a temper tantrum.

I look over to my right and I see Sherri. I asked her to attend today for the traffic session and when I told her why she was more than happy to come. To her those few seconds were a lifetime.

I sit beside her and I ask her how everything is going.

"Very good now. I have moved back home and my parents are really cool about it. I have signed up for school again and I am very excited to do that."

"And?" I say as I turn to look at her bruised face. Rings of green still flow around her eyes from the broken cheek she got from Shane. Her lips are still swollen and I can see bandages still on her arms.

"Oh fuck, are you kidding me? Shane and I are so done. That was the last time for me."

I smile at her and through her injuries and swelling I can see a beautiful and determined woman forming. It is as if since she decided to fight against Shane, she has gotten the self-confidence and self-worth she always lacked.

She smiles back. "Sorry you had to get hurt helping me." Her eyes fill with tears.

"Oh this?" I raise my cast and my blue-green forearms. "Nothing to it. I got some time off because of the hand. And, I am getting through some of the paperwork that I have been avoiding. It is all good."

She knows I am full of shit but it is the answer she wants to hear. She has enough to deal with anyway without hearing my sad story of how much I hate desk work.

Court is called into session and I am called onto the stand first to testify. When I am done the crown requests that Sherri be called as a next witness.

The crown had to push for Sherri to be able to testify as the judge did not see what this had to do for the offense that the accused had committed. The crown told the judge that it gives weight to the offense and that not allowing the victim to say what effect the seconds played in her life would be unjust. The judge allows it.

He wants to hear a good story like everyone else does. This tale will add some spice and interest into a day filled with boring testimonies.

Sherri walks up and swears on the Bible that what she is going to be telling is the truth, the whole truth, so help her in front of God. As she tells the story of how she was getting assaulted by her common-law boyfriend, the room sits stunned in silence.

The mass hears of her screaming for help as she was strangled, beaten, and thrown about. She tells the court how she felt she was going to die and that she just kept on praying that the police would come to help her.

Sherri looks over to me as she starts to break. She sees me smile at her and she takes a deep breath. Her voice calms and she tells the court that she feels that if the police showed up seconds sooner she would have not received some of the injuries that they see on her. If the police arrived seconds later she feels she would be dead right now.

I breath in deep because I feel like I am going to break. I breathe out slowly and look at Sherri, who is smiling at me. My waters calm as

I look at her newfound strength.

The judge concludes that the accused is guilty, and as the sentence is handed down, all eyes look at her. All the eyes rip her apart for her actions while driving a car without any care or attention to her surroundings.

All those eyes will remember this story the next time they hear the whine and wail of a police siren. Maybe some of them will stop.

The Futility of It All

The Futility of It All.

There are times when I get depressed with my job. It is not the gore, the death, or the sadness of seeing victims from the darker side of human behavior.

My depression is from the futility of my job.

Anyone who isn't a cop and wants to be one will tell you that they want to make changes. They want to help people and they want to catch bad guys and put them in jail.

A noble job.

When I was becoming a cop I thought the same things but now, I know the reality of it.

Policing is futile because we get no support for our work. Society has given the rights to the accused and taken them away from the victim.

I have been to sexual assault trials where I felt sorry for the victim because the defense lawyers make the victim feel like he or she wanted to be violated in such a manner. In court you become a victim a second time.

Even if there is a conviction, which is few and far between, the time in jail is so menial that it is a joke.

A prime example of this is auto theft. Most cars that are stolen today are older models because the newer model cars have some pretty good antitheft devices. So, the charge that will be laid for stealing a car would normally be "possession of stolen property under $5,000." So, if caught and convicted the average sentence that I have seen dished out is time served or a $500 fine. If the bad guy went to cells to be processed that time in cells would have been considered his sentence time. So he walks and is done. If he was released on an appearance notice and not brought to cells he will have to pay the fine.

That is if he is convicted.

If he has no prior criminal record he will go onto the Alternative

Measures Program and he will have to write an essay on why it is bad to commit crimes, serve some food at a homeless shelter for a few hours, and he is done. To top it all off he gets no criminal record even if he admits to the offense and does the alternative measures. Clean slate, society's one free "Fuck Up and No Punishment Card."

If I work hard my service never gives me a pat on the back. Unlike present-day companies and businesses, and I do refer to policing as a business.

I make this reference because I have a clientele base, I have a job description, our service has a budget, and our clients want to have the best service possible for the money they pay. So, in the grand scheme, we are a business!

Besides, my service always likes to fly the political flag that they are:

"A progressive police service. On the cutting forefront of public transparency."

What a load of shit that is. Sure when we fuck up they raise the wall and push outside and point fingers at us. Our management will leave us out to fry if words such as "excessive use of force," "discrimination," or "unlawfully placed" are used. They want to wash their hands of us so they will never support us in our actions. Heaven fucking forbid you have to shoot someone. You are fucked. I have seen it. Good cop shoots bad guy when bad guy tries to stab him with a knife. Good cop left out in the cold to fucking freeze because bad guy is black and a political hot potato.

In the corporate world where I came from before I came to the service, if you worked hard you were acknowledged. You would be praised for your ambition and drive. You would get bonuses and recognition. These are things that hard workers strive for. Hard workers love to do their job and take pride in it.

A little gratification goes a long way.

What happens when I work hard? What happens when I go the extra mile to service my clientele base?

I make more arrests. I have more contact with the public and bad guys.

I get more paperwork. I increase my complaints because I piss more bad guys off.

I have more court on my days off. I have more time in our Internal Affairs office explaining why I am giving bad guys a hard time.

I come in on my days off to catch up on my paperwork and files because my inspector is now on my ass. He only sees the complaints come across his desk and when he looks at my file he sees a lot of open cases. Our management will not look to see how many calls you take, how many arrests you do. They look at the stuff they can bitch at you about. Open files and citizen complaints.

So, I have no bonus to working hard on the street except that I have pride in my job and take my work ethic seriously.

There are some major dog fuckers out there that will slough your complaints and never get grief over it. The workers that fuck the dog will still get courses and be promoted because they spend their time kissing ass.

The guys in the Ivory Tower never like a street cop. We are dirty, rough, and driven. We have self-thought developed by years of street work and we stand up for what is right or wrong.

To them we are not "Yes Men" so they shit on us.

PRINCESS

PRINCESS

A call comes across our screen about a small disturbance at a liquor store in our zone. My partner and I scoop it up as we are only a few blocks out from the location.

As we pull up we see a limousine bus parked on the side of the road and several kids drinking out on the side walk. It looks like a grad night as the kids are all dressed well in black gowns and white pressed shirts.

A quick glance over tells me that they have been partying for a while as several of them are using the bus to steady themselves.

As we walk up to the liquor store to talk to the complainant about some people entering the store and smashing bottles while they were in it, we see the owner walk out towards us.

He has locked the store behind him and as we get closer he points to the busload of kids. In a rush of excited words he tells us how several of those kids entered his store and smashed the liquor bottles that they had just paid for. He tells us of the mess of spilled liquor and glass in his store and how angry he is about it.

Now our focus changes as he speaks and we watch the group of kids yell and holler as they congregate around the bus.

When the complainant finishes his story I tell him that we will look into it and my partner already starts to walk towards the bus.

When the kids see us walk towards them, they scuttle onto the bus, leaving only a few of the truly hammered outside to try to shuffle their way towards the door. As we walk closer to the bus I see a male about nineteen years of age stick his head out the window.

"Fuck you, fucking pigs! I will fucking kill you, fucking pigs!"

I shine my flashlight into his face. I want a good look at him and I want him to know that I have seen him. He cannot hide behind the mass of kids. He ducks quickly back into his seat.

"Hi there," I say to the uniformed bus driver. He looks at my partner and me with a look of worry.

He should be worried that his clients are out on the street drinking alcohol. His clients are in his bus drinking alcohol. All of which can land him some heavy fines.

"We need to go onto your bus. There are a few people we need to talk to about their behavior."

"Yeah, feel free." He motions to the door.

We are golden. We have permission from the driver to get on. I know it sounds stupid but it is better to have permission than to tell a lawyer that you just walked onto the bus. It gives us better grounds to function on even though, due to the threats, we could do it anyway.

As I walk onto the bus first the entire group hushes. I see a line of faces ranging from eighteen to twenty-one years of age. I see well-dressed youths sitting in leather-bound seats and a copious amount of open liquor bottles lining the cup holders.

I scan for the face I am looking for and I see him. He is looking down at the floor, his bleached blond hair tips tipping me off to his identity.

I point at him.

"You." He looks up. "You have to come outside, we have to talk about something."

He acts like I am talking about someone else. "What, me?"

"Yes, you. Get out of the bus now."

I draw my line into the sand and he knows he has to come outside. He gets up and starts to walk towards me. Just then a young girl stands up in front of me.

"You can't take him off the bus. It's my birthday"

I can smell the booze from her breath. Her eyes are glossy from drug use and slurred speech adds to her indignity. The layer of expensive clothing she wears does nothing to add to her false level of class.

"Yes, I can take him off the bus and your birthday has nothing to do with it." I put my hand on her shoulder and move her out of the way. I sit her back down and watch her. I have dealt with her kind before.

She is a "princess." She has lived her life in comfort and lack of discipline. She has thrown temper tantrums only to be met with coddling and compliance for her actions. She whines, yells, and screams and she gets what she wants. A spoiled child in an adult body.

As soon as I grab onto the male and slide past the princess she stands up again and grabs my shoulder.

"Fuck you! You cannot take him! It is my birthday!" She pulls my radio off and rips my shirt as she tries to turn me around. Her hands reach for my face and neck. I move my head back out of her range.

My partner is all over her. He grabs her and pulls her off of me. He pushes her towards the door so that we can get off this bus. It is a bad place for us. No room to maneuver. No room to move away from the angry crowd that is massing.

The male with me starts to scream at me. He yells for us to let her go. He yells again that we are fucking pigs and assholes. His yelling adds fuel to the crowd inside the bus.

I body-check him as he stands at the top of the stairs to the bus. I want him out of our way. I want him to stop firing up the crowd. I want off the bus, this cage filled with drug animals ready to turn into a mob.

He flies off of the stairs and onto the sidewalk outside. His body rolls and tumbles and he hits the rough concrete. I grab onto my partner's shoulder and guide him off the bus as the princess keeps swinging and clawing at my partner. She lands several blows to his face in her mad fury.

I look into the windows of the bus as we step down and I can see everyone standing up. I can see angry faces and I can hear shouting. I see a group of kids turn into a mob. I can feel the adrenaline kick in as I know this is going to be all bad.

My partner is still fighting with the princess as we get off. With my hand on his shoulder I keep pulling back away from the crowd. I want to get my back to something. I do not want this mob to surround me and my partner.

I see my partner land several blows to the girl's face in attempts to try to subdue her. These attacks just infuriate the crowd more. In the princess's drug-induced state, the strikes seem to be just shrugged off. The blows to her face seem to make her even more aggressive. Her hands are lashing out with intent to claw and gouge. She kicks, screams, and fights every attempt made to try to control her by my partner.

As soon as we get our backs to the cruiser I let go of my partner's shoulder and tell him this is where we stand.

I can see that he is still in deep combat with the little girl and I hope that he has heard me and doesn't try to move from this spot.

I turn my back to him as I step out in front to face the mob. I see a rolling mass of people coming towards us. In the distance I can see a local bar emptying out. The fight outside has attracted the majority of the crowd inside. They too are caught up in the mob.

Now as a couple of hundred people come bearing down on us I feel the dread of fear. My stomach tightens as I look at the crowd and feel lost. For a fleeting moment my mind goes into a black sphere of death. I see my death coming towards me at the hands of hundreds. I know that death is watching me today and if I do not perform he will take me tonight with a hundred angry fists.

My baton slides into my right hand and my pepper spray is grasped in my left just as the first few come close to me and my partner. A large male about twenty-one years of age with the look of a high school football player closes in.

My world slows down. I am getting filled with my fix. My fight-or-flight chemical, and flight is not an option anymore. I want to fight. I want to crush. I want to damage anyone who will come close enough to try to hurt me or my partner.

I slam the butt end of my baton into the shoulder of the jock football player. I can feel his collarbone snap and pop as all my energy is focused on the baton base. I see his face wince and his body starts to give way to my downward momentum. I reel my right hand back and drive the base of my weapon into his face. I see his cheek split and his head snap back.

His hands reach up and grab his broken face. He turns his back in panic and runs through the crowd. He is just running, he wants to get away. His fix is telling him to run. Run far away and then hide because his brain tells him he is hurt.

A second male tries to close in on my left but he is met with a face full of pepper spray. He screams and covers his eyes. He also turns and runs in sheer panic. He is blind and in serious pain from the chemical agent.

The massive wave falls back out of my range. The damage they have seen from the first two that fell has held back the front line of the mob. But they are still angry, still shouting. Their faces are filled with hate and the air is filled with threats of death.

I can see out of the corner of my eye that my partner is still fighting with the girl. When I see that she lands a blow to his groin, which breaks his hold on her, I give a full shot of pepper spray into her face. Her screams fill the air. She covers her face with her hands and she is in full panic. She cannot see, she cannot see what she wants to kick. She has lost her targeting systems and she knows that she is in for a whole lot of trouble.

The crowd surges forward again. A sea of bodies, and this time I do not worry about my fate. I do not feel dread. I am in the heart of combat. I am in a world that I dream of when I sleep. I am in a place that I train to be in. I feel confident, almost euphoric. Time slows for me even more. My world is filled with an invisible water that everyone is moving through. Slow movements, long groans instead of audio voices.

I slam the point of my baton into the ribs of my next attacker. He buckles like he has been pierced by the point of a saber. I jerk up my knee and hammer it into his face. His body snaps back into the mass behind him. My rage builds, I am entering a special place. A place where time slows even more and my inner beast rises. I become overtaken by this animal and it wants to crush, pummel, and hammer everything. I am filled with blood lust, lust for combat and destruction.

The next thing I see is a beer bottle flying through the air towards my head. I move to the side as it sails past me. Sailing by my head by a few inches. As its twirling vortex passes me I can see the beer fly out of the open top. Globs of brown liquid slowly cascade out, frothing out into the air.

I instantly focus on the next person attempting to break the shield that I have created by standing between my partner and the masses.

He lunges at me and I fill his face full of my chemical agent. The same effect, he recoils back because of pain and suffering.

A female runs at me and I chamber my arm up to strike her.

"What the fuck are you going to do? Fucking hit me?" I hear her words as she keeps coming in closer.

I strike her to the center chest with my fist holding the baton. I hit her hard, as hard as I would have hit a man. Right now she is a target, a person wanting to do me harm. I will lash out at her as hard as I would lash out at anyone else.

My heavy fist crumples her. I can see her dress wrap around her as her body is sent backwards. She lands on her back and she rolls around on the ground, grasping her chest as she tries to get air into her lungs. I see hands reach through the crowd as she is dragged up and is engulfed into the fluid mob of people.

More come forward and I strike hard and fast. I drive people down to the ground. I smash bodies with my baton and I fill eyes with my burning pepper spray. I let loose of myself as the mass keeps coming in. More and more targets to hit, to crush. More and more people are closing in.

My combat lust grows and I feel even more vicious. I have let my beast go into the combat and I am loving it. If I would die right here, right now fighting, I would go to wherever that place that is meant for me to be happy. This is the way I want to live. This is the way I want to die.

I step back only to feel my partner's back as he is putting handcuffs on the still ferocious girl. I know this is as far back as I can go. I now stand at the edge of the cliff. I plant my feet hard as another wave moves in. I smash them, crush them, and spray them. They are just pulled back into the crowd, only to be replaced by others. I am fighting in an environment filled with limitless targets. I lash out hitting and crushing. I want them to pile up at my feet, I want to stack them broken up for all to see.

I can hear the sirens, the screech of tires. I can see the red-and-blue reflection of police lights on buildings. The troops are here. A world of hurt is coming to the crowd now as cops from all over the city are rolling in. My partner had called for backup when the crowd first surged in.

I drop my baton into another person's ribs and feel my hand touch his flesh. The four inches of protruding baton have made its way into his body and his face tells all. I can see pain and fear flash in his eyes. I see spit fly from his mouth as the air is forced from his lungs. His body wraps and contorts to try to get the foreign object out of him.

I see the crowd break and I can see fear flow through the once angry mass. Blue uniforms are flooding in, batons are swinging. Like a reaper's scythe, a path is cleared through the crowd. I catch a glimpse of another beer bottle smashed off the windshield of our cruiser. I follow its path back; I can see a male hammered to the ground from enraged uniforms.

I strike at my last target. My baton hits solidly into the quad of a large fat guy still filled with rage and mob mentality. I feel his soft fleshy leg get pinched between his femur and the base of my metal baton. He falls immediately and pulls his cramping leg close into his chest. I lash out with my boot, driving the tip of it into his face. I see blood pour from his face onto the black asphalt. His eyes open and blank as the blow has rendered him unconscious.

I want to hit him again and again. I want the streets to be filled with these people's blood. My beast demands it. It tries to move from fighting to punishing, but I hold the leash tight. I do not want to let go of the animal. I respect its ability to fight but I fear its ability to destroy.

"Fuck you, not so fucking tough, are you?!" my rage screams out inside of my head.

I look for others to hit, for someone else to rush in. But, the crowd is breaking. People flee as more cops flood the area. I see faces with fear in their eyes as the sunfire light from our police helicopter illuminates the area. I can taste pepper spray in the air and I can feel the chemicals sting my face as it floats past me.

I see a confusing medley of red-and-blue car strobe lights. I can feel the delirium of the crowd as they move from a killing mass to a fleeing body.

I see people getting hammered everywhere. I see strong hard faces in the crowd as they grab onto and arrest all those who do not flee from the area.

I want to lash out and crush. I want blood, my inner animal wants to feed. I pull hard on my inner demon. I reel it in and lock it up again. I can feel it smashing against its cage, straining the locks that bind it. It wants out. It smashes on the cage until it tires and sleeps again.

I look over to my partner as he pushes the girl into the car. I see his face is reddening on the side from her blow. His eyes are filled with frustration and anger.

"What the fuck is that bitch's issue?! Fucking bitch!" he screams as we stand there amidst the streets filled with the remains of combat.

I look around and I see a battle scene that would be shown only in the movies. There are people lined against the walls in handcuffs. People are lying on the ground holding their faces and crying from the pain of pepper spray. I see guys sitting on curbs with blood soaking their heads and shirts. I see people getting carted off in paddy wagons.

I walk up to my sergeant, who is trying to establish control and order to the chaotic scene.

"Sir, those people there as well as that girl over by the ambulance all need to be arrested and charged for assault P/O [Police Officer]. They were the ones that rushed me. They are pretty well the most active of the crowd."

"Okay, you all right, Smith?" he asks me.

I don't know if I am okay. I am still pumped on adrenaline. I am still high on combat. I just look at him and shrug my shoulders. "I guess so, nothing's bleeding or broken."

I feel the rush leave and I start to get the shakes. I make my way from my sergeant as fast as I can. I do not want to show signs of my shakes. I do not want to seem affected or weak.

I move to our cruiser and sit down. I act like I am taking notes but I am not. I cannot, my hands shake too much.

Later on, after the carnage is done I will look at the dispatch printout. I will see that from the time that my partner asked for backup, till the time that the first car was out, it was only two minutes. I feel like I was fighting for three hours.

I will also find out that I cross-contaminated one other cop while I was spraying a guy. He ended up getting a short blast to his face as the guy in front of him moved in the last second. As he fills out his part of the paperwork his right eye will be red and hot. I saw him fighting with the crowd. He was fighting hard even though he was contaminated with my pepper spray.

He worked through it and kept fighting. Not for himself, because he could have left the scene to decontaminate. He was fighting for me and my partner. Fighting and suffering through pain the same way I would for him.

When I finally get home I fall into my bed. I am exhausted and spent. I feel hollow and empty inside. I will sleep for nearly ten hours. But those ten hours are not filled with darkness. I dream of the occurrence over and over again in my mind. I live the moment dozens of times, each time with different endings. My death, my partner's death. The death of people around me. I see myself through the mob's eyes as I am overwhelmed and forced down under their sheer mass. I see myself die as hundreds of feet kick and trample me. I see my uniform get ripped from my body as my head is smashed relentlessly against the pavement.

I call these dreams, work dreams. I sleep in a fit of low cries and body jerks. I live the fight over and over again. My mind is sorting out what happened and what could have happened.

Ten hours later I awake and make my way downstairs. I see my wife enjoying the weekend newspaper. She looks at me as I pour a cup of coffee. As the black surface becomes still I am reminded of the wet asphalt beneath my feet. The asphalt that had blood roll onto it from the face of the fat guy I knocked unconscious.

"Busy night, babe?" she says as her eyes leave the paper and make their way over to me.

"Yeah, it was pretty crazy."

"I guessed it. You were moving all night in your sleep. Everything okay?"

"Yeah, just work dreams." I look away from her. I do not want her to see my eyes. I do not want her to see deep into me and know that I felt the fear of death. I still have some sorting out to do before I talk to her about this.

I look into my coffee cup and see its black familiar surface.

A blood red smear flows across the top as my eyes glaze over. My mind travels back to the night before.

GROWING PAIN

If you ever hear a cop tell you that the job he or she does has not changed them, they are lying.

We all change through time. Since most of our self-identity is created by our career, to say that policing has not changed you is a false statement.

When people look at you they will associate you with your career.

Oh, that's Bob, he is an accountant. That is Jim, he is a manager, and that is John, he is a cop.

With each career comes a prefabricated image of what the person looks like even though you have never met them, talked to them, or know them personally.

So, being a cop has an image that goes with it. Most people think that we are boozing party animals that are tough, rough, and cold.

Most people that meet me for the first time and find out what I do for a living instantly assume that I am a mean, hard mother fucker. They do not want to see the side of me that is not associated to the image that television has made for police officers.

Don't get me wrong; I am a mean fucker on the street but only to the bad guys. When it comes to the civilian population I smile, I laugh, and I am very tolerant of poor behavior.

I always have to tell myself that the person I am dealing with right at this moment might be a really nice guy when he is sober. Maybe he has had a shitty day and he is way too drunk.

I have to remind myself to have patience.

I try to keep myself level-headed so I work hard at having normal friends. You know, the manager, the accountant, and the mechanic, they are normal friends. Cops, even though they may understand the special world I live in, it will not help me mentally. If I hang out with them the whole world becomes assholes.

Why? Because all we are going to talk about are the assholes we deal with.

Even with all of the work that I put into trying to keep myself whole, there are things and times that I cannot control. Occurrences that make me wonder how much of myself I have lost.

How much of the old me has been replaced by the new knowledge I have gained working this career?

How much of the old me has changed since I have started this job?

How tainted have I become, how mentally fucked has my sense of right and wrong become?

What a week it has been at work. We have had a rash of shootings in our city. I have humped these calls for service that lead to long hours of overtime. The gangs here are getting more and more brazen. Drive-by shootings, gunfights on our main entertainment street, and broad-daylight executions are becoming commonplace.

It is a matter of time before a civilian is shot and killed in these events and that thought bothers me. I want to catch these gang-banging fucks and have my chance to deal with them. I pray they try to kill me, that the bad guys push the envelope enough that I can teach them who the meanest dog on the block is.

Day shifts pound the sense just as hard as the night shifts, the city is big enough that one cannot say the days are slower any more. It is busy twenty-four/seven now. Get into your car and hump calls, that is the motto now.

My first shift started with a guy jumping out in front of a car to kill himself. Well, it did not work all that well and he was all twisted up and broken when I got to him. Who knows what or why but after he was rolled under the car he must have realized that dying was not a good option.

Now he lay there in the street with the flesh from his arms rubbed to the bone, legs that showed no skin only bones and tendons, and half of his skull ripped open, he begged me to help him. He pleaded with God to save him and cried to his mother.

I just knelt there beside him and lied to him.

I told him that everything was going to be all right and that he did not look all that bad. I lied to him as dark purple blood oozed out of his head. I lied to him as I saw half of his brain exposed to the cool night air.

As the ambulance siren came into earshot I saw his eyes widen and death creep in. I saw his breath roll out into the cold night.

My second shift was taken up by a drunk driver who was an absolute pain in the ass to deal with. I wasted half of my shift getting through the paperwork knowing that our court system will let him off with the standard bullshit fines. No real damage for his stupidity but a whole lot of paperwork for me.

The next shift I had to fight with some twenty-year-old chick that was high on meth. She was in a world of paranoia and aggression. When we showed up she just ran at our cruiser and started to swing at anything she could. She could not fight worth a shit but since her body was filled with pain-numbing chemicals, a lot of damage had to be done to subdue her.

Even once she was in cuffs she still bit her tongue, smashed her head off of the car's inner cage, and tried to bite us if we got close.

I feel hurt and scarred inside from hurting her, my father's voice echoes in my mind:

"You must never hurt a woman. They are precious, fragile gifts."

I had no choice.

I know that when she wakes up in the morning, her pounding headache, her arms slung tight from dislocated shoulders, and her bruised body will remind her, she is killing herself with her drug use.

But I also have no false illusions; I know that I will see her next week on the streets strapped to a glass pipe.

The last shift I had to stuff my chunk into a guy's face because he was contemplating reaching for a knife on the table to kill him or me with. I could see it in his eyes, the sketchy targeting of the knife as his eyes looked at the blade, then me.

He chickened out; I never had to put my finger on the trigger. I was sure that he would have to be shot.

I had it all planned out. If he reached for the knife I would drive two .40-caliber rounds into his chest. If he did not stop I would drive two more rounds into his body until he was filled with enough trauma that he would stop.

I was sure he was going to do it. I was just waiting for him to make his decision.

These were just the apex points of my shifts. The rest of the noninjury accidents, the lost property, the standard "he said, she said" domestic abuse calls, and the property break and enters fall into a thick fog of monotony.

All this for a week's worth of day shifts.

Now I am done my shifts and I am exhausted. I have hit the wall and all I want to do is crawl home and sleep. Put my head down beside my wife, hold her, and sleep.

I want to lock the front door behind me and have my dog run around in an excited frenzy as his high-pitched shepherd whine fills the front entrance of my home.

I want to pick up my favorite book and read. Read until I fall asleep.

All I want are the simple things in life.

I pull into my driveway and shut off the engine of my car. I sit there and stare at my gym bag in the passenger seat.

Do I leave it and get it later?

It looks so heavy, I am so tired.

I know that if I leave it here I will not come back out to get it. I know that the clothes inside the red nylon bag need washing.

I pick up the bag and it feels like I have packed lead into it.

I slowly step up to my home. I see the front door and I take slow-paced steps up the front concrete walk.

As I put my key into the front lock, I can see my dog's shadow filtering through the stained-glass window that frames the metal main door. He makes me smile and I start to feel awake again.

I barely get in the front door and I am forced by my dog to go through a ritual of scratching and belly rubbing. He spins in circles as his tail crashes into the antique table that I slide my keys and wallet onto.

Long hard steps are taken to get me to my bedroom.

A few digital keys ring out as I press in the combination to my gun lockbox. When the lid pops open I slide my heavy .45-caliber personal firearm out of its hard plastic concealable side holster.

My hand wraps over the top of the cold metal slide as I make the weapon safe for storage. Pulling back fast on the polished metal top rail I eject the loaded round out of the gun's chamber.

A large brass-coated hollow point round is ejected into my hand. I can feel the dead weight of the bullet as it rests in my fleshy palm.

I never go out of my home without a weapon, not since I have started this job. I have seen way too many victims, I do not want to be one because I lack the tools to protect myself or others.

A hollow click slides across my empty bedroom as the gun locker is closed.

My clothes unceremoniously fall to the floor as I get ready to crawl into my bed. I am exhausted. It takes only a few seconds for me to fall into a deep sleep, my last thoughts being of my wife, how I wished she was not on evening shifts.

How I wish she could be here with me as I slip into the black oblivion of exhaustion.

Soft bedsheets wrap around my legs as I imagine her next to me.

Morning has come too fast for me. I still ache as I stretch my arms over my head.

I stagger out of the blacked-out room, making my way past our bed to the door like a blind man. I walk slowly and cautiously through the darkness, as quietly as I can, because I know my wife will be sleeping for a few more hours.

It is early Saturday morning and I know that my lovely wife will not be awakening until at least two or three in the afternoon.

I smile to myself. I remember my wife creeping into our bedroom the same way late last night after a busy night shift for her.

The smell of coffee fills the kitchen as I start my daily morning ritual. The bittersweet smell of rich earth awakens me far before I drink the hot caffeine-infused fluid.

With a full cup of hot black coffee in my favorite mug, I sit down at our dark cappuccino-colored kitchen table.

I watch the blue screen of my computer flash as I start it up. I start surfing for movie times at a local theater. I figure that I will go see a movie while she sleeps, I want to keep the house quiet and empty.

In a matter of minutes I have my day planned out. A movie will fill my time and give me some distraction to help me decompress; I still feel the nagging effects of work lingering in me.

The heightened vigilance that sits inside of me will not calm down today.

I feel anxious.

As my car's engine starts up I light a small cigar. I still feel tight, wound up. I light the dark blend of tobacco leaves in hopes that it will draw out the demons inside of me.

I just can't put my finger on it. I cannot find the reason why I feel so wound up. I am on edge, grumpy, tired, and anxious all at once.

I tell myself to relax. I tell myself that a movie will be good for me. It will get me out, give me a chance to detach from the feelings inside of me. It will be healthy for me.

My cigar is almost done as I walk across the parking lot towards the theater. Pulling a final few draws of hot bitter smoke into my mouth I drop the last bit of the earthen roll into a storm drain.

The theater doors ahead of me are filled with people. Fuck, I did not expect all of these people here. Not really what I wanted.

Should I go back home?

Should I just go see this movie?

A debate runs through my head. The end result is that I have to go see this movie, after all am I going to let a crowd of people deter me? Am I afraid of a crowd of people?

The theater is huge. It is packed with people from different lifestyles. The seats are filled with people eating popcorn and chocolate bars.

People are laughing and joking with each other.

Smiles are on everyone's faces, all but mine. I cannot shut off what I do at work. I am "Heat Scoring."

I am watching hands, remembering what people are wearing, where they are sitting.

I see a bulge under a shirt. Gun? Knife?

Nope, Blackberry.

I can feel my heart rate increase.

Too many people, I cannot keep track. I look at the emergency exit. How fast can I get out if shit goes wrong here?

I hear more laughing, I watch more hands. I try to remember more faces.

My heart rate raises more.

I want to fight. I want to run. I feel my animal inside getting primed for combat. I do not know what is going on with me. My heart rate jacks even more.

A voice rings in my ears. "Do you want to leave? You can leave."

"No, I will be fine." I don't want to run away from this feeling. I don't want to give into this anxiety. I don't want to give in, I cannot give in. If I lose this battle now I will have to fight harder if it happens again. It will happen again if I lose it.

I concentrate. I focus on my breathing. I slow things down. Emotions can be controlled. I can control this. I cannot let it beat me. My heart pounds harder.

I want out. I want to run away from this crowd of people. I can smell them, I can feel their warmth. I want out right fucking now.

I fight the urge. I know it is not a good emotion. I fight it. I can hear my beast banging on my cage. It wants out; I can feel it banging in my chest. It has taken the place of my pounding heart.

I relax, I give up the fight. I focus on my breathing. I focus on calm, not fighting. I calm my beast, I cannot shake its rage, wondering why it is so mad.

The pounding slows. The closing feeling of people slides away and I can feel my waters inside smooth out. I breathe deeper, my heart slows, and I am calm again.

I finish sitting in the theater but still to this day I do not remember what the movie was about. I also have not bothered to rent it.

An anxiety attack afflicted me. I know it, but I really do not want to accept it.

I have read a lot of books on police stress, post-traumatic stress symptoms, and combat-induced stressors. I have used them to work with fellow co-workers through times that they did not understand.

I have explained to them that when we get a huge adrenaline dump we may lose our hearing; we may experience time distortion or tunnel vision. Our sense of smell may be acute, our sense of vision may be completely refined. Our memories of that combat may be triggered by sounds or smells in the future. Very common, very normal stress-induced side effects.

But now I have had an anxiety attack. I have to understand that this is normal also. I have to realize that I need to talk to someone to know this demon better.

On the police force, though, talking to a psychiatrist is seen as weak. It is viewed that you may be a threat to your fellow officer's safety because you are unstable.

In an ironic way, our Tactical guys have to see "Dr. Rubber" every two months. They have to sit there and tell her how they feel. Most of the guys I talk to in the TAC unit tell me it is good for them. It allows them the chance to learn more about how and why they are reacting to the stress they get.

Any TAC guy will also tell you the highest stress on the job is being a street cop. You get shit on from all angles, you never know exactly what you are getting yourself into, and when shit goes wrong, it goes wrong fast.

But as street guys we are not mandated to talk to Dr. Rubber. In fact it is looked upon badly if you mention that you want to talk, need to talk, or have talked to Dr. Rubber.

I look into myself and see that a moment with Dr. Rubber will be good for me.

I secretly book an appointment with her and I am very nervous when I first meet her. I do not want her to think I am a quack, that I cannot hack the street.

She says the opposite. She is happy that I have enough courage to come see her and tell her about what happened to me at the theater. She goes on explaining how such reactions are normal and can be handled. The way that I worked through it was good. It allowed me to work past it. I hear that a long full week of shit can build inside and since I did not go through my ritual decompression I still had all that crap inside of me.

When I leave I feel much better. I have learned something about myself. I have fought an inner battle and won. I have looked at a personal fear and challenged it.

As I walk down the sidewalk to my car, I am Heat Checking. I am looking for familiar faces, bulges in pockets and shirts.

I walk and I feel good, I am a soldier, and I battle on the streets. I will be on alert when I am not in my own home. I have changed from innocent to wise. I have moved from sleeping to the conscious. I am happy where I am going. I am happy with my changes.

If anyone says that policing has not changed them they are lying.

OPEN HEART SURGERY

"1424 can you respond to a 911 call at 44 Apple Hill Lane? We have a woman on the open line that is giving us sparse information about her husband getting stabbed. EMS is en route but will not enter until you have cleared the residence."

I accept the call and fire up the siren. My partner reads off any more information that is coming in over the CAD. My foot edges the throttle to the floor and we soar through the streets. I break hard at intersections and crawl through them making sure I look at all the drivers. Even if I have the right of way I slow for the intersections.

I cannot help if I get into an accident, in fact I will slow shit down if I do. Units will have to attend my site and another car will have to go and attend the original call.

I would rather waste a few seconds looking for unaware drivers, drivers with HUA or "Head Up Ass," than get into an accident.

It is a never-ending rocking of the car. Hard and fast on the straightaway and then the front end of my cruiser will drip to the earth as I threshhold break. It is a ballet played out until we arrive on scene.

I park one house away and we walk up to the house on foot. I scan with my eyes, listen with my ears, and open all of my other senses for any clues to what might have happened. The door is open but not damaged, the concrete sidewalk is clean and free of blood.

I yell:

"City Police!"

My partner and I go in. As soon as the open door is pushed open I can see a kitchen to my right, the living room immediately to my left, and a long hallway right in front of me. My eyes fix immediately on the hallway. I see a guy propped up on the wall with a knife in his hand.

I draw my sidearm.

I yell again.

"Police! Don't fucking move!"

My partner rushes past me then dips to the right. His gun is drawn and he is yelling at someone in the kitchen.

I do not look over as I hear him challenge someone else. I have a job to do.

"Drop the knife! Drop the knife!" My sights from my gun are leveling on his chest. I can see blood covering his shirt. I can see blood on the walls behind him. I see globs of blood on his bare feet.

Fresh, hot sticky blood. Deep red and dripping.

I slow my breathing down. Inside I have made a plan that if he takes one step forward I will drop this fucker. I will dump round after round of hot metal with an expanding lead core into his chest. I will fire until he is dropped. I am ready. I slow my breathing down. I am ready to fire.

He looks at me with sullen and spent eyes. I can see the smear of blood across his face. I see his right eye is watering from the blood that has entered it. I can see his eyelids dropping. His face is turning pale and it looks like he is getting ready to pass out.

I see the knife slip from his bloody hands and he slowly starts to fall forward. His hands are down to his side and his large body just topples over like a great redwood tree being cut down. His face smashes into the carpet.

I see his body in slow motion, a slow bounce as his full dead weight strikes the carpet. I start to close in on him, keeping my gun high and ready. As I get up to him I scan the room behind him but because he is in the way I cannot reach him to ensure that there isn't anyone else in the other rooms. I can hear more cops come in behind me.

"The rooms in front of me are not cleared. The basement is not cleared. I have one down here and he needs EMS."

I keep track of my breathing. I keep it slow and steady. I do not want the fix, I do not need it to flood me right now.

Cops blast past me stepping over the body and leaving footprints of blood on the carpet behind the fallen male. The soles of their boots stamped with blood.

I can hear several other officers open the basement door and make their way down into the unknown.

"Clear!"

"Basement is clear!"

271

"Send in EMS!"

Shouts fly through the air as I holster my gun and slide on my blue rubber gloves. I grab the fallen male's arms and slide the lifeless limbs behind his back. My handcuffs go on and I roll him onto his side to check for injuries and look for other weapons besides the knife he discarded.

My hands travel down the front of his chest and I can feel open ribs and raw meat under his shirt. I lift up his blood-soaked shirt to see a huge gash in the center of his chest. It is square between his nipples and runs down for about three to four inches.

His body jerks slightly as he rolls into consciousness. His movement causes the wound to open even more and a glob of chunky blood spills onto the floor.

He gasps and blood spurts from his mouth. A red line trickles to the floor. I can see death taking hold of him.

"Tell my mom I love her," he gasps, again sending small specks of blood onto the painted walls in the hallway.

I grab his t-shirt and rip it off.

"You're gunna be all right. Just fucking hold on. EMS is on the way." I wrap his shirt in a ball and it press hard on his gaping chest wound. I can feel the warmth of his blood soak through the shirt in an instant. I feel his warm blood pool around my fingers. I can feel his life slipping away from him.

He groans as I apply pressure.

"I have to push hard, buddy. I want to stop the heavy bleeding you got going on."

Little do I know that there is no way I can stop the bleeding. His heart is cut in half. The knife went deep and cut his heart wide open. With every pump of his mangled heart, blood fills his chest cavity. He is bleeding out. There is nothing I can do to stop his death.

I can see his eyes grow faint. I can see that he is slipping into the darkness.

"Tell my mom, tell her." More blood flows from his mouth.

EMS runs into the room and as soon as they see me they know shit is bad. They set up equipment and tell me not to release the pressure until they are ready.

"Okay, let us have a look." One medic motions for me to move my hands and the wad of clothing away.

I let go of my pressure and pull back the rolled-up shirt.

"Oh, fuck!" shouts a medic as a stream of blood pumps out of the guy's chest. It has built up pressure under my compression of the wound. I see a thick stream of blood squirt across the wall ahead of me. It looks like someone took a hose filled with red paint and sprayed the wall with it.

The open wound in his chest pumps out blood under pressure every time his heart beats.

I can smell the stench of human blood. The earthen salty smell that human blood has to it.

He groans again and I see his legs and feet start to shake. I see the effects of death slipping into him.

"Fuck me, he is fucking coding here!"

I get pushed to the side as two other medics scramble in. I can see drugs getting administered, vital signs being read, and wound assessments getting done.

Information is sent over the radio and the fallen male is unceremoniously thrown onto the gurney. I follow the medics out to the ambulance. I watch with awe as the orchestra of the well-tuned medics is played. One medic pumps air into the man's lungs, the other places an IV into his arm, while the third medic pushes the gurney along. Short terms are shouted back and forth. Blood pressure, respiratory counts, pulse count, the list goes on.

Once we get into the ambulance I quickly sit on the bench out of the way of the medics.

"Here! Rip strips of tape about twelve inches long and tack them to the bar on the ceiling." A medic points up to a shiny chrome bar that is used to hold on to and hang medical supplies.

In a fury I rip pieces of tape off and they are scooped up as fast as I can rip them. I see clear rubber tubing taped to his blood-soaked arm. I see the tape being applied to hold down IV tubes, heart monitoring devices, and a vast array of other items.

The medics are working frantically to keep this guy alive. Needle after needle is requested and administered. Huge pieces of gauze are held over the wound, only to turn red as soon as they touch the male's skin.

Blood flies across the ambulances as the male goes into a rage of convulsions. He groans and moans. His hands want to reach for the hole in his chest. He is in the last throes of his life.

His body relaxes. Peace has met with him. Death has come and taken him. His body slumps and feet fold off to the side. I hear the air flow from his mouth in a rushing low roar.

The ambulance is suddenly filled with medics moving from CPR to the defibrillator. More drugs are pumped into the male as they try to bring him back from death.

"Clear!" yells a medic as I can hear the defibrillator squelch out the voice-automated warning. Large plastic pads have been stuck onto the male's chest. The medic hits the button to engage the machine; his body moves slightly from the electrical jolt.

With the blast of electricity meant to revive the heart, comes a pulse of blood that pounds out of his chest. Large globs of red chunky blood flop out and roll across his bare chest and splash onto the floor.

The medics no longer try the defibrillator. They can tell that there is no longer a need to try to help the man in the ambulance.

We all sit in silence. We all stare at the mess in front of us. Blood flows freely onto the gurney. Pooling under his back and by his arms. Like a river it finds a new path to follow and flows onto the floor. The pool of blood there is stopped by all of the clothes, gauze, and other medical supplies lying around.

I can smell the blood. The earthen salt smell lingers in my nose.

I look up at the medics, who are covered in sweat. They are just staring at the guy who has just died in their care. They did all they could but I know they wish there was more they could do.

"It was his time. No matter what you did it was just his time," I say to the medics, who still stare.

As if awakened from a daydream they both look at me. A small nod is given and they slowly move to other tasks. They call the hospital to let them know that they will only be arriving to deliver the body to the Coroner's room.

I let them know that this ambulance is off-limits soon as it will be seized as evidence, an exhibit to be documented and photographed.

They radio in to let the hospital know. They request another unit come by and pick them up.

We all step out of the ambulance and I let my sergeant know what has happened. I remove my blue latex gloves, which have red streaks of drying blood covering them.

My hands feel better now that they are in the cool air. They feel better now that they are not stuck in latex covered with someone else's blood. I like the feeling of cool air against my bare skin. I slowly forget the warm flow of blood covering my hands.

Yellow police tape goes up around the house and ambulance. The sight of the police line attracts people to walk by and stare. Their morbid curiosity drives them to stand as close to the line as they can before we tell them to back up.

I have always wondered what they would do if we just let them see the death. Let them see how we become a lump of cooling meat when we die. Let them see how blood turns purple and sticky when it cools and coagulates.

If the curious smelled death and blood, would they still gather in such annoying packs to see someone else's suffering?

I turn my back to the crowd that is gathering and walk back inside the house. I walk into the living room to see cops doing a variety of tasks.

One is logging who is coming in and out of the house, what they are doing, and what time they leave.

"Hey, Smith. How's shit?" he asks.

"It's okay, fucked up night, eh?" I say as I look at a large fish tank against the wall near me.

"Yeah, I heard you almost had to drop the fucker with the knife."

"Almost, pretty fucking close actually. If he had not started to bleed out and drop the knife I would have shot him. Fuck, what a night for the sorry fucker. Stabbed in the chest and then shot by the police." I reach over and grab a can of fish food. The large gold fish in the tank waddle their way to the top and I can hear their mouths sucking at the top of the water. I smile as I sprinkle food over the top of the water. The fish feast as if they have never been fed before.

"Oh nice, Smith. Let's see, notes of crime scene; 2035 hours, Constable Smith feeds fish." He laughs as he comes over to watch the fish eat also. "Man, those are some big fucking fish."

"Yeah, bet they have a story to tell, eh? They could at least tell me what the fuck happened here."

"Oh shit. No one told you? The bitch covered in blood admitted that she stabbed the guy. It is her husband and they were up all night drinking and getting high. They had a big fight and when he went to sleep she walked in and drove the fucking knife into his chest."

"No shit."

"No shit. She then called the cops, saying someone broke in and stabbed her husband in a lame-ass attempt to try to cover up her stupid move."

"Fuck me, so that poor bastard went to bed only to awake to a knife in his chest. Fuck, what a way to die." I feel bad for the guy. I really did not care before because I thought he had something to do with the break-in. But now he is a victim of a murderer.

I brush it off. I did not know him. To me he is just a lump of cooling meat.

I look back into the fish tank. I wonder to myself who will feed them when we leave. Who will take care of the fish when their providers are either dead or in jail? The fish are helpless without someone taking care of them. They are prisoners, trapped in their watery cell. Helpless.

I close the lid to the tank and shut off the light. I walk away towards my car to write my notes for the event.

I am tired and getting hungry. I still wonder who will take care of the fish.

JUST ANOTHER DAY

His name is Cory.

He is twenty-eight years old and he was released from prison ten days ago. He served a four-and-a-half-year sentence for an armed robbery beef that went bad.

Cory ended up stabbing the clerk. The clerk was not moving fast enough for Cory and he stabbed the guy. He did not kill the clerk but it was Cory's forty-first conviction, most of which focus around violence. So, Cory got some hard time, if you want to call it that.

Cory has a heavy crack cocaine addiction and feeds it by committing crime.

He feeds it every time he gets released from prison.

He was released on parole two years ago and was Unlawfully at Large thirty days after his release. He failed to contact the parole board on a weekly basis, his only conditions for his release.

Within two months Cory had committed a slew of other crimes and was back in jail

This happened again last year when Cory was again released on parole. Twenty-five days after his second release Cory was again arrested by police and brought back to serve his original six-and-a-half-year sentence.

That is when Cory and I first met. My partner and I scooped him up on a warrant for his breach of parole at that time. Cory was full of shit and lied his ass off to us to try to avoid getting caught. He stuck to his guns about the name he was giving us but we found flaws in his story.

It took some time but we ended up finding out who Cory was when he went for fingerprinting.

I had conducted a search of Cory's pocket, as I saw what "appeared to be a spike in his left pocket." It was actually a crack pipe but you have to word it so that you can conduct a search for "Officer Safety

Reasons." For some stupid reason I cannot search a guy's pocket if I tell the judge that I was looking for drugs or drug paraphernalia.

So, to play the game I saw a spike and heaven behold it was actually a crack pipe. So I busted Cory on a cheesy crack pipe but I had my grounds for fingerprinting. So he got nabbed for his warrant.

Cory talked shit on the way down and told us over and over again that he was a bad mother fucker. He told us he was not afraid of jail time.

I told him that if I deal with him again and he fucks up I will put a world of violence against him.

Cory laughed and told me that he has been hammered by the cops before and he can take it.

Now Cory has done four-and-a-half years of his six-year term and he is out on parole again. He told the parole board that he is a changed man and that he wants to integrate back into the real world to become a contributing member.

He is sitting in a stolen 2004 Ford Mustang convertible. A beautiful black car that was just bought by one of his girlfriend's best friends. A friend that has allowed Cory and his girlfriend to stay with them as Cory "gets back on his feet."

Cory has been unlawfully at large for the past eight days now, because he failed to meet his parole officer the second day after his release. Cory just lies back as a soft plume of smoke escapes from his lips as he "blasts off" a small rock of crack. He is doing what he loves to do. Getting high on crack cocaine.

He is running from the police now. He knows it but he doesn't care. He has been through this before. He knows he will get caught, but he will run the gambit because he knows that nothing will really happen to him when he gets caught. He will just go back to a system that feeds him, lets him clean up, and allows him to work out. He can even still get high in jail if he can get some cash together.

He is just looking to score that elusive high as he feeds his crack addiction, he is "chasing the dragon."

Cory pulls out into the downtown traffic in his stolen Mustang. The engine gives a dull roar with the trapped power under the hood. He drives along and he feels unstoppable. He is high on crack, but he is coming down. He has two credit cards sitting in his pocket that belong to the girl who owns the stolen car.

Cory needs to get stuff to sell and he has the ability to do it. He needs cash or items to trade for his crack. Cory plans to go to a gas station first to fuel up and get a few cartons of smokes. Easy money, just charge it to the credit cards. If the cards don't work Cory will rob the station. He doesn't care; he wants his crack. He needs to chase his high.

As Cory slides with the downtown traffic he Heat Checks his rearview mirrors and sees a brown dodge Durango behind him.

He knows that he is getting followed by an unmarked police unit.

"4416," a traffic unit calls in over the air. "Can you run Alberta license DDE146 and tell me what it comes back to?" The traffic unit has already run the plate; he knows. He is behind a stolen vehicle.

I immediately dump that license plate into our computer. I know what it will come back to. It will be stolen. I have heard the routine before. The cop will air the plate and get our dispatch to check it. Next he will tell dispatch the direction that he is traveling and the make of the car. He is letting everyone know that he has eyes on this car. He is poking the dogs with a stick, letting them know that things might get pretty interesting, really fast.

"I am behind a black newer model Ford Mustang with a tan top to it. One Caucasian male driver with a grey hoodie operating the vehicle."

"4416, that plate comes back stolen on a match for the car. The suspect for the theft is Cory Muldoon and he is considered armed and dangerous. It also has an attachment on the call that he is a high suicide risk and wanted Canada-wide for Breach of Parole."

The calls get acknowledged by our street sergeant and the traffic unit. Units start to suck up valuable air time as they want on the call.

I look over to my partner and he knows I want in on this call. We usually avoid stolen cars as the drivers will usually take off and do stupid shit.

Not only is the chance of someone getting hurt very high over a mere theft charge. There is a whack of paperwork that is needed if it is called a pursuit. And it is rare that anything like this is not called a pursuit. If the guy evades police it is a pursuit. I have been there and done that. I don't like to get in shit for trying to catch a bad guy but that is the game we play.

I listen in on the radio as the other units get into place to try to do a "box" on the car. It is a funny thing when a sergeant asks for a box on a vehicle. Funny because we avoid pursuits due to the possible liability issue if the bad guy strikes a citizen while fleeing from the police.

But, we will box a car with no training on how to do it. We have had no formal training on how to box a car, how to engage the occupant of the car, or even how to set cars up so that all the cops on scene are functional.

I have stared down the barrel of another cop's gun as we are all engaged in a deadly cross-fire. Seen cops stuck inside of their cruisers as the partner has parked too close to the car to allow him to get out. I have seen a world of shit come down and luckily I have not seen anyone get hurt. It is a matter of time till it happens.

We all know this fact, yet a box is still called for a prepursuit tactic. The guys in the Ivory Tower will always worry and think about legal ramifications from citizen getting hurt but they will never pull their head out of their ass to think about the guys on the street getting hurt. Much like war, we are cannon fodder. We have a job to do, a goal or objective to reach, and they care not for injuries or casualties from the guys in the trenches.

Collateral damage.

But now, because of his history of violence, I want in on the action. Cory is suicidal. Cory is considered armed and dangerous. Cory is wanted Canada-wide, and I want Cory.

I listen more to the call. The black Ford Mustang blows through a red light. The driver hammers the gas down and drives without hesitation through a second red light. He is gone, driving the car recklessly.

My partner says he wants to circulate close to the last known location to see if the offender has dumped the stolen car and is out on foot.

I disagree because I believe that the guy is going to drive the car hard and fast. I feel that the driver is going to grind out all that he can from the high-performance Mustang before he dumps it. But my partner is driving and he opts to circulate close to the last known location.

Cory pushes the car hard. His heart rate is jacked and he is high on another drug now. He is running from the police and he is high on adrenaline. He blasts through two red lights and hits a short straightaway. But Cory knows that the pack of dogs has been released, and they are out to get him. He can feel them circulating for him and he knows he is the hunted right now.

Cory also knows that he cannot drive in a straight line. He sees a left turn coming up and he takes it hard. The rear tires of the Mustang screech as he rounds the corner at a high speed. He sees construction workers jump out of the way of the car. He forces the accelerator down to the ground and gains speed down the street.

I keep my eyes out for a guy matching the description given by the traffic guy. I know either way, whether we circulate close or far, it is now just luck of the draw. My partner has good instincts and lots of street experience. His call to circulate close is as good as it gets.

We drive down the last street the black Mustang was seen. Just as I scan an alley to my left my partner slams on the breaks.

"There's the fucking car. He is down the street."

I look over to see the black Mustang convertible with the tan top racing down the street towards us. I can also see that half of the street is blocked by a Freightliner truck.

Without saying a word my partner jacks the cruiser into the only open spot of the street.

Cory sees the other end of the street blocked off by a construction crane. He jerks the steering wheel to the left and spins the car around. Blue smoke rolls out from the tires as he skids to a dangerous stop.

He looks around and pins the accelerator to the floor again to get out of the street the way that he came in. The roar of the engine and the whine of the tires cover the screams and curses of anger from the construction workers that he has almost run over.

Cory slows down as he sees a police cruiser block the only exit he can see. The car has stopped. A large truck is in his path and the front of the cruiser is blocking the rest of the road. Cory sees two cops running towards him. He sees guns drawn and he sees that these cops want to get a piece of him.

Cory has dealt with us before and he knows that if we get him we are going to go old school on him. He knows that today he will pay a price for his crimes.

I am out of the car before it comes to a complete stop. I am in full sprint towards the car that has stopped halfway up the street. I have my gun in my hands and I yell at the driver to show his hands. I feel like I am running through water. I feel slow, heavy, and I can feel sounds move past me. I can feel the flood coming, the adrenaline fix flowing through me.

I am hunting, I have cornered my prey, and I want to attack now. I level my chunk on the chest of the guy in the car as I slow my run down to keep a steady shooting platform.

If I see a gun I will hammer the window in front of the driver with enough rounds to stop a charging bull. I will aim high on his chest as I know that the rounds from the .40-caliber Glock pistol will deflect down when they penetrate the front window. I am ready to drive several rounds into this fuck if I see a gun. I am hunting and I want to attack my prey.

Through the muffled waters created by my adrenaline dump I can hear the engine rev and I see the car's front end lurch up. Cory forces all the power out of the Ford Mustang, and now the 2,000-pound bullet races towards my partner and me.

I see my partner run to the right to avoid the car so I move to the left. I know that if Cory wants to run us over with his new weapon he cannot target both of us running in separate directions.

The car roars loudly as it races down the street. I can see Cory's eyes. They are locked on my partner. I see the front tires turn toward him and I can see my partner pick up speed to get out of the way of the mass of steel and fiberglass. I can see Cory's eyes wide open and his hands locked onto the steering wheel. Cory is hunting and we are his prey. Cory wants to attack us.

My partner just makes it clear of the car. The black bullet slices by him at breakneck speed.

I see the tires turn towards me. I see the front end of the car racing toward me. I can hear my partner yell out my name to ensure that I see the car coming towards me. I can see Cory's face.

He is now looking at me, his next target since he missed his last one.

My legs pump hard as I move laterally from his forward movement. I cannot outrun the car but I can outmaneuver Cory's attempts to put me under his wheels.

I feel the flood of my fix pour into me. My legs feel heavy and burdened but I know that every time my foot hits the hard asphalt I am picking up speed. All that I can hear right now is my heart pumping hard. I push harder and move faster. My world slows down even more.

I can see the black Mustang pulse by me. I can feel the wind of the car passing me. I can smell the caustic exhaust as he races past. I have made it clear of the deadly projectile and now I am running after it.

I am pissed as I race after the car. I know that Cory has now gone from fight to flight. Cory was not able to attack so he is now looking to escape. Cory sees a small opening between the rig and a house.

The Mustang crashes over the sidewalk and when it hits the dried grass all is lost. The front end bounces and pieces of black fiberglass splinter off across the concrete. Cory keeps his foot on the gas and the rear tires break free on the lawn of the residence. The high-performance tires are not meant for travel on grass.

I see the rear of the Mustang kick out as the engine screams. The tires are spinning out of control, kicking up blades of brown-yellow grass as they burn a track deep into the ground.

I feel a wave of sound rush into me as the back end of the car tears through the wooden porch of a nearby house. Wood splinters fly around me as the energy of the out-of-control car gets delivered into the grey-painted deck. I smell the old wood, the musky odor of the dry grass, and the acidic smell of burnt gas from the car's frothing exhaust pipe.

I curse to myself when I see that the black Mustang might get away. I can see an opening large enough for the car to slide through. My cursing turns to inner cheers as I see that the car still spins out of control. I can tell that the driver is going to hit a large old-growth tree.

I am in a full sprint again. I can feel my heart pump, my legs thunder with energy. I know that I am on the hunt again. I know that I am going to be able to attack soon.

The car crashes into the tree head-on. The front end buckles as fiberglass and steel give under the force of the collision. I can see the car strike the tree in slow motion. I see the airbags deploy in slow motion, the white gas-filled pillow slowly expanding as the driver collides into it. I can see that the driver is stunned, reeling back from the force of the airbags hitting him.

I feel the rush of combat hit me. I am pumped; I have my gun back on the driver as I try to open the door.

"Show me your hands!" I want to see a weapon. I want to shoot him, drive round after round into this fucker. I want to see his driver's side window explode into small little pieces as my Glock humps hot rounds into his body. I am ready to shoot, I want to test my training. I am ready to use deadly force against this guy. I am hunting.

The door is locked; the driver shows his hands to me. They are empty. No gun, no chance to test my training.

Time to switch tactics.

I quickly holster my chunk and without effort draw my baton from my belt. I yell at him to keep showing me his hands as I drive the baton's metal end into the window. I hit it hard but I just hear the tinny tang of metal onto safety glass. I strike it again, but the same effect occurs. Just a loud metal-on-glass gong.

Time to change tactics.

I expand my baton and hold it by the opposite end so that I can strike the window with a better reach. The large arc delivers more energy, hits the window harder. The change in positioning works and I see a cascade of broken glass roll down the side of the car.

I let my baton travel further into the car. I purposely let the baton travel its full arc. It slides through the falling glass like a sword flowing through a waterfall. I let it travel into the car, I let it fulfill its arc. It moves through the air and finishes its arc as it smashes into the left cheek of the driver. I can see the heavy metal end punch deep into the soft flesh of Cory's face.

I see his head snap back as the force of the weighted club hits him hard. His eyes slam shut and his hands reach for his face. I reverse the energy on the baton and pull it back towards me. As soon as I can see that Cory's hands have covered his face to try to stop a second blow I drive my baton into its hard black plastic holder.

My hands are now free of any tools. They are free to do what they know best. I reach into the car to destroy Cory. I can see that he is wearing his seat belt and I grab onto his left hand, which is shielding his face.

I lock on hard to his hand and pull it out of the car to stretch his arm out. I pull harder when I see his arm straight. I start to pull him out of the car until I feel his seat belt holding him tight to his seat.

"Stop resisting! Get out of the car! Don't fight me!" I yell as I start to drive blows into his face. I can see it in his eyes that he has already given up. I can see the confusion set in. He wants to give up, he doesn't want this abuse anymore.

But it is my call when the damage stops. It is my decision to stop, I will stop when I think that he has received enough to remind him of his actions. I want him to remember what putting the lives of people that I have sworn to protect will cause him.

I hammer more blows into his head. I can already see swelling start around his cheeks and eyes. I can see his eyes flow back into his head as Cory starts to drift off into unconsciousness. I keep yelling at Cory. I make sure my tone is steady and strong. Loud and focused, forcing the words beyond Cory. I want all of the people around watching to hear what I am saying. I am cultivating witnesses.

In their mind the world is code black. They are watching something right out of the movies. They are experiencing something that they will never experience again. They have seen a guy try to run over two cops, then hit a house, then collide into a tree. They now perceive the world as I am giving it to them. I am programming them by telling them what they need to hear. Later on they will all write statements stating that the driver fought with me, that he resisted my attempts to arrest him.

And they will totally believe what they have heard as true accounts of what happened. They will swear on the God they love that what they are about to say is "the truth, the whole truth and nothing but the truth."

I land my last blow into Cory's face. I can feel his body go limp as he teeters on the brink of darkness.

I lean over and talk to Cory loud enough that only he can hear.

"Undo your seat belt or I am going to pound your head into a fucking mess."

I can see his hand slide down to his seat belt and he undoes it. I yank hard again on Cory's arm, sending him soaring out of the car. I am pumped. I am furious, I am hunting, and I have nature's wonder chemical in me. I feel fucking amazing and unstoppable.

Cory flies through the air like a leaf in a harsh winter storm. He lands hard on his chest as my partner moves around from the other side of the car. He was making sure that the vehicle was cleared before he came over to me. He wanted to know that Cory was the only occupant of the car. He now knows that he can help me deal with Cory, that there are no other hot spots in the car for us to worry about.

I drive Cory's face into the dry grass. I see my partner's knee ram into Cory's back. I can see my partner drive his body harder into Cory as he slides Cory's right arm back into an arm bar. I know that my partner is applying maximum force onto Cory's shoulder joint. Just enough for Cory to writhe with pain but not enough to dislocate the shoulder.

My partner wants to drive Cory to react to the pain. Make it look like Cory is trying to fight us.

My partner also yells out commands to cultivate better witnesses.

Cory's legs jerk back as his body screams in pain from the arm bar. Exactly what we wanted from him. My partner delivers a solid open-handed head stun, which bounces Cory's face off of the ground.

"Stop resisting!" he yells.

I switch my footing to place my knee into Cory's back so I can also secure his free arm. I drive my boot into his face as I switch my footing. I know that the onlookers will not see this as an intentional blow to Cory's face. It is hidden but effective.

I feel the mashing of flesh and bone on my hard leather boots. I see Cory's legs go limp on the ground. He is done; he is just lying there, broken. He will just lie there and accept what we have to deliver to him because his will is broken.

Cory will lie there knowing what it feels like to be a victim of violence and punishment. Cory will know what his victims felt like when he attacked them.

My partner and I stop. In perfect harmony only achieved by working together for years, the cuffs are slid on and Cory is searched. As my partner talks on the radio to let everyone know what has happened, because we were too busy taking care of business to talk on the radio, I get off of Cory.

He starts to mumble. He asks why we beat him so bad and I tell him to shut his mouth. I tell him he is under arrest. I let him lie on the ground cuffed as I let my fix leave my body. I look around and see all the faces of the construction workers looking at us.

A burly man with big hands forged from years of hard work looks at me.

"That is the most crazy shit I have ever seen. Are you guys okay?"

I give him a nod and let him know that I am all right. I move him over to his buddies and ask them to write some statements on what happened. In a frenzy of excitement they start to tell me what they saw and as they speak I can see they too are filled with adrenaline. They are pumped from what they have just seen.

I ask them to write it down before they forget and they all stop their work to help us out with their statements.

I look over to see other cops gathering witnesses. I can hear my partner talking to some other guys as he too is collecting the information needed.

I walk back over to Cory, who is still lying on the ground. I drag him up to his feet and lock him up in the back of our cruiser. I sit in the cruiser as I feel my leg start to shake. I breath deeply as the fix works its way out of me. I relax, except the downswing of the rush. My hands shake and I keep them low out of sight. Just a few more minutes and I will be fine. I have been here countless times before, I know that the shakes will go away.

I look at my hands and they are cut up from all the glass shards from the shattering window. I flick out small pieces of glass that are sticking out of my skin like crystal needles.

I look at my sore hands and see my knuckles. They are red and puffy from the blows to Cory's head. I can see the thick skin over my knuckles chafed from the repeated strikes.

I massage my hand and am happy to feel no broken bones. I curse myself because I should know better than to hit a guy in the head with a closed fist.

"A good way to break your hand and spend time working the desk, you fucking idiot," I say to myself.

I see our sergeant arrive on scene and start to coordinate a tow truck for the smashed vehicle. He asks what everyone is doing to ensure that all the tasks are covered. He is a good street sergeant. He doesn't order his men, he guides them, leads them with his examples.

I can feel my body returning to normal as he walks over to my car. I act like I am writing in my notebook but my hands are still too shaky to write.

"All good, Smith?"

"Yes sir."

"I need to know one thing."

"What is that, sergeant?"

"Did you guys pursue that car?"

I almost fucking snap. I know what he is asking. I know better than to get into a pursuit because of the reprimand that can come from it. I know that my ass would be in a sling if I pursued that car and he got into an accident because of it.

My sergeant reads me like an open book and answers the question for me.

"I know you guys told me that you went in on foot but the Duty Inspector still wants to call it a pursuit. God knows fucking why but he does. I am going to settle this out. Don't worry."

"A fucking pursuit when we chase a car on foot? How the fuck can he think of that?"

"Policy states, 'A pursuit is initiated when a vehicle's operator makes any attempt to avoid police,' so technically this is a pursuit. You and I both know that it is intended for vehicle-on-vehicle shit but the Duty Inspector has his fucking shorts in a twist over this and he wants to give out paper. But like I said, I will take care of it. Don't worry."

My partner sits in the car as my sergeant leaves. I let him know about the pursuit bullshit and he too looks at me like I am going crazy.

I run the unit roster to see who the inspector is and I know in an instant why this is happening. The Duty Inspector is a guy with severe "short man's syndrome." He is an asshole to all those who just may happen to cross his path. Ever since I stood up to him and refused to do something that I viewed as an issue to my safety he has been gunning for me. He wants to flex his mighty authority on me. He wants to pound me until my will is broken. But, to his dismay I have been right before and I will be right again. He will just have to sit and fume till he can try to find something else to get me with. It is a funny battle of cat and mouse.

I laugh to myself and start to focus on what is important. We drive the loser to jail and start a long set of hours processing paperwork on Cory. He is going back to jail to serve the rest of his time for his robbery beef.

But Cory is different this time. The last time we brought him to jail he just talked the shit the whole time. He told us how bad he was and how he did not care about his jail time.

I warned him then that if we crossed paths again and he fucked up I was going to happily inflict violence upon him.

Violence has been inflicted and Cory now knows that he has suffered for his crimes. Cory goes back to jail broken and bleeding. But even more important Cory goes back to jail with a broken will. Cory now knows what his victims felt like.

SELF-IMAGE

SELF IMAGE

Self-image is a funny thing.

Ask any warrior, soldier, or fighter to envision themselves and you will never get the same answer.

Some will tell you images of knights in ancient metal armor.

Others will give you images of present-day warriors: SEALs, Green Berets, Rangers, snipers, all of which are unique in style and character.

Some envision Vikings, heroes from movies, or even mythological persons.

The Samurai is the warrior I envision.

I have no Asian heritage but I still look at the ancient Asian culture with respect.

To me the Samurai embodies the principle of a soldier. They were honorable till their death.

They did not fear death but simply accepted it. Death to them was just a test of honor and faith.

Loyalty was the Samurai's mantra. To lose honor was worse than death because one cannot control his death, but they can control his ability to retain honor.

A Language All in Its Own

A Language All its Own

I live in a world that has its own code, its own language, and its own hierarchy.

A gun is a "chunk."

A car is a "Veh." And a traffic stop on that car is a "T-Stop."

A criminal is a bad guy.

An experienced criminal is a "ringer" and if you want to let him know you want to fight he is a "goof."

Choking out someone by grabbing them by the throat is called a "C clamp" or "turkey claw."

If I do some heavy damage to a bad guy I have "crushed" him.

If people are watching what is happening, there are "eyes" around.

There are 10 codes for virtually everything that we do. Our location is our 1020. If we are dealing with a drunk it is called a 1018. If he wants to fight it is a 1019. So in a quick verse of numbers and words I can give forth all the information needed in a flash.

As an example: "I am out with a 1018 male that is about to 1019. My 1020 is at...."

So, even when I got out with other cops for a beer it is hard for us to shut off this other language that we know. Our entire conversations will flow with numbers and quick little blurbs of information.

We will talk about the bad guys we crushed and we will laugh. We will talk about the bodies we have seen and the accidents that were brutal. We will laugh.

Why do we laugh? What else are we to do? Cry, break down, and hurt inside? No, that is not a way to deal with what we see. You would not last five minutes if that was the way you dealt with the horror and shit on the street.

A black sense of humor is developed and you laugh at other people's misfortune. Especially when it is caused by their stupidity.

A car on the radio is calling in a motor bike that has just blown by

291

him.

"Roger that, dispatch. It is a late-model Harley Davidson Fat Boy. There was a male driver and a female passenger. Their last 1020 was going westbound down 17th Avenue." The voice on the radio is calm but I can still tell that he is pissed off by his tone. "They blew past me as I was conducting a T-stop on another veh. The passenger threw a Slurpee at me as they passed."

My partner and I laugh as we start to head into the area. We laugh because it sounds funny. We know that we would not like a drink thrown at us but if you conjure the idea in your head it is funny. Fucking funny, in fact.

"The driver of the bike is a heavy-set male wearing black leather jacket and a skull cap type of helmet. The female passenger is even heavier set and wearing a white shirt and blue jeans."

I can hear sirens in the distance. Cops are moving in. It should not be hard to find this guy and his fat girlfriend.

I scan the side roads as I drive at a casual speed.

"Up ahead," my partner tells me.

I look forward and see a large woman on a Harley. She is so large that I cannot see the driver of the bike from my angle. As I start to drive up to score a plate the bike takes off. The driver guns every little bit of power out of the Harley and it moves. The roar of the exhaust fills the air and I am sure it has attracted any police car within earshot. The distinctive blast from the exhaust can be heard for blocks.

Just as my partner is ready to air the location of the bike we hear another car voice the location of the bike that just rocketed past them.

I can see the driver of the bike veer off to the left as he sees a cruiser to his right waiting at a traffic light. I am amazed when I see the passenger give the finger to the car sitting at the light as they blast past.

The bike has rocketed up to over 100 km an hour when I see disaster appear. A large flatbed truck has pulled out to turn towards us in the opposing lane. The driver, to no fault of his own, thought the intersection would be safe to pass through. He of course would have no idea that the driver of the Harley Davidson bike half a block away would suddenly accelerate.

I see the back tire of the Harley lock up and a blue-black cloud appears from the locked back tire. It is too late for his sudden breaking. The bike slams into the back end of the truck.

All I can see is metal flying everywhere and the massive female gets catapulted off of the back of the bike. I can see her fly over the flat deck of the truck and as she is moving through the air she hits a light standard.

She bounces off like a rag doll as her body twists in the air. I see a mist of fine red blood plume from the pole as her head is crushed into a mass of splintered bone and brains. I cannot see her hit the ground behind the flatbed truck. I can only imagine her body tumbling and rolling.

Her lifeless corpse is getting ground to bits by the asphalt as she tumbles and rolls to a stop.

I look back to the scene and I have to take a second to make out the visual that I am getting. I see the bike crammed under the truck and the lower mass of the male stuffed into the rear axle with it. I cannot however see his head.

As I stop the car to block off traffic my partner calls in over the air that we have a severe accident and to rush Fire and EMS here. We both know that they are dead but we cannot make that assumption. That decision is for the medics to make.

I walk over, totally enthralled by the way the fat guy's body has mashed into the truck's undercarriage. My mind is trying to put his body together like a three-dimensional puzzle. I keep looking for his head because I am confused as to where it is.

Then I understand. It is not a matter of where it is but where it has gone. When I get really close to the fat guy I can see that there is a trail of blood sliding over the wooden planks of the flat deck. I see hair and bits of skin stuck to the protruding slivers of the worked wood planks.

My eyes follow the trail and then I see the guy's head.

I see the bloody stump facing me and his grey beard covered in blood. I walk around the truck to the head lying on the ground stuck between the sidewalk and the curb.

I am fixated on this head and the closer I get to it the more fixated I become. I am soon standing right over it and as I look down at it I can see that his helmet has flown off and his skull is ripped right open. I can see his hair is cut neatly back like it was surgically removed.

As I lean forward to see what his skull looks like with the hair and scalp cut back, I am surprised at what I see. I see nothing. A hollow cranial cavity. I see the outer rim of the skull that has been mashed and broken open. I see a hollow skull cavity but no brain.

"Where the fuck is his brain?" I speak out loud in my amazement.

My partner has been walking beside me the whole time. He too is mesmerized by the sight before him.

I keep staring at his empty head. I look closely at the slight trail of blood that sticks to the cranial wall. I look at the sharp edges of bone that are the skull itself. I am amazed.

"Fuck, look at this," my partner says in a hushed voice.

I look over to him and he is staring down at the ground like I am staring at the opened head. I look to his feet and see a glob of jelly. It is red, pink, and grey in color and even though I have never seen a real brain before, I know what I am looking at.

"Fucking weird, man. It looks like nothing happened to it."

I look at it closer as my partner speaks. It does look like nothing happened to it. It looks like someone carefully placed this guy's brain on the ground.

I suddenly realize that there are people gathering. I look up to see a police line tape getting strung across the street to keep the curious and plain old stupid out and away from our scene.

I look around for something to cover the brain. It is evidence and of course I don't want some kid to see a guy's brain on the grass. Even though I know that they have been exposed to much worse gore on television.

As I scan from left to right I see something out of the corner of my eye. It is the black skull cap helmet that obviously was worn by the fat guy before his head was popped open.

Casually I walk over to the helmet and with rubber gloves on I pick it up and place it over the brain sitting on the lawn.

"Got to protect your melon, man," I say as I place the small helmet over the drying brain matter.

My partner and I laugh as we walk over to look at the dead woman's body. She is a mess as she skidded about thirty feet down the road on her belly. Her head is caved in and all the skin is ground off of her face, arms, and feet. I see the tips of her bloodied sneakers are worn off as well as the nails of her toes.

I see shreds of jeans stuck to the asphalt. I also see a white sheepskin seat cover that she was sitting on. I see chunks of skin smeared all over the ground. A red trail of human waste leading to her final stop.

There are four of us standing around the dead woman when a fifth cop comes over and covers her in a yellow plastic blanket.

As the blanket falls over her body and sticks to her blood-splattered skin, we are all silent.

The cop that brought the blanket over speaks.

"Bad fucking accident, this one is."

"Yup," says another cop standing there.

"She must have been hit pretty hard," he says as he starts to chuckle to himself. "It knocked the pelt right off of her." He bursts out laughing as if he has the joke of the century. He laughs as if he had this joke lined up for weeks. He laughs as he points to the sheepskin seat cover that lies a few feet behind her.

We all start to laugh. We laugh as we turn our backs to the body and walk away.

Fucking funny shit.

THE DEAF GUY

The Criminal Code gives black-and-white guidelines for how I do my job. After all, my job is to enforce the Criminal Code.

In the ever-growing book lay my powers and how I use them. Once again, very black and white.

But there are times when a situation can become grey. This grey zone comes when extras are thrown into the mix.

This grey zone is especially apparent with young people and alcohol.

Consensual fights, unwilling victims because they do not want to look like a loser and a rat to their friends, and of course just plain young stupidity expand the grey zone of the Criminal Code.

Once drunk, they all seem to think that they know the Criminal Code and the laws that govern Canada. Most of their education comes from television and since most of the television that we watch here in Canada is from the USA, they are filled with a mass of misinformation.

If ignorance is dangerous, misinformation is deadly.

So things usually go bad.

It will start with us dealing with someone who has had too much to drink and is looking to fight someone. A standard behavioral guideline for a young inexperienced drinker.

Then when we do start to deal with him, someone else will come up and start to tell me that what I am doing is an invasion of his rights, and that they know the law.

This statement right away is followed up with me usually telling the person why the loser is getting arrested and my grounds. Sometimes this works as they take the knowledge and fuck off. Most of the time all it does is allow the "legal beagle" to tell me again that I am violating this guy's right to freedom.

It makes me laugh because I ask if they know the drunken guy and it is always "No."

I usually ask them what they do for a living. No matter what they say I will give them this follow up:

"Well, how about I come to your place of work and tell you how to do your job? How would that work?"

Sometimes it shuts them up as they realize that they really don't know shit.

It amazes me that people are willing to get in the face of a police officer, tell them how to do their job, and start to walk the line of an "Obstruction" charge when they do not even know the guy we are dealing with.

So, once the drunk is in the back we try to just leave because a crowd will always gather around the mouthpiece legal beagle guy.

If we cannot leave because this guy or gal gets the crowd fired up enough to start to close in on us, then we get the troops in. We call it "getting swarmed."

Now things will always get interesting.

The troops that are coming in will take care of business. We do not take any shit from the crowd now so that we stem the possibility of a riot happening.

The cops move in and we arrest everyone who decides they do not want to leave or get back into the nightclub. Now the vans are filled with legal beagles. Cars are on their way to the drunk tank, or cells with the back cages filled with the bar goers.

It always happens that way. One minute all you are dealing with is one stupid drunk, then the next thing you have is a mass of human stupidity.

If it goes really bad there are bleeding noses, smashed faces, and crying kids. Some will be saying they are sorry and begging for the charges to be dropped.

Some will be crying and telling us that we cannot do this to them, that it is an invasion of their rights. Legal beagles will always insist to the end that they did nothing wrong. They will also tell us that they are going to have our jobs, they are going to sue the city, and we are truly fucked.

Sometimes the drunken losers that we deal with throw me a twist.

Something that makes it funny, in a dark humor way.

Our dispatcher ask for a unit to assist a unit at a local nightclub.

My partner and I pull up to a popular bar in our district.

It is called Bar Coyote and it serves a crowd ranging from eighteen to twenty-five years of age. This age group is always hard to deal with because they are young, inexperienced drinkers.

And the bar overserves the clientele base.

As we pull into the parking lot before the nightclub we start to scan the area and see if there are warning signs of a crowd becoming a swarm.

To our surprise the crowd is relatively happy and still moving about. No large masses of people and no shouting of death threats.

We drive up closer to a unit with a van and once out I see a junior cop walk towards me.

"Hey guys, we got a guy in our cage that is fucking losing it. The crowd is getting a little bit tense. Can you transport our bad guy for us?"

"Sure, what's his issue?"

I see another cop walk towards me. He has a lot of time on the job and is a really good cop. He knows his shit and I wonder why he would not just transport this guy himself.

"Hey, Smith. We are here on a pay duty and we cannot leave. Otherwise I would have driven this putz to jail myself."

"No problem. We can take him." I can hear the bad guy in the back of the cage yelling and kicking the metal liner of the large cage in the back of the van.

"Fuck, he is tripping. Any drugs on board that you know of?" my partner asks.

"Uh, well, that is where things get tricky." The senior cop rubs his face. "You see, he cannot hear and he cannot really speak."

"You mean that you got a deaf mute back there?" I point to the van.

"Yeah, we tried to just get him home but he is an asshole." I see the junior cop pull out his notebook. He hands it towards me. "As you can see I wrote in there for him to write down his name and where he lives so that we can drive him home. When I gave him my notebook he read it and wrote 'Fuck You' in it."

I look at his notebook and in big block lettering the two words make me laugh. "FUCK YOU" written in bold lettering.

I laugh as I pass the notebook to my partner, who also chuckles at the answer written in the white pages.

"Okay, we can transport him." I reach for the back of the van door and open it.

As I look in I see a Caucasian male about twenty-two years of age. He is about six feet in height and about 200 pounds in weight. He is screaming at the top of his lungs and has his hands in fists. I can barely make out the words that come from his garbled speech.

But what I do make out is him telling me that he wants to fight. Him telling us to fuck off. He is hysterical and ferocious.

I look over to the other two cops. "Um, why doesn't he have handcuffs on?"

"We tossed him in the cage without cuffs on. He was being such a pain in the ass that we just grabbed him and threw him in."

I look at the new copper. I see that he knows he has done bad. Not only did they not put the cuffs on a violent bad guy but I am sure that they did not search him. I suspect that they treated him differently because of his handicap.

"Well, we got an issue now. I do not want to take this guy out of the cage here because the shit is going to get bad if we have to go in and get him. One of you two will have to drive the van back to cells so that we can take him out there."

The senior cop speaks up. "I will drive the van back, junior here can stay with the bar until I get back."

I look over to the new cop and see that he is embarrassed.

He looks over to me. "Sorry about the cuffs."

"Hey, no issues, man, the job is a learning experience. Just don't make the same mistake twice."

I see him nod at me as I hear the van start up.

We arrive in an alley that is filled with video surveillance equipment. It is the alley to our cells. We park here and take our bad guys up the elevator to the booking in area.

As I get out of the cruiser I can hear the guy in the cage still banging away on the metal. I can hear his violent screams as he tries to kick the back cage door open.

We all set up and when we are ready I open the vehicle doors and then the cage door.

The bad guy slides to the back of the van and continues to scream at us. He huddles himself in the corner and raises his clenched fists at us.

His speech is contorted because of his hearing impediment but we all know what he is saying. He wants to fight. He is telling us to fuck off.

I make eye contact with him. I need him to know that I will be dealing with him tonight.

I put my hands out in front of me and show him my palms as I wave them to the ground. I clearly mouth the word "relax" but he just fires up more.

I try this two more times but he is still just fired right up. He wants to fight. He knows he is dealing with the police and he has been given his chance to relax and behave.

He still screams and yells. He still keeps his fists clenched and high in a boxer's stance. If I go into the cage he will have the advantage. He has his back against the rear of the cage and he is ready for anyone.

If I enter he can kick and punch me before I can even get into my striking range.

I know better than to go into the cage and go head-to-head with this guy.

I have no doubt that I would win this metal-box battle but I know that I would also get hurt in the event, and I avoid injury as much as possible. Besides I have other tools on my duty belt that are designed for people just like him.

I reach down to my belt and pull out my pepper spray. Once I have the bright red can in my hand I look again at the deaf mute guy. I again attract his eyes so that he knows that I am talking to him.

Our eyes are locked. I shake the small can in front of me to show him what I have. His eyes follow the canister and I know that he has registered what I am about to do.

Once again I motion for him to relax. Once again I am met with a flurry of obscenities and threats that can barely be made out through his muted speech.

"Are you actually gunna pepper spray the guy?" the senior cop asks me as he looks at the can of spray in my hand.

"Fuck him. Mute and deaf don't give you a right to be an asshole. I have given him enough slack as it is." I straighten my arm out by my side so that all I have to do now is raise my arm up and hit the button to issue forth a foamy spray to the face of the guy.

I wait for the right time. I let my co-workers know that I am going to spray this guy as soon as I get a good opening. I want them ready to drag him out and away from the contaminated area. The spray will be contained to the cage in the back of the van but as we reach in we will feel some slight cross-contamination. We will cough, sneeze, and wheeze. The less time we spend in the area the better.

I wait and listen to the yelling as my partner now steps from the side of the van, into the view of the enraged bad guy. It is a distraction technique and it works perfectly.

The bad guy thinks that my partner is going to climb into the van to deal with him. So the bad guy focuses his attention to my partner. Just then my arm comes up and I release the burst of the chemical spray into the bad guy's face.

It is a perfect shot. A wad of yellow-red foam spits into his eyes. Instantly the deaf mute guy jerks back and his eyes tell him that something bad is happening to them. His hands go up to his face and he goes to wipe out the oily paste from his eyes but he just forces the irritant in deeper.

I hear him scream as he falls to the floor of the cage. His hands cover his eyes as he writhes on the floor in pain.

Hands reach in and drag him out unceremoniously down to the ground outside the van.

I hear him scream, his words slightly distorted from his speech impediment.

"It burns! It burns!"

Strong black leather-covered hands grab his arms and fold them behind his back as metal handcuffs lock into place.

I can see his eyes are watering and swelling shut. Mucus flows from his nose so fast that long clear strings flow to the ground.

I grab his shirt and pull in over his head to prevent the snot and mucus from splattering onto us.

It is a short walk to our cells from here and while we make our way through the secure doors all I can hear from him is his scream about the fact that "it burns."

Just as we get to our cells we let the sergeant behind the counter know that our bad guy has been sprayed and needs to be decontaminated as soon as possible.

The white-haired sergeant looks over my shoulder and looks at the mess of a human being we have under arrest.

He sees the bleach-white belly of the unfit bad guy as his red shirt covers his face. The shirt is already wet with the mucus from the guy's mouth and nose as his body tries its best to decontaminate itself from the pepper spray. The deaf guy's words echo through the concrete halls.

"What the fuck is wrong with him? You guys break his fucking jaw?"

"Um, no, Sergeant," I am almost embarrassed to tell him. "He is deaf."

The sergeant's eyes open and he looks harder at the bad guy. "You're fucking shitting me?"

"Not at all, sir. He is a drunk deaf guy that totally refused to cooperate with us and then wanted to fight with the police. I sprayed him to get him under control."

He starts to laugh. "Poor fuck. Not only can he not hear but now he can't even fuckin' see. Take the guy to the medic's office and clean him up."

As I turn to get my prisoner and move him down the hall to the medic's office I hear the sergeant again as he talks to his staff behind the counter.

"Fucking Smith just sprayed a fucking deaf guy. I have never heard of that before."

A rush of other officers peek around the corner as my partner and I walk our bad guy down the hall.

As we move the screaming deaf guy down to the medic's room I can hear a roar of laughter and a banter of words come my way.

"Nice move, Smith, picking on handicap people now, eh?"

"Glad to see that you have found someone that you can beat up on, Smith."

"Hey Smith, my mother-in-law is really old and losing her hearing; can you come over and spray her?"

The laughter continues as we get into the medic's office.

The medic already knows what is going on as he walks out of his office to see what the screaming was about. He just looks at me as he fills a sink with cold water. I just shrug my shoulders.

"Some people just need to be sprayed."

The medic smiles. "I am sure they do. Have fun cleaning this guy up." He motions to the sink.

I start to go through the routine that I have gone through before with other people that I have sprayed.

Without thinking I start announcing the automatic succession of events.

"Okay, this is dish soap; it will break the oily bond that the pepper spray has." I start to rub the dish soap all over the guy's face. My rubber gloves protect me from the mucus and snot that is covering his face. The green dish soap mixes with the yellow and red and forms a thick brown slime all over the guy's face. I take my time to be sure that there is no way that I can get this shit onto me.

"Fuck, Smith, the guy can't hear you. You forget that already?" My partner laughs as he hears me talking to the guy.

"Ah, shit. This is the way I do it all the time. Did not even think about the fact that this poor fuck can't hear a single thing I am saying."

I rub the soap deeper and harder to break the chemical off of his skin. He screams more that it burns. He stomps his foot trying to suck up the pain. His arms shake as they are still shackled behind his back. He works hard at sucking up the pain.

Once the soap is well mixed in the biological mess on his face I now contemplate how in the world I am going to put this guy's head into the sink of cold water without having him think I am trying to drown him. It is easy when they can hear you. Someone with a face full of pepper spray is more than happy to dunk their burning face into the cold water. That is what they are crying for. The water is like a gift for them.

I look over to the medic and my partner and they know what my dilemma is. "Any suggestions?"

They both just shake their heads and start to laugh.

"Oh, what the fuck. It is going to have to go this way then." My blue latex-covered gloves grab a hand full of hair on the back of his head.

With both hands on his head and his body trapped on the counter, I shove his head down towards the sink.

He starts to fight and scream.

"It burns. I'm sorry. It burns."

I feel for the guy. He probably thinks that the cops are now going to take a round out of him for wanting to fight.

I wait till he goes to fill his lungs up with air again to issue his screams once more. Just as I see that he has filled his lungs up with air I force his face into the water.

His legs kick and water splashes across the room. His thrashing forces water out of the sink and across the walls in front of us.

I give him two seconds in the water and then I pull his head out.

He pushes back so hard to get his head out of the water that an arc of snot and water spray across the room. The medic and my partner all dive for cover and I quickly duck to prevent myself from getting hit.

His lungs pound and he fills them with air again. I slam his head back into the water. I hold his face in the cold water and he once again thrashes about.

Two seconds. I pull his head back out, now expecting the spray of water and mucus.

"Fuck, Smith!" my partner yells as a gob of water and human slime spatters on the metal filing cabinet near him.

I look at him and smile. "Can't stand the heat, get out of the kitchen!"

He gives me the finger.

The deaf guy relaxes. He can feel that that water is calming the effects of the pepper spray.

"More. Water. More!" he says as he stomps his feet in the pool of water forming below him.

"That's it! Now you got it." I move his head close to the water and splash it onto his face. I let go of his wet hair and he dunks his own head into the water.

I step back and look at my uniform. Amazingly enough I am not wet. My boots have some water on them but I have escaped the whole thing and remained dry.

I look over to my bad guy and he has his head in the cool water. He is shaking his face furiously back and forth in the water. He wants this shit off his face.

I move back to him and take his cuffs off. I know that the fight is out of him. I know that giving him the ability to wash his own face is a reward for not still wanting to fight.

The cuffs are off and my bad guy washes his face. The room is quiet. Every so often we hear him thank us as he splashes more and more water on his face.

I look at the medic and the mess in his office. "Sorry about the mess, man."

"No problem. It is like this all the time with guys that come in with spray." He starts to laugh. "It doesn't matter whether they are deaf or not."

About twenty minutes pass before the deaf guy can finally open his eyes and the medic cuts off the water.

"That is enough of that, we are getting behind now and I have to get the cleaning staff in to mop this place up," he says as he taps his foot in the puddle of water on the floor.

A quick medical exam is conducted and then I walk the guy down to our cells. As we start to walk down the hall that takes us to our cells I can tell that the deaf guy is getting agitated again. I feel his arm tighten under my grip and I can tell that he is trying to slow down to get beside me. I push on his arm to keep him in front of me where I have the best control. He knows that I am on top of him and he doesn't try to do anything stupid.

The cell door opens and as I give him a final push to move him clear past the sliding cell doors I look over to the guard that came with me to open up the metal barred doors.

"Fifty-yard hero," I say as we make eye contact.

The heavy gate slides shut with a ground-shaking thud.

"Oh yeah, without a doubt," he replies.

As we walk out the deaf guy comes racing to the cell doors and starts to call me a cunt, fucking asshole, and all the other words he can slur out of his mouth.

I laugh as the final door to the drunk tank is closed. It is a full metal door and it blocks out most of the sound from the cells. I laugh because I pegged him right. He is a fifty-yard hero. Not enough man balls to square off with me. He has just enough courage to call me on when he is locked behind metal bars and he knows I will not go in there to get him. He has guts as long as he is far enough away to be a hero.

I walk into the processing area to do my paperwork, and as I fire up the computer I hear a huge commotion in the front. A mob of us make our way over as I hear a familiar scream.

It is the deaf guy. I look out the door down the hall. I see that the staff here have him splayed out on the floor, a person on each arm and leg.

The deaf guy is picked up in this fashion and moved off to an isolation cell. I hear his screams as he is moved down the hall and handcuffed to the floor of an isolation cell.

"What is all that about?" I ask one of the cell staff members that is standing by the front counter.

"He started to fight in the tank. He was getting his ass kicked so we had to rush the cell. As soon as he saw the uniforms he turns on us. That was not good for him. Fucking idiot."

I laugh to myself again. "Yup, fucking idiot is right."

Back at my computer I print out his criminal history and it is no surprise to me that he has one. Standing at the printer as the green-colored criminal record sheet is printed I scan it as it rolls out. One thing catches my attention right away.

Offender's DNA on file. Sexual Assault. Age under twelve years.

"Fucking skinner." I no longer feel any pity for this piece of shit. He is what we call a skinner. He has been charged and convicted for sexually assaulting a person under the age of twelve. He is the biggest pile of shit known to humankind. If I had known his criminal history earlier I would have gone into the back of the van to get him out. I would have risked getting punched or kicked so that I could dish out a heavy beating. I would have sat at a desk while I healed with a huge smile on my face. "Fucking piece of shit."

I walk over to the sergeant on duty that is approving paperwork. I show him the completed paperwork and he barley looks at it. I am here three times a shift on average and he knows that I do a good job. Besides, this is no robbery file, no major event in our world.

"I assume that this is up to the usual shit work standard you have?" he says as he lifts up the sheets of paperwork. He looks at me with a smile.

"Yes sir, full of shit as usual." I smile back.

"One question, Smith, don't you like coffee?"

"Yeah, I love coffee. Why?"

"You are in here way too fucking much. The more you are here the more we have to deal with the shit you bring us. Find a fucking coffee shop and take a Goddamn break."

My partner and I leave cells and as soon as we turn the corner we duck down an alley.

We are hunting again.

No coffee for us.

OLD DEATH

Old Death

One of the most common questions that I get (besides the one asking if I have ever shot anyone) is if I have seen dead people.

My response to that question is a quiet yes.

I know what is coming next. A follow-up question that is driven from people's curiosity. Curiosity of the unknown, not necessarily from a morbid obsession like some people think.

"What is the weirdest one that you have seen?"

My response to this question is, "Define 'weird.'"

I have seen people die in car accidents, from stabbings, gunshot wounds, suicides, natural causes, freak accidents, and almost every other way imaginable.

If they want me to tell them what I think is weird, it may not be the story they want to hear.

One has to understand that when a person is found dead and the death did not occur in a medical facility, the police are called. So, we attend a lot of scenes that have the smell of death in them.

And yes, death does have a smell.

Old death is a putrid odor of shit, urine, and possibly human rot, depending on the time that has transpired before someone found the deceased person. This smell hangs in your clothes and will contaminate anything you sit in or sit by. It is a smell that can fill a house. An odor that you can start to smell even before you open up the front door.

It is another early day shift and as noon breaks I am already well through my day. I am tired and looking to stop at a Tim Horton's to acquire a coffee fix to carry me through the rest of the day.

As I pull into the drive-through I hear that Chris's car has been dispatched to a call that I know she will not want to take care of.

"1430 can you take a look at the 109 on the board? The possible victim is an eighty-five-year-old female that has not answered the door or returned calls from her son. He has not had contact with her for over a week now."

"That will be a good one. She is toast for sure," I tell myself in a whisper as I pull out with my hot coffee sitting in the center console cup holder.

I pull over to a vacant stall in the parking lot. I try to take my first sip of the overly hot coffee. Carefully balancing my lips on the open tab of the plastic lid so that I do not burn my mouth on the beverage, I CAD a note to the car that was responding to the call.

Hey there. It sounds like she will be in the residence; I will swing by to give you a hand with that call.

In a matter of a few seconds she responds.

Thanks.

There have been countless calls where this copper has taken calls that I dislike to deal with. Sexual assaults especially. It is hard to interview a woman that has just been victimized by a man. Especially when you are another man. Very tough call. Chris has always taken the calls that involve sexual assaults.

I have always taken the calls that involve violence and death. I have heard her say countless times that she did not join this job to look at dead people if she could avoid it. I have heard other cops ridicule her because she does not want to see dead people.

I make sure to remind the other guys that they are always happy when she shows up for a sexual assault call or a nasty domestic violence call. She takes it without hesitation so we should take her death issues without hesitation.

So, here I am now pulling up to an old 1970s-style house. Ivory white sheer curtains covering the windows, contrasting with the bleached yellow siding that wraps around the box-styled house.

As I look over the house a little bit more I see another sign that there is a problem here.

Mail is stacked in the mailbox and a pile of dated newspapers sit on the concrete step. No one has taken the mail in for several days now.

"Hey, did you do a door knock yet?" I ask Chris, who is standing on the sidewalk waiting for me to show up.

"Um, no not yet. I walked around the house and saw nothing that showed me anyone was at home. Maybe she is away visiting?"

"Maybe," I say but I already know the answer to that question. We walk up to the door and I give the door a few solid kicks to the bottom kick plate.

Nothing.

I press the doorbell and hear the soft chime echo through the house.

Nothing.

I hit the door with the base of my fist as I try to peek into the house through an arched window at the top of the door.

My limited view shows me a short hallway that spills into a living room. Brown tile leads my eyes into a kitchen that has dishes on the counter.

No movement. No response. No life.

But then I see it. There is life in the house. Flies are collecting against the window. They buzz around and bounce in a confusing dance off the glass.

I turn towards Chris. "Yeah, there is gunna be a dead person here. I will check it out if you could wait here. I do not want family members or neighbors to be showing up without anyone here to stop them from coming in."

"How do you know she is dead? You see her through the window?"

"Nope," I say as I point to the window. "Flies, Mother Nature's decomposers. I have a feeling she is going to be really stinky."

Chris looks at me and she knows why I want her to stay outside. She knows that I do not want her to see what is inside because she has told me that she doesn't want to see death. For whatever reason she wants to avoid seeing death.

I key my radio and tell the on-duty sergeant that I have a locked house and a possible death. I ask him for permission to kick the door in to get entry. I have to ask his permission if the call is not one that demands my immediate reaction. No rush here, she is dead. Our victim here will not be going anywhere.

My sergeant gives me permission without any hesitation. It is just a formality really but if I did it without asking I would have broken that tedious chain of command. Breaking that is showing disrespect and I do not want to start to piss of the guy who handles my shifts and organizes who I partner up with.

In a fast and hard mule kick I blow the door open. The thin wood frame shatters under my black combat boots.

I turn around to start to walk into the house when a waft of warm air hits me. It reeks of rotting flesh and decay.

My face wrinkles up as the odor fully fills my nose. I turn my head away as I try to avoid the awful smell.

I see Chris move away from the corner of my eye. She walks further down the sidewalk to get to the clean, untainted air.

I stop breathing through my nose. I regain my composure and make my way into the house. As I break the threshold of the door I can feel small flies bounce off my face. I can feel them hit my short hair and wisp past my eyebrows.

I want to swat them away. I want to walk back outside and get away from the smell of death. My primitive animal inside of me is yelling that this is no place for me to be.

It screams that there is death here and I should not go further.

But, I move on, fighting back the urge to leave.

In a futile attempt, more of an involuntary action due to the repetition of training, I yell out:

"City Police!"

Nothing. Dead quiet.

I look quickly into the kitchen and see what one might expect. A simple kitchen with clean plates stacked by a spotless stainless-steel sink.

Entering the living room to see an open television guide. It is on the fifth of this month. It is now the tenth. Five days of rot. I have seen five-day-old bodies before and they have never smelled this bad.

I move through the house and float through another person's world. I look at pictures on the wall as I silently make my way into other rooms looking for the death I know I will find. I see family outings, weddings, reunions, and high school graduation pictures.

I also see flies sticking to the walls and picture frames.

The smell is putrid. It is all around me and there is no escaping it.

I turn a light on to the bathroom and to my surprise I do not see her there. Most people die on the crapper. Especially if they are ill. I guess it is the body's last attempt to try to make itself feel better. Not a place I want to die.

I move to the last room on the upper level. It looks to be the master bedroom and before I put my hand on the door handle I breathe slowly. I set my mind for the worst sight that I can imagine. I envision a scene out of the worst horror movie, I want to be mentally prepared if the sight here is one out of hell.

My hand reaches out and touches the cold brass door handle. I open the door and move in as my eyes scan the room.

All I see is an old woman embraced in death on her bed. She is in the furthest decomposition that I have ever seen.

Her eyes are wide open and completely white. Her skin is brown and her body is severely bloated. Her feet, which are sticking out from under the covers, are so swollen that they look like someone was pumping them full of air.

I make my way around her bed looking at her ballooned body pushing up the bed sheets. I can see her body fluids soaking into the mattress that she was sleeping on.

I continue to walk around the bed and I see a small fly crawl out of her ear. I want to smack it off. I want it to go away and leave the old woman alone. But I know that this is just Mother Nature taking care of the dirty work. The fly has a roll to play. It will lay larvae and they will eat the body until nothing is left.

It occurs to me how we are kept so far away from death. How we try to keep the dead looking alive as much as possible to keep us from seeing what nature has intended for us. It is a natural occurrence, our hiding death is as unnatural as it gets.

I move to a window to open it up to vent out the smell that seems to be flowing right through me. As I slide the window open I can see a car pulling up to the front of the house. I see Chris approach and talk to a male, who is on the verge of hysteria.

From what I can hear, he is the son that called about not talking to his mother. He was worried about her.

I look at the bloated dead woman. "Not much to worry about anymore. Just peace and quiet now," I say to her as a final respect. I look at her night table. There is a mass of pills and painkillers. I can only imagine that life for her was at the point of pain and suffering. A good time to let go and die.

As I move my eyes across the night table I see a glowing orange light. It is the light to a heating blanket.

"Oh fuck, that is what is making things go so bad here." I reach over and shut off the heating blanket. She died five days ago but she has been fermenting under a heating blanket. A blanket she probably turned on to keep herself warm when she was not feeling good in the middle of the night. Warmth she needed because death was creeping into her.

Now, the heat of the blanket was just speeding up the natural decomposition process. That is why she was so far into her rot. That is why the house smelled so much of death.

I start to make my way back outside. I can hear the male becoming more and more insistent that he wants to go into the house to see his mother.

I slowly walk back to the front door and when the cold fresh air hits me I feel myself become invigorated.

I breathe in clean air that is not filled with the strong stench of death.

I take a brief moment on the concrete steps to let the sunlight hit my face and arms. The sticky feeling of death burns off my skin with the warm sun's rays.

I fill my lungs deep with clean air.

With slow-paced steps I walk down the stairs. I want to enjoy the peace a few more moments before I have to deal with the now crying son.

I can tell that he is gay. One of those flamboyant gay men that probably had a hard time being accepted by the world. I look at his sorrow and see that his mother was his keystone for his life. She probably did what all mothers do. She never judged him, never questioned his life style choice. She just loved him.

"I want to see my mother. I need to see my mother!" he cries as he tries to push past Chris.

I put my hand out to stop him. He looks up at me and doesn't push to get past. He knows that I will not let him pass.

"You can't see her," I say in a low quiet tone.

"Why? I need to see her. I need to see her one last time."

I can feel the wind change. It moves from a head-on breeze to a swirling wisp coming in around my back. I can smell the death in my uniform.

Chris and the male both stop for a second to try to figure out what smells so bad.

I keep my eyes on the male and when he looks at me, his face registers that I am what smells like rotten meat. I can see in his eyes that he now knows what death smells like.

"The last time you saw her is the image that you want to keep. She is dead, you do not want to see her that way." I stand there with death hanging off of me. The odor of death is seeping out of me.

He stops crying. He just stands there while the smell swirls around him.

"Why don't you go back to your car and sit down?" I look over to the car he drove here. I can see another male sitting in the driver's seat. He is looking at me.

I motion to him to come over. He gets out of the car and without words he holds his partner as they make their way back to the car.

Once they are both seated, Chris goes over and lets them know that the medical examiner still has to come. She gives them all the information as to how to get a funeral home to retrieve the body from the M.E.'s office.

She walks back to me as I stand there, turning my head into the wind so that I cannot smell myself anymore.

"He said to say thanks," she says in a low quiet tone. "Pretty bad in there?"

"Yeah, she was really stinky. They are going to have to take the whole mattress out to get her body out of there. She had a heating blanket on. Really fucking messy now."

Chris looks at me. "Yeah, well, um, I guess I should also thank you for..."

"No need to say anything," I cut her off in midsentence. "I know you are not crazy about seeing dead people. Maybe you are the sane one here anyway." I smile and pat her on the back.

I ask her if she is going to wait for the body removal guys because I need to get out of this uniform. She agrees and with a smirk she tells me that I really stink.

I smile back. "Thanks, I kind of guessed that."

I go back to the office. I shower and change. I seal up my uniform in a plastic bag. I can still smell death. It creeps up on me during the whole shift.

A little waft of rot catches me.

I get home at 4 in the morning. I shower and clean up. I walk outside to my back yard carrying a black plastic bag with my death-soaked uniform.

The crabapple tree is in full bloom. I can smell the sweet blossoms in the cool morning air. It mixes with the smell of death.

I slide off the metal mesh that covers my fire pit and toss in the black bag.

My hands squeeze a can of lighter fluid all over the plastic. A clear liquid gushes from the can. The splattering of fuel onto the bag reminds me of rain on a tent. The steady stream pounds the thin black plastic bag.

Flammable liquid pools on the bag, the smell of gas mixes with the sweet smell of apple blossoms and human rot.

I stand there and pull out a cigar from my shirt pocket. I clip off the back with my knife and throw the cap on top of the wet black plastic. It slides into a pool of fluid and is instantly soaked. The fragile leaf wrapper soaks up the liquid feverishly.

My senses are flooded with sulfur as a wooden match is lit. I roll the hot flame across the tip of the cigar until I see the once-rich brown filler turn coal black.

After two heavy draws off the cigar my mouth is filled with warm earthy smoke.

The match burns between my fingers as I hold it over the fire pit. I look down at the shiny black plastic bag and watch the match as it falls towards it.

With a low roar the bag lights on fire. Plumes of black smoke roll up towards that early morning sunrise. I slowly guide myself into the lounge chair.

I lean back and let another mouth full of smoke roll away from me as the bag burns. As the cremation happens my senses pick up my environment.

I smell the warm earthy smell of my cigar. I pick up hints of sweet apple blossoms. I catch the smell of early morning dew.

I no longer smell death. I have put it away, forgetting the smell until the next time I have to greet death.

I sit and watch the sunrise.

Fresh Death

Fresh Death

Fresh death has an odor.

Human blood smells like salted earth. It is a sticky smell that tells you something is wrong.

The smell warns you that there is danger far before you see the first drops of blood.

I sit across from my wife, both of us clad in the same uniform. We sit together as we share some coffee and company together.

She tells me of a call where she goes into a house and finds a woman with her throat just cut open and multiple stab wounds.

The victim's boyfriend decided to stab her to death because he always dreamed of killing his ex-wife while he was in prison. Mind you he was in prison for viciously assaulting his ex-wife. She went into hiding and when he got out of the clink he was never able to find her. So, he killed his new girlfriend.

As I sat across from my wife and listened to her story my heart sank. She is a tough girl and she can take this job as well as any man can.

But we are all affected, man or woman, by what we see.

She goes about describing the amount of blood, the deep red hues splashed about the white bedsheets. I hear how her neck was cut right open and how the blood oozed onto the bed that she died on.

She describes the way the body laid, the brutality in her death. I hear her use words that I have used before.

"Dead quiet," she says. "The room was dead quiet."

The story continues and she tells me how she went into the basement and arrested the boyfriend for the murder of his girlfriend.

I listen as she tells me how fellow uniforms, her brothers on the street, either congratulated her or scolded her for going in alone. There will always be armchair quarterbacks on the job. Guys who will tell you how they would have handled the call.

How what they would have done was the right thing to do.

How you fucked up. But, they were not there.

They did not have to make the split-second decisions. If you were not at the call you have no right to tell me how to do it.

I sit and listen because that is what we do for each other.

I know that she just needs to tell me, needs me to just listen to her.

"Fuck them. I have a badge and a gun. I will do what needs to be done," she says as she raises the cup of hot coffee up to her lips. "It is a crock of shit that guys on the job think that just because I am a chick I cannot do the same fucking job they do."

The place she is at when she talks to me is the same place I go to when I talk to her. She and I communicate and share. We are able to put our hearts out to bleed the black blood out, bad blood that will corrupt and taint our very soul if we do not let it out.

I prefer to talk to her because she is a woman and naturally a good listener. I know I will not be judged for showing emotion or hurt. I know that she will never tell me that I am fucked up or that the way I feel is wrong.

If I open up to a male officer I know I will be seen as weak and unfit for combat. It is simple bravado.

She talks to me because she knows I will just listen. I will not judge her and see her emotions as a weakness. We have had this bond since we first met. She holds a very special place inside of me. She is the true meaning of friend.

Some things have to be left unsaid to protect our loved ones. Things I would never talk to my mother, father, sister, or brother about. The evil things that boil inside of us.

Things that only another person who lives in the hate and dark side of human nature can understand. I can tell my wife that I saw a person murdered but I will never tell her how it looked, smelled, how I felt inside, or how bad the victim looked after a violent death. It is the little things that I share with this cop that wring the darkness out of me.

After our coffee session we part ways with a simple hug and kiss. I ignore the prying eyes around us. Eyes that look at us with disbelief, amazed to see a cop couple being affectionate with each other. The uniform is not associated with love, family, and compassion.

I am happy to be a sounding board for her today. The fact that she was smiling and happy when we said good-bye means a lot to me.

As I turn the ignition over in my cruiser my mind floats back to a time that I was surrounded by fresh death.

A time that I looked into a dying man's eyes as he gasped his last breath of sweet warm air.

"Attention, all units, we have shots fired at the Mac's on 17th Avenue and 8th Street SE. Witnesses say a black Nissan SUV fled the scene after shots were heard."

I don't even bother to key my radio. I know that more information needs to come over the air. I know that other units will be wasting valuable air time letting our dispatcher know that they are en route to the call.

A real waste of time. Anyone who is free and likes violence will be en route to the call.

I round the corner and see that no other police cars are out. My partner points to a man lying on the ground by a gas pump. There is no one around. People are hiding in the Mac's looking out like fish in an aquarium.

This is their brief experience with real-life violence. They are all glued to the window like they are watching the world's biggest television screen.

I stop our cruiser in the entrance of the strip mall parking lot. I do not want anyone to leave the scene. People will never leave their prized possession. No matter what, they will stay with their cars.

My partner and I bolt out of the car with guns in hand. I scan to my right and he scans to his left. Even though we have been told that the offender has left we do not believe it for one moment. I will act like the shooter is still here until I can verify it with my own eyes that there is no threat here.

In a matter of seconds the small parking lot is clear from any visible threats.

"Clear!" I yell towards my partner as he completes his final search around the last parked car.

"Clear!" are words that we hear back.

My partner gets on the radio to let our dispatcher know that the area is clear and that she can send EMS in. In a hot situation the ambulance will hold back until we make it safe for them to come in. It just makes sense. Send in the dogs and when they are done you send in the medics.

I approach the downed man with my gun pointed right at him. To me he is still a threat.

I move in slowly and scan his waistband for a weapon. I scan his hands, which are around his neck.

Nothing. No weapons.

I take one more moment to make sure. Gang wars are erupting here and I know this will be a gang-related shooting. I know the guy on the ground. He is a well-known gang banger. I have hunted him before.

Once I am sure it is safe I holster my gun.

I slip a blue pair of latex gloves over my hands to protect me from all the blood that is now pooling around this guy's head and neck.

It is dark blood, thick and flowing. A deep red pool of blood is rolling out from under him. His eyes are looking at me as I kneel down beside him.

I tell him everything is going to be all right. I tell him the ambulance is on the way and that he needs to stay calm.

"Adult male conscious and breathing!" I shout at my partner as he relays the information back to our dispatch. I take my hand and place it over his. I tell the male that I am going to have to take a look at his wound to let the ambulance know what they have to be ready for.

He nods to me as I gently move his hand away from his neck. His eyes are glued onto me. His hand barely moves off his neck and I see a gaping hole in his neck. Blood pumps out with every heartbeat. I calmly put his hand back on the opening.

"You are going to have to keep the pressure up on that to slow the bleeding."

"Gunshot wound to the neck. They gotta speed shit up!" I shout at my partner. I hear him relay the information back over the radio.

I look back at the guy on the ground. I can hear the sirens of the ambulance in the background.

"You hear that? That is the medics. You hold on and you're going to make it." I try to keep him in reality. Gang banger or not, I don't want to see him die.

I see his hands start to lose their strength. A flood of blood leaves his neck. Blood oozes through his fingers and squirts across the asphalt. I can smell the blood, fresh and salty.

"Fuck me." I reach over with my thin latex gloves and apply pressure to his neck as his hands slip off. I feel the heat of his blood through my gloves. I can feel his pulse as his heart pumps out his blood onto the street. I can feel the wet and warmth of his blood as it forces its way through my fingers.

I apply more pressure and I can feel shattered bone and raw open flesh.

I look at the gang banger on the ground and his mouth starts to move as if he is trying to say his last words. Nothing comes out as his lips move. I feel his pulse slow down.

He tries to talk more, his mouth and lips moving but no words escape them. He looks like a fish that has been taken out of the water.

Frantically gasping for air, frantically searching for life.

His eyes look right at me as his pulse stops. Blood slowly pours out from his neck, no longer pulsating out onto the street. I look into his eyes as he leaves the land of the living.

His chest falls down as the final breath escapes his body. A long exaggerated exhale as he dies before me.

His body goes limp and his flow of blood slows even more.

I let go of my grip and stand up, looking down at him.

I stand there with red blood dripping off of my blue latex gloves. I watch the drops form at my fingertips and slide off towards the ground. Red drops of blood splatter on the black asphalt.

My hands feel the cold as air rushes over the wet blood, cooling it. The blood is already becoming tacky and thick.

I carefully peel the gloves off and toss them to the ground. I step further back, but I am unable to break my gaze into the dead man's eyes. They keep looking at me. His eyes never break their stare.

Silent words escape my mouth. "How is that gang banger shit working for you now?" I turn my back on him and walk away to my car. I have no remorse for him because he is on the other side of my world. He is a wolf and I have hunted him.

He has been killed by his own kind. There is justice in that.

I walk back and sit down in my cruiser and start to write notes into my notebook. I see the medics roll up on scene and they do nothing to try to save the dead man. They look at him like I did and walk away.

He is dead, beyond saving no matter how good today's medical science is.

A yellow plastic blanket is put over the body and bright red cones are placed all about over important evidence.

The police tape is set up and people are getting interviewed. The scene is contained and we are all taking notes.

Our Identification section is called out as well as Homicide.

Now the paperwork really starts.

CHILDREN OF THE DRUGS

CHILDREN OF THE DRUGS

The rain falls hard in a horizontal sheet of liquid glass. It is a horrible night to be working. Mother Nature has whipped up a fury. She is letting us know that we are just mere mortals.

I drive slowly as the rain blankets our cruiser. The damp has soaked into every small crack as the humidity clings to the inside of the front windshield. I reach over and turn on the defrost fan to clear up the patches of fog appearing on the glass. My face is covered with a thin layer of moisture; I can feel the clinging wet covering me.

The wipers fight hard to keep my vision clear enough to see the road. Small waves roll across the jet-black streets as the winds pushes harder. Gusts blast our car hard enough to rock it back and forth as if being cradled by a giant . The piercing winds create small screams that echo through the vehicle's weather stripping.

My partner breaks the silence generated from the raging storm. "Let's hit the parking lots, the crackers are going to need to get out of this shit storm."

Water rushes out from the wheel wells of our cruiser as I roll through a large body of water pooling along the entrance of a parking lot. The gutters are fighting in vain to keep up with nature's torrent.

Our car slides under the concrete ceiling and our windows roll down so that we can hear what stories the silence wants to tell us.

I run my hand along the door's windowsill and push away drops of water that fall into the cruiser from the roof. My wet fingers are wiped onto my chest, the wet sticking to my dark blue uniform. The open window allows air to rush across my damp face. The cool is refreshing, removing the clinging damp rag that seems to be covering me.

The cruiser rolls quietly along the smooth concrete flow as the water rolls off of its smooth gloss paint job. A snake-like trail of water droplets follows our cruiser, leaving a temporary track of our passing.

My ears search the heavy humid air. My eyes scan the far reaches of the parking lot. I look for movement. I look for anything that might be out of the ordinary. Our car's radio is off, the headlights have been turned off. We are quiet and dark. We are hunting.

I spot some wet footprints in the floor. I look over to my partner to let him know that I see something that is of interest. I motion to the temporary track of wet prints.

As my head turns to look at him I see him nod as he too is focused on the trail. His eyes reach far into the darkness of the parking lot. He has seen it too and he knows that we are both hunting.

We are functioning as one being right now. I follow that track closely so that we don't lose the trail. His eyes scan the distance, so that he can see if our prey lies ahead. Two sets of eyes and ears working as one. Each of us doing a different job, our body language is our only form of communication.

Our cruiser rounds a corner as a flash of lightning illuminates the harsh concrete walls. The surge of light causes a moment of shadows. Shadows hiding behind a set of parked cars.

I slowly stop the car so that our tires do not chirp on the polished concrete floors. The engine shuts off and my key slides out of the ignition. No ringing door alarms will sound when we exit the car. It is a well-rehearsed scene. My partner stays focused on the shadows with hand on the door handle. Ready to explode out of the car if a threat appears.

I book out on the computer. No communication over the radio, everything now is done with noise abatement in mind, a quiet execution. We are hunting our prey.

I reach for my door handle and exit the car; so does my partner. We both shut our doors with total control, our hands holding the doorframe until they are barely closed, the only noise that can be heard is a low click of the door locks.

My ears reach for any noise from the shadows. My eyes grasp for information as we walk through the darkness.

Lightning flashes again and the quick flash of light again casts shadows against the walls. I can make out two figures. I cannot tell anything more than that.

I hold up my right hand with two fingers pointing up to tell my partner that I can see two bodies. I catch a slight head nod from the corner of my eye.

My beast starts to roar inside. My heart pumps. The adrenaline fix is chambered and ready. This the low-adrenaline fix of hunting humans.

Everything runs through my mind. I look for areas to move to if one of the persons hiding has a weapon. Places where I can move tactically to allow me cover and a good position to deal with the threat.

Like an activated computer my mind highlights objects in my memory. Concrete pillars, other vehicles, tripping obstacles, and shadowed areas to just list a few. The stairwells and other natural escape routes are also put into my mental filing cabinet. I want to know where I can move to but I also want to know were the bad guy might move to.

I think about what will happen if these are just crack heads "blasting off" and what they might do when we interrupt their high. Some are okay to deal with but others can be violent drug-induced animals. A determined cracker or Jibber (methamphetamine user) are some of the toughest opponents that I have ever had to get dirty and nasty with. They are indestructible, no concept of pain, no source of logic. Just a frothing animal that will kill to escape.

I cut to the left of the car and my partner moves to the right. We are circling in on the two. We are both hunting. We are moving like two pack dogs prowling up upon their prey.

I see them first, as I am much taller than my partner. I see the two of them facing each other, a young female with her back to me and an older male facing me. They have no clue I am there as they are solely focused on the crack pipe that they are sharing.

I peer over the two bodies and give a quick scan around to see if there is anything that they could use as weapons. I see blankets thrown about, open food containers, and discarded plastic bags scattered around them. I can smell them now. Wet unwashed hair mixed in with the sour smell of sweat-soiled clothes. These animals have not washed for weeks.

The back area is lit up with the glow of a butane lighter. I see the male stuff the hot flame into the front of the glass crack pipe and in a flash he is off. I see his eyes roll back and his hands drop as the rush of the chemicals floods through his lungs. I can smell burning flesh as I see him put his thumb over the end of the hot glass pipe. A short sizzle escapes his hand as his skin sears from the heat. He holds his thumb over the pipe so that small rock of crack doesn't fall out and onto the floor. He wants to hold onto the rock so that he can blast off again without having to search through the darkness for his lifeline chemical.

I see his head move forward again and when his eyes open he sees me look at him.

"Oh fuck," he says as he tries to slide the crack pipe between his crossed legs.

"'Oh fuck' is right. Keep your fucking hands where I can see them."

Both of them are fixed on me right now. "I fucking told you once and that is all you are going to get. Show me your fucking hands and keep them away from your body."

"Relax, boss," the male says and slides his hands away from his lap; I can see the end of the crack pipe sticking out from his pants.

Really fucking shitty job, asshole, really bad job at trying to stash that shit. You are going to have to do much better than that. I snicker at how bad some guys are at trying to hide shit from the cops.

Just then the girl sees my partner standing on the other side of the car. I can tell from her sudden glance over in his direction that she has seen him. She knows that there is no way out, they are trapped between the cars.

"Okay, so let's play a game. I call it the honesty game. If you don't fucking lie to me I am pretty good to deal with." I stare at the two, letting them know that I am all business now. I let them know what the rules for my game are. "But play me like a fool and I get really fucking pissed off."

Both heads turn towards me in the faint darkness of the parking lot. I can see their eyes, eyes filled with age and despair. Their faces are gaunt and frail-looking from malnourishment. The male is sporting boils on his arms from infections that are raging out of control. His body is rotting. I don't give a fuck and amazing enough he doesn't give a fuck either. They just stare at me.

"Are we clear on these rules?" Death-filled eyes stare back at me.

"Good, so now how about I ask you two what you are up to?"

The male answers first as the young girl just dips her head. "We are just sitting here getting warm and dry from the rain. Just cut us some slack, boss."

"Boss"; the word tells me that he has spent time in jail. Calling a uniform "boss" is common language for anyone who has done time; it is a warning sign for me. I scan his hands and open forearms and I can see jailhouse tattoos, lots of them. He has done some heavy time.

"Don't ask me for slack, dipshit. I told you that I am good to deal with if you don't lie to me and I have just caught you in your first lie. I was fucking standing here when you blasted off on your shit. Do not fucking play me for a fool."

I look at the male on the ground. He looks back at me with eyes that have nothing to lose.

"How much clink time you done?" I ask as my finger points to the tattoos on his arms. I want to let him know that I know that he has done time, that I am paying attention.

"I just got out five months ago. Did eight years for robbery."

Eight years. That is a long time in our court system. It is so rare to hear anyone get eight years, even for a sexual assault or some other unforgivable sin like that.

"You have identification on you?"

His head moves from side to side. "No, boss, I don't have any papers."

"Well, let's go to my car and find out who you are." I motion for him to walk towards my partner. I watch him like a hawk as I can feel my body start to get pumped full of adrenaline. My instincts are kicking in, telling me that his body language tells another story. My subconscious is yelling out that he is going to try to run or fight. I listen to it closely as this inner voice, "Spidey senses," some of the guys call it, has allowed me to go home to my family alive more than once.

I glance at my partner and I can see he is reading the same thing I am. I see his body blade the male as the cracker starts to get up. We are still hunting and this guy is giving us all the signals that he wants to be our prey today.

Just then the guy blasts up and rushes my partner. The guy has made his decision to go after the smaller cop, the less in-your-face guy. Wrong fucking move on his part. I love to fight, I was born to fight, and violence is what fulfills my soul. I am a soldier. My partner is a soldier too. He is just made in a smaller package than me but he is just as fierce and determined as I am.

Just as the guy gets to his feet and his momentum starts to move towards my partner he is stopped. My partner steps forward and hammers the guy to the chest with his elbow.

My fix is flowing inside of me. The adrenaline drives my heart to beat fast. It makes me clench my teeth and draw my lips back over them. It fills me with power and strength. The adrenaline fix dumps into me and I am on the attack too.

The bad guy drops back holding his chest from my partner's blow. In a flash I see a fist hammer into his jaw, which rolls him over the car that we have been using to trap the two crackers.

I slide my hand out and lock into a fist full of hair as I drag the guy towards me, over the hood of the car. I control the head, I now control what this guy can see, which way his body moves, I control his world as long as I can control his head.

I don't move my spot. I keep myself in a place were I can see the girl on the ground. She is as much of a threat as he is.

In my peripheral vision I can see her cover her face with her hands as she cowers in a fetal position on the ground. I can hear her cry as my partner opens up a world of shit on the bad guy.

I slam his head off the hood of the car. I drive my fist down into his face like a hammer. My first blow lands hard and I can see his lips split and blood flow from his mouth, covering his teeth in a red gloss. He is not fazed, his eyes keep trying to lock onto me. He is looking for something to hit.

My partner hammers the guy to the stomach and drives another elbow into his chest. I feel the gasp of warm air escape from his blood-covered lips.

I slam another hammer fist into his face again. I can feel his nose bend and snap under my leather-covered hands. The hood of the car echoes with a resonating gong as I drive his head hard into it again.

I can hear the girl scream to God as she can hear the fury we are unleashing on the male. Her cries are loud enough to break the muffling barrier as her trembling hands over her face.

I drive my fist into his face again. It lands hard into his jaw and I hear the echo of bone on bone, teeth grind into teeth. Small splinters of pink-colored teeth scatter across the black polished hood of the car that he is lying on. His eyes still flash, he is still functioning. He is high on crack and he is not able to feel a single blow we deliver.

His hands reach up and lock onto my hand that is clenching his hair. He is trying to stabilize his world enough to get a bearing and recover to fight better.

I yank his head to the left and expose the side of his neck. My right hand drives towards it target. As it moves through the air my fist opens and I hit the side of his neck with my palm. As I strike the side of his neck, I imagine my hand pushing through his neck. I imagine driving his spine out of his body.

I then see his eyes roll back in his head. The brachial stun I delivered worked, all the blood sitting in his jugular vein surged into his brain. The sudden rush of blood caused the brain to shut down. The effect is momentary but if my partner and I work fast the two seconds of unconsciousness will be enough.

He is flipped onto his stomach, his hands are rolled behind his back, and the cuffs are locked onto him before he gains consciousness. It is a well-rehearsed task we have performed hundreds of times in our brief time working together as partners. The bad guy is in handcuffs and is being unceremoniously tossed to the cold concrete floor. He is finished.

His head rolls back and forth on the ground as he starts to wake up. His blood drips into the pools of rain water on the ground. The water turns red and flows in small rivers down the parking lot's smooth floor. A red swirl rolling down on the floor that turns to dark black in the shadows.

I look at the girl on the ground, I never really stopped looking at her. I always kept her in my sight. She just stayed there, in her fetal position, crying.

I watch the trickle of bloody water slide across the floor past my black shiny work boots. I wait for my adrenaline fix to subside. I don't want to deal with her all jacked up. I am still frothing from my fight, I have to settle my waters first.

Calm floods me. I am coming down from the fix and the surge of calm is the light to the darkness. From an extreme high to the exact opposite. I could just sit down and let time pass me by right now. I am tired and this was not even a big dump. This is just a little fix, a regular daily dose for me.

"So, how are things going to be with you? Are you going to make wiser decisions than the goof on the floor?" My hands shake as the adrenaline fix slides out of me.

I look over to the guy lying on the floor. He is now conscious and he looks over at me with his face already swelling from the blows he took.

"Fuck you! You're the fucking goof!" he yells at me. He is trying to still save face because the name tag of "goof" in jail is an immediate insult and fighting words.

"Fuck you!..." His next rant is cut short from my partner's hard boot strike into his kidneys. I can see the pain swell in the bad guy's eyes as he rolls over onto his stomach, trying to release the spasm that is now rocking his body from the blow.

"Still not learning? Don't worry; you will learn soon enough to keep your fucking mouth shut." I look back at the girl on the floor.

"So, what do you think we might need to know?"

She sits there, hiding her face in her hands. I wait for her to think things out. I don't want to push her into making a bad mistake tonight. A mistake like the guy just made.

Her hands push the tears off of her face. She pulls back her wet dirty hair and tries to put it into a ponytail. She is trying to recompose herself, regain whatever dignity she has felt that she has lost from crying.

Her hair is still a mess and her face is puffy and red from crying but she works hard, pulling in her feelings. She is trying to build a brave face.

"Can I stand up?"

"Sure, just keep your hands away from your body." I give a nod and a small smile at this little girl who wears such a brave face.

When she is standing up I see how little the girl is. My eyes open and my heart sinks as soon as I get a full visual of her.

"How old are you? Thirteen? Fourteen?"

"I am thirteen," she says as she pulls her soaked red sweater straight. She fixes her oversized jeans and her hair again. I just stare at her.

Maybe five feet two inches in height and all of 100 pounds in weight she looks like death has been sleeping with her for the past few weeks.

"How long you been binging for?"

"Um, dunno, I think five or six days now." She rolls her palms over her hair again as if the meager attempts will push away the days without showering or hygiene.

Fuck, no food, no sleep, or rest for five or six days. She is at the breaking point of her drug binge. She had maybe another day before her mind would want to shut down but her body would just keep on rocking as long as she pumped in the crack. The breaking point of most binges is where we deal with them.

Crackers and Jibbers snap at this point. They are hysterical, delusional, and paranoid. Very dangerous animals that not only are all fired up on their drugs but they are completely immune to pain. That is when it takes six or seven cops to subdue them. When the public sees that, it is instantly tagged as police brutality. Heaven forbid someone has videotaped the occurrence; then it is front-page shit.

I always want the civilians raving at our use of force to be put in a cage with these animals. You want to point your finger at me? Take my place and stop this fucker. It would take only a few seconds before the "Do Gooder" would be screaming for the police to help him. Then would he say the force we used to save his ass is excessive? I think not.

"How are you when you 'Jones'? Do you get violent or do you just crash hard?"

"I just crash hard. I am not a violent person." Her voice cracks and I can tell that the tears want to come back. She glances over to the guy lying on the floor. Blood is still flowing from his mouth but he has learned a valuable lesson again. A lesson I am sure he learned repeatedly in prison. He is quiet.

She works hard but she is still just a little girl. She tears up and starts to cry again.

I ask her for some picture identification and she reaches towards her purse to get it. I shake my head and her hands move away from her bag as I reach for it.

"Where is it at and is there anything I can cut or poke myself on in here?"

"No, nothing sharp in my purse. I keep my school ID in the front of my purse." Her trembling hand points towards the small zipper on the front of her worn black leather purse.

I see her hand shake. "Don't worry. If you play it cool nothing bad is going to happen to you tonight." I motion my head towards the guy on the floor. "He fucked around and decided to break the rules. You know the rules, don't you?"

She nods her head. "Don't lie to the police and don't fuck with them."

"Perfect, if we are like that with each other tonight nothing bad will happen." I slowly move my hand into the front pouch of her purse. I always move slowly after looking inside the purse. I worry about the day that I am careless and I get a dirty rig (syringe) stuffed into my finger. The price to pay for my carelessness: "Welcome to the world of Hepatitis C or AIDS."

Fuck, not a price to pay for having your head up your ass. I always keep sharp.

My leather-covered hands move slowly through the purse, waiting for anything that might feel like a needle, knife, or any other sharp.

Nothing.

I slide out her school identification and hand it to my partner. He sits behind our car's computer and starts to load her information in. His face is lit up in a ghostly blue from the screen's light.

I wait to hear what my partner learns from our criminal records search system. I watch her, look for any movements that might tell me that her behavior is going to change. She runs her hands through her hair again. She is nervous, her palms are sweating, she tries to dry them in her hair.

Warning sign, what is she so nervous about?

"Why are you here with this loser?" I motion to the male still lying on the cold concrete floor.

"He is my uncle."

"Your uncle?" I am stumped. I look over to the shitbag on the floor. "Is this the fuck that introduced you to crack?"

She hesitates, I know the answer is yes. I look over to the piece of shit, I want to rip him to shit. Fucking puke gets a young girl hooked on death.

"Five fucking months out and you get this young girl hooked up?"

I can feel my voice change with rage. I calm my beast, I want to rip him apart.

I look at the girl's purse. I grab the bottom of it and dump the contents of it out onto the hood of my cruiser. I need to distract myself from the guy on the floor. I can feel the anger build in me, I want to punish this fucker for his sins. I know that the court system will never punish him.

I scan the items scattered over the hood of my car. In the dim parking lot lights I can see various crack paraphernalia. Plastic tubing, wire mesh, lighters, thin metal rods to push the used wire mesh out of the pipe. I grab empty lip balm containers that used to hold crack. A quick shake tells me that the storage items are empty.

I see nothing that a normal thirteen-year-old girl may have.

My hands brush over a small cloth bag. Condoms fall out of the small open top.

"You're working the streets for your dope?"

She dips her head and nods. I look through the front window of my cruiser and see my partner's face. He has two little girls at home and they are about her age. He looks at her with sadness and despair in his eyes. He sees his girls standing there.

She has lost her life now due to one mistake. In this era youth are no longer allowed to make mistakes with these designer street drugs. No wisdom to be gained from experimentation.

"You are hooking at thirteen? That is really fucked up. And let me guess, this piece of shit on the floor gets to chip off of the drugs you get from hooking?"

She nods her head again as tears start to swell in her eyes. She dips down and sits on the floor and starts to cry. Shame fills her rotting soul.

She tries to talk. Her sentences are short and chopped. She tries to speak between her sobs but the words just make her gasp for air.

"I can't help myself. I want the drugs. I can't stop. I don't want to fucking hook for the drugs but I have no money." She sobs more. "You cannot know my world. Don't fucking judge me." She sobs more.

My eyes never leave her. She is broken. She has lost all innocence. The drugs call to her and she follows. Her body is no temple, no sanctuary. She will now use her body to get the chemical that calls her.

She is dying a slow death and she knows it. Her world is spiraling out of control.

I hear my partner tell me that she is 1055, a runaway. She will have to be going home to her parents tonight.

I know she will be back here tomorrow.

I have seen it far too often.

I look over to the guy on the floor. "If there is a hell, you are going to be getting a front seat on the bus, mother fucker."

He looks back at me, blood still dripping from his face. "Fuck you, pig, you are going to be driving the bus!"

My partner starts to chuckle. He knows that the line has once again been crossed. He knows what is coming next.

I look at my partner and signal for him to watch the crying girl. He steps out of the car and move towards her.

"You're right, you fuck. I am going to be driving the bus to hell. I got no issues with that." My eyes are locked onto him as I move towards him.

I can feel my animal inside yelling to be let out. I can feel the rage building. The animal is roaring with excitement, it wants out to do what it does the best.

Punish.

Crush.

Destroy.

I do not stop it.

"Hey boss, take it easy." Fear, his voice echoes with fear.

His eyes open up wide as he sees the rage inside my eyes, he sees the animal and he wants to run, fear rips through him.

"Fuck you. I am going to give you a taste of hell, mother fucker. Gunna rip off a pound of flesh for what you did to this little girl." He tries to push himself away from me. His rubber-soled runners squeak on the wet concrete as the metal handcuffs behind his back echo a metallic scrape.

I step over his scrambling feet and grab his neck with my left hand. Flesh disappears under the black leather of my gloves. A noose tightens around his neck. I see his eyes open wide as he loses the precious air that he needs.

I drag him up off the ground and slam him into a concrete pillar.

His head makes a hollow sound as it strikes the manmade stone.

"You want to fuck around, mother fucker?" My hand tightens around his neck. "Now you get to know how this girl feels. Helpless, like you are in your handcuffs."

I slam my right fist into his stomach. My teeth grit as I grind them together. My animal is let loose. I have taken off the leash.

My fist slams again and again into his body. I can feel his soft stomach give to my hard blows. I look into his eyes as he tries to scream. I look into his eyes as they flare in pain.

I drive another blow into his body, right into his kidneys. Urine flows to the floor as his bowls release themselves from the punishment. I drive my fingers under his ribcage and then grab onto his lower ribs.

I let go of his neck and he screams. The scream is quiet and filled with gasps. His lungs are pinched into his ribcage as my hand tightens its grip. He tries to fall to the floor to escape the pain. I hold him there. I squeeze harder.

My animal wants more. It wants blood, true punishment. I have felt this beast so many times now. I know how to leash it up. I know how to call it back into its cage.

"Remember this feeling, mother fucker. The crushing pain in your chest. She gets this every time you let her go into some fuck's car for her to get hooked." I let go of my grip.

His body falls to the floor. He huddles into a fetal position. He legs dragged close into his chest as he tries to lessen the pain surging through his body. His body jerks as he tries to hold back his pain. His lips let out small gasps of air, he tries to hold back his tears. He is fighting the pain.

I wind my right leg back and kick him hard to his stomach. His pain threshold is breached.

"Stop, oh fuck. Please stop," he cries. His sobs are now mixed in with the sobs of the young girl.

I turn my back on him and walk to the car.

My partner looks at me. "Feel better?"

I nod my head. I do feel better. The fucker got his karma returned back to him.

My partner starts to dial the cell phone in the car. He is calling the young girl's parents. "I feel better. Glad you did it. I wanted to kill

335

him." He puts the phone up to his ear and listens to the drone of the electronic ringtone.

I take deep breaths to slow down my heart. I wanted to kill him too.

The phone is answered after only three rings.

My partner speaks.

"Hello, is your daughter Trish Smith?" A short pause. "Yes, this is the City Police and we have her at 7th Avenue and 10th Street. Can you come by to pick her up?" Another short pause as my partner listens to the person on the other side of the phone call.

"Yes, that is 7th Avenue and 10th Street, twenty minutes? No problem, we are on the second level of the parking lot." The phone gets seated back into the cradle.

"Mom and Dad are coming to get her. They will be here in twenty minutes."

"Cool." I sit back and breathe in deep again. I close my eyes and imagine all the good things I have. I can smell my wife's hair. I remember my dog. His tail wagging as he spins and whines out of excitement. I put my brain in a good place.

The rumble of thunder stops my mental travel. Cold air rushes into the open-air parking lot and with it small wisps of mist roll over my face. I can hear the sobs of the girl still echoing off of the slick concrete walls.

For twenty minutes my partner and I sit in silence.

Silence that is cut only by the moans of the guy on the floor and the slowly subsiding cries of the girl. Sounds that are soaked up by the steady rush of rain outside.

I sit and smell the damp air. I sit and stare out into nothing.

I want to feel nothing. I feel everything.

My head turns as I hear the chirp of wet rubber tires sliding over the concrete floors.

Mom and Dad are here.

A newer model Nissan SUV rolls close to our cruiser as I set out into the bright headlights. My eyes squint and burn as they adjust to the white lights cast out from the vehicle headlights.

Just as I start to turn my head away to protect my eyes, the headlights turn off. The Nissan's engine dies as the ignition is turned off. In a flash the young girl's mother and father exit the SUV and I can feel the panic in them.

The father is trying to look conservative and strong but I can see the fear in his eyes. Fear that comes when the police have found your missing child. Fear that grows over long nights where your baby does not call, does not even give any hint of her existence. Fear that has cut deeply into his soul.

The mother wears her heart on her sleeve. She looks tired and worn. Her eyes are red from crying. Her body looks weak and drawn. She has been awake for way too many nights worrying about their daughter.

I reach out to shake the father's hand just as the mother peers past me and sees her daughter sitting on the concrete.

"Oh, my God" are the only words that escape in the silence. She rushes forward and reaches for her daughter. In a heartbeat the child is wrapped in her mother's shielding arms. The two start to cry together as her mother rocks her child in her arms.

How many times did her mother rock her like this as a baby? How many times did she have her mother wrap her protecting arms around her? How does this little girl feel now? She knows that her mother's arms and the protection that they give will not save her from the demon that she dances with.

The father and I just stare at the sight before us.

I stare. I can see a mother holding her child in her arms. A child that is dying and there is nothing her mother can do. A child that will live for the next five or six years as her drug addiction rips her apart. She will become a living nightmare for her parents. Dead in soul but still living in body.

I break my eyes from the pitiful sight before me.

"How long has she been missing for?"

My eyes look into the father's eyes standing before me. I see his shattered soul through his eyes.

"For about thirteen weeks now. This is the first time we have heard from her in thirteen weeks. She has been gone for too long." His voice quivers as it echoes his shaking soul.

"You know that she is hooked on crack?" I point to the drug paraphernalia on the hood of the car.

"Yes, we do." He clears his voice. He is trying to pull his soul together. Piece together the puzzle. "Before she left she told us that her uncle, my brother, had her try crack. She told us that she was addicted. She wanted help, we did not know what to do. I thought she could just stop." He starts to cry, his hands cover his face as tears stream down his cheeks.

"I got angry when I caught her stealing money from us to by drugs. I yelled and she cried. She ran off that night. I have been dying every day since she has left."

He looks over to his wife and child. "I am so sorry, I never knew that this would happen."

His voice is directed to his wife and child. "I am so sorry."

I dawn my iron mask, ensure my suit of armor is locked tight. I cannot lose myself in his world. I shut down my feelings as I distance myself from his hell.

"It is not your fault. I have seen this time and time again. One hit from that drug and they are lost." I put my hand on his shoulder and motion him towards my open cruiser door. "Why don't you sit down for a bit?"

The father sits down into the driver's side of the cruiser. His legs hang out the door. His hands still in his face. I walk to the trunk of the car and grab a couple sheets of paper towels.

I hand it to him. "Sorry, that is all we have."

"Thanks," he says and wipes his face clear of tears; his eyes are red and puffing. He lifts his head up and draws air in deep into his lungs. He is grasping at the puzzle inside of him. He is trying to put forth a brave face. The same brave face his daughter wears.

"No problem. Has anyone told you what to expect from your daughter now that she is hooked on this crap?" My voice is steady, my armor is on, and my face is etched in stone.

I no longer look at him with pity or empathy. It is all business now. I wear my mask now.

"Uh, no. We have not talked to anyone about this addiction she has."

The mother gets up off the floor with her daughter still cradled in her arms. They move past us as the mother and child walk towards the SUV.

"I will explain to you both what my experience is with these matters." I watch as the two pass me. I watch as the mother carefully puts her baby into the back seat. I watch as she ensures that the seat belt is locked around her baby.

The father speaks. "Did she tell you where her uncle is?"

Oh fuck, I almost forgot. "Oh, we have him here. He got aggressive with us so we had to arrest him. He is laying over on the other side of our car." I point to where he is laying. I point into the darkness.

The mother looks over to my partner. "He is here? You have him here?"

I hear the rage in her voice. I hear the animal that is stored within every mother. Her animal wants to protect her children; her animal will gladly die to protect her child. I can feel her fury.

"Yes, like I said he is on the other side of the car."

They both race over to the other side of the car. I can feel their fury. My partner is the only thing that separates the uncle from the wrath that mother and father will give him.

I catch my partner's gaze as the parents stop. They see him standing in the way and they will not question his authority. They are good people and they will not push past him as he stands in their way.

They stare at him.

He speaks. "I have two daughters, one is fourteen and the other is sixteen." He steps aside and turns his back to them. He walks towards me. His voice is cold and dry. He wears his stone mask. "Just don't kill him."

The father grabs the guy laying on the ground. A rush of words escape him mouth.

"How could you!"

"My baby, you hurt my baby!"

"I am your brother!""

A fury of futile slaps hit the uncle's face as the mother shouts at him. Her blows are all she can give.

"You bastard! How could you?" Her shouts turn to tears as she keeps slapping him.

I watch and I can hear my animal scream, "Fuck him up. Carve his fucking eyes out! Kill him!"

I watch.

My partner watches.

We let the rage flow, let the fury echo through the parking lot. The father shakes the uncle, the mother slaps him. They will not kill him, they are not of that creature. They cannot kill.

Then the rage slips loose. The fury stops. The father throws his brother to the floor. The mother stops her assault. They both turn towards us as we stare at them.

The husband speaks. "Sorry, I don't know what came over me." His hands shake. His heart pounds. His body quivers.

I know what came over you. Rage, anger, vengeance, and violence. Emotions rarely felt unless someone destroys something you love.

"Don't worry about it," I say as my stone face cracks a smile. I can see that this release has allowed him to find some pieces of his soul.

My partner walks over to the mother. Her eyes are still fixed on the uncle.

"If I were you I would never let these people see you again." His voice is cast down to the uncle on the floor. Blood is flowing from his face. The blows from the mother opened wounds that were starting to close. "They would have killed you if we were not here." He hands over a sanitary wipe to the mother so that she can clean the blood on her hands.

She looks at her hands as she wipes the blood off. Her hands are shaking. Her body quivers as she washes her hands clean. She too has found some of her lost soul.

"Can I speak to you two over here while my partner deals with him?" My head nods to the uncle on the floor.

The mother and father move over to me with newly gained dignity.

"What I am going to tell you is what I have experienced from working the streets and seeing with my own eyes what this drug addiction will do to your child." I fix my stone mask. "I am not saying that this is that path that your daughter will follow but I am saying that I have never seen anyone follow a different path."

Their eyes are fixed onto me.

"If you want this information I will tell you but it is not going to be good."

The mother speaks first. "Tell us, please." Her hand slides down and locks into her husband's. Their grip tightens as they hold into each other.

Such a simple embrace, hand in hand. Such a powerful bond, I work at keeping my stone mask on.

"Okay," I breathe in deep. "Your daughter is dead. The girl that you raised is dead. She has been replaced by a person who will do anything for her drugs. She will not sleep, she will not eat, she will not care what she does to her body if it means that she gets her drugs."

Her parents' eyes open up as I point out the condoms that scatter the hood of the car beside us.

"She will steal from you, manipulate you, and destroy your world to get her fix. Nothing else matters to her now that she craves this drug. Your daughter is dead now."

I can see it in the father's eyes: acceptance. I can see that he knows that my words are true.

"Neither of you can blame yourself for what has happened to your daughter. It is way out of your scope or control. Blame him." I point to the uncle that is now leaning against the back window of our cruiser. His bloodied head is propped against the cool glass.

The mother looks at her husband. "But, we have to try. We cannot lose hope."

I expected nothing less from her. A mother will never lose hope in her child.

"I am just telling you what I know."

My partner's voice moves across the parking lot towards the couple. "But for tonight, take your child home. Feed her, clean her up, and let her sleep. She has had a long few days of no sleep. I think that you two could also use some sleep." He knows that they will sleep better tonight knowing that their baby is at home with them.

The husband and wife thank us for our time and I shake their hands. I watch them as they get into the SUV and drive out of the parking lot.

My door closes on the cruiser as I slide the key into the ignition. The car turns over and starts. A low rumble from under the hood floods the now silent parking lot.

"So, what do you think her chances are?" my partner asks me.

"She is fucked." I put the car into drive and move out of the concrete parking lot back into the rain.

341

JAKE

JAKE

Sometimes the hardest thing to do is not shut down.

To not close off the outside world, which seems to constantly show how evil and monstrous it can be.

As time passes I find it easier to shut down. Lock my soul up in the dark recess of my body. A place where it is safe but hidden.

As time passes I find it harder to find my soul after I have locked it away. When I shut down I am cold, hard, and made of stone. I am protected behind my stone mask. A defense mechanism I have learned to save me. One that I fear will one day destroy all that I have.

I fear it will crush my marriage, snap precious links with friends, and burn ties to my family. Shutting down is a way I protect myself from the outside pain and suffering. I need to shut down to save me but I have to work harder and harder each time to awaken from this emotional slumber.

I arrive at an old house. The wood siding is faded and the brown paint is flaking off in the mid-day sun. Large chunks of paint are pealed back, exposing the rotting wood underneath.

My short walk up to the house causes sweat to roll down my back. The sun cooks my body as the dark uniform soaks up the heat it punishes me with. I smile as I approach another uniform. It is a bylaw officer that deals with animal complaints.

I wipe my brow with the back of my hand. "Fucking hot day."

"Yeah, not a good day to be working. Much rather be having a beer on a patio somewhere." His eyes squint and he pulls at his belt trying to get his pants to sit properly. His large belly forces his pants back down with every attempt.

I look at the water pooling on his balding head. He is feeling the heat of the sun also.

"So what do we have here?" I ask as I look at the aging house. The grass is long and uncut. The widows have large bedsheets draped across them to keep the sun out. "Besides your everyday shit pit?"

"Well, the neighbors have lodged a complaint that the dog at this residence is always howling. I have to issue this guy a warning but your dispatcher told me that I might need you guys here. I guess he has a history of violence."

I shrug my shoulders. "Cool, I will help you anyway I can." I laugh internally; I too have a history of violence. I guess in a reversed world if the bad guys came to my house they too would bring backup.

The overweight but really pleasant bylaw guy rings the doorbell. We wait and he rings the doorbell again. Nothing.

I bang on the door hard with my fist and to both of our surprise the door creaks open.

"Hello, City Police!" I yell into the house as I open the door further.

I smell rot, filth, and defecation. The odor rushes out towards me and I turn my head in an attempt to escape it. There is no escape as the hot air wraps around me.

"Oh fuck, that is fucking all wrong," I say as my face twists into a contorted ball.

The bylaw officer steps back out into the hot sun to try to find fresh air. "No shit, what the hell is that smell?"

I know that the smell cast out from this place will welcome me into just that: hell. I key the mike to my radio and let our dispatcher know that this call is going bad. "Dispatch, can you send another unit here? The front door is unsecure and there is a foul odor in the residence. Possibly a coded person in the residence."

"A coded person" is our language for a dead guy. This place smells of death, old rotting death. I know this sticky smell well.

I look at the bylaw guy as the second car unit pulls up to the house. "Can you stay out here and warn us if anyone shows up?" I know he doesn't want to go inside this house. But I also know that he would follow us if I did not tell him to stay outside. I can tell from his demeanor that he is a good strong man that would confront his fear of this house if he needed to.

He nods his head and the backup unit follows me into the house.

The smell is overpowering. It tries to steal the air from my lungs. I work to fight off the nausea that is creeping up, making my mouth water. I can feel the warm acidic bile eating its way up to my throat. I think past the smell and the nausea dissipates. It is a natural ability I have and one that I am so thankful for.

"Fuck, hold up, buddy! I have to open up some windows." I see my backup quickly walk over to a large window, slide it open, and gasp for fresh air. He balances his body against the frame as his arms are outstretched, his hands gripping onto the windowsill. His body wants to retch and throw up. He is fighting his gag reflex as good as he can.

The wretched smell in this house is warning us that we should not be here. Our subconscious mind registers it. It makes us sick, waters our eyes, and fills our nose with mucus. Our subconscious is yelling at us that death and rot are sleeping here and we should get out.

But our conscious brain is what we control. So we press forward into the hellish smell.

"Hey, I am going to clear the rest of the rooms up here. Can you slide more windows open so that I do not toss my lunch from this fucking smell?" I see him look at me as I speak; his face turns pale. He is fighting the desire to throw up.

I speak again, before he can tell me that he will follow me through the house. "Don't worry, brother, all I am going to do is find a dead guy. I am all good. You open up some more windows and I will be done in a minute."

I walk away and don't let him answer me to object. His gag reflex is kicking in. Nothing he can do about it but get some air. He has to give in to his subconscious mind.

I walk around the top floor. I open each door, round each corner, expecting to find a rotting dead person. Nothing.

I walk past the kitchen and move towards the basement door.

I wonder where this fuck has died. Is it a suicide? Will I find the body with the head opened up like a popped balloon from a gun suicide? I have seen lots of those. Will he be hanging? Will he have bled out from cutting himself? My mind walks through all of the scenes I have witnessed before.

My hand reaches for the doornob, and I twist the brass sphere and swing the door open.

"Fuck!" I twist my face again. The smell is far worse now.

"What's up?" A voice echoes with concern from the backup unit opening a window in the kitchen.

"Nothing, but it fucking smells way worse down here. This fucker must be rotten bad to smell this way." I force down the odor again. I shut off my gag reflex as I turn on the light to the basement and walk down the steps. I wipe the mucus that is gathering on the tip of my nose.

As I make my way down the steps I see an unfinished basement with a bare concrete floor. Dogshit covers every available inch of the floor and the smell of stale urine mixes in with the foul odor. The raw ammonia from the urine burns my eyes.

I carefully walk towards a string hanging from the ceiling. It is attached to a light bulb and with a tug down it blazes to life.

In the basking light I stand and stare. My mind draws blank as it tries to understand what information my eyes are giving it.

I can feel my mouth open in disgust and awe.

Among the shit and piss, chained to the corner lies a black mat of hair and exposed flesh.

I can see the eyes of a dog, a black Lab staring back at me.

Eyes filled with fear and pain.

I can see cuts to his face, infected wounds oozing yellow puss from them. His legs are filled with open sores and his ribs are exposed from malnourishment. I stand and stare. My mouth opens wide as my jaw drops.

Holding onto the string that I used to show me this hell I slowly bend over. My stomach clenches and I can feel a torrent of water flow through my teeth and over my gums. I vomit all over the floor. My stomach heaves harder as I push out bile and partially digested food.

I just stand there holding onto the string as I throw up all over the floor. I can see my vomit pool on the concrete over the dogshit and piss. Vomit splatters over my boots as I heave again.

I can hear my backup call down to me, asking if I am all right.

I keep heaving. I am lost in this hell and I do not know how to pull myself out of it.

Then I hear it. A low whisper in the foul air. A whine from the dog as he moves in pain.

I stop throwing up. I pull myself up on the thin string that acted as my lifeline. I look at the dog and I feel such sorrow for him.

"Yeah, I am okay, just tossed my fucking lunch. Don't come down here. It is not a good sight. Tell that bylaw guy to call a vet. I got a dog here that is all fucked up." I wipe my hand across my chin, wiping off the vomit that is hanging from it.

I walk over to the dog and I can see the fear in his eyes. I can only imagine how many times this dog was beaten. How long this dog suffered under the hands of someone who was supposed to cherish and protect him.

As I walk closer to the dog he winces and cowers. I see the wounds on his body and I can feel his pain.

I raise my eyes off of him to look for something to wrap his body in.

My eyes flow across the room to a blanket sitting in the corner. As I turn to go get it the dog starts to whine and cower more. I look at the old dirty red blanket; I can see why my actions have filled him with fear. I see a metal coat hanger that has been bent straight like a whip. The back end of it is wrapped in duct tape to allow a firm grip. It has black dog hair sticking to it, glued onto the wire with dried blood.

"Don't worry, buddy. I am not going to hurt you."

I want to scream, I want to take away the dog's pain and suffering. I want to cry. I crouch my stance and open my palms towards him as I walk slowly. I want to show him that I am no threat to him.

As I reach to touch him he turns his head away from me as if to shield himself from a punishment that he knows will come. He folds his ears close to his head, scarred and split from old beatings. His eyes shut and quiver as he braces himself for pain. His nose tucks as far into the corner of the wall as possible.

"Not today. No one is going to hurt you today." My hand slides slowly over his head. My fingers move gingerly over infected cuts and blood-crusted hair. His flesh jumps from my touch.

I hear footsteps from other cops coming into the house.

I reach over and open a chain that is wrapped so tight around his neck that it has worn its way into his flesh. He whimpers and whines as I slowly remove the bond from his neck. Everything I do seems to hurt him.

"Sorry, buddy, but I have to get you out of here."

His head turns towards me as I speak and I catch his eyes opening.

Open eyes, not afraid of my actions, look at me. Huge brown eyes that hold such innocence in them, begging me for more of the love that I am giving him.

He looks at me as if to ask me why I am not hurting him. They are filled with confusion; he has never been treated with anything but violence and hate. Now he feels loving and caring hands roll over his fur. His eyes tell me that this is all that he wants.

Love and affection.

As the chain unravels itself from the dried blood and matted hair I slowly lower it to the floor. I keep my movements slow and calm because I do not want to frighten the Lab any more. My palm moves over his head again, stroking his face with affection.

I slowly reach up to my radio mike and calmly speak into it.

"Yeah, can all the attending units hold back? I have a badly hurt and spooked dog down here. I am trying to get it so that I can move him."

I hear units acknowledge me over the radio as the heavy thuds of issued combats boots make their way out of the house to allow me to do what I need to do.

I stroke the dog's head again. "Hey buddy, I have to get you out of here. But it is going to hurt. I am sorry." I slide my hands under his body. I feel his ribs sticking through his thin fur coat. I make my way over old cuts, my hands feeling infected scabs beneath them.

His starts to whine as I pull his body close to mine but he has no energy to try to move. He would weigh in at about eighty or ninety pounds if he were healthy but I lift his meager body easily. His whining stops as I pull him close to my chest and roll his head over towards my shoulder.

"I'm sorry, buddy."

I can smell his rot. I feel his hot body warm my arms as fresh blood rolls out from old wounds. I hold him closer to me as I speak quietly in his ear.

"Don't worry, I got you. No one is going to hurt you now." His chest heaves as he pants heavily from the pain. His whining stops as I stand up. His head turns and his nose touches my ear. I feel him smelling me. His short nasal breaths search for a smell of happiness in this putrid hell.

I walk up the stairs holding him tight in my arms. I feel the dogshit squish under my boots as I pass the string hooked onto the ceiling light. My lifeline that held me only a few minutes ago.

As I make my way up the stairs I see faces of fellow officers peering down at me.

"Jesus fuck!" Words from a close friend of mine. He quickly opens the back door to allow me the fastest way out of the house.

I slowly take step after step up the stairs. I can still feel his warm breath on my neck. Step after step I take, lifting me and the dog out of the hell below us.

As I pass through the back door I welcome the hot sun on my face. I see other cops standing outside and they all just stare at the dog in my arms.

"We got to get him some help," I say as my voice works to not crack. I feel so helpless, I want to take the dog away and heal him. I want to make him forget the pain and suffering. I want to show him how good life was supposed to be for him. I want to take him home and heal him.

With my words a flurry of activity happens from the cops around me. It is as if someone sounded a horn and woke up sleeping giants. The side door to a police van is opened and I am called to it. I hear the driver tell me that he is going to take us to the nearest animal shelter. I hear him say that there is no fucking way we are all going to stand around here and wait for the vet.

As I move myself into the back seat I can feel hands hold onto me, fellow officers making sure that I do not fall with this precious package in my arms. I sit on the back bench and another officer on the scene hands me a cold bottle of water.

"Here, he looks thirsty," he says as he moves away to close the door.

A female officer in the front passenger seat talks to the driver as she turns to look at me. "Don't drive like an ass to get there. And leave the siren off. The poor thing has gone through enough." Her hands reach out and she gently strokes the dog's head.

I can feel his breathing slow from her gentile touch. I am always amazed at the ability of a woman's touch to calm a crying child or a hurt creature. Human or not.

I can see pity and passion in her eyes as she strokes his head. The van rolls out and we start towards the animal shelter.

I open the top to the water bottle and slowly pour cold water over the dog's head and mouth. His tongue jets out, licking up the water as I rest his head on my lap. I fill my hand with water as his tongue licks my flesh, pulling the precious cool water into his mouth.

"Careful, don't give him too much. He will get sick. Just a bit." The female officer's hands touch mine to slow the pour of water.

I look at her as if to tell her to fuck off but I soon know that she is right. She sees that all I want to do is help the dog, take away the suffering.

"Here, why don't you wet this cloth?" She pulls out a rag from the glove box. "I am sure he will enjoy some cold water on his cuts. That will do him better, don't you think?"

I nod as she takes the bottle of water away from me and pours it over the white rag.

She hands the rag to me and then starts to talk to the dog as she strokes his head.

She tells him that he is going to be okay and that he is safe. She tells him that there are no more bad men to hurt him. She tells him that we are here to save him. His eyes roll shut as her voice soothes him. He doesn't wince or whimper as I slowly run the wet cloth over his wounds.

I clean his fur, wash his wounds, and hold him tight on my lap as we pull into the animal shelter.

"You stay here; I am going to get the vet to come out and look at him." The driver jumps out of the van and quickly makes his way over to the front doors.

The female officer strokes his head and calls him "Jake."

"He looks like a 'Jake,' doesn't he?" she says as she looks at me.

"Yeah, Jake is a good name for him." I continue to wipe his coat with the rag and when I stop to wet it again I can see that the rag is no longer white but red spotted with dark purple lumps of sticky blood.

I just add more water to the cloth and slowly press the cool rag against his wounds.

The side door opens and Jake doesn't even move from the sudden noise. I see a veterinarian; with precision and expertise he doesn't even flinch at the sight before him. His hands move over the dog's face and body as I hold him.

He pulls out a stethoscope and listens to the dog's heart.

As he wraps the stethoscope around the back of his neck he looks at me and asks if I can bring the dog inside.

"Sure, but Jake is in a lot of pain. Can you give him something to make the walk over easier for him?" I ask.

"Constable, Jake is no longer in any pain, he is dead."

I just sit and stare at the vet. I am quiet.

I hear nothing from all the other cops around me as they stare at the dog's lifeless body.

"John, why don't you carry Jake inside for us?" the female constable asks me.

"Uh, sure." I wrap my hands slowly around the dog's body. I act as if he can still feel his wounds, that he is still alive.

As I exit the van I can feel the hands of cops hold onto me to make sure I do not fall with this precious cargo.

I walk step by step towards a set of double doors that mark the entranceway to the animal shelter. The large glass doors swing open as other officers hold them for me.

I feel like I am floating through the lobby as I follow the veterinarian in the green overcoat. Down a hall with polished tile floors I carry Jake in my arms. His head rests on my shoulders, his nose no longer sniffing for a sent.

"Just put him down on that table there, I will take care of Jake from here." The vet points to a stainless-steel table that sits in the middle of a well-lit room.

I set Jake down slowly onto the table, careful not have him hurt from his old wounds. The female officer holds his lifeless head, preventing it from hitting the table as I set him down.

My arms slide out from under the lifeless body. I pull away as my arms fall to the side of my body. I am still floating.

I walk over to a large sink that the vet points to as he tells me to wash my arms and hands. He starts to describe the infections and diseases that Jake might have had. He presses the point that I have to make sure that I have cleaned myself as best as possible.

When I am done the female officer washes herself next. We walk out together back down the polished floors. I feel as if she is pulling my body along as I float along in clouds.

I slide into the back seat of the van again. This time the ride to the station is a quiet one. No one speaks; we all just stare out the windows as we make our way down the streets. I feel the hot sun wash onto my face. I still feel like I am floating, as if I am walking on clouds.

As the doors open I move to reach for the handle to open the side door. The female officer turns to look at me from the front seat.

"Hey John, you okay? That was a shitty call."

"Yeah, I am okay."

She asks me again if I am okay and I respond the same. She tells me that it is okay for me to be upset over what I just went through. I tell her I am fine.

I look at her and tell her I am fine. Her hand reaches out to touch me and I pull back. I wince like the dog did when I reach for him. I am afraid of what a touch might release.

She stops her hand. "You talk to me if you need to, okay?"

"Yeah, I am okay though."

"Yeah, I know you are. But sometimes we just need to talk, to sort out how good we are. You know, you gave Jake something that he never had. You showed him love and affection. Even though he died he knew how that felt."

I exit the side of the van and float into the locker room. In a foggy haze I cannot remember changing or hanging up my uniform. I am suddenly sitting in my car as the night surrounds me.

Just as I slide my key into the ignition I feel like someone has pushed me off of my cloud. I feel my body slam into the ground like I am being pounded by a massive sledgehammer.

I bend over in my seat and hold my face as tears stream out. I do not make a sound. Tears run down my face. I barely breathe as tears flow down my cheeks.

How much time passes I do not know but my tears have stopped. I can feel my waters calming as I start to breathe again.

I drive home.

I sit on the floor with my dog as the morning sun cracks the horizon. I promise him that he will never be hurt. That he will never feel the fear and pain Jake did. I pet him and watch his wagging tail and comforting eyes gaze at me. His head turns from side to side, tilting his big ears as he tries to understand what I am saying to him.

I feel the cloud start to move over me again. I can feel the fog rolling in.

I take in a deep breath and shut down. I shut off my emotions and lock away my soul in the private dark place I know where to hide it. I cannot handle another fall off of the cloud.

I walk up to the bedroom and fall asleep without holding my wife, who is sound asleep.

I am shut down, locked away.

Safe.

For now.

THE WOLF HUNTS THE LAMB

THE WOLF HUNTS THE LAMB

I quietly take the color picture off of our team meeting table as the rest of my fellow uniforms exit the room to start another shift.

As I walk I fold it in half to hide what I have removed from the parade clip.

"Smith, that shit is supposed to stay here."

I look at our team sergeant. He eyes the folded piece of paper that I hold in my hands.

"I am going to need this more than the next crew. Besides, that picture is on the overhead Powerpoint presentation."

"So why do you need to have that picture?"

I smile, whimsically holding the picture in my hand. "Come on, Sergeant. You know why I need a photo of this dirtbag. And if you don't know why, it is better that I do not explain it to you."

A grunt escapes from his lips. He knows how I police; he knows what I need the picture for.

"Keep your shit straight, Smith. I don't want to see this shit on the front page."

I smile and tear apart the Velcro on my duty pants pocket before sliding the photo into my pocket.

"Smith."

"Yes, sir?"

"Is that the pedophile snooping around the playgrounds?"

"Yes, sir."

"Happy hunting."

He moves past me with a stone face, acting as if we never talked.

Out at my police cruiser my partner and I load up our gear. Bags containing arrest reports, appearance notices, and other criminal documents. Evidence bags, biohazard containers, disinfectant gel, and police tape fill another. Lunch kits are stuffed in last, as well as our entry bags, which have extra shotgun rounds, lock cutters, raingear, and anything else that one might need for a long-haul weapons call.

I fire up the computer and see what work is waiting to be done. A few shit calls glow on the screen.

A minor theft and a landlord/tenant dispute.

"I am going to ask dispatch to stack us this shit so that we can take care of it. But first we are going to start hunting for this piece of shit." I pull out the photo from my pocket.

My partner looks over to the picture in my hands.

"I figured you were going to pinch that. I would be happy to catch that fuck." The car gets put into reverse as I ask the dispatcher over the radio to send us those calls waiting.

We start our usual routine.

On the way to our minor theft call we stop by the schools in the area and slowly crawl down the streets. We are jacking car license plates, looking for tinted-out vehicles that have been sitting for too long. We are looking for anything that is out of the ordinary.

We drive past the school; teachers and parents wave to us. They smile at the dogs that are roaming their fields looking for the wolf. They are always happy to see us here. They know that we would never bare our teeth to them or their children.

Once we have finished our theft call and tied up the paperwork for it we are back on the hunt.

I ask my partner to hit the strolls in the area. We have three major hooker strolls, and what separates them is simple: price and looks. The better looking you are, the better stroll you work.

We stop first at the "A" stroll. I know all the girls here. They know me.

I don't give them a hard time. I know well enough that I cannot change the oldest profession in civilization. So, I share information, make sure that they know who the bad dates are, what vehicles to watch out for.

They in turn give me street news, descriptions of guys that "creep" them out. I figure that if you can creep out a working girl you have something really wrong with you. I have made some good arrests on their information.

A few words and a flash of a picture and I know that the guy we are looking for is not here.

I tell them why I want him so bad. I tell them that he is a pedophile and that he is out prowling for little girls and boys.

"What are you going to do when you catch this fuck?" asks a young girl with knee-high white vinyl boots and a short skirt to match.

I shrug my shoulders. "I am going to have a little chit-chat about the proper behavior of human beings."

She leans into my window. Looks at me with cold empty eyes. She is an out-of-town girl. I have not seen her before.

"You better find this fuck before I do. I will cut the fuck's balls off." She still looks at me with cold eyes. "I got fucking messed up when my uncle messed with me." Her eyes flash fire and hate. "A fucking chit-chat is not going to cut it for that bastard." Her hands tighten on the car's door sill.

Another working girl steps into the window frame and sets her hand on the out-of-town girl's shoulder.

"Take it easy, Britney. Constable Smith is a good fucking guy. He looks after us." She looks at me and smiles.

I know her as "Paris"; she has been working this corner for the last four years. She came down from Vancouver. I have never asked her why and she has never told me.

She is a good girl, shoots me straight, and never feeds me bullshit.

"Besides, I had a bad date once and he punched the shit out of me. I had a black eye for months." She touches her left eye and cheek, running her fingers over the soft skin that was once black and filled with blood. "Smith found him and I saw what kind of 'chit-chat' he had with him. I have never even heard of anyone else seeing his freaky ass after that day."

The two girls move away from my car.

"You ladies have a safe night."

"Same for you guys. Take care. Stop by later and we will let you know if we know anything."

A quick wave and I leave the area. I never stay too long. I do not want to dent their business. They have money to make and a cop car parked on their corner is bad business for them.

We make our rounds. My partner talks to his informants, I talk to mine.

We grease all the bad guys that we know are sick fucks. Bad guys with drug habits and sexual twists. Not a good mix. I talk to them like I don't want to kill them. I act like I am their friend. I make them think that I believe their shit. They say they are cleaning up, and that they are seeking help for their issues. I just want information from them.

The night goes on and we hump some more useless calls.

Another pass through the "A" stroll creates a frantic set of waves from Paris and Britney.

"Pull over. It looks like the girls have some shit for us."

Our cruiser slows down and grinds small stones into the ground as it edges towards the curb. Before the car has even stopped rolling the girls are at our window.

"Fuck, you guys are never here when we need a cop!" I can see it in Paris's eyes. She is excited, jacked up.

"That guy was here about ten minutes ago. He looks exactly like the picture you showed us. He was chatting up Sherri." She points over to a very young-looking girl that is standing on the far corner.

Sherri has a schoolgirl look to her. Young looking face, short plaid skirt and stockings. Black shoes and a white t-shirt tied up high on her chest. A set of pigtails to finish off the look.

"No wonder he was chatting her up. She looks like she is fifteen and on her way to school."

"That is her gig. She is nineteen but she gets a lot of business from the Johns because of her look. She gets a lot of freaks too."

Paris rattles off the plate and description of the car he was driving.

I dump the information into the computer and thank the girls. I point to Sherri on the corner as I speak to my partner.

"Let's go thank her. She totally baited that fuck for us."

Our cruiser pulls up to Sherri and a look of fear crosses her face. I have never talked to Sherri before. She is a face that rarely surfaces here. I figure her for more of an escort call girl. She must need some extra cash if she is working the corner.

"Sherri?" I lift my arm onto the car's window sill.

"Uh, yeah?"

"Thanks. I really appreciate your help." I reach out to shake her hand.

She is hesitant. With fear and hesitation she reaches out and shakes my hand. Her grip is full of hesitation and confusion. I let go after a brief shake.

I smile at her as we drive away. I look into my passenger-side mirror and see Sherri step back onto her corner. I can still see her confusion.

"She doesn't trust cops. I think she has had some bad shit go down with the uniform," my partner says as we round back into our patrols.

I let out an acknowledging grunt and nod my head.

It is getting dark now. The sun is setting in the distance.

Purple clouds and silver skies cast a beautiful carpet above us.

"Fucking beautiful," I say to my partner.

He just stretches his head forward, closer to the front windshield, and peers up high to take in the sight.

He moves back behind the steering wheel. He is all business again.

"Listen, he went after the hooker that had the little schoolgirl look so he is out hunting too. He is looking for a schoolgirl. He got turned down by the hooker so now he is really fucking fired up."

I listen to him speak. His mind has been looping this information over and over again. He has come up with an answer.

"But the parks are closing, the public schools have been closed for a long time. Darkness is hitting us and we know he is here. We have to find him tonight, if we don't he will have a whole day of hunting tomorrow while we sleep." His hands grip the steering wheel hard. I can see his knuckles whiten as his grip wraps around the hard rubber covering.

"That is not fucking acceptable in my world."

"What is the plan?" I ask him.

"We find where all the afterschool classes are. We look at the music lesson schools, the afterschool care, the sports clubs for kids."

Then the Gods talk to me. I can see the building appear in my mind. The large wooden doors with old black iron runners. The red brick, the stained-glass windows. I can see it perfectly.

"Hey, there is that church over on 18th that has those ballet and band classes running late into the night. Remember, we had to take that rummy out that was sleeping in the pews?"

The car turns sharply and I know that my partner is on the way to the church.

I know that this is a good hit. I can feel it in my bones. I can feel my heart start to pump harder. I know deep inside that this fuck is going to be around there. It feels just right.

We drive down the avenue with no sign of his car. Nothing fitting the description of our guy.

"He is here, I can smell the fuck," my partner says as we pull into a poorly lit alley.

"Let's get out and walk that green belt."

I look over to my right and see a set of low-lying trees and shrubs that surround the back part of the school. A line of green that our civil engineers think are great ways to keep the natural world in our communities. Nice to look at but a real headache for high crime area. Crack heads use the space to hide and blast off. Low-class hookers pull tricks in the bushes, and criminals use it for cover and concealment from the world. If you live by a green belt you have a much greater chance of having your house broken into and your car vandalized or jacked.

A quick stroll through the underbrush usually reveals used condoms, dirty needles, and stashed stolen property.

"If I was hunting that would be a good place for me to wait and prey on my next victim."

"Sounds good to me," I say to him.

We get out of our car and make our way to the green belt.

Our heavy-duty boots fall silently onto the grass-covered trail. We move slowly into the deep thick brush.

I can smell the deep musk of a dense forest. In a matter of a few steps we are transported into it. The city seems far away as my eyes adjust to the low lighting. Summer leaves drown out the streetlights, brief speckles of artificial lights remind me that I am not in the deep heart of Mother Nature.

My eyes focus as we move into the darkness.

I am hunting now. My ears scrape the winds for any sounds. My eyes reach far into the shadows for movement.

My senses are peaked. I am a hunter of humans.

My partner and I slide through the brush, only slight sounds of our uniforms touching soft branches escape from our prowl.

Just as we are ready to break out the other side of the green belt, my eyes catch some movement.

I am fixated on a truck parked on the other side of the street from the green belt.

My body freezes. My eyes are locked onto the last spot I saw something move.

My partner stops behind me and I can feel his eyes cut past me, hoping to find what has caught my attention.

Movement. I see it again. A shadow moves in a half-ton truck parked directly across from where we are standing.

I hear my partner whisper to me.

"I see it. A guy in the blue and white truck."

A slow nod of my head lets him know that he is looking at the same thing I am.

Now we wait and watch.

Mosquitoes start to hover around my face. My ears feel their high-pitched whine as they close in on my neck and face.

I feel them land, the tiny pinprick as they pierce my skin. I do not move, I have spotted my prey. I will not move, I do not want him to know that I am here hiding in the soft shadows of the green belt.

My skin twitches as more and more bugs bite. I push them out of my mind.

Like two sheepdogs looking at a flock below them, we watch this wolf hiding in the bushes. We just want the right time, the right place, we need to know that we have the right wolf we are hunting.

My eyes move to the left as I hear soft footsteps coming towards us down the sidewalk. My head slowly turns to see a young girl walking down the sidewalk.

She looks to be no older than thirteen years old. Her head is down as she smiles and lightly sings to music that is playing in her ears.

She walks as if the wind is carrying her. Small feet in runners move eloquently as she moves along to the music playing in her headphones.

My eyes catch a bright blue i-Pod on her belt. She is a young deer, able to run if danger is sensed. But the ability to hear the danger is long drowned out by her music.

My heart starts to beat stronger.

My eyes move back to the truck. I can smell the wolf now. I know that we have stalked the right prey tonight.

The girl moves closer to the truck as the shadow inside moves around. The wolf is readying his trap.

The driver's side door opens up and I now see the wolf. The wolf we are hunting.

My heart beats harder. I want to jump out, to attack this wolf hunting the sheep I have sworn to protect.

But I cannot. I have guidelines to follow. I have rules to work by that are set out by the sheep. They forgive the wolf for preying on them. They will never forgive the sheepdog for preying on the wolf.

I can see the predator, his face, his body all tell me that he is hunting too.

He moves out of his truck into the sidewalk. He moves with grace and skill. His actions are preplanned and skilled. He has hunted before.

With ease and comfort he moves over to a pole and slides out a piece of photocopied paper that he sticks onto a lamp post with bits of tape.

His actions are slow and deliberate. He wants to attract this young girl. He wants to play on her curiosity.

He steps back from the tacked-up paper, acting like he is looking to make sure it is the right height and affixed properly; she stops to look at the picture.

She slides off her headphones.

"Oh, you have lost your cat?" Her voice is pure. Her eyes are naive and filled with innocence.

"Yeah, she ran away yesterday. Have you seen her? She is such a great cat. I just love her." His voice is slick and rotten. His eyes are filled with greed and pain.

"No, but she is sure pretty."

"Do you have a cat?"

"Yes, I have a tabby cat. His name is Tommy."

The wolf's eye light up. His trap is set and she is walking into it.

My heart pounds. My legs want to push me between the wolf and the hunter. My mind screams at them to wait. Wait a few more seconds. I have to see the wolf drop his disguise.

I have to wait.

"Oh, I am sure Tommy is a great cat. My name is Steve, what is your name?"

She hesitates. All her instincts are telling her to run. They are yelling at her to duck away and flee from the wolf. But her grooming, her social upbringing, is telling her not to be rude. Her internal battle has started.

"Uh, my name is Trisha." Her hand slowly reaches out to touch the wolf.

I see his hand reach for hers. I see his claws that will shred her apart. He smiles as they shake hands and I can see his bare-toothed grin spread across his face. The same teeth that will rip her soul from her.

"'Trisha,' that is a beautiful name. Where do you live, Trisha? "

Her guard falls. She has touched the wolf and is unharmed. She feels safe now.

"Just a few blocks down." Her slim arm points down the street.

"Oh, great. I was going that way to hang more fliers. Why don't I give you a ride home? I can see Tommy then." The wolf's eyes squint shut, the evil in the stare makes my heart pound even more.

"Uh, well...." Her instincts are fighting with her again.

"It is no problem, Trisha, I would be happy to help you. My favor to you."

He hits all her politeness buttons. He knows how to make her feel guilty for not taking his gesture of faith and help. He knows how to trap his prey.

"Okay." She swallows hard, pushing down her fears.

His hand touches hers again and he turns with her towards his truck.

In harmony we step out of the bushes. Branches move and rustle.

The wolf snaps his head towards us. I can see his eyes. They are filled with hate and lust. His lips move back over his teeth. This wolf wants to fight. He has his prey so close to him, so close to his cave. He is so close to temporarily satisfying his lust.

The young girl turns towards us and when she sees the uniforms she pulls her hand free from the wolf's grasp. His eyes follow her as she slowly walks towards us.

I look at this little lamb. Her eyes are filled with fear and embarrassment. She knows she has done wrong. She knows that she has walked with the wolf.

"Hello, Trisha," I say to her. "Why don't we have a little talk while my partner has a chat with this fellow here?" I motion with my hand for her and me to walk further down the sidewalk.

She follows me. A few steps and we are out of the reach of the wolf. I stop and turn so that her back is to the predator. I can watch him as I talk to her. Watch my partner deal with him.

"Trisha, I know your name because I was standing in the bushes while you talked with that man. Did you feel scared talking to him?"

She hesitates. Her head dips down.

"Yes, but…"

I cut her off.

"No, Trisha, this man is evil." I pull out the photo from my pocket. "He hunts for little girls like you. He takes them away and hurts them."

The wolf overhears my conversation.

"Hey, you can't say things like that. That is defamation of character! My lawyer is going to have your job."

I glare at him. I let him see my eyes. I want to show him my teeth, let him feel my bite. Not yet, I have to wait. I cannot show this lamb my ferocity. She would not understand that my violence would be in her defense.

My partner tells the wolf that he is in breach for being within 100 meters of a schoolyard and that he is under arrest.

The wolf is caught.

"Fuck you! I am not in breach. I want to call my lawyer!"

I look at him as the cuffs go on.

"Don't worry, you will have your chance to talk to a lawyer." I smile at him as he gets put into the back of our cruiser. I see a flash of panic cross his face as he sees my smile.

My bare-toothed grin.

I look back at the young girl.

"Now, Trisha, what is your address and phone number? I am going to bring this guy to jail and after that I am going to need a statement from you."

She gives me all of the information that I need. I call in the radio for another unit to attend our location to transport Trisha home.

A car slides by and the two cops in it are good men. They look over at me when I walk the young child to their car. I give them Trisha's name and address and thank them for driving her home. I ask them to get a statement from her and let her parents know that I will be calling them in about an hour.

They give a quick glance over to our cruiser and see the shadow of a man sitting in our back seat.

"Do we need to know anything more?" asks the senior constable in the driver's seat.

"No." My answer is short and cold. They know what this means.

"Cool, let us know how jail is." They smile as the car gets put into drive. Red lights flicker off as the brakes release and they drive off.

I look into the parked truck and see the tools of his trade. A paper bag filled with candy treats, a high stack of photocopied pictures of a lost cat, and CDs for a younger generation.

I take out my duty knife from my pocket. I look at his car stereo and I see his face, his grin, and his evil eyes. I slide the blade into the stereo's CD port. I cut and jam it into the machine. I hear plastic snap and metal grind. I take joy from trashing some of his tools.

I snap CDs in half and rip the photocopies apart. I take the bag of candy out and leave it on the hood of the truck for the local crack heads to take.

I want to pour gas in this truck and watch it burn.

I lift the handle on the cruiser's passenger's side door and slide into my seat.

My partner looks dead forward as he forces the shifter into drive.

"Jail?" is the only word that escapes from his mouth.

"Nope, a pit stop to hell first." My gaze is set dead forward.

"What the fuck does that mean? A pit stop in hell?" The wolf's voice is frantic.

He reaches for any hope he can. "My lawyer is Jacobs. He is the best. He is going to love...."

"Let me guess, he is going to get us fired. Oh wait! He is going to sue us also!" I snap at him. My bark at him reignites with hate and disgust.

We drive in silence to a spot that we know. It is a large underground parking lot. No cameras, no vehicles after 8 p.m., and the best thing, our car's GPS cannot transmit out of the thick concrete walls. This is a place we have been saving for such an occasion.

The far back of the parking lot is poorly lit and filled with human shit and waste from crack heads and Jibbers flopping here when they can.

It was not too long ago that we found this place and moved the mass of chemically-dependant occupants on their way. The first time I saw this place I called it "hell" because the stench almost made me retch.

We pull in and the smell instantly seeps into the car.

A wave of the odor of old urine and shit covers us. Our car slows and slides into the cover of the shadows. I look over to our computer to see the flash of three red small spheres.

Our computer has lost contact with its server. Our GPS map is shut down as the outside satellite signal cannot reach us down under the depths of the concrete.

No link to the outside world.

We have entered hell.

As I open my door the smell wraps around me. I embrace it. It is not my hell today.

"Get out." I open the back door to the police cruiser as my partner steps out of the driver's seat.

"Why?" The wolf's eyes flash with fear.

"Get the fuck out of the car." I stare at the wolf. I am frothing to let out my inner beast.

"Oh, I get it. Good cop, bad cop, eh? You think you scare me? Fuck you!"

"No, not good cop, bad cop. Just plain old bad cop." My partner opens the other door of the back seat. He stares at the wolf in the back seat.

"Fuck you. You guys are talking shit because I am in handcuffs."

I grab a handful of his hair and pull him out of the car as his screams echo down the parking lot.

"Don't worry, hero. No cuffs today." I pull him straight as he tries to duck away from the pain of having his hair yanked from his skull.

I push him onto the trunk of our car. My hands move over to his cuffs as a key slides into the small keyhole.

"Fuck you. My lawyer is going to have a field day with you

fuckers!"

He rubs his wrists, which are now free of the handcuffs.

"I have two young daughters. You are going to be lucky if you live through the night."

His eyes are cold, a look of death in his eyes.

The wolf sees this. He stops rubbing his hands as he scans the area; he wants to run, to escape the hell that we have brought him to.

"Don't even try to run, you fuck. We closed the roll gate behind us, there is no way out for you tonight." Hate, my voice is filled with it. Destruction, my eyes are burning with it.

"Soon you will get the chance to know how those kids feel when you lock them up in your cage." My partner starts to walk towards the wolf.

"Fuck you! Those kids wanted that shit. It is not my fault they are curious."

My partner snaps with that comment. I see the animal escape from him. I see his teeth get drawn back and his eyes flare open. My skin crawls with excitement from the savagery that I see before me.

We have trapped our wolf, the animal that feasted upon our flock. We now get to deliver pain and suffering back onto this predator. Pain and suffering that should have been granted the first time that this fuck hunted lambs.

The wolf too snaps forward to attack the animal before him.

The trapped wolf knows that he must fight. He is cornered, he has teeth too, and he will use them against his adversary.

As the rush comes, my animal bursts through my walls. My soul is flooded with the primal lust to crush and destroy. Man's inner evil, that dark side that lurks in our species.

My partner drives a heavy blow into the wolf's face. Bone splits from cartilage as the wolf's nose snaps.

The wolf tries to fight but he is used to timid prey. Innocent creatures that succumb to his growl. His blows miss the target as my partner continues his assault.

The wolf puts his hands up to protect his broken nose. Hard punches slam into the side and ribs of the wolf. His body crumples forward as he twists from the pain.

The broken wolf switches from fight to flight. He spins from my partner and in blind panic runs right towards me, his hands covering his face as blood spews forth.

With my feet planted firmly on the ground I snap my arm out fast and low. My arm swings out in a vast arc as I drive my right hook deep into his kidneys. He drops to the ground as piss roles down his pant leg.

The wolf falls. He crawls his body into the fetal position and covers his head.

My partner cuts the leash off of his inner animal. Black leather boots drive blow after blow into the wolf's side. I see blood spray across the floor as every last breath is driven out of the wolf's body.

I want to crush. I want to rip his body apart. I want to take part in this retribution.

I hold tight onto my beast. I pull in the leash. I cannot let my animal run free. I know what I am capable of, the damage that I can do.

With my partner and I both biting into the wolf we would kill him.

I know it.

I pull back my animal.

As the wolf rolls onto his back, his arms dropping away from his head, I see the look of pain cut into his face. His nose is split and bleeding heavily. His face is already swelling from the blows delivered.

My partner stops the carnage. His animal is reeled in and in an instant his beast is caged.

With total composition and calm he straightens up and stands tall.

"That, you piece of shit, was for all the children you touched. This is for the next time you think of touching another child." My partner steps onto the wolf's groin. Thick-soled black boots grind his groin into the concrete below him.

The wolf screams, it echoes everywhere as the pressure is continued.

The pressure releases as my partner removes his foot.

"Fucking piece of shit. Now you go to jail."

We drag his body over to the car and put the handcuffs onto him again.

My leather covered gloves grab onto the hair on the wolfs head. "Tell your lawyer what you want, fuck. You ever come around here again and we will bury you alive."

In silence we drive out to the street again. Our computer fires back up and our GPS map shows our car again.

I tap the screen. "Technology eh? It is always fucking up."

Not another word is said between us.

In prison we sit our wolf on the metal bench with other prisoners waiting to get processed and go behind bars.

They all look at him as blood drips to the floor. Small drops melding with larger ones as the blood spills out of his face.

I look over at the others on the bench. They are all hard-core ringers. Prison tattoos and jailhouse stares. They are seasoned wolves, long in tooth and vicious in nature. They are predators but not like him. They do not prey on the lambs. I know this because I know most of them.

The staff sergeant of cells looks at me and then looks at our prisoner.

"You got a story for me, Smith?"

"Yes sir, we got this skinner in a school park." My eyes glance over to the bench. The ringers look at the wolf and I can see their teeth. I can see their eyes filled with hate.

"Skinner" is prison talk for pedophile. That breed of wolf has no friends in jail. Even the hardened ringers have kids. Kids that live on the outside. Kids that this fuck will hunt.

I continue my conversation with the staff sergeant. "He tried to take a pop at my partner and, well, he lost."

"Looks that way. Maybe he will learn not to fight with the police." The staff sergeant looks at me and smiles.

I smile back. I know that tonight the cell walls will echo with whispers of a skinner in their midst. Any ringer doing hard time will bite into this wolf. Jail will be a whole new hell for this wolf.

Months pass and we are in court with the wolf seated across from us in a pale blue jumpsuit.

It is court day and the circus is about to begin.

The lawyers play their game. The defense wants to deal and the crown doesn't want to go to trial.

The judge decides that the breach of the conditions that the wolf had doesn't warrant any more time in jail than what he has spent.

"Time served," that is all that I hear from the judge.

The wolf walks free. Our old injuries on his face are still healing and new ones given to him from his cell mates are showing.

The wolf looks at us and smiles as he walks away.

Two weeks later I find out from another cop that they arrested and jailed the wolf for sexually assaulting a ten-year-old girl.

My chest feels like it is going to collapse. I feel my heart rip as I think about that monster with a child.

I push down the hurt, the anger, and the feeling of helplessness. I bury it deep inside of me. Lock it away to be dealt with another day.

The wolf is back in jail.

The lamb is injured for life.

So the cycle continues.

Paying for Your Sins

Paying for your Sins

A mother's hand reaches for her son.

"You are doing a great job, Terry."

A mess of broken bones lay on the green medical sheet covering a boy, her baby. Her fingers gently slide over the bandages and plastic tubing that cover him. His breath is short and labored.

She touches her son on the only space free of gauze and medical tape. Her hand touches his cheek. I can see the warmth of her touch on his skin. The peace it brings to him, the strength it gives him.

"You have to let the constable know what happened so that the guy who did this can pay for his sin."

Her words echo in my mind.

He is, was, in his prime. Now this young man is a mass of crushed bones and internal bruising.

No more than a few minutes ago I was talking to his surgeon. I was told how the young man was lucky to be alive.

I listened to his injuries. A shattered hip, crushed spleen, bruised liver, and severe intestinal damage. Not to forget the loss of over 30% of his skin from being dragged under a vehicle.

No more than an hour ago I was holding onto this young man's head as blood oozed across the thin latex gloves that shielded my hands from any possible biological hazards. A shield that feels the warmth of blood. I look at my hands, I can still feel the warm fluid cross my fingers.

A broken voice tells me a story of innocence. A story that starts and ends with the young man crossing the street at night. A twist of fate slammed him into the grill of an impaired driver's vehicle.

But, unlike the movies, a body rarely goes sailing over the vehicle, it is quite the opposite. Under the vehicle is the most common path.

I arrived on scene to see a trail of blood, skin, and hair tracing across the black pavement in the night. My cruiser's headlights glance off of the fresh blood, highlighting the clumps of hair.

As I walk closer to the car that is high centered on a concrete median, I see that the driver's door is open and no driver is to be found.

"1145 to all attending units. The driver has fled from the scene. Dispatch, can you run a plate for me and air any information on the registered owner please?"

I report the license plate of the car and as I peek into the driver's side of the car I can see blood on the light brown leather seats. A star pattern shines brightly on the safety glass directly above the steering wheel. Small bits of hair are stuck in the impression.

"1145 to all attending units, the driver might have facial or head injuries. It looks like he wasn't wearing his seat belt and struck the window upon impact."

I hear the units acknowledge. I now know that I must look under the car. I know there is a body there. I have seen the blood and hair on the road. I know that the person that was hit by this car is under it. I have to look. I have to assess what I can so that I can ask for the right medical assistance. I have to talk to them if they are alive. I always talk to people if they are alive, conscious or not. I guess that if I was there under the car I would want someone to talk to me.

As I kneel down onto the cold asphalt I can see a pair of runners on the far side of the crosswalk. I look at them briefly; no matter how I try to focus past the shoes it bewilders me how the shoes are always knocked off. Shoes left in the last moments of footsteps. They sit there as if they were glued to the ground, laces still tied.

I take a deep breath in. I can smell hair burning, skin searing from a hot exhaust pipe. I take a deep breath and duck my head into the small space between the asphalt and the engine block.

My flashlight casts a ray of light under the car. My eyes follow its beam.

I see a mass of twisted flesh. Jeans twisted into meat. Bones melding into the iron of the car's frame. I search for a face, a head. I cannot distinguish it from this pile of human meat lying in front of me.

I lie on the pavement to get under the car.

"City Police, can you hear me?"

A groan echoes. Low and filled with pain. I follow the sound until I can make out a face. I can see his face. I freeze at the sight.

His eyes open slowly as the light focuses in on him. Blood pours from his nose. Blood pours from his ears. I see blood pouring from an open wound on his head. Blood flowing over an exposed skull.

He moans again.

"Take it easy, buddy. The ambulance is on the way. Whatever you do, do not try to move, okay?"

Under this small cave of steel and asphalt I can barely key my mike to tell the dispatcher that we have a conscious breathing male trapped under the car. I do not want to tell her that he is a mess. He would hear me say that and that is the last thing that he needs to hear.

"Okay, the ambulance and Fire Department are on the way. Just keep breathing nice and slow. Everything is going to be all right."

I see eyes slowly close in front of me as he lets out another groan. I feel the heat of the car's engine soaking into my skin. A constant crack and ping sings from the hot engine block as it slowly cools.

A blast of scorching air pushes on my face. A cooling engine pours off the odor of metallic sulfur.

Hot air mixes with burning flesh and sticky blood. A smell floats around me. An odor filled with blood, heat, pain, and death.

My mind wanders. "This must be what hell smells like."

I reach over to his hand, which is wrapped around the drive shaft. I pinch his fingers.

"Can you feel that?"

A long drawn-out "No" splits the silence.

I see the young man start to cry. I can see that he is losing faith in himself. If he lets go here he will never come back.

"Listen to me, man. I have seen way worse. Yeah, you're banged up but it is not all that bad." I lie to him. He is fucked up in a bad way. I cannot even tell where his body begins and where it ends. I only see exposed shards of bones. Blood flowing from flesh that has had its skin ground off.

All I can see is pain.

I reach for his face. Blood is flowing into his eyes. The skin on his skull has been pulled back like a peel on an orange. I can see the bone, veins crossing over it like red lines on a bleached white map.

Blood is flowing from the exposed skull into his eyes. I have felt the sting and frustration of blood in my eyes. I know that the loss of vision is so aggravating for me.

I gently touch his brow and force out the pooling blood in his eyebrows. I push the thick warm blood off to the side and away from his eyes. I feel the warmth and wet of his blood on my flesh. The thin latex gloves I am wearing do not protect me from the sensation of his warmth.

"I fucking hate it when I get blood in my eyes. I will keep that shit out for you."

"Thanks," he says in a long drawn-out tone.

I reach up with my other hand and I wince as I touch a hot oil pan. I can feel the burn instantly. I wince but I keep the pain in. I have no right to complain.

I can see from his last words that his jaw is broken. Every time he tries to speak I can see it slide from side to side.

I put my right hand onto his face as I hold his jaw steady. My light embrace seems to comfort him. My human splint takes away some of his pain and discomfort. The human contact reminds him that he is still living. It tells him that this is real, not some nightmare he just cannot wake up from.

I pull myself closer to his body with my left hand and once I know that I can brace myself properly between the car and the concrete median I brace the other side of his jaw with my left hand.

Blood pours from his nose onto my hands. A shallow stream of blood flows down from his forehead, across his eyebrows, and down his cheek. It follows the new path I gave it.

I can smell the stench of burning flesh. Singed hair fills my nostrils.

An eternity passes while I talk to the young man. I keep telling him that he will be okay. I tell him that the ambulance is on the way and will be here soon. I tell him that he may be feeling bad but he is not in that bad a shape.

I can hear the sirens in the distance. I can hear other police officers gather at the scene.

"Hey, Smith, you okay? Are you trapped under there?"

"Yeah, I am okay, just talking with the guy that is pinned under here." I try to smile, I try to look positive. I know that he is looking at me. I can see his eyes open and close. He is trying to stay focused; he is trying to stay alive.

Now I hear the firetruck pull up and more units. The earpiece I have attached to my radio is buzzing with information. There are witnesses to the accident that are calling in. It is repeated over and over again that the driver is expected to be impaired. All the other witnesses that saw his driving pattern are sure he was plastered.

My lips grind together. I want this guy caught. I want him to pay any price for this. I want him to be here holding this young man's face together. I want him to feel the car's heat, the warm blood, and to smell the chaos in this small space.

I listen to my radio transmit more information. Our helicopter is out searching the area. Our K9 units are out on patrol. The troops are organized and mobile. I know we are going to be getting this fuck soon. I can feel it. The players on the chessboard are moving into position perfectly.

A firefighter slides into the small space beside me. He smiles as he scoots right up to me. He fills the last remainder of space down here in this iron and concrete coffin.

"Hey, how are we doing tonight?" the firefighter looks at me, then the young man under the car.

Another groan escapes from the young man. He is unable to talk as my hands brace his jaw shut. Blood drips from his nose as he breathes out. The air passing over my blood-covered hands cools my skin. It is hot as hell under the car.

"Well, things are going to be getting much better soon. We are just blocking up the car so that when we move it, we don't crush this fine constable holding your jaw." He smiles more. This is his game, this is what he is trained for, this is what he has done hundreds of times before. "Then we will lift the car up enough to let some medics under here to stabilize your body. From there they are going to be giving you some good drugs for your pain. Then it's off to the hospital for you." He is still smiling.

While he spoke to the young man his hands moved over and took a pulse from the young man's neck. He shouts out numbers to another fireman outside, who writes the information down on his latex glove.

More medics show up as the fireman under the car with me still talks to the young man. Since the young man cannot speak a system

373

is worked out. Blink once and it is no. Blink twice, it is yes. A medic has slid his body close to the front of the vehicle and I can hear him relay the information given by the firefighter. I hear codes yelled out, equipment called for, and men mobilized.

I hear the banging of hammers onto the wooden blocks that are used to prevent the car from rolling down onto us. Power tools fill the air as the car is getting ripped apart. I see light pour in from the outside world. The doors are cut off and the entire top of the car is already being removed. I am amazed at the speed and organization of these men.

Hands slide in from every small opening. They cover the young man's body parts with medical compresses, shielding the open wounds from flying metal and sparks.

The work continues. The fireman and I talk to the young man. We tell jokes and let him know what is happening next when we can see a look of fear fill his eyes.

The medic that was at the front of the car is now free to work on some of the young man's body as the front end and the radiator are cut free. I see the medic find the young man's other arm and check for a pulse. I see an IV tube put into his arm and medication put into the IV line.

"There we go, buddy. Some painkillers are on the way. You are going to feel much better now. Just stay calm, okay?"

I see the young man's eyes open as the flood of painkillers enter his system. A small groan escapes again as some of the pain leaves his wrecked body.

I feel the fireman reach back and grab something behind him. He reaches over my face and slides on a clear set of plastic safety glasses.

"Here you go. Have to put some safety glasses on you. We are now going to cut out the floor of the car so we can see what else we need to do. There is going to be sparks and shit."

His hands move over to the young man as he slides safety glasses onto him as well. The safety glasses sit half-assed on the young man's head as my hands are in the way for a good fit.

"Okay! We are good here!" yells the fireman to his fellow uniforms.

Saws whine and cutters shear away at the vehicle's steel skin. I can hear the snapping of metal bars as the entire floor of the car is cut out. In one slow and monitored movement the car's floor is free.

Air pours into our small hell. Fresh air fills the crevice we have been stuck in for the past thirty minutes. Clean cold night air slides across my face. I close my eyes and embrace the gift. I imagine a better place, a place filled with tall leafy trees, cool earth, and clean air. It is the world I have created to escape to. I have just entered my place when hot putrid airs fills me again. Quickly I am extradited from my magical realm.

It doesn't matter; the brief reprieve is enough for me. The brief sip of heaven has filled me.

I hold his face still as my arms scream from pain. I have been lying here on my belly in this unnatural position for the past forty minutes and my body is letting me know. I stuff down the pain, the discomfort. I bury it with the rest of my anguish. It is buried with the other sufferings I have felt on these streets.

I feel like a hindrance to the working machine around me. I feel like my big body is in the way of their skill. But, I hear all the people around me continually tell me not to let go of his head, to not let the jaw drop. I hear them tell the young man that he is doing a great job. I feel them pat me on the shoulder and tell me that it will be a few more minutes.

A stretcher is slid in from the other side of the car. Hands from every direction slide under the young man. I see hands move in from all the openings around me. Helping hands from everywhere, they seem to magically appear from the heavens.

They move as if controlled by one maker. The body is carefully lifted as the stretcher is slid under the young man. It pushes its way under my arms. I peer at the bright orange plastic stretcher.

The orange plastic has streaks of black oil mixed with green engine coolant and red blood. The medley of colors reminds me of paints running off of an artist's pallet.

Hands now move to the neck of the young man. The medics work around my hands. They direct me when it is good for me to move certain fingers. I listen to their commands with precision. If I am not clear on the instruction I ask for them to repeat the command. I do not want to make a mistake. They have enough to deal with, no need to make things more difficult by assuming I know what they want. The neck brace is slid on and now my hands are free.

I do not leave.

Before I felt trapped under the car, now I feel that I cannot handle my freedom yet. I lie there and ask the fireman what else I can do.

I have no idea what they want from me. This is not my game, this is not what I am trained for.

Rolls of medical tape are now being unraveled. I see the tape wrapped around the young man's head to secure him to the stretcher.

"You staying?" He looks at me then turns his head towards the young man. "Well, look at that, leave it to a cop to stay under a car to hang out with a fireman." He smiles and jokes as he moves about in this small space with ease and precision.

"He must like all of your jokes," the fireman tells the young man.

The fireman grabs my free left hand and guides it over to the open and exposed skull. He uses my clean gloved fingers to roll the large hanging piece of scalp back over to its original position.

"Here, hold this here." His hands hold mine into place over the loose piece of skin and thin flesh.

"Apply a little bit of pressure to slow the bleeding." His hands push onto mine to show me how much pressure to apply.

I see the left hand that was wrapped around the transmission shaft now free. It is curled tightly against his body now. Instinctively I reach out with my hand and touch his hand. I see his eyes open.

"Can you feel that?" I ask him the same question as I did earlier.

He blinks twice. Yes.

I keep holding onto his hand.

He blinks twice again. Yes.

"Don't worry, buddy. We are almost done here. Now you have to think of how you are going to handle the ride in the ambulance. I don't want you to quit on me because you feel safe in the ambulance. You have to fight until they force you to sleep with medication. No quitting," I tell the young man as I hold onto his hand.

I have seen too many people die when they are taken out of a bad situation and put into a safe place. It is like they quit their fight because they feel safe now. They just die in a safe place.

The last bit of metal is removed from around us and then the body is slid out towards me. Helping hands grab onto my uniform and slide me out with the body. Angels' hands pull me off of the ground to stand. I feel like I am weightless, like I am being lifted to the heavens. I want to be carried out of here, taken away.

No such luck. The helping hands only help me to stand. Then, once I am up, they let go. I am alone again. I stand on my feet again.

As I stand I see the young man's eyes follow me.

"Don't worry about me. I am all good, buddy." I smile as hands raise him onto a stretcher.

"I cannot take the ride with you to the hospital. Too big to fit in the ambulance, but I will be waiting for you there. Remember what I said about fighting till they force you to sleep." I still smile at him.

His stretcher is loaded into the ambulance and the roar of sirens fire up as it drives away. I can see police cruisers roar down the road to run blocks at every intersection. This ambulance will have a police escort. It will not need to slow for traffic.

I hear the voice of my sergeant.

"Hey, Smith!"

I turn towards him. He stops and stares at me. He stares at my body, covered in blood. Blue latex gloves with a red gloss, clinging over my hands as they swing low on my side. Pools of blood have soaked into my dark blue uniform; oil has soiled my arms and back. Speckles of blood stain my face. Dirt covers my pants and face. I look like I have opened the door to hell and taken a good long hard look at it.

I smell like fresh blood, the earthy musk covers me. The odor of burning flesh and hot engine oil has permeated my uniform, soaked into my very own flesh.

"Let's get you into that ambulance. They are going to get you cleaned up as they escort you to the hospital. That fireman told me that it would be good for the young guy to see you when he gets there." My sergeant's finger points to the man that was under the car with me.

He looks over our way and smiles. With a simple wave he gets into the back of his firetruck.

"Oh yeah, we got the driver of the vehicle. We found him about eight blocks away from here drinking up a storm in a park. He is drunk as a fucking skunk but he is telling us that he drank booze after the accident. Fucking asshole knows how to get himself out of an impaired driving charge. We got nothing but a careless driving beef here." My sergeant shakes his head as he ducks under the bright yellow police tape.

I jump into the back of the ambulance and a female medic goes to work on cleaning me up, looking at the burn on my arm, and ensuring I have no other wounds. Precision is their world. Organized chaos, I call it.

The large ambulance rocks and twists as we make our way to the hospital. I gently move with the flow of the vehicle. The medic moves with me and we are now in a little dance as she wipes the dirt and grease off of my face. We say nothing to each other.

"Okay, here we are. You're all cleaned up and ready to go."

I look out the front of the ambulance and see the other medical unit already stopped and a few medics readying the stretcher to be removed from the back.

Jumping out the side door I quickly make my way to the medics. Metal legs fold out from underneath the stretcher holding the young man's body.

As I close in I can see the young man. His eyes are open; his head is locked into place with tape and a hard plastic neck brace. A medic next to him holds an IV bag high, watching that the thin plastic tube connected into their patient doesn't get caught during this transport.

I lean over to look into his eyes. I know he cannot turn his head to look around, and as I move over his head I get locked into his gaze.

"So, that wasn't such a bad ride, eh?" I smile at the young man. He held on, he has made it this far. His chances for survival are getting better as time goes on. He is in the hospital now.

He smiles slightly. No groan escapes his lips. I can see the subtle glaze of painkillers gloss across his eyes.

"Remember what I said about you hanging on until they want you to get some sleep." I touch his shoulder and feel shattered bone under the medical blanket. I do not react to it. I leave my hand there ever so lightly as I follow the stretcher down the well-lit hall of the emergency ward.

As soon as we approach triage I let go of my grip. I stop moving my feet and I let the mass of medical staff slide past me. I can feel the slight wisp of wind from them passing. I do not go further. This is the end of the line for me.

His life is now in the hands of the doctors and his will to survive.

I start to shut down. I can feel my energy draining from me. I can feel it flow into the floor below my feet. My life is flowing out of me as I stand.

I slowly guide myself into a chair outside of the operating room. My hands grip the chair's arms as I squish my body into the small chair. My duty belt barely allows me the room to squeeze in.

I put my head back onto the wall behind me. I can still smell the oil, the hot steel, the warm blood, and the burning hair. My uniform is covered in this mess. I put my head back and close my eyes.

I am walking in my forest now. Green leaves flow on tall old-growth trees. Soft moss cushions my bare feet as I walk slowly through my forest. I can smell the damp cool earth. Rays of sunshine glace between the tall trees.

A cool mist dusts my face as I walk towards a lumbering waterfall.

I do not smell death here.

I do not taste suffering in this place.

I am at peace here.

"Sir, sorry to bother you but we have a situation outside in the waiting room." A gentle hand rocks me away from my forest.

My eyes flash open as I look at a nurse.

"Sorry for waking you, but we have a woman in the waiting room that is going crazy."

I can hear the screams of a woman in the distance. Hysterical yells for her son. I know who she is, why she is here. Her son is the young man. She is here because she was told that her son was here.

I push myself out of the chair. "Don't worry. I wasn't sleeping anyways." I smile at the nurse as her body shrinks. She is all of five feet tall, I tower over her. Her eyes open as the blue uniform in front of her continues to grow in height.

I walk towards the sound of the screaming and a quick tap on the access pad opens the emergency room door.

Eyes from all around the room look at me. Eyes asking for me to stop the ranting woman. Eyes wondering what sight that they will see now.

I see these faces look at me. Look at my size and build. Faces seeing the blood and dirt on my uniform, wondering where I have been and where I am going to go looking like this.

I slowly start to walk to the hysterical woman. Two hospital security officers are trying to hold her back from the door that I just walked out of. Her back is towards me as the security officers try to hold onto her arms in an attempt to walk her outside.

Her arms are flying about and her anguish builds. She wants to see her son, she wants to know that he is all right. Now people are telling her to leave.

She is in her later fifties and her hair is turning grey. Her five-and-a-half-foot frame is leaning towards the heavy side. She is no longer in the prime of her life but, as mothers do, she will fight to see her son. She will be a caged animal soon, Mother Nature's most furious animal.

I walk behind her and place my hand on her shoulder. The security guards let go of her arms when they see me.

The mother spins around to make her way back to the door that she thinks will lead her to her son. She turns to only look at my chest. Her eyes move up and look into mine.

I see eyes lit with fear. Not for herself but for the safety of her baby.

Eyes red from crying and flowing with tears. They flow down her cheek and fall onto her light blue shirt.

She just stands there not saying anything. Her world is spinning out of control. First the late call from a neighbor telling her that they saw her son in an accident. Then the hysterical drive to the hospital.

Her anguish building as she would not be given any information about her son. Security trying to remove her, take her away from her child.

Now the police are here. And not some warm and fuzzy-looking cop. A big hard-faced cop whose uniform looks like it has walked a path in hell.

I bend over to the mother's ears and whisper, "Your son is okay. I was with him the whole time and came here with him. He is in the operating room right now. I need you to be strong now. Your son needs you to be strong now."

I straighten back up to see her face change from fear to joy. Tears rush out as she weeps into her hands.

"Let's get away from all of these peering eyes. How about we go for a walk outside and I will tell you what I know?" I put my hand on her shoulder and she turns around with me to walk outside.

I look around the room and the older faces nod congratulations for a difficult situation put to rest with a few words they did not hear.

No violence, no harsh tones, just a soft whisper.

Young faces show a different tale. They wanted to see the TV world they are so used to. They wanted to see her get tossed out. Arrested by the police. They wanted to see violence.

I walk around the hospital grounds in an endless circle with the young man's mother as I tell her the tale of his being pinned under the car. I tell her what a strong character he is, how good of a fight he is putting up.

Her tears have dried up. She is listening and asking questions. I answer them the best that I can.

I learn his name is Terry and that he is a good kid. Never got into trouble. Never did anything to deserve this fate. I have heard this tale before. The innocent, the pure of heart, get tested the most from fate.

We walk back towards the hospital when Terry's mother turns to me.

"Your uniform, the blood and dirt on it?"

"Yes, that is from the accident. It is Terry's blood." I look down at the stains turning to dark purple blotches. The blood no longer sticky and tacky. It is dry and cracking now.

Terry's mother looks at me and the tears well up in her eyes again. Her head dips to the side as she starts to smile. Her hand reaches out and I can feel her cool fingers touch my face.

"Thank you for all that you have done." Her palm rests on my cheek.

A mother's touch. A touch no man can learn. Perfected through years of child care and family strife. Loving hands that can lift away all sins with a simple touch.

I feel all the suffering and chaos inside of me fall away. The pungent odor of metal and death have slid from my senses. I feel free from the metal coffin I was lying in not so long ago.

I smile back. "Let's go and see Terry. Another cop has just told me that the attending physician is out of surgery."

We make our way quickly to the emergency room; we move through the doors that Terry's mother was denied. A surgeon in green scrubs looks our way.

"Are you Terry's mother?"

She nods frantically. She wants information, any information. She wants to know if her son is alive.

I can tell he has survived because of the way the other nurses are acting. They are hanging around. If the kid had coded in the operating room they would all be leaving this area to avoid seeing the depressed mother. I can't blame them.

"I have finished Terry's initial surgery. He is doing better. Why don't we have a seat in my office so that I can fill you in on the extent of Terry's injuries?"

The mother and surgeon move into a small office used to counsel the bereaved.

The doctor turns to me just before he enters the room.

"Thanks for your time, constable. Can you attend here tomorrow at about the same time and I will have more information for you? I know that you need certain information for your paperwork but I will not be able to complete it tonight."

"Yes, sir. No problem, I will be here tomorrow. I have to go and get cleaned up anyway."

With a smile and a nod to Terry's mother I leave the hospital and return to my work. A unit drives me back to the office and we talk lightly about the call I was just at.

Once in the locker room I carefully slide off my soiled uniform. A few minutes later it is bagged into clear evidence bags and tossed onto the top of my locker.

Hot water pours onto my face and rolls down my chest. I have been yearning for this shower for the last few hours.

The hot water cleans the dried specks of blood off of my arms, rinses the blotches of Terry's blood from my legs and shoulders, places where the blood soaked through my uniform to stain my skin.

I think of the extra paperwork I will have to fill out because of this blood exposure.

"Terry seemed like a straightforward kid. I hope he doesn't have fucking Hep." Low words move from my lips as more water flows across my face.

I am in court now. I have finished testifying and displaying my soiled uniform. As soon as the bag was opened the smell covered me again. The stench of that night awoke the memories inside of me.

I had to take a moment to myself. I paused when the odor hit me. Internal walls had to be built, barriers made because the demon of this memory, the feelings that it brought welled up inside. I had to hammer it down. Lock it away.

I will deal with it later. I will breathe out this demon in the future.

I had to act like I was examining my uniform as I pulled it out of the plastic bag. I did not want to seem weak or unsure. I did not want the vultures to come in because they thought that they saw a moment of weakness.

The judge calls for a brief recess to the trial.

He needs time to assess the proceedings to make his decision. There is no jury, no grandstand theatrics here. It is not TV land. Things are simple and plain.

Terry and his mother stand outside the courtroom. I can see Terry's father there with them. They are all happy that Terry is alive but from Terry's walk I can see that there is going to be months more of rehabilitation for him.

I walk over to talk to Terry's family. They all thank me for staying with their son when he needed someone there. His father shakes my hand with a firm grip that one man would use to thank another man for his help. I smile back at him.

Just as Terry goes to thank me I stop him.

"I had nothing to do with your fight, Terry. Never forget that. Never say to yourself that you could not have made it without someone being there. You climbed your mountain by yourself."

I shake Terry's hand, the same firm grip that I received from his father.

"I have to thank you for letting me be there with you. The chance I had to see someone work through such an accident will sit with me forever. If I am ever in your situation, I will hang on because I know it can be done."

We shake hands for a long time.

I set the family up for what I think the judge will hand down. They know that the courts will be lenient on this fellow because he has never committed a driving offense before. They are ready for what the courts give him.

I tell him that they should never forgive this man who hit Terry. Never tell people that they forgive the drunk who ran Terry over. I think that people should stop forgiving and express the hate and anguish that this has caused them.

We forgive the sinners and they will sin again. The sinners should have a lifetime of people looking at them with disgust for their actions.

Terry's family is happy he is alive.

Court is now back in session.

The sentence is handed down: Dangerous Driving. Six-month driving suspension, a $5,000 fine, and 100 community hours.

Terry will have to do two years of rehabilitation. Countless hours of pain management.

He will never walk the same, and when old age creeps up on him he will feel the pain and suffering of old injuries. Terry is damaged for life.

The impaired driver, the real bad guy here, will suffer for six months without a license.

Sin? No one pays for their sins anymore.

As I Walk Through the Valley

As I Walk Through the Valley

My name is John Smith and I am a cop.

One may ask why I do what I do after reading this book.

Believe me, I ask myself that over and over again as I see more blood, more violence, and more shattered innocence.

No matter how bad it gets I keep coming back. I am drawn to this world. I follow a path through a valley of death that has been marked clearly for me.

I know that this is my place in life, the role that fate has decided for me.

My path in life has never been clearer, more focused.

Maybe it is the addiction to the adrenaline fix.

Maybe it is the gift that a smiling child can give when they feel safe behind the dark blue armor that I wear.

Maybe it is the excitement of hunting for my prey, bad guys.

I do not know, I cannot explain it.

I just hope that if there is a heaven, I get a free pass into it because I have walked a lifetime through hell.

I just hope that there is a higher witness to remember what I have sacrificed being the sheepdog that watches over this flock of sheep.

"Character cannot be developed in ease and quiet. Only through experiences of trial and suffering can the soul be strengthened, vision cleared, ambition inspired, and success achieved. You gain strength, experience, and confidence by every experience where you look fear in the face.

"You must do the thing you cannot do.

"The finest steel is forged in the hottest furnace."

Unknow author.